THE EARTH LORDS

GORDON R. DICKSON

ACE BOOKS, NEW YORK

This book is an Ace original
edition, and has never been previously published.

THE EARTH LORDS

An Ace Book/published by arrangement with
the author

PRINTING HISTORY
Ace edition/January 1989

ISBN: 0-441-18044-2

Ace Books are published by The Berkley Publishing Group,
200 Madison Avenue, New York, NY 10016.
The name "ACE" and the "A" logo are
trademarks belonging to Charter Communications, Inc.

PRINTED IN THE UNITED STATES OF AMERICA

10 9 8 7 6 5 4 3 2 1

TO PAT OANES,
who appeared in our lives just in time
to rescue both my mother and myself.

Acknowledgments

I want to express my appreciation in particular to David Wixon and Sandra Miesel, whose research and work in a large number of different areas helped make this book possible; as well as to a number of other experts in various fields to whom I turned for help and was given it.

chapter
one

IT WAS EARLY spring yet, this high up, and the pony came gratefully to the top of the little hill. Bart Dybig stopped to let the beast catch its breath, while he looked over the tiny settlement in the river valley below before riding down into it. He was too heavy for the pony, that was the truth of it; though so compact was the bone and muscle of his solid body that most people would have guessed him thirty or more pounds less than his real weight.

Now that he was here, he found himself of two minds about riding down into that place. The whole reason for his coming this long distance was to do so. At the same time the habit of being by himself had brought him almost to the point of avoiding society completely. He had a strange feeling of uneasiness about what riding down the hill into the settlement before him might lead him into.

But there was nothing in what he saw to justify such a feeling. The settlement itself was ordinary-looking enough. Some eight buildings were strung out on either side of a single street, a small distance back from the thin blue line of the small river that had its home in this valley. All the buildings were of logs; and only one, in the center of the settlement on the far side of the street from Bart's point of view, had anything resembling an actual second story. It also had a couple of fairly good-sized windows fronting the street, and an open porch—accumulation of luxuries on this west Canadian frontier in 1879—that strongly suggested that the front part of the building, at least, was more store than living quarters.

He rode the pony at a walk down the hill toward the settlement.

The closer he got, the more the place rang a note of warning in a part of his mind that the time with Louis Riel had honed to constant awareness of possible danger. Since leaving Louis in his exile in the United States and returning to Canada, he had been passed on westward from group to group of métis—those people who were the result of the interbreeding of the early European furtrappers and the native Indians. Bart's father had been European —even if other men, Indian, white and mixed-breed alike, had combined in avoiding him—and Bart's mother had been a Cree Indian whose name in English translated to "Listens to Trees."

Both of his parents were dead now—Bart's mother by a raging fever when he was six years old, and his father, in Montana, in the United States, by a rifle bullet from a distant assassin—a bullet clearly intended for Riel, as the two men rode side by side. Riel had escaped below the border, after the métis had risen for their rights and had their uprising put down by soldiers from eastern Canada; and Bart's father, with Bart, had gone with the métis leader.

His father had been a close adviser to Riel, who alone besides Bart had come to understand the innate gentleness in the physically powerful and brilliant, but misshapen little man. When his father had died, after nearly a week of fever from an infection brought on by the bullet, which had lodged too deep in the older man's body to be removed, Bart had considered himself released of any further duty to Riel. After working a few years to raise money that would set him free to travel, Bart had returned to Canada in search of a relative he had never known he had until the delirium of his father's dying hours.

All that Bart had been able to gather, putting together the fragments of his father's brief, fevered utterances, was that the relative was a woman and named, or called, "Didi," and that she was to be found somewhere in the Canadian Rocky Mountains, most probably somewhere on the western side of that range.

The métis who had remained in Canada had aided Bart and passed him on from group to group. His clothing, the brown Indian eyes which he had inherited from his Cree mother, his very way of walking and riding, was his passport among them. He was métis himself, and looked it. In their small settlements he had felt, momentarily at least, at home and for the moment safe, although there was a price, if a small one, on his head from the days of the rebellion.

But he did not feel at home or safe as he rode down into this settlement marked on the map in his saddlebags as Mossby. The blind but always to be listened to instinct within him was sounding a signal.

Unobtrusively, he loosened his rifle in its saddle scabbard and checked the heavy revolver in the holster at his belt, hidden under his leather jacket. For the first time it struck him what was bothering him about the group of houses before him. There were no children to be seen about, nor any dogs.

True, there were no adults to be seen, either; but at this time of the spring afternoon they could be up and out, away from home, or inside the buildings, out of sight. He headed toward the large building that he had assumed to be a store, though this place was beyond the very end of the high western plains, in the beginnings of the Rocky Mountains. Any goods that came in here for store sale would necessarily have come by pack horse. There was a hitching rail before the store building, but no horses at it.

It was the more surprising, in light of the quietness of the place and his own feeling of inner warning, that just as he rode up to the hitching rail a man he recognized came out of the front door of the store—and the feeling of fate chimed loudly within him.

"Arthur!" said Bart.

The other turned and stared, still holding the bale of furs he had brought out. Slowly, he put the bale down on the floor of the porch, against the log wall, and stared at Bart, clearly without recognition.

The lack of recognition, at least, was not so surprising.

Now in his twenty-fifth year, Bart had changed from the barely adult young man Arthur Robeson had last seen in the town of Sainte Anne, far to the east on the central plains, where they had grown up together. For one thing, Bart had come into his full weight and strength—that strength he had inherited from his father, but in as far greater measure as his larger body had outstripped the older man's small one.

With that development had come a squareness, a blocklike appearance that made other men walk around him unthinkingly. These things had come with the years of the 1870s. Now, in 1879, that growth had hardened on him. He stood five feet eleven inches in his stocking feet, which was tall compared to the average of the people around him; but there was no lack of men taller—and bigger—than he was.

The difference that set him apart from everyone else was not in his height, but in the unusual development of his body. His shoulders, as his father's had been, were almost unnaturally square and wide, and his chest was massive; but the real difference in him was his legs, disproportionately thick though now hidden by the wide leather trousers. The power of those legs had even surprised him, at times. At eighteen he had lifted horses, quite easily, on his shoulders until their hooves cleared the ground. He had done this to win bets and to show off, on several occasions—until he found that advertising his strength this way only seemed to increase the isolation which both he and his father had always seemed to feel from the world in general around them. Once he had realized this, he had stopped showing off. In fact, he had ended by sidestepping situations in which his strength might be noticed at all.

So it was not surprising then that the slim, white-skinned, brown-haired Scotsman who had known him as a boy did not recognize this thick-bodied stranger in the leather shirt, trousers and jacket. This armed stranger with the large head in which the heavy bones of brow and cheeks were prominent under the black hair and the tanned skin, and the face below the cheekbones hidden by the full, bushy, black beard Bart had grown to disguise himself when he slipped back across the border from the U.S.

For a moment Bart felt again the empty sense of isolation. Then he reminded himself that they had never been close anyway; and it did not matter about Arthur. What mattered—and he felt a sudden leap of joy within him—was that if Arthur were here, it was more than possible that Arthur's sister Emma was also here—even possible she was still unmarried. Emma, with whom Bart had fallen in love as a boy in school—those few years of school before the tide of the rebellion claimed him, young as he was. It might, in fact, have been Emma's liking for him that fed Arthur's dislike; for Arthur, although he showed little affection for his sister, had always wanted all of her attention. Their family had been storekeepers even then, back in Sainte Anne; and their mother, particularly, had always thought of their family as better than the métis around them.

But suddenly Bart was ashamed of himself for remembering Arthur so unkindly. If the other was willing to let bygones be bygones, now that they were all grown up, he could be willing also to start over from scratch in their acquaintanceship.

"Don't you know me, Arthur?" Bart said accordingly, halting his horse by the hitching rail, dropping its reins over the wooden bar and looking up at the other man, who stood on the porch above him. "I'm Bart Dybig."

"Bart?" Arthur still stared at him, but now as if trying to see through the beard to the boy he had known. "What are you doing here? The last I heard you'd gone to Montana with Riel."

"I'm looking for someone I heard was here—Telesphore Daudet. You know him?"

"Yes," said Arthur, his face still uneasy. "He lives here. Or at least he did—his squaw still does. But he went hunting, off into the mountains, some weeks ago, and he's never come back. Something may have happened to him out there."

Bart frowned. Telesphore Daudet, he had been told at the last settlement of métis he had visited, had been the man who could direct him on into the mountains, to where his father had, in his ravings, mentioned that some relatives of theirs lived.

The name of Telesphore Daudet was all Bart had to go on; such clues as Bart had been able to glean from his father's dying words had been vague, and it required the right man to be able to listen to such words and suggest the place they might refer to. The last such man, far east of here, had said Daudet might be a man to talk to, and he had tracked that name here to Mossby.

"You knew him?" Arthur asked, from up on the porch.

"No," answered Bart cautiously, "I was just dropping by with a message from an old friend of his." He put the problem of Daudet from his mind for the moment.

"Have you been here yourself, long?" he asked Arthur. "What about Emma? Is she still with you?"

"About five years," said Arthur.

"And Emma?"

"Yes." The word came out of Arthur slowly and reluctantly. Evidently Arthur was still possessive of his sister.

"Then she'd be inside there?" said Bart, nodding at the store. "I'll just step in and say hello to her. It'll be good to see her, too."

Arthur took a short step toward the front door, almost as if he would move between it and Bart. But Bart was coming up the steps, moving with all the casual but unstoppable progress of a boulder rolling downhill; and at the last moment Arthur turned and opened the door for him.

"I think she's probably up to her ears in work in the back," Arthur said. "It might be better not to disturb her now."

"Come on now, Arthur," said Bart, continuing past the other man into the interior, "she won't mind a moment or two, after all these years. . . ."

Within, the front lower half of the house had been partitioned off and fitted with counters and shelves to hold the goods of the store. So, thought Bart, he had been right. The air was strong with the aromas of pelts, woolen goods, liquid parafin—that fuel for lamps some people were beginning to call "kerosene"—and several dozen other odors. In appearance, it was no different from any of the small settlement stores Bart had been stepping into all his life, not only in the western Canada fur country, but down in Montana territory as well.

Except that behind the main counter at the back of the store, just coming in through a door that must lead to a back room, was a slim, small young woman. She had straight blond hair and blue eyes, in a round face that was not conventionally pretty but had a serene happiness about it that made it, and had always made it, Bart thought, beautiful.

"It's Bart Dybig, Emma," said Arthur, quickly and harshly behind Bart.

Emma's expression of pleasant welcome for a stranger was wiped out by one of happy recognition.

"Bart!" she cried, dropping onto the counter the armful of pelts she was carrying and coming out through an opening in it to grasp both of Bart's outstretched hands with her own. "And with a beard like that! Oh, it's good to see you again, Bart!"

He was suddenly warm with happiness. Not merely the happiness that being with her had always kindled in him, but a particular powerful joy that she should be so pleased to see him again. The sense of isolation and loneliness was utterly wiped away.

"It's wonderful to see you, Emma," he said.

He had completely forgotten Arthur, the store, everything but the two of them and their joined hands—when the voice of the other man jolted him out of it.

"Bart's just passing through, Emma," said Arthur. "He came by with a message for Telesphore Daudet from a friend of Telesphore's."

"And Telesphore's been gone for weeks!" said Emma without letting go of Bart's hands. "We're worried about him. Was he a friend of yours, Bart?"

"No," said Bart. "I never heard of him until I was asked to drop by here. I didn't know you two were here."

"But we've been here for five years. Do you realize how long it's been since we've seen each other? You'll stay with us while you're here, Bart; and we'll have a special dinner tonight."

"There's no extra room," said Arthur.

"We can clear the furs off that bunk in the back room, the bunk we always give to the pack-train handlers when they come—what's wrong with you, Arthur?" said Emma, for the first time taking her eyes off Bart and looking over at her brother.

It had always been Arthur's habit to bully his sister and order her about; and Emma had almost always let herself be bullied and ordered. But on the few occasions when Bart had seen her face up to Arthur, he had noticed that it was always Arthur who backed down. It was that way now.

"We've got all these furs to sort and get ready before the pack-train comes to take them east," he muttered, looking away from his sister. "And what'll we do when the pack-train handler gets here if we've somebody already staying in that bunk?"

"He can find a place to stay with someone else in town. Don't be stupid, Arthur!" said Emma. She let go of Bart's hands and reached up to her hair. "I'm covered with dirt and dust. We've been cleaning out the back room, as Arthur says—getting the winter pelts ready to send off to market."

"Tell me what I can do," said Bart.

His words were automatic. Anyone, even a complete stranger, was always offered food and shelter. And any such stranger always turned to immediately to help his hosts with whatever chores or other work had them busy at the moment.

"You can help me sort the furs that're left. Arthur grades well, but sometimes I'm a little faster at it than he is. And Arthur can bale the sorted furs, while you carry them out to the porch ready for the pack-train to pick up."

"I'll help you sort," said Arthur. "Bart can carry them out."

It was a small meanness, to deprive the two of them of being together during what remained of the afternoon; but Bart did not greatly mind. Just to be under the same roof with Emma had always seemed to bring happiness to him. Also, the prepared and tied bales were heavy. Arthur had made a load of just one as Bart was riding up. But Bart himself could have carried four of them without thinking. He reminded himself to take them one at a time, like Arthur, to give the other as little reason for annoyance as possible.

The two men followed her back into the storeroom. This room at the moment was a place of dark and dusty corners, glaringly lit at its center by the white-hot, glowing mantles of two parafin lamps set on flour barrels. The air, too, was full of dust and hair from the fur of the pelts; and boxes of goods were stacked everywhere.

"This whole place really should be put in some sort of order," said Emma, replacing a stray strand of blond hair which had fallen onto her forehead, "but we never seem to have time."

By which she probably meant, thought Bart, that she could not get Arthur to give the time to cooperate with her in straightening out the room. The odors of the skins and all the detritus of the previous winter that had come in with them, was thick in Bart's nostrils as he began to work.

"There's two bales of beaver pelts already tied up and ready to take out, Bart," said Emma, as she reached the small mountain of furs she had evidently been working on. "Arthur, you can start baling up these lynx pelts I've just sorted out. . . ."

As Emma had said she was faster than her brother—and evidently sorting was not the only work at which Arthur was slow. He made hard work of getting the pelts baled and since Bart could not carry them one by one out to the porch until they were tied up, both men were well behind Emma by the time she dusted her hands together and stepped back from the section of bare split-log floor that was now showing before her.

"That's that, then," she said. "I'll clean up and start to work on dinner while you two are getting the rest of those baled and outside."

"You could give me a hand baling, then, Bart," said Arthur.

"Glad to," said Bart, moving to this new work and still being careful not to make up his bales so fast as to show up Arthur's slowness and clumsiness. Together, they finished up the baling and carrying out of the bales to the porch, where Arthur covered them with a tarp and tied it down against possible wind and rain. He turned to Bart, dusting his hands as his sister had, but with no mention of cleaning himself up.

"Care for a drink?" he asked.

"It'd taste good," said Bart.

Arthur led him on back through the store and back room to a stair that brought them up into the living quarters occupying the whole second story of the house. It was apparently divided into a living room with a table for eating at one end of it, two bedrooms and a kitchen. From the kitchen now came the sounds of Emma moving about and the good aromas of food.

Arthur led him to a tall cabinet, opened the upper of its two doors, and from a shelf produced a dark bottle and a couple of small glasses. He filled the glasses three-quarters full and handed one to Bart.

"Well, here's luck to both of us," he said and tossed his drink down. Bart followed his example. It was a western-made corn whisky, not so raw as trade liquor, but not much of an improvement over what was sold across the counters of most stores like this—though Bart had seen none downstairs.

The whisky seemed to have given Arthur the gift of reading thoughts.

"I don't sell alcohol," he said. "Only causes trouble in a place like this. But for our own use . . . another?"

"Thanks," said Bart.

Arthur refilled the glasses.

This time, Arthur sipped more slowly at his glass, but not very much so. Bart followed his example. Even so, it was only a couple of minutes before Arthur was pouring them a third drink, without even asking Bart if he wanted to be refilled.

". . . You were asking if anyone around here had a horse for sale," Arthur said, picking up the conversation where it had been interrupted by his pouring. "What's wrong with that pony of yours?"

Bart thought it best not to mention the matter of his weight.

"I'd like to carry more gear and supplies," he said. "I'm headed into the mountains, and if I have to end up wintering up there, I'll need more than I've got now. More blankets, more clothes and flour. More ammunition . . ."

"Well, anyway, there's no horses available around here. You know these—" Arthur checked. He had clearly been about to say "these métis," but the alcohol had not had a chance to work enough in him to give him the courage for it. "—these people. They go just about every place on foot. What horses there are, the ones who own them won't want to part with—"

He broke off to turn his head toward the doorless entrance to the kitchen where Emma was audible but invisible around a corner.

"—Isn't that right, Emma?"

He had shouted the last line. Emma called back.

"Isn't what right, Arthur?"

"There're no horses for sale around here!"

"No, I don't think so. The pack-train handler may have an extra one he'd let go."

"Don't believe her," said Arthur, dropping his voice and turning back to Bart. "That pack-train may lose horses along the way. Any spares the train-handler's bringing along he'll want to keep. No, I'm afraid you're out of luck."

He poured himself another drink and moved the neck of the bottle into position over Bart's glass. But Bart already had it covered with one square, thick hand.

"All for you, is that it?" said Arthur. This time the alcohol put a noticeable jeer in his voice.

"Enough for now, anyway," said Bart.

It was a question, he thought, why Arthur should be forcing whisky on the two of them like this. If Arthur had turned into a drunk since he had last seen him—but there had been no sign of that in the man Bart had first seen on the porch. On the other hand,

Arthur could hardly be expecting to outdrink Bart, who clearly outweighed the Scotsman by a considerable amount.

Actually, Bart could have drunk half the bottle before dinner without losing his own manners; but it seemed to him that by refusing to drink himself, he might put a period to Arthur's drinking.

In fact, that was what happened. Arthur defiantly finished his fourth glass of whisky but made no further efforts to refill his glass. That at least, thought Bart, made it clear that the store owner had not become, like so many on the western frontier, a slave to the bottle when it was available.

Some ten minutes later, Emma called them both to the table, which was now set with plates, silverware and filled dishes.

"You killed a chicken!" said Arthur as soon as he had finished saying grace after they had taken their seats at the table.

"It's an occasion," said Emma calmly.

Chickens were a delicacy out here. It was not that they could not find their own food once snow was off the ground, but that they had to be protected against hawks from the sky and four-footed marauders on the ground—to say nothing of humans unlikely or unable to raise their own fowl. Then in the icy, below-zero winters the birds had to be housed indoors and their quarters cleaned and cared for.

But the tone in Arthur's now noticeably alcohol-tuned voice seemed not so much to be objecting to the slaughter of one of the prized birds as to the guest for whom it had been slaughtered.

"Will you pass the gravy, Bart?" said Emma, handing on the plate of chicken parts herself. "And you, Arthur, hand me the biscuits, if you will."

The bowls of food were passed from hand to hand above the circle of the tabletop. In her quiet way, Emma was a good cook; and the chicken, gravy and potatoes, to say nothing of the young spring asparagus, added up to a meal such as Bart had not had in a long time. Afterward, Arthur went to sit in one of the livingroom chairs while Bart helped Emma clear the table. But once the dishes were in the kitchen, she merely rinsed and stacked them.

"I can wash up later," she said, drying her hands on a small towel. "Right now, while there's still some twilight left, you and I are going for a walk, Bart."

"Fine!" he said.

They went out through the living room.

"We're going for a turn up and down the street, Arthur," said

Emma as they passed him.

He sat up in his chair.

"You're going out walking—"

"Just sit there and digest your dinner, Arthur," said Emma. "I'll do the dishes later. And you'd better bring the accounts up to date with the worth of those furs we sorted and baled today."

"I'll do it," said Arthur. He all but scowled at Bart. Otherwise, he made no more objection to his sister going walking in public with a man.

They went down the stairs, out of the building and into what passed for the settlement's main street. It was trodden free of grass and other growing things, but it was late enough in the spring that the ground was no longer muddy—and yet early enough that the little evening breeze was not able to raise clouds of dust. They strolled down between the double row of structures.

The store building had been made of peeled logs; but most of these others were constructed of logs with the bark still on them. The shagginess this gave their appearance seemed to make them part of the ground on which they sat—ground which ran clear and free from the river and the valley wall on the far side to the more gentle slope that was the valley wall on this side, down which Bart had come.

"Arthur said at dinner you were hunting for your relatives and you thought they were off somewhere in the Rockies," she said.

"That's right," Bart answered. "Father only mentioned them once. I don't even know their names. But I got the clear idea they lived at some place in the mountains. Any place in there is bound to be small enough so that if I mention the name Dybig, and I've got relatives around, someone should be able to tell me."

"After you find them, what'll you do? Stay?" she asked. "Or will you be coming back this way?"

"I'd be coming back this way in any case," said Bart, looking down at her. "Emma, I've never forgotten you, you know. I used to think of you, no matter where I was."

"I thought of you, too, Bart," she said—and his heart jumped; but she went on in the same soft voice, looking straight ahead of her, "but Arthur needs someone to look after him. Now that both Mother and Father are gone, there's no one but me to do it."

The message was clear enough; but Bart's feelings were so strong they broke out into words in spite of himself.

"There's no one to take care of me, either," he said.

"You're a great deal more capable than Arthur, Bart." She

looked up at him. "And I've an obligation by blood to care for my brother."

"But not to throw your life away on him!"

"God will decide whether I throw my life away or not," Emma said. She put her small hand on the sleeve over his massive right forearm. "Dear Bart, you know how I'd feel if I was free to feel any way I wanted. But a person's duty comes first, before anything. Didn't you follow Louis Riel down into exile in the United States because of duty to your own father?"

"He wanted me to," growled Bart.

"And my father would have wanted me to be a help and aid to Arthur as long as I was needed," she said. "I'll tell you what you do, Bart. Go find your relatives. Maybe when you come back things'll have changed and I'll be more free. Then we can get married—that is, if you still want me."

"It'll be a cold day in—on the face of the sun when I don't!" he growled.

She ignored his near slip into profanity.

"It's too bad our fathers, yours and mine," she said thoughtfully, "won't be around to see it."

Bart checked himself from saying what he badly wanted to say—that his father, in spite of his short stature and spiderous ugliness, had been a brilliant, responsible man with a strong sense of independence and what was right. While Emma's father had been another Arthur, if more religious about it; a selfish, narrowminded and bigoted man who had leaned all his weight on his wife while she lived, and on Emma after his wife's death—for all that Emma at that time had been only thirteen years old.

Emma, he knew, had not seen her father that way. In fact, Emma found good in everyone, whether it was there or not, he told himself grimly. Which was perhaps a noble thing to do but led to situations like this one, which was unfair to her and hard on Bart.

He remembered a woman visitor to Sainte Anne, where they had all lived when both he and Emma had been young, asking Emma if her family were Quakers.

"Oh, no!" Emma had answered, shocked, for her father and mother had been strict Presbyterians; and at that age neither Emma nor Bart, who had been with her at the moment of the visitor's question, had had any real notion of what a Quaker was. They only knew that it was something religious other than Emma's Protestantism, and Bart's father's absent-minded observance of Roman Catholic rites.

It had not been until he went down into the States that Bart had encountered some actual members of the Society of Friends— those nicknamed Quakers—and for the first time understood how Emma could have been taken for someone brought up in their forms of religion. In all his life he had never seen Emma angry at anyone or without an excuse for anyone else, no matter what he or she had done. Her own life of automatically doing for others, she seemed to believe, was nothing unusual or remarkable.

"Her goodness is built into her bones," Bart's father had said in one of his rare moments of paying anything much more than passing attention to the people they lived among.

It was true. Emma did not think of herself as good, or kind or dutiful. Whatever she did, from putting in long hours at their store in Sainte Anne, or doing all the housework by herself after her mother's death, was simply what she assumed anyone else would do in her position; unless something beyond their power prevented them.

And one result from that was that it had always been a waste of time for Bart to argue that she owed something to herself.

chapter
two

THEY HAD REACHED the end of the short street of buildings. There was a small graveyard with seven wooden crosses, of varying ages and sizes, standing in it, beyond the last house on the right side; but that hardly counted as part of the living settlement. They turned about and began walking back toward the store.

So far no one had come out of any of the houses to look at them. This was, of course, still the dinner hour, since Emma, Bart and Arthur had eaten, if anything, a little early. But no one had emerged to meet the stranger, which was peculiar in a little out-of-the-way place like this where strangers must come seldom. A couple of faces had looked out the tiny windows which were the most in the way of a view on the world the buildings owned; but they had been the faces of children.

There was, it occurred to Bart, the unpalatable possibility that Arthur and Emma—or more likely just Arthur alone—were disliked enough in the settlement so that no one wanted to have anything to do with a friend of theirs. The possibility reminded him of another, disquieting question. Bart would have preferred not to ask Emma about it; but since he was headed into strange territory from which he might not come back, he wanted to know how she was placed with these same neighbors who surrounded her.

"Emma," he said; and the word seemed to come out suddenly, so that she looked up at him at once. For, after his giving up on any hope of getting her to consider leaving Arthur, they had been walking side by side in silence.

"Emma," he said again, more quietly, "there were rumors when we went down to Montana that Arthur had become involved with the Scottites. I told people it made no sense. But . . . he wasn't, was he? I mean he didn't get himself into anything that would give people reason to jump to that conclusion about him?"

"Arthur?" Emma laughed. "A storekeeper has to keep the goodwill of his customers unless he wants to lose them, you know that, Bart. Most of our customers thought the world of Louis Riel.''

''Are you sure he couldn't have done something without you knowing it that could have got such a rumor started?'' Bart said. ''It could be dangerous if he had, and neither of you'd realized it. You know how the métis still feel about Thomas Scott.''

''Of course I know,'' she said.

And of course she did, as everyone did.

In 1867, the Canadian Federation had been formed, and soon thereafter it began to look as if the Hudson's Bay Company, which had title to almost all the land between Ontario and the Pacific coast, would turn over its holding to the new nation.

The métis community in the area of the Red River Valley—which was to be the center of Louis Riel's power base—generally had little desire to be Canadian. But a vocal minority that was pro-Canadian soon made itself heard, particularly among the non-métis elements of the population; and their presence caused a friction that soon led to an uprising.

Into this turbulent situation had walked Louis Riel. He was a métis and a lawyer from Montréal with radical leanings. He had returned to St. Boniface, near Winnipeg, after receiving a letter from Bart's father, who did not visibly involve himself in politics, but who kept his eye on all that was going on around him. Not even Bart understood exactly what his father's position was, and where the older man's interest lay. Lionel Dybig was considered by most, who did not know of the strength in his small body, to be essentially an invalid incapable of ordinary work—but one who did not need to do so, since he was well enough off financially to live without working. A smart but harmless bookworm, was the general concensus of people regarding him. A few other, brighter-than-average people who knew him, like Louis Riel, knew better.

Riel was a racial patriot, proud of both his French and Indian ancestry. He also believed in nonviolence, and had been proud of the fact that he had been able to bring the métis of the Red River Valley under his leadership without any violence.

Some of the people in that territory did not agree either with him or his policies; and in the self-defense of a peaceful community, he was forced to jail them. Mostly, these were the open advocates of violence among the so-called ''Canadian Party,'' and one of them was the man named Thomas Scott.

The majority of the métis were French and Roman Catholic. Scott was a Protestant Irishman and a thoroughgoing bigot, originally from Ontario; and he was one of the jailed group that later escaped and tried to create a countermovement among the local people. Scott himself tried to assassinate Louis Riel.

He was recaptured and once more imprisoned, but continued from his cell to try to fight for his way of doing things. The trouble he created was dangerous enough so that Riel's party brought him to trial for his crimes. He was found guilty and executed.

The execution aroused violent feelings in eastern Canada. A military expedition was sent out, and it put down Riel's party. Riel himself, and Lionel Dybig with him, decided to go into exile in the United States. And because his father was going, Bart went over the border into Dakota, and then to Montana. Bart stayed in the U.S. until his father's death emphasized his sense of difference from those around him; then his loneliness drove him back to Canada, to try to find the relatives in the western mountains he had heard his father refer to on that one occasion. Surely, he thought, he had someone he belonged to.

He knew that meanwhile, back up in Canada, a group of followers of the dead Thomas Scott had banded together, calling themselves Scottites; and apparently still dreamed of an armed control of the Canadian government, so as to run it their way. They were generally despised among the métis, but they survived. If Arthur had had his name associated with them, even by purely casual rumor, the eventual result could mean trouble for him—and for Emma.

"I'll be truthful Bart," said Emma now, "Arthur does things he doesn't tell me about. But as I say, the store is our living. I can't believe he'd be foolish enough to get mixed up with the Scottites. If there was any rumor like that, one of them would have told me about it, and no one has."

"Good, then," said Bart, relieved.

They were almost back at the store. In part, the quickness of their return was caused by the shortness of the street itself; but it was also partly due to the silence between them that had followed Bart's words—a companionable silence, however.

It was strange, thought Bart, that after so long a time apart, they should need to talk so little, and be so comfortable without words needing to be spoken. No, he corrected himself, it was not strange at all. It was because they knew and understood each other so well. For the first time, the small coal of a dangerous anger kindled itself deep inside him. Why should Arthur be allowed to stand in the way

of their being together, as surely all Emma's instincts must tell her
they should be?

But to that, there was no good answer; and as long as Emma
refused to change the situation, Bart himself was helpless. Abruptly
now, he felt baffled. When the rebellion had been quashed and they
had left Canada, Emma's family had already left Sainte Anne—
following the death of their only surviving parent—their father—
eight months before. When Bart had followed Riel into exile,
therefore, he was leaving a place where he felt he had no close ties
to anyone; and he had given up hope of ever seeing Emma again.
Now, this sudden rediscovery of her and the sudden rekindling of
the hope that perhaps he might have her with him for the rest of his
life, after all, had left him no longer sure that he wanted to continue
searching for his lost relatives—or anything else except staying here
and somehow forcing her to free herself of Arthur.

However, to do that would be to force Emma against the grain of
her conscience—and that he could not do.

As if she had been able to read his thoughts, she suddenly took
his hand in hers now as they walked—a shocking thing for a single
woman to do in public in a small community of this time and place;
but then Emma had always been a law unto herself. On the other
hand, thought Bart, if there was anyone anywhere around that
wanted to make some objection to what she had just done—Bart
felt the sullen coal within him flicker with the first brightness of
flame, and the heavy muscles across his stomach tightened. He
looked deliberately up and down the street into the windows of the
houses there, but there was no one to be seen looking out at them
now, not even children.

"Bart," Emma said; and he thought he had never heard anything
more soft and gentle than her voice when she lowered it as she did
now to speak to him privately. "You know if it wasn't for Arthur
I'd follow you anywhere. Have faith, dear. God is always on the
side of those who do right; and what's right is for me to stay and
help Arthur while you go search for your people. I'll wait and hope,
Bart. Can't you do the same?"

His hand closed around her much smaller one.

"If that's what it takes," he said. "I'll wait—"

He broke off, for Arthur had just walked into sight around the
farther front corner of the store. He was towing by a halter a
heavy-headed, long-eared beast.

"Look what I got you, Bart!" he called triumphantly. "You

needed a horse. Well, here's something better than a horse; especially up in the mountains where a horse might panic and go off the side of a cliff with you on him. A mule's got too much sense for that; and here's a mule for you.''

Bart and Emma had come together with him by the time he had finished speaking, and they all stood together in front of the store.

"Not that it's for sale," Arthur went on.

Either the drinks he had had before dinner were still working in him, or he had had a few more. His gestures were a little loose and his face was flushed, his voice uncontrolled. He laughed now, and the laugh was louder than was called for by the situation. "It needs returning to the man who owns it; but you can use it along the way, since he's where you want to go, anyway. I've got a map, too. I'll show you."

"Arthur, what is all this?" demanded Emma. She had let go of Bart's hand at the appearance of her brother.

"Bart here wanted a bigger horse so he could pack more gear and supplies," said Arthur to her. "Well, this is a mule that Guillaume Barre's cousin borrowed from a man named Charles Waite, up at Shunthead; and that's where you want to go from here, anyway. That's the place where it's most likely somebody might know where your relatives are."

He passed the rope from the mule's halter into Bart's hand.

"You can peg him out back overnight and decide how you want to use him in the morning. Probably want to ride your horse until you hit the steep mountains; and until then, of course, there's no better pack animal than a mule. After you peg him out, come on upstairs and I'll give you the map Guillaume drew me."

The twilight had been fading steadily. But there was enough light left for Bart to see that Arthur had found him a good, healthy animal of generous size.

"I'll do that," he said, and started leading the mule around the back of the store. "Thanks, Arthur."

"Think nothing of it," said Arthur, and laughed again a little too loudly. As he went around the corner of the store, Bart heard Emma behind him, speaking to her brother.

"Shunthead?" she was saying. "I never heard of it."

"Why should you," said her brother, "you're only a woman!"

The daylight was almost gone. Bart found a sledgehammer in the store and a decent piece of wood out back for a stake and drove it into the ground too far for the mule to jerk it out. Then he ran his hands completely over the animal's body; and, as far as eyes and touch could tell him, there were no galls or sores and the mule was in fine condition.

He went back into the store to put the sledgehammer back where he had found it, and found himself wondering at Arthur's efforts to help him out. Of course, Arthur would want to see him gone as soon as possible. The whole world might trust Emma to keep her word and stay with her brother; but that brother had no faith in himself and therefore little faith in others.

By the time Bart got back upstairs Arthur had gone to bed and the snoring of someone heavy with drink could be heard coming from the larger, front bedroom. A map drawn in ink on the back of a public notice sign lay on the kitchen table. Bart looked at it and put it in a breast pocket of the shirt inside his jacket. He looked toward the sound from the front bedroom.

"Does he do this often?" Bart asked Emma, who was finishing up the washing of the dishes.

"Almost never." She frowned. "He gets terrible hangovers if he drinks at all; and he usually stays clear of it."

"Is this Guillaume Barre a drinker?" Bart asked. "If he is, he could have led Arthur into it, tonight. We had a couple of drinks before dinner, but the food should have taken care of that."

Emma shook her head.

"I don't really know Guillaume Barre," she said. "He came in with a load of prime pelts only a few weeks ago, and he's been around ever since, though he's gone days, hunting I guess. I suppose he drinks. Most trappers drink themselves insensible whenever they come out of the woods and get their hands on a bottle. In fact, they buy their needs for next winter, drink until the money left over runs out, and that's the last we see of them until next year. He's staying with the Pinaud family—that's two houses down on the right."

"I think I might drop down there," mused Bart. "Barre could tell me a little more about this Shunthead place and the way to it; and I could thank him for letting me take the mule back."

He stood next to her at the sink, hesitating.

"Unless," he said tentatively, "you've got some time to just sit and talk . . ."

She turned to face him.

"No, Bart," she said, "I'm going to bed now; and so should you, as soon as possible. We both have to get up early if we're going to get in a good day."

"Yes," he said emptily. The urge to put his arms around her was almost overpowering, but his early upbringing and hers, as well as her attitude, made an invisible wall around her. "Then . . . I'll see you in the morning."

"In the morning, Bart dear," she said.

He turned and left her, going down the stairs out of the door and into the settlement street. He found the house she had spoken of, but its windows were dark. In itself, this was not surprising. Most people out here went to bed right after dinner and rose with the dawn or before it; and most of the other houses along the street were also already dark.

Bart knocked on the door anyway, and when there was no answer, opened the door which custom would naturally have left unlocked, and stepped into the darkness within.

There was no light within the house whatsoever, not even that from the coals of a fire in a fireplace just used for cooking or banked against the owner's return. Bart searched in one capacious side pocket of his long leather jacket until he found a wooden match, struck its head with his thumbnail as he held it up in his right hand, and looked around in its sudden, yellow light as the head burst into flame.

It was an ordinary cabin, untidy and dirty as such a cabin could be when its occupant had no interest in keeping it clean. There were a couple of stools, a table, a fireplace with nothing but some cold burnt ends of logs and white ash in it, and a bunk against one wall beyond the fireplace, with the blankets half out of it and spilled on to the floor. No one had been here for hours, nor was there any sign that anyone was likely to return here soon.

The match burned dangerously low toward the skin of the fingers with which Bart was holding it. He shook it out, turned to the door and went out again, back to the store.

Inside, in the back room there, he found a parafin lamp burning on a flour barrel, beside a bunk fastened to a wall by the foot of the stairs. Blankets that had been washed and aired recently had been neatly spread on it to make up a bed. Bart smiled, for Emma's hand was as visible here as if he had seen her making the bed ready herself.

He glanced up the stairs, but everything was quiet and dark above. He shrugged, took off his outer clothes and went to bed—but from old habit he put his revolver and knife under the flour-sack pillow.

He woke instantly to the sound of movement overhead but, realizing he had roused at the first noise, lay still and waited while

Emma—it must be Emma—completed her getting up and walked into the kitchen area. His senses told him that while it was not yet dawn, sunrise could not be far off. Probably the dark sky was lightening a bit in the east, but he of course could not see that from here in the back room. He continued to wait while Emma moved about the kitchen for fifteen minutes or so, then rose silently and dressed, putting his knife and pistol back in place at his belt.

Then he went upstairs.

"Arthur?" he asked, to Emma's back as she stood at the stove, frying what his nose told him was bacon.

"Arthur'll sleep late today," she said. "He'll feel too bad to get up until long after you've gone, Bart."

She turned to face him, and smiled at him. He smiled back, happily.

"Emma," he said, "I love you."

Abruptly, her face became serious.

"You mustn't say such things," she said, "not until I'm free to hear them."

But then she smiled again.

"I think of you always," she said softly. "Now, sit down and have your breakfast."

She gave him the oatmeal they had both grown up on, with brown sugar syrup to pour on it, half a dozen eggs and possibly half a pound of bacon along with the better part of a loaf of bread and currant preserves, all washed down with freshly made black coffee in large amounts.

"I haven't eaten food this good in years," he told her.

She beamed at the compliment.

"Would you like some more bacon and eggs?" she asked.

He shook his head. She would be familiar with the need of travelers to load up at the beginning of the day, not knowing when their next real meal would be or what shape it might take; but she could not know the size of his adult appetite. He could have eaten another meal like the one she had just given him, and not been overfull; but there was no need for her to know that now, and it was another of the differences he was a bit shy about; but he had already eaten better than he had for a very long time.

"I've had breakfast," he said, "and I've got to start loading up ready to leave. Can I buy some things from the store downstairs?"

"Of course."

She led him down into the front room. He picked out some sacks of flour, bacon, salt, matches, dried beans, extra tarps, blankets and a rain slicker; most of the homely necessities needed by a man alone in the wilderness—as well as a few little luxuries such as crackers and tinned peaches and sardines. From one of the match boxes he took a small handful of matches and put them in the side pocket of his jacket.

"I always keep some there for emergencies," he told her.

"Emergencies?" she asked him. "You've got flint and steel, of course?"

"Of course," he said. "But sometimes a match is handier."

He paid her in American silver. She pushed the coins back across the counter at him.

"You don't have to do that," she said. "We can carry you on the books the way we'd carry any trapper, until next spring—or forever, if it comes to that. There's always those who don't come back the following spring."

"I'll be back," he told her, pushing the money once more to her, "and besides I've got plenty of cash from working below the border."

She picked up the coins.

"I'll put you on the books anyway," she said, "and keep this for you. If you ever need it, all you have to do is ask me for it."

"All right," he said. "If that's how you want it."

They went back upstairs, and she handed him a bag filled with lumpy objects, its opening closed with a drawstring, then further sealed with wax.

"I made you some hardcakes," she said. "Be sure you remelt the wax to seal it again after you've taken one out, or seal it again with something like pine resin. The cakes are loaded with dried blueberries and sweetening, and the flies will want to get to them, given half a chance."

Hardcakes were small, fried cakes in which cornmeal, or anything else available, essentially held together the greatest possible mixture of fat and sugar; the fat usually being animal fat and the sugar, out here, being anything from ordinary sugar to the dried blueberries she had mentioned, raisins or anything sweet. The hardcakes were treats. They also were a food that could be eaten without cooking, and were a source of quick energy for someone lacking the time or opportunity to stop and build a fire for a proper meal.

"You think of everything," he said, taking the bag from her. "How can I thank you for things like this?"

"You know I love doing it," she said.

He carried the sack of hardcakes, along with most of the items he had selected in the store below, out back to the mule. He would have carried the whole load himself if his arms had been long enough. As it was, Emma brought the smaller and lighter items behind him. It was a fresh, cool, bright morning, a little damp from a brief rainshower probably just before he had awakened; and the peaks of the mountains stood up on the western horizon. The mule took uncomplainingly to being packed with not only the things he had bought from the store, but some of the extras he had been packing on the pony. The horse would now find its load lightened by that much, at least.

"Well," he said finally, turning to Emma. The sun was just up over the far wall of the valley opposite the direction he must go, according to the map Arthur had left for him. "Goodbye for a little while, Emma."

She held out both hands to him. He took them . . . so small they were . . . in his own two hands. Again the urge was all but overpowering to put his arms around her, to kiss her—but he could feel that she did not want him to do more than hold her hands, for the moment.

"For as long as it takes, Bart," she said.

Her eyes were very clear blue, looking up at him. He could hardly believe that she could look so lovingly at what he knew she must be seeing, the brows and cheekbones large and prominent under the densely black hair, tight-curled against his large skull. The beard, full and dark and thick, hiding a jaw as fiercely prominent as the cheekbones and forehead; hair and beard together framing eyes of a glinting, dark brown. A face to make people stand aside from it, not love its owner as she plainly loved him; for all that she would not give up her duty to Arthur and go away with him.

But then, Emma had always seen more in people than others saw. His father, in particular, had given her credit for having unusual perception and intelligence; and when his father gave that sort of compliment . . .

But none of it mattered now. It was time for him to go. He made himself let loose her hands, and they dropped to her sides like slain birds.

"I'll be back," he said again; and swung himself up over the pony, which he had saddled some minutes earlier.

Emma handed up the end of the rope fastened to the mule's halter, and he took it.

"Here."

"Thanks. Goodbye, Emma. I'll be back."

"I know you will."

He shook up the reins of his pony and rode off. The mule followed after without protest.

chapter
three

IT WAS NOT until he rode out into the settlement street that the feeling of uneasiness struck him. From where he was he could see, only a little way farther beyond the houses and the tiny graveyard, the valley slope down which he had approached Mossby. That slope continued a short distance past the town to the edge of the river; and it ran alongside the river, rising to the place where the river first came into sight between two hills.

When he had come, no one had been expecting him. But the slope before him was wooded. The way he must go, up alongside the river, he was open and exposed to any rifleman who now might be hidden in the trees that covered most of the ground to the far wall of the small valley. There was absolutely no reason to expect such a rifleman, but he had a sudden, inexplicable feeling inside him that someone was up there. He turned to look behind him and saw that Emma had followed him out of the yard behind the store, still smiling.

She continued to follow him as he rode past the buildings and the graveyard, out into the open land. By the last house she halted, and stood watching him as he went. And the apprehension lifted. Just as he had felt the reasonless certainly that a gun was waiting, aimed at him from the trees on the crest of the valley rise, perhaps beyond the river, he also was suddenly certain that it would not fire as long as Emma was standing there, watching.

She watched him out of sight and no gun sounded.

Nearly a mile from the settlement, the trees on the left bank of the river, up which he rode, closed in on the water; and the underbrush between them was too thick for riding. He turned and swam the river with both animals, emerging on the tree-crowned bank of the far side. But as he passed into the trees, he passed beyond the point where he could see back to the settlement—or Emma, watching there, could see him.

The uneasy feeling he had had was gone. After all, he thought, even if there had been someone there with a rifle, that person might have had nothing against him specifically, might not even have known who he was, but been on guard against a possible enemy who had nothing to do with Bart. There were many men on the frontier who had reason to be wary of strangers.

He rode on, alone but cheerfully now that the feeling was gone.

The map he was following was simple and straightforward enough. Like most maps in this country that had been opened to Europeans by the fur traders, whoever had drawn it originally had thought in terms of canoe routes; and so the paper Bart had been given had shown a route following a sequence of three rivers, with the first important one—not the one he was on now—eventually flowing into the second, and a route over land where he would leave the second river to take the third, on the western watershed of the Rockies.

It was easy enough going; and the mule gave him no trouble. However, on the afternoon of the sixth day after leaving Mossby, the uneasiness that had touched him as he rode away from Emma came back on him. Only now, it was the feeling of someone deliberately stalking him. He continued to travel just as he had been doing, but he kept eyes, ears and nose alert for any sign that could back up the feeling.

However, there was nothing. And yet the feeling, instead of going away, persisted and even grew until it was strong within him as he camped for the night.

Here, where the end of day had caught him, the second of his three rivers ran narrow and deep between vertical cliffs of eighty to a hundred feet. So the camp he made was on a shadowed, mossy ledge among thick but stunted spruce and pine; and the roar of the river below hid any sound he might hear of someone approaching. And once the sun was gone he was effectively blind as well as deaf.

He did not like camping under these conditions, but the end of the daylight left him no choice. He unloaded the pony and mule and tied them out among the trees only a couple of dozen feet from his fire. Then he set about preparing some of his bacon with an amount of the dried beans he had had soaking in a closed flask, tied to his saddle throughout the day.

The beans took longer than the bacon to cook, even with the day's soaking, so that it was deep dark and no moon visible because of thick cloud cover by the time the food was ready to eat. He had made an amount that suited his large appetite, and he stuffed himself with everything he had cooked, leaving nothing;

for he had decided to get out of here at the first glimmer of daylight, without waiting to make any kind of breakfast.

Meanwhile, both the pony and the mule had been quiet, which gave him a certain amount of reassurance. He let the fire burn down to coals against the boulder before which he had deliberately built it; and, warmed by the reflected heat from the fire-warmed stone, rolled himself in his blankets and let himself go off to sleep.

He woke suddenly, at once fully awake and alert. The cloud cover had thinned, and a small pale moon could be glimpsed through thin parts of it at stray moments, high overhead. It must be well past midnight, he thought; and he closed his hands, one around the rifle he had taken to bed with him, the other on the butt of his revolver.

He lay still. The feeling of an inimical presence nearby was as strong as a rank smell in his nostrils. But as he continued to lie still, waiting, no betraying sound or odor came to him to help him identify it, or tell where about him it might be.

There was an uneasy stir from one of his animals. He glanced in their direction, wishing the moon would come full out; or that he dared to give away the fact he was no longer sleeping by putting some more wood on the fire, so that he could see better. The pony moved; he heard though he could not see it. It was completely hidden in darkness; but he could just make out the head of the mule, who had not moved but stood now, stock-still but head-on to a niche between two huge boulders, with its rear hooves facing outward and its ears upright and listening.

Plainly, both beasts were feeling what he was feeling. Perhaps, with their animal hearing, they had heard what he had not. The mule, at least, had moved into a position of defense—anything coming at it would face those lashing rear hooves. The pony, less intelligent, was the likely target if what was out there in the dark was animal, rather than human.

If it was human, the chances were that he was the target.

It was strange, as strange as his fear of a hidden rifleman among the trees when he had left Mossby. The price on his head was enough to attract a casual bounty hunter who just happened to cross Bart's path. But it was not enough to make it worth anyone's time to trail him for it. Particularly since any such person must know that Bart would not be an easy man to take or kill; so that trying to collect the bounty could be a dangerous business. And Bart's habit of avoiding closeness with people generally had kept him from making personal enemies—at least the sort of enemies that might take the trouble to hunt him down.

The minutes slipped by without a sign or a sound. Still, Bart waited. The pony neighed, suddenly, a frightened sound.

Moving abruptly, Bart reached out from his blankets, snatched up a handful of small twigs and threw them on the red coals of the fire. They did not catch for a moment, but the coals, disturbed, brightened; and a small flame licked up from one blackened bit of log. In that extra light, Bart caught a glimpse of the pony; and, on top of a boulder six feet above it, a pair of glowing eyes.

Cougar.

He was out of the blanket, on his feet and firing the rifle even as the eyes sailed through the air toward the pony. The crash of the rifle, the kick of its butt against his shoulder combined with the thud of a body falling almost at his feet. The twigs had caught, now, and flame was rising from them, illuminating the two equines and the camp area clearly.

The cougar lay still, stretched out and dead on the stony ground a long step from Bart's feet. The rifle bullet had gone through its throat and head as it leaped. Bart lowered the rifle. A cougar. The only predator other than a grizzly or a hungry wolf that would be likely to try taking a prey as large as the pony in single attack; and often a night hunter. He should have guessed that it might be a cougar that had been shadowing them all day, hoping for a chance at one of his animals.

A flicker of movement seen out of the corner of his right eye made him duck instinctively; and a heavy blow sent him tumbling to the ground, losing his grip on the rifle. Even as he went down, a thought flashed through his mind.

There had not been one cougar but two, a mated pair, perhaps, hunting together. It was rare but it happened. He scrabbled at his belt holster for the revolver, found it fallen away, too, and reached instead for his knife. At the same time he was rolling over on his back and drawing his knees up tight against his body to protect his stomach and chest.

He had a glimpse in the dim firelight of a gray body leaping at him—from the direction of his legs. He had his hand on the hilt of his knife now, but no time to get it out, and the angle of the beast's attack made the knife awkward to use. He lashed out with both feet and all the heavy power of his massive thigh muscles behind the movement.

His heels slammed into the leaping body in midair. The big cat glanced off to one side and upward; then, dropped—over the edge of the cliff to the riverbed a hundred feet below, with a yowl of surprise and alarm that fell away into silence below. For a moment Bart lay where he was, catching his breath.

There were no more enemies to fear now; and the instinctive feeling in him was now gone. For more than two cóugars to hunt together was unheard of.

The pony was neighing shrilly and pulling wildly at its neckrope. The mule still stood in a position of defense and turned itself slightly to put its rear hooves toward Bart as Bart got to his feet and shakily went about collecting his dropped rifle and revolver. The mule's eyes continued to be rolled back, watching him, ready to act if he came within kicking range.

Bart stayed well clear and the pony began to calm down. He sat down by the fire and threw several more, larger, branches on it. Then he got back up and walked over to where his saddlebags lay, with the saddle on the other side of his fire. From the left boot he removed a pint bottle of whisky and took a couple of swallows. He recorked the bottle tightly, then put it back into the small nest of hay that protected it against accidental blows and breakage.

The fire was blazing strongly now. He got out his coffee pot, which he had cleaned and packed away before going to sleep, in preparation for his planned early start in the morning. He threw a handful of new coffee grounds into it and added water from his canteen and put it on the coals. He sat there, watching the flames of the fire as the pot came to the boil, feeling the alcohol inside him gradually beginning to make its calming effect felt.

Then he sat, drinking, and as the level of the coffee in the pot slowly dropped, he began to notice a lightening of the sky. They were closer to dawn, then, than he had thought. He finished the coffee and set about getting the pony saddled and the load on the mule. By the time they were ready it was almost light enough to travel. He had another half cup of coffee, carefully put out the fire and left.

The rest of the trip was uneventful, and he was not visited again by the feeling of being watched or pursued. He came at last to the portage across to the third river. Like most portages, it was passable enough for human animals on two legs, even those loaded down with more than a hundred pounds of canoe gear or supplies, but impassable to four-legged beasts like the two with him. He had to cut a way through for the horse and mule, including the chopping through and clearing of two good-sized trees, over which the human portagers would merely have clambered, before he could bring them all safely to the third river.

The portage came out at the point where the third river joined a fourth that was not on his map and that was navigable downstream by canoe. The third river itself was not. It was a racehorse of water from the high mountains, forty yards wide and not much more than a yard deep, foaming around boulders of all sizes and stampeding downhill at twenty to thirty miles an hour. He began to pick his way up along one side of it, riding around obstacles when these intervened on the bankside. The far bank looked like it would be easier going; but to try to cross the river, alone or with the horses, would have been suicide.

In the late afternoon, he encountered a wagon trail from somewhere else downslope, which he could follow upriver in the direction he was going. The road curved in toward the river from somewhere else off through the mountains—evidently there was another town or settlement not too far away, and perhaps having a quicker route by river to larger centers of civilization in some mountain valley or even down on the coast. The road showed the signs of frequent use. It was a ''corduroy'' road, surfaced with the narrow, trimmed stems of small trees, laid down side by side, to form a surface that would not go into impassable muddy ruts under the wagon wheels.

He took it, as an easier route to Shunthead; and one late afternoon he came up over a steep crest of rock to look down into a narrow, rocky valley with a lake at its bottom hardly wider than the river had been. Buildings constructed of boards clung to the side of the nearer of the two steeply inclined slopes. The road went at an angle down the slope, to a precarious platform of rock and earth; where it did a switchback and then angled in the opposite direction to deal with the steep pitch of the valleyside until it reached the gentler slopes just above the lakeshore, on which the buildings were erected.

One glance at those buildings was enough. The name of the place should have told him, as well as the fact that it was a mule he was returning. For that matter, the corduroy road itself had been a strong indication that it must lead to a mining camp, since only a mine would require the bringing in of equipment and supplies heavy enough to require the use of wagons. There was no farming this far up in these mountains. The only use for mules here could be for hauling, in and out of and around a mine—and this was a mine.

Now that he had made the identification, it was easy to pick out the miners' bunkhouse, the cookshed, the offices and other buildings used by the staff, as separate from the one or two residences that would be occupied by those in charge here, who ran the mine. There was even the waterwheel-driven sawmill, sited on a stream that spilled over the valley wall about two hundred yards away and plunged down a steep ravine into the lake below. At the moment, the sluice gates in its wooden dam were open and its waterwheel stood motionless, clear of the water. He saw no other human or animal in sight. It was possible that everyone was at work. But as at Mossby, the absence of people moving about between the buildings roused an uneasiness in him.

He picked out the largest of the staff buildings and rode to the three steps that rose to the small landing before its front door. He dismounted. The pony had been trained to stand with its reins trailing, "ground-hitched." The mule he untied from the lead rope that had tethered it to his saddle leather, and retied the rope to the end of the two-by-four handrail of the steps.

As he was doing this, a man came out of the door and stood on the landing. He was tall, middle-aged, very erect and with a noticeable pot belly. His hair was gray and thinning, and a gray mustache drooped its ends around the corners of his mouth.

"Here, you!" he said. His voice was baritone and slightly hoarse. "This is private property. I don't think we know you."

"I rather think not," said Bart, glancing up at him.

Bart had deliberately colored his voice with the accent of someone who was upper class English; and as he had expected, the contrast between his appearance and the accent checked the other for a wordless moment.

Bart, however, had unavoidably reminded himself once more of his father; and of his real schooling, which had taken place between his father and himself in that private life they shared and which the world had never suspected. As a boy, Bart had necessarily to attend the small school that was held in Sainte Anne so as not to attract attention to himself or his father; but it had been a chore—until he got to know Emma and the school became a place where he could see her. It would have been too easy in the classroom for him to score a hundred per cent correct on all the tests, and even to correct the occasional mistake of the teacher, who himself had only had a high school education.

Bart's father had taught him many unusual things, including a number of different accents, not only in English, but in French. If the man on the landing had spoken to Bart in French, he could have replied as easily with an upper-class Parisian accent. His father had also taught Bart smatterings of other languages— some German, Italian and Latin; as well as a great deal of the science and technical knowledge of the nineteenth century world, from beyond the boundaries, and in most cases beyond the imaginations, of the Canadians and Americans Bart was later to deal with.

What the older man had not taught his son was anything about his father's boyhood and family—an exception Bart had not realized for a long time simply because he had known no other way. And somehow the boy had been brought to understand that questions about these things would not be welcome to him.

"I was headed up this way, so the storekeeper in Mossby asked me to deliver a mule he said you'd lent to a man named Guillaume Barre," Bart said in the same accent, mounting the steps. "There it is, tied to the handrail down there. I don't suppose you'd care to sell me another one—or this one, if you've been getting on all right without it. As you see, I've got quite a bit of stuff to pack. I may be wintering here in the mountains."

He was on the landing by the time he had finished this speech, and was interested to discover that the other man was a good deal shorter than his first appearance on the raised platform of the landing would have given anyone to believe. The mine man had an imposing upper body and arms, but his legs were short, so that, as they stood facing each other on a level, the other was revealed, in spite of his erectness, to be a good four or five inches shorter than Bart.

"Oh?" he said now, still clearly off balance from the contrast between Bart's language and appearance. "Well, I don't know. I mean—well, come in."

He opened the door behind him and backed through it. Bart followed him through into what seemed to be an outer office. There were two tall secretary's desks and writing stools, although no one else was in view at the moment, and a sort of bench along the wall with a couple of instruments that Bart took to be microscopes. There was a dustiness and an air of relative unuse to the room. An open door in a far wall gave a glimpse of what seemed to be another office in the rear of the building.

"Well, we . . ." The mine man was clearly floundering. ". . . appreciate your bringing the mule back. If there's anything we can do by way of return . . ."

"As a matter of fact, there is," said Bart, and he repeated

much of his previous words about needing another mule.

"Sell you a mule?" said the man. "By the way, my name is Alan Morrison." Bart chose not to ask about the man Arthur had named, Charles Waite.

"Bart Dybig," said Bart.

They shook hands.

"About selling me a mule . . ." said Bart.

"Oh yes. I'm afraid that's not up to me. I'd have to have you talk to our stock handler. Of course, I'll explain to him . . . come with me; and we'll go find Sorley. He's the stock handler."

Morrison started up and reached for the door handle. Bart moved so that he stood in the way of its being opened.

"First," he said, "you might want to give me a receipt?"

"Receipt?"

"Yes, you know," Bart came down a little harder on the accent, "for the mule I've brought you. Just so I've something to show the man I got it from that I did what I promised to do with the animal."

"Ah. Of course," said Morrison. He turned back to one of the desks, took a piece of paper, dipped a pen into an inkwell and scribbled on the piece of paper.

Bart watched him curiously. There was something wrong here but he could not put his finger on exactly what it was. Receipts were normally never asked for or given out in the western prairie and mountains for animals lent and returned like this. This man Morrison might be from the east of Canada, but he would know that much if he was on the staff at a western mine like this. Of course it had been Bart who had asked for the receipt, as a sort of test and stall . . .

Granted, the man had been surprised and for some reason shaken by Bart's arrival. The fact still remained that he was acting strangely; and Bart's ever-ready wariness was stronger than ever. He studied Morrison as the other stood at the desk, writing. Plainly, he was not armed in any way; and unarmed he should be no serious threat to Bart, even if Bart had not had both knife and revolver at the belt under his jacket.

The situation was puzzling. But Bart actually did need a replacement for the mule, if he was to give it up. Also, Arthur had said that here there would be people who would know about Bart's relations, if the knowledge existed. But when Arthur had said that, Bart had taken it for granted that he was being directed to a town or settlement. Why should miners, who were usually from some other part of Canada or the U.S. originally, and normally did not know any territory but that immediately surrounding the mine, have any information about where relatives of Bart might be living?

Morrison finished his writing and handed the receipt to Bart with a snappiness that was almost a flourish. Evidently he was getting over his initial uncertainty with Bart. Bart glanced at the receipt. It was a simple few lines giving the date and noting that a mule named Sidewinder, originally lent to Guillaume Barre, had been returned this day by Bart Dybig—with Morrison's signature at the bottom.

"Come with me," said Morrison. "We'll find Sorley and ask him about selling you a mule. We're having to make some repairs at the moment and there's only a few men around to do that and some general cleanup while the mine's idle. We'll look over in the bunkhouse. Sorley was up late last night as I seem to remember. I think he may be catching a nap."

Morrison led the way out of the building and down the steps. The day had turned cloudless and now in the later hours of the afternoon, the shale rock under their feet and the naked granite walls of the two close valley sides had warmed from the sun and now threw back their radiated heat at everything in between them, so that Bart felt the heat like a blow as he walked with Morrison across to the long, two-story building.

So the mine was all but shut down at the moment? That would explain the fact that he had seen no one moving outside the buildings when he came in; but it did not feel right. The whole mine did not feel right; and Morrison himself rang as false as a lead dollar.

When they reached the bunkhouse, which again had three steps up to a small landing before the door they approached, Morrison reached the landing, then stood aside to let Bart go first. Bart stopped and shook his head. His suspicions must have been showing, for Morrison did not urge him to go forward, but put his hand on the knob and pushed the door open, shouting as he did so.

"Sorley?"

There was the mutter of something unintelligible from within and Morrison entered. Bart stepped through after him, and stopped, one pace inside the building.

The whole lower floor of the building was one large room. In that room, only the near end was occupied with cots, spaced apart by small chests of drawers. There were ten cots in all, and six of these were occupied by men half asleep and just waking up, in various stages of undress.

It was none of this, however, that rang a sense of danger, loud and clear inside Bart. What had checked him so suddenly barely inside the door was the fact that from the dust on the empty section of the floor to the clutter around the beds that stood close together at this end, clearly the whole space had not been filled with cots for a long time, if ever. And it was clear from inside that the second story that had been promised by the outside appearance of the building did not exist, or if it did it had no floor, and was open to Bart's view from the doorway. The open expanse almost shouted at him that the building was a fake, a mock-up.

But he had no time to do more than notice this. He became aware suddenly that Morrison had stepped to one side and back against the wall to the right of the door through which they had both just entered. Even as he turned his head to see what the other man was doing, he caught sight of Morrison's hand closing on and pulling down a wooden lever set in the wall, a lever connected by a movable joint to a length of two-by-four going upward—and in the next second something fell on and all around him.

It was a net.

Instinctively, he tried to throw it off, and his arms became entangled; while at the same time, as he tried to turn, his legs became tangled also in the meshes and he fell. A moment later, the men from the cots were all over him.

Something hard hit the back of his head, and that was the last sight he had of the interior of the bunkhouse.

It seemed to him that he was only unconscious for a second, no longer than the time it takes an eye to blink; but when he opened his eyes, he was someplace else. Just where, he did not at first notice, for with the return of consciousness a blinding headache had exploded in his skull.

He fought that as his Indian childhood had taught him to fight all pain—by putting it off at arm's length from him, treating it as if it was something separate and apart from himself. It was a knack, no more. As a very young child he had tried earnestly to master the technique and failed utterly; until one day, suddenly, it worked. As he later tried to describe it to his father, it was a sort of forgetting of the pain even as it happened, split-second by split-second. The pain had not gone away; it had simply become something that could be recognized or disregarded at will.

So, now, with his headache from the blow on the head.

". . . Good," he heard Morrison's voice saying. "I was afraid your man had hit him too hard and wasted him. You've got to train those men of yours, Sorley. We need them to get us people like this, but we need the people they get us to be alive and able."

Bart looked up. He was lying on a sort of tray with one foot over a blacksmith's anvil, in what seemed to be a rocky cave about twelve feet in diameter. The blacksmith, a short, square man with a gray spade beard and a leather apron under a checked shirt pocked with small black burn-holes, was just finishing up the fastening of a hinged ring, made out of three-inch wide bar stock, around Bart's right ankle. He was closing the ring by hammering the white-hot legs of a staple through two holes drilled in the turned-up ends of the open part of the ring. The legs of the staple were several inches from Bart's leg, but their heat was close enough to his skin to make Bart put his pain-control trick to work a second time.

Morrison stood watching. With him was a tall, thick-shouldered, clean-shaven man of about forty, with a smoothly polished, three-foot length of inch-thick wooden rod tucked under his arm. He was dressed in dark, baggy trousers and a dark red shirt that was open at the collar, showing a muscular neck.

"Just lie still," said this man to Bart, taking the rod from under his arm and holding it ready in his fist. Bart made no move. They were three to his one. Still, on his feet, he might have tried his luck against them even though the man holding the stick handled it as if he had had some experience using it. But attempting anything starting from his present awkward horizontal position was plainly foolish.

The stick-handler, thought Bart, must be the Sorley whom Morrison named earlier and who he had been talking to just now. Bart tried to remember if Sorley had been one of those they had wakened on entering the bunkhouse, but could not. The question was chased from his mind by the realization that already encircling his other ankle was a ring like the one now being put around his right ankle.

"What do you think you're doing?" Bart said to Morrison.

"We're a long way from courts of law out here," said Morrison, "so we make our own justice. Did you think we wouldn't recognize Guillaume Barre because you've grown a beard? Or that we'd forgot you stole the mule in the first place? Borrowed it, indeed!"

"Mule stealing—just like horse stealing—," said Sorley. Incongruously, he had a high-pitched, rasping tenor voice. "In lots of places they'd hang you for that. You've just been sentenced to ten years' work in the mine."

Bart ignored the clean-shaven man. He kept his eyes fixed on Morrison.

"Along with those other workers you need?" he asked the pot-bellied man.

Morrison did not look at him or answer him.

"Your story about Guillaume Barre's as much of a lie as that so-called bunkhouse you took me to," said Bart. "Who are you anyway? What're you mining here that you can't do it with regularly hired miners, aboveboard and honestly?"

Morrison turned to Sorley.

"Take him to the latrine," Morrison said, "then chain him up to wait for the shift just coming off work."

He went out. The blacksmith, his work finished, shoved Bart's leg off the anvil and it fell heavily to the floor. Bart started to sit up and found the stick hovering in the air inches in front of his face.

"When I tell you," said Sorley, "and only when someone tells you, do you do anything from now on. Get that straight!"

Bart said nothing. Perhaps half a minute went by and the stick did not move. Then it was withdrawn from before his face.

"Now you can sit up," said Sorley. "In fact, stand up! Stand up and move where I tell you to move to."

Bart got up. On his feet again, he was able to see that Sorley wore a revolver in a holster at his belt. It was a good thing, thought Bart, he had not tried to attack them all from his lying down position.

Sorley herded Bart out the door of what was obviously an underground blacksmith shop, into a tunnel lit at only the point where they emerged, by a parafin lamp fixed to one rocky wall. A faint breeze blew in Bart's face, back past him through the doorway. It must, he thought, be caused by whatever vent connected the blacksmith's shop to the surface—the gases from such work would have to be carried away somehow.

"Stand still!" said the voice of Sorley behind him; and he felt a blow against his back in the area of his right kidney—probably from the end of Sorley's rod. A moment later Sorley came around in front of him, carrying a cap with what looked like a small lamp attached to the front of it. He lit the small lamp with a flint-and-steel sparker, and a pale glow washed out from it into the darkness of the tunnel. Sorley jammed the hat onto Bart's head and stepped once more around behind him. The blacksmith, hammer in hand, followed along.

"To your left. Move, now!" said Sorley from behind.

He moved, the light from the lamp on his cap showing the rock walls of a tunnel about six feet wide and the same distance in height, opening out of darkness before him as he progressed. They came close to an outhouse odor which turned out to come from a dark opening in the rock off to his left.

"Stop!" said Sorley. "The latrine. Use it while you can. You won't get another chance for twelve hours."

Bart turned and went in, leaving Sorley waiting outside. What was called a latrine was clearly an abandoned length of tunnel which was now given over to be a place for the disposal of human bodily wastes. He took Sorley's advice and when he was done came back out again.

"Now," said Sorley. "Straight ahead."

They continued to another opening, this one also lit by a lamp fastened to the rock wall of the tunnel beside it. This opening also smelled, but more of unwashed bodies and clothing than anything else. At Sorley's direction he turned in and his lamp lit up a chamber hewn out of the rock, with what looked like a long wooden table down one wall. The table was empty except for a man with a badly swollen leg. The man lay flat on the table, secured there by a chain that was fastened to the rocky wall at the far end of the room, and then ran through the staple on one of the man's leg irons; it was held to the near wall by a massive padlock.

Sorley lit a lamp inside the chamber.

"Go lie down beside him!" He prodded Bart forward. Bart moved down along the table, climbed up and lay down next to the man with the swollen leg, who stared at him with interest—or seemed to. It was hard to read his expression, for hair and beard tangled together hid nearly all his face. His clothes were torn and worn to rags.

Sorley had meanwhile unlocked the padlock. He came down with the free end, poked it through the staple on Bart's right leg-iron and pulled it on through. He pinched out the wick of the lamp in Bart's hat. The blacksmith stood close at hand, watching, hammer in hand.

"Save your carbide for work hours," Sorley said.

He went back up to the far end of the room, carrying the end of the chain, which he refastened to a heavy bolt set in the rock of the wall there, locking it in place with the padlock.

"Now lie quiet until your shift comes back. Then you'll be fed."

He turned out the lamp he had lit and left, leaving Bart, with the other man, in darkness except for what little light reflected into their rocky prison from the lamp in the tunnel, outside the opening.

The man beside Bart stirred his leg on the bare boards. His voice came hoarsely out of the darkness, like the voice of a man who has gone so long without talking that his vocal cords have nearly forgotten how to work.

"Welcome to hell, friend."

chapter
four

THE LENGTH OF the chain that dragged behind Bart, like all the lengths of that chain that bound the moving line of raggedly dressed men together, pulled at his ankle and rang on the rocky floor of the tunnel. But he no longer noticed its sound or its weight. As always, his mind was at work on other matters; and his body automatically followed the movements of the man one step in front of him, the length of that step determined by a pin dropped through the link of chain just before the chain passed through the staple on the right leg-iron of the man ahead.

They moved in unison because they had to, because their legs were spaced apart and linked together by the chain; but long practice had made that unison almost an instinctive movement.

"Duck," the word came back down the line of men, passed from each one to the man behind him.

Bart was fifth in the line of eight, and far enough from the guard in front with his lantern so that the warning was ordinarily necessary. As usual, the small lamps by which they worked and which were a part of the caps they wore had been put out before they were moved, so that they would be that much less likely to know where they were being taken. But Bart knew anyway. Just as he now knew the low point in the tunnel ceiling was coming. However, he ducked and dutifully repeated the word back over his shoulder even as he bent his knees and his neck.

He was taller than most of the men on the chain; and during the first few weeks here in the mine where they lived and worked, he had taken several hard blows on the head before learning to respond to that warning immediately and without question. The sickening crack of the rock against his thankfully thick skull was in his memory now, even though time had turned the lesson into an unthinking reflex. But now he knew when such bumps were coming, just as he—evidently alone among all the men on the chain—knew the route they were on and the destination in the mine to which they were headed.

He knew these things because he had qualities of survival in him that his captors did not guess, nearly all of them the result of things learned either during his childhood years in the Indian camp or later from his father. Most of the captured men driven to work here died in a matter of months, if not mere weeks; but long before they died, they sank into an apathy in which they did not talk and hardly seemed to think at all. Seeing this, Bart had deliberately kept his brain busy every moment of his every waking hour, in the long months he estimated he had been imprisoned here.

He had found in himself two tools for doing this; and the first was a legacy from his father. His father had not only been an omnivorous reader, always surrounded by books; he had also had a prodigious memory. And Bart, growing up at his side, had thought it only natural that anyone should remember word for word a book he had read once; consequently, with his child's retentive memory he had stored in the back of his head everything he had read, so that by concentrating a little he could see it all, page by page in his mind, and reread it as if it was physically before him.

When he got older he gradually became aware how unusual this ability was, not only in himself but in his father; but he owned it nonetheless by that time and learned to follow his father's example of not drawing the attention of others unduly to it.

But now, here in the mine, it was a lifesaver. He searched through his mental library for anything that might amuse and instruct him; and so, even as he worked, or lay in the damp, odiferous darkness of the sleeping platform, he was able to put his surroundings away from him while he reread the books in his memory—both for mental relief from those surroundings, and for anything that might help him get away from them.

It paid off. Knowledge, he knew, was power; and from the beginning he set up systems to collect information about his situation.

All knowledge was potentially useful. It did not matter if an immediate use for it was not visible at the time the knowledge presented itself. It could still be learned and stored against the moment when it would become useful—as his training in the use of accents had been momentarily useful with Morrison, even though it had not kept him from ending up here.

Consequently, from the first day he had been taken out to work, he had estimated the length of step that the chain permitted him. He had counted the distances, the turns, the climbings and descendings of each trip; and in the succeeding days put them all together in a map that was constantly growing in his mind.

For days at a time they would be taken from their dormitory to work in only one part of the mine. But eventually, they would be shifted to some other place, when the vein of gold ore they drilled for, blasted for, and collected after blasting, had run out. On the way to each different destination they passed other tunnel mouths. At rare times they had glimpses of larger, lit caverns, blasted out of the solid rock. All of these places and the routes to and from them had been stored away on the map building in Bart's mind.

"This way . . ."

It was the voice of Gregory, their guard and leader, also the man who actually handled the explosives. The explosives were packed into the holes they drilled, to set off explosions that loosened the ore they then gathered; and which they then put in the small, high-sided metal cars, pulled by the mules, who also worked here in the darkness and dampness. Gregory, up front with a revolver at his belt and a ready rod of polished, three-foot hardwood in one fist, a lantern in the other.

"Stop!" It was Gregory's voice, this time unusually subdued.

There was the feel of a new draft of air on Bart's face as utter darkness suddenly descended. Up front, Gregory had suddenly blown out his lantern, and now not even faint glimmers of light were lancing back occasionally between the moving bodies in front of Bart. Bodies which had obediently stopped.

"All right, come on now. Pick up your chains." It was Gregory again, but now speaking in something barely above a whisper. "I don't want to hear a sound, you understand me? Not a sound!"

Bart reached down like the others to pick up the length of chain that connected the shackle on the ankle of his right leg with that on the right leg of the man in front of him. As quietly as possible, they moved ahead—and came out into a room so large that the few lamps burning on its far wall were dimmed by distance.

"We wait here," Gregory whispered. "There'll be people coming through. If one of them so much as looks this way because of a noise you've made . . ."

Bart moved, as silently as possible, out sideways, half a step from behind the man in front of him, to get a better view. He was aided by the fact that the tunnel they had just emerged from had now entered this larger cavern at an angle, so that they now stood almost in echelon, able to look clearly across at the other side where the far lights burned like yellow glowworms, at distances Bart estimated to be about thirty feet apart. The walls of the roughly circular chamber in which they now stood ran clear to his left, without an opening until it came to an entrance against the lighted far wall, wide enough for three people to walk through side by side and obviously the opening of the main tunnel leading forward to the front entrance of the mine. But to his right an undulation outward of the rock wall hid the continuance of the main tunnel deeper into the mine.

Their work gang had been in the process, Bart knew from his mental map, of being taken to a new workplace. They had crossed this particular large cavern before, he was sure, but always it had been simply a vast dark space, with no lights on the other side to show it to their eyes—the light they ordinarily traveled in was too weak to illuminate such a space.

Now there were lighted lamps, stationed at intervals along the far wall, and Bart could see the length of that wall and a blackness that must be a tunnel opening, off at the left end of the wall. It was unusual for so much light to be anywhere in these tunnels, he knew, even though it was still not enough light to illuminate the work party that crouched at the other side of the chamber. It must be that something was about to happen.

They waited in silence, and Bart pondered. He suspected that Gregory—who answered to bosses of his own—had made some mistake, such as misjudging the time, so that they were here when they should not be. Which would mean Gregory's retaliation for any noise that would betray their presence would be even more savage than his usual wont—and in the past months, Bart had seen men die under that polished wooden club.

He tried to think what could be happening, that shackled slaves like themselves should not be allowed to have sight of. He came up with the notion that someone important might be passing through the mine—although he could not for the life of him imagine who such people might be, or why they might be there. He, himself, had never lost hope of getting out of here, someday; but he knew that most of his fellow prisoners had long given up hope and that their overseers had no real fear of anyone escaping. Even if one of them could get loose from the chain or slip off without being seen at some time when they were off the chain, whoever did so would get lost in the lightless tunnels; and even if by some miracle such an escapee found his way to the front of the mine, he would still have to pass a sort of guard post that Bart had been told of, up where the mine opened to the surface.

He remembered no such guardhouse himself because he had

been unconscious when he had been brought in. But the other men had talked of it. The thought of it did not stop him. Just as he was slowly putting together a knowledge of the pattern of the tunnels in his mind, so he would work out ways of getting past whatever guards might bar his way at the mine entrance. There might be more than one and they might be armed; but they would also be complacent about the inability of any one of their charges trying to escape. They would be unsuspecting when he finally came to them; and all he needed was to get his hands on the revolver of one guard to get past them all.

Happily, the one thing their captors did for them was feed them as much as they could eat. The food was mainly vegetables in a sort of meat gravy. But in spite of the fact that the food was plentiful, he had felt a weakness growing on him, and he knew he had been losing weight. He would have to make his escape soon. There was no such thing as medical attention for the slaves. Their guards' one cure for any hurt or illness was rest. And with that rest the slave either recovered or died.

The man with the swollen leg—Hatfield, his name was, Bart remembered—had died three days after Bart had first been brought in. The rock that had broken his leg had also gotten dirt into the wound, and the leg had been already gangrenous by the time Bart was made to lie down and be chained up alongside him on the community plank bed.

But before he died, Hatfield had told Bart some things. One of them had been a description of the guardhouse, because Hatfield had been brought in on his feet, at gunpoint. Another—

Bart's thoughts were interrupted by the first sounds that signaled someone was either approaching the large chamber they were in, or passing by it in one of the tunnels connected to it. The echoes in this underground labyrinth reflected sounds around in all directions, so much so that under certain conditions you could swear someone was coming toward you, when actually they were going away from you.

But, in this case, it became clear shortly that the sounds were not only coming toward them but coming directly and relatively rapidly. For a moment, Bart puzzled over that rapidity, then realized that he was not hearing the customary sound of feet marching in unison and the sound of chains being dragged.

Whoever approached was not bound with iron like Bart and his fellows.

What he was hearing was only the clump and shuffle of boots, and occasionally the sound of voices, distorted by echoes to incomprehensibility. Even as he thought that, the first of those he was hearing stepped into view from the tunnel entrance under the lamps to his left—the tunnel evidently came in at an angle that had prevented him from seeing lights approaching down its length.

The figure he saw was one he knew—though he had not seen the man since his first day at the mine. It was Sorley. He wore his revolver in its holster as usual; but his stick was not in his hand. It was hung on his belt at one side.

A second figure came into view behind Sorley; and—wonder of wonders, Bart knew this one, too. Not only did Bart know him, but the man who followed the leader of the mine guards was almost the last person Bart had expected to see down here, walking freely and apparently willingly to some destination along the lighted section.

It was Arthur Robeson.

The rumor, then, about which Bart had asked Emma had been true. For before he died, one of the things Hatfield had told Bart had been that the people running the mine were Scottites. The gold they mined was for the purpose of mounting an armed Scottite revolution that would overthrow the present Canadian government in eastern Canada. That was why they could not operate the mine with ordinary hired miners. They must get out the gold in secrecy, refine it in secrecy, and sell it secretly, exchanging it for the supplies they would need or the allies who could be bought.

So Arthur was one of them, after all. Not only that, but if the rumor about him had been true in this, it was probably true all the way and he had been one of them from before the time Bart, his father, and Louis Riel had gone down over the border into the States. And probably Arthur had knowingly connived in luring Bart to Shunthead and captivity, then.

Bart watched Arthur now, walking past in the lighted distance. From Arthur's viewpoint, the place Bart stood with his co-workers would be seen only as black darkness. Arthur strode freely and lightly, as a man does who wears no leg-irons and no chains; and the trousers, shirt, boots and jacket he wore were clean and unworn.

Following Arthur came several more guards carrying lanterns, mixed with people Bart did not know, but obviously free and dressed as if they had just come from the surface. Then, without warning, there emerged into his line of sight a figure that checked his breathing.

It was apparently the figure of a younger man or a boy; but even at this distance, in this light, Bart was not to be fooled. It was Emma.

She was dressed in men's clothing, with her hair either cut off or done up high on her head. In either case, it was hidden by a man's cap she wore.

Arthur, he had not been too shocked to see, now that he thought of it. But Emma—he could not believe it. She could not be one of the Scottites. She could not have lied to him about her brother. It was not in her. He had never known her to lie to anyone in her life.

But there she was; and there she passed, cut off from view suddenly by the outcurving of the rock wall to Bart's right. Within seconds the rest of the party had also disappeared.

They were gone; and the momentary glimpse of a life beyond the mine that they had brought for a moment into it was gone.

"Move now!" came the hoarse whisper of Gregory. "But keep it quiet. Pick up those chains and don't let them clank. You know what'll happen to any of you who makes a noise!"

They moved off, Bart's mind full of the brief image of Emma. Through the long hours of work that followed, he carried it like a private picture in his memory. Through the same hours, also, his mind was busy, fitting what he had just seen and what it might mean, into his already accumulated information about the mine and its operators. He was still studying its possible meanings when they at last stepped back into their sleeping chamber, left in darkness for the eleven or so hours before they would be wakened to another time of work.

He lay waiting for the few muttered conversations to cease, and for his chain-mates, particularly those who lay on either side of him, to fall asleep. At last, he was sure that those two in particular slept, and that it was likely most of the others did also.

He sat up silently in the utter darkness, reached down to his right ankle and felt with careful fingers for the staple through which passed the chain that bound him together with the others on this bed.

The fingers of both hands found the staple; and in the lightlessness, Bart smiled. Last night it had given a bit more to the pressure of his hands.

The nights of all the time he had been here, he had been working on that staple. It was made of three-eighths-inch diameter iron rod bent into the shape of a loop; and the legs of its open side driven into holes in the iron band of the leg-iron around his right ankle.

The leg-iron itself was made of three-inch-wide iron bar stock, and the white-hot ends of the staple had been driven through two holes drilled in this metal so that the staple stood at right angles to the flanges of the leg-iron. The staple's curved end stood two and three-eighths inches out beyond the surface of the leg-iron, and so gave room for the chain to pass through it. The links of the chain were made of seven-sixteenth-inch bar stock and the total chain weighed, at Bart's estimation, two to two and three-quarters pounds per running foot; and since there were about fifty feet of chain, that made for a total of nearly a hundred and fifty pounds of chain holding the sleeping men prisoner.

Ordinarily, that staple was capable of resisting the strength in any human hands. In fact, for the first months it had seemed to ignore all the pressure even his strength could put on it.

But sometime after that, he had found it slightly bent to one side.

One of the things Bart had learned from both his mother and father had been patience. All those first months he had worked on it, not only with fingers, but with the heels of both hands, putting pressure on it to bend to his right. It was not until well into the third month that a rare chance came for him, during working hours, to momentarily direct the glowworm illumination of his caplamp directly on the staple. Then for the first time he had seen confirmation of what his fingers had seemed to feel in the darkness. The staple was now visibly, if only slightly, leaning toward the right.

That very night, he began to put pressure on it to bend it back toward the left.

A couple months later, in another stolen moment of illumination when the guard's attention and that of his chain-mates was elsewhere, Bart had seen the staple now leaning at a slight angle to the left.

Once more, that same night, he had reversed the pressure he was applying; and in a bit over a month, according to the calendar he kept in his mind, he once again stole a moment and saw the staple leaning to the right.

He kept the calendar by using a memory method of visualizing what he wanted to remember—another of those tricks his father had taught him. In this case he visualized it as a massively heavy, square board, painted white and upheld at one corner by Morrison, at the other by Sorley, and with the numbers painted inside large black-edged squares in thick red ink, as the work-periods passed.

So he had continued working, with imperceptible progress at

first, and then visible nightly changes, bending the staple first one way, then the other.

Last night he had been able, with the fingers of both hands, to bend the staple as far as the chain would allow it to go. He had been sure that he was near the point where the fatigued metal would break under his hands. But he had made himself let go of the staple, forcing himself to sleep for the rest of the period allotted them for that purpose. The metal was weakening fast, breaking down under the constant flexing, but he did not want it to break until he was ready to try his escape.

But the sight of Emma, here, had brought a fever to be free upon him. He took hold of the staple again now, and began to bend it once more to the right.

He could feel it move as he put pressure on it. It bent slowly to his right, and he reversed his efforts. Now it bent to the left. To the right again . . . Again, and again, the time needed less and less each time . . .

There was a sudden ping that seemed to sound as loud as a revolver shot in his ears, even over the snores of those of his chain-mates who slept noisily.

He had frozen, instantly, at the sound that had seemed to him to echo through the room. Now he stayed still, holding his breath, waiting for any evidence that the noise had roused any of his fellow workers. But it had not.

He waited, still without moving, counting the passage of the slow seconds in his mind like a child . . . "un Napoleon, deux Napoleons, trois Napoleons . . ."

Unmoving, he counted ten minutes that way, counting to one hundred and then keeping track of the hundreds on his fingers. But by the end of that time, still, none of those around him had made any sound or movement to indicate that the sound of the breaking staple had wakened them. He let himself move.

He felt down around the staple, and found that the left leg of it had snapped, just at the point where it had flexed against the flange of the leg iron. He was able to get his right thumb through the curve of the staple, now, and he flexed the unbroken leg to his right. Once . . . twice, faster and faster—another ping.

Again he went through the slow process of waiting to see if the noise had awakened any of his chain-mates, this time holding the broken-off top end of the staple in his fingers.

But they slept on. At the end of another ten minutes he put the end of the staple into the one pocket of his leather jacket which still had no hole. There should be no evidence left behind that would let his guards guess how he had escaped. He got a grim pleasure from imagining their puzzlement. He would simply, inexplicably, be gone from the chain and the chamber.

He moved more carefully and silently than he had ever moved in his life before. Now, with escape close, he was determined not to be tripped up by any small clumsiness or mistake. Carefully he checked with his fingers along the lengths of chain to right and left of the leg-iron that had held the staple. There was slack in the linked metal both ways and that slack lay silently on the boards of their common bed-surface.

His fingers felt their way back to the now topless staple. They closed on the chain that lay between the broken uprights. Slowly and as silently as possible he began to lift up, freeing the chain from what was left of the staple.

The links of iron chinked against each other as they were lifted—but there was no change in the night sounds around him. No sign of the sleepers waking. His movement of that part of the chain he held necessarily made audible movements in its further links where they lay on the wooden planks at each side of his right leg. Small movements, but to him the noise each made in moving was heart-stopping.

But the sleepers continued to sleep, the snorers to snore. The moment finally came when the chain was completely free of the staple, and he was able to draw back his leg—carefully, so that the leg iron itself would not scrape on the boards below it—and lay the freed length of chain silently down.

He waited again for a couple of minutes. Then, slowly and in utter silence, he began to lift his body on his arms to the foot of the bed, then to extend first his right leg, then his left, silently over the edge of the bed onto the floor below. And finally to lever himself forward and stand upright, legs well apart, so that the irons still on his legs should not strike against each other and make more noise.

At last, he stood upright and free in the utter darkness. He felt behind him with the palm of his hand for ends of the planks that made up the bed. When he found them, he turned, using them as a guide, and began softly, step by step, to move toward the entrance that would let him out into the tunnel beyond.

He knew the distance to that entrance to the inch. His eyes had measured it at every opportunity. His mind had divided that distance countless times by the length of the foot movements he was used to taking as part of the chained line of men, so that he knew the number of steps he must take to leave the sleeping chamber. With his left hand touching the ends of the bed-planks as he went, he moved slowly past the sleepers . . . until at last his outstretched right hand touched the rough rock at the right edge of the entrance.

His left hand went on to find the left edge of the entrance. He found it; and he turned, following his left hand around the corner of the hewn rock, into the tunnel, facing now in the direction the map in his head had told him would lead him eventually toward the front of the mine and the exit; past whatever guardhouse existed there, to the surface and freedom.

Rapidly he left the sleeping chamber behind him. His shoes, like those of all the prisoners who had been there more than a few months, had fallen apart quickly in the damp air and on the rocky surfaces; and he moved silently in bare feet protected by the thick callouses on their soles.

The barriers to escape for the prisoners had always been massive but clumsy, just like the mining itself. One of the prisoners who had come after Bart into their chained working group, but who had lasted only a month or so before dying, had once been a miner; and he had told the rest of them that those in charge here were working the mine both carelessly and amateurishly. They were working only on the richest veins they could find, and driving more tunnel than they needed in proportion to the ore they brought out. They seemed to prefer to use brute strength rather than cleverness in getting gold from the rock.

The same attitude was apparent in the way they held their prisoners. The prisoners were not worked effectively. The killing conditions under which they lived wasted a large amount of the strength they originally had when they were first brought in, and the work that might have been gotten out of them under more humane conditions. In the same way the barriers to their escape were obvious but simple. The leg-irons and the chains were one; the lightlessness that the prisoners were kept in at all times except when they were either working or going to and from work, was another.

But Bart had now defeated both things. True, his mental map did not show all of the tunnels and workings of the mine, but it showed enough of them so that he could deduce the mine's general pattern.

That pattern, happily, was excessively simple. For all practical purposes the mine was all on one level. When an ore-bearing vein plunged downward too steeply, the mine managers simply went and found another vein, rather than digging down and creating a lower level of tunnels and workings. Also, even on its single level, the pattern was a simple layout of workings and tunnels branching out on both sides from a single main tunnel, that lit way through which Arthur, Emma and the rest had moved as Bart and his team had stood and watched them pass.

Those who managed the mine evidently had assumed that even if a prisoner should get loose, he would still be helpless by reason of the utter darkness of the tunnels. They had evidently believed this because they, themselves, would have been helpless, there in the dark. So they had not imagined someone like Bart, who would learn to live by touch, to know by feel the very walls he passed; and who had counted his steps, translating them into actual feet and inches. Essentially, he told himself, now, all he had to do was find his way to the central tunnel and then follow that toward the front of the mine rather than to its rear.

In the darkness, even the guards like Gregory would never have been able to do this. But Bart went as confidently, once he had left the sleeping chamber, as if the route was brightly lit all the way.

Ironically, in this case, he was discarding all the other routes he had worked out over the months in his head, and was simply following the route Gregory had taken them on earlier this same laboring period, to the new working. That way had led them directly to the large chamber and the main tunnel. It had to be the main tunnel, or the party containing Arthur and Emma would not have passed through it. To say nothing of the fact that their route had lamps permanently fixed to its wall, which was a sure indication that it could only be the main tunnel.

He could hear as he went the sound of his regular breathing and the light scrape of his foot calluses on the rocky floor underfoot, even these slight sounds magnified by the echoes of the mine, and by the lack of competing sounds for his ears. Under the light touch of his fingertips—right hand against rocky wall, now—the rough surface of the tunnel side slipped past.

His legs still automatically moved in the short, regular steps conditioned in them by the length of chain that had measured him from the man who had walked just in front of him. He was content that they should move that way, so that he could be sure of the distance covered with each step and the accuracy of his count of the distance to the entrance in the wall of this tunnel that he sought next.

Twice his fingertips lost contact with rock and touched air for a brief moment before they made contact with the stone side of the tunnel again. But these were side tunnel entrances he knew and had expected.

Only forty-two more steps now, according to his mental map, before he came to the tunnel junction he sought; the one at which Gregory had made his first turn yesterday on his way leading them to a new work-place and site of that chamber where he had glimpsed Arthur and Emma.

Forty-two, forty-one, forty . . . he counted off the steps; and, as he counted the numeral one his fingers slid once more into empty air.

He halted; and turned right.

His right hand reached out and found the wall of the other tunnel leading away from the one he had been following at an angle of some forty degrees. He began to move along this new route. Roughly an eighth of a mile of underground going; and, five turns later, he stepped into the large chamber.

There were no lamps illuminating the far wall now. Bart stood for a moment, staring into darkness but seeing, in his mind's eye, the chamber just as he had seen it that one time previously. So far he had encountered no light in any tunnel, nor heard any sound that might indicate anyone else was moving in the mine near him. But now, as soon as he should cross the chamber to the wall where the lamps had burned, he would be both in unfamiliar territory and in the one tunnel where his chances of encountering someone would be considerably increased.

He hesitated, searching the darkness before him with his nose sniffing for any scent of burning lamp fuel and his ears strained to pick up any sound, no matter how distant, of movement along the way he planned to go.

But he smelled and heard nothing.

Satisfied, he began to move again. Fifteen hours before there would have been no doubt about which way he would have gone. He would have turned and followed the left wall with his hand—a wall he had seen had only one other tunnel opening before the opening of the main tunnel leading to the mine entrance, so that he could not go wrong.

Now there was still no doubt. But it was not to the left he would turn. It was to the right, in the way the party they had watched had taken Emma.

chapter
five

THERE WERE TWO ways of crossing the lightless space before him. One was to feel his way around the wall to his right until he came to the opening that would be another entrance. Whatever entrance he found that way should stand a very large chance of being the opening to the main tunnel that Emma's party had taken. He remembered, though, that outward-curving wall he had seen in silhouette against the dim lighting in the chamber, before—he had not been able to see past it, and there remained the chance that between where he stood now and the main tunnel he wanted to follow, there might be other tunnel openings. If there were one or more such intervening entrances and he simply turned into the first opening he came to, thinking it was the main tunnel, he could indeed become lost.

His other route was to trust to the image of the room in his memory, and walk directly forward across the open middle of the chamber until he came to the far wall. Any wall encountered by going straight forward in a straight line must be the wall he had seen lit up, essentially that part of the main tunnel with the fixed—if now unlit—lamps, which ran through the chamber. He need only turn right then, keeping his fingers touching the wall, and he would be certain to be headed down the main route in the way Emma and the others had gone.

The second way was the sure one—unless he went astray in the darkness with no wall to touch; and walked in a curve or off at an angle, so that he hit the wall to his left or right before he came up against the wall straight ahead. He knew that in the dark most men tended to walk at a slight angle or a curve when thinking they were traveling in a straight line. If he ended up doing that, he would already be lost. For he would then have no way of knowing which way to turn, right or left, to go where he wanted. He could end up at the mine entrance or in some abandoned tunnel.

He stood for a second more, thinking it over. Even as he thought, he could see clearly in his mind's eye how the chamber had looked. It could not be more than fifty feet to the wall he wanted to reach. He must take the bold way.

He closed his eyes and let go of the wall he presently touched. Touching nothing, hands outstretched, he concentrated on the picture in his mind. Then, step by step, he began to walk across it—not the real, darkness-filled chamber which his body occupied—but that remembered room in his mind.

He counted his steps as he went. Fifty feet had been his estimate at the time; and he must trust himself. Fifty feet would have been a little over thirty-four of his chain-limited—and now accustomed—steps. If he hit a wall more than half a dozen steps before then, he had most certainly curved off and gone astray. If he went more than a few steps beyond those thirty-four it was possible that he had simply made the distance longer by angling off in coming to the wall he sought—but there would also be a strong possibility that he had taken a large curve into some farther intervening section of the chamber, or toward a side wall. In either case he would then face the question whether to continue to go to his right, hoping that whatever entrance he came to was the right entrance.

". . . twenty-four," he counted in his mind, "twenty-five, twenty-six, twenty-seven . . ."

—so far, so good.

". . . twenty-eight, twenty-nine. Thirty." He was getting close to the critical number of thirty-four. "Thirty-one, thirty-two, thirty-three, thirty-four—"

He paused at thirty-four and reached out as far as he could in front of him; but felt only air.

He began to move again, slowly, one step at a time.

"Thirty-five . . . thirty-six . . ." He was walking now with his arms at full length before him like a blind man feeling his way in unfamiliar territory—"thirty-seven . . . thirty-eight . . ."

His fingers still touched nothing but air. He stopped. He could feel his heart pounding in his chest; and, almost savagely, he willed it to slow down. He ordered his mind and body to calmness. Panic would do nothing to help him if he was indeed astray. He took up his careful movement forward with arms outstretched.

"Thirty-nine—"

His fingers bumped hardness. He stepped hastily forward in the first long stride he had taken in a year and a half; and the toes of his right foot bumped cruelly against rough, vertical stone. He flung his whole body against it, the right side of his face pressed to it, his arms outstretched and his hands laid flat against its surface in a feeling of relief as strong as love.

For several moments he merely stood clinging to it as someone lost overboard from a ship might cling to a piece of drifting timber he had been swept against by the waves.

Gradually, the feeling of relief ebbed.

He had found a wall. But was it the wall he sought?

If this was the one he had seen Arthur and Emma pass, there were the lanterns fixed to it, half a foot or so below ceiling level, and at a distance from each other that he had estimated at some thirty feet. He reached with his hands high on the wall and went right.

He reached up to touch the corner above him where wall met ceiling. He could reach it easily with his upraised arm half bent. Holding it so, he shuffled along, counting his steps to measure the distance.

"One, two, three—"

His forearm below his wrist jarred painfully against something hard and thin, projecting at right angles from the wall. Almost in the same moment his elbow touched something underneath it.

He felt downward with his hand, and his fingers touched the slick glass sides of a mine lantern in its metal case. He felt a second's longing for one of the matches he always used to carry, but they had been taken from him long ago, with anything else that might have been of use to him. Then common sense reasserted itself, and he remembered he dared not light it, in any case. Not only would its illumination attract the attention and curiosity of anyone looking down the tunnel, but the fact of the matter was that the darkness gave him an advantage over anyone coming toward him. In fact, if anyone should come, his first effort should be to put out any light the other was carrying.

He dropped his arm. The lantern did not matter, anyway. It was merely proof of what he had needed to know. He was against the wall he had had to find. He needed now only to keep it on his left, to go in the way Emma had gone.

His sense of relief was a calmer, but a more lasting thing, this time. He made himself stop and think.

He had been in a number of different parts of the mine in the past months. Sometimes the workings they were taken to required crossing the main tunnel, according to the map in his head, and sometimes they simply went deeper into the rock, but stayed on the same side of the main tunnel.

It should be safe to assume that they would always be working at the farthest point at which the mine had followed the veins of gold ore into the mountain. If that was so, then it was only reasonable to assume that the main tunnel—though Bart's working group had never worked on it—was only driven forward when necessary to keep up with the progress of the workings that were being dug forward on either side of it.

He had always assumed, therefore, that the main tunnel went merely to a dead end; no farther than the farthest of the workings to which he had been taken.

So, since only yesterday Gregory had taken them to a new working, crossing the main tunnel here in the process, then the main tunnel itself should go for only a short distance more, then stop.

But if that was so, what was that considerable party doing, headed down it, beyond the chamber in which he had seen them? Above all, where had Emma and her brother been taken? Certainly not just to see the wall of rock at the end of a tunnel.

Where was Emma now?

She could not have been brought into the mine for any good reason. The only reason for being here was to take out gold-laden ore; and she was not physically fitted to be a miner—for that matter, Arthur would probably have lasted no more than a week or two in one of the chained groups.

They must have been headed toward something Bart could not even imagine. There remained, he knew, the possibility that Emma and her group had returned up the tunnel in the time that had passed since he had seen them. But he did not believe that. Whatever it was that they went to, it must be important, and that implied time—it was more likely than not that they were still down that tunnel to his right. Something inside him was certain Emma had gone down it and not come back. Perhaps Arthur had been condemned by his fellow Scottites to something, and Emma had insisted on sharing whatever sentence had been given to her brother. It would be just like her to do something like that.

Two strong desires tugged at him, pulling him in opposite directions. With all the emotion built up over his time of living and laboring under killing conditions, he yearned to turn back and get out of this mine. But something even stronger pulled him onward, the way Emma had gone, to find her and get her free if she was held in any way.

He went on, turning his back on the hope of daylight and freedom for a while longer. Guiding himself with the fingertips of his left hand against the main tunnel wall, he followed its pit-dark way in the direction he had seen Emma disappear.

Out of old habit, he counted his steps as he took them; he had reached six hundred and fifty-one steps when the toes of his right foot, moving forward, struck painfully once more against something vertical and solid.

He moved up to find out what it was; and it was a solid wall of rock, the tunnel's end.

He stood, unable to believe what he had found. And in that moment of stillness, things began to happen.

It was as if the whole tunnel end around him suddenly tilted downward. The rock wall pulled away, vanishing from before him; and he lost his footing, pitching forward onto an incline whose surface seemed as polished and slick as if it had been greased.

He slid down the incline, gathering speed swiftly as he went. Without warning he plunged into moving water, shocking in its iciness, water too deep for him to stand up in. He went under and came back up, sputtering, fighting for air and against the current that was whirling him away. His head banged hard against rock, and he was forced under water again. Now there was no longer any air above him. He understood suddenly that the underground stream had entered a stretch where it filled its tunnel completely to the rock roof above it. There was no choice for him. His only hope was to swim forward with the current on the chance that he could reach a point where there was once more air and space above him, before his strength and breath were exhausted. He was a powerful swimmer. He swam now, knowing his life depended on it, coming up every so often to paw at the rock overhead. But each time he failed to find any air space. His senses began to slip away . . ..

. . . It seemed to be some long time afterward—at least, he was vaguely aware that there had been moments of memory before this present, definite awareness. They had been moments filled either with strange dreams or glimpses of things that made no sense. Of people passing about him as he lay in some sort of bed. Of the bed itself moving, with him in it. Of a huge room holding what seemed to be an enormous tangle of crystal and highly polished metal, and an aperture into which he and his bed slid for a moment before darkness descended again.

But this time he was not only awake, but aware of being

awake—only things were still not right. He lay on his back, still in the bed; but he was filled with a dreamy lassitude so great that to move the smallest part of him was simply too much trouble. It was not, he understood, that he could not move if he wanted to, but that the energy of wanting to was greater than he cared to expend.

Meanwhile, around him stood three small, thinly bearded figures, not much more than four feet tall, any of them, and all wrapped in togas of white cloth like those worn by ancient Romans in the pictures in the books he had read as a boy. The three were talking to each other in some garbled tongue that he yet somehow understood.

". . . how disgusting!" one of them was saying, staring at Bart's body, which had somehow become dressed in only a pair of dark trousers, "and to think—"

"We can't be sure there's anything to speak of, there," snapped one of the others, the middle one, young, with glittering eyes and broad shoulders. "What I say is, don't coddle him. Put him down with the Steeds. If there's anything worthwhile there, it'll show up."

"Clearly, he was escaping from the mine, when the safety trap at the entrance caught him," said the third, whose beard was white and who had not spoken before. "That's an indication of some unusual qualities, surely."

"Nonsense!" It was the broad-shouldered one again. "Found himself loose and wandered by chance into the main gallery, I'd say! Oh, by all means, give him the benefit of the doubt, but make him show us there's something there, first. You can't argue with that."

"I suppose not," said the third. Bart thought he heard a faint note of regret in the small, piping voice. These before him were not children, he realized without any real interest in the matter. All of their heads bulged unnaturally above the eyebrows, and they were small; but their arms and legs, emerging from the white wrappings of their clothing, were muscled like the limbs of the adults they were—even the arms and legs of the white-bearded one.

"Well, that's settled, then?" said the broad-shouldered one.

He flung his right hand upward with the index finger extended as if he was about to stab Bart with it, and unconsciousness returned.

When Bart woke the next time he was in what seemed to be a sort of barracks. Two rows of beds faced each other, with the head of each bed against one of the long walls of the rectangular room. Next to each bed was a piece of furniture that seemed to be both nightstand and chest of drawers. The walls and ceiling were of some smooth, white material; but the floor was a maze of tiny red or black tiles no more than an inch square, laid together in a multitude of interlocking geometric patterns that, however, made up no overall shape or picture. There were twenty beds on each side of the room and perhaps a dozen of these held the sleeping figures of men dressed as Bart was, in trousers of one solid color or another, but naked from the waist up. Three others were playing what seemed to be some sort of dice game on the tightly stretched blanket of a made-up bed, and four more were sitting talking in another group farther down the room.

Like Bart himself, they were all young men, clean-shaven and with hair cut short. The sight of them made Bart suddenly conscious of a coolness about his ears and the lower half of his face. He put his hand up and felt that his own beard was gone and his hair had been cut short.

He looked again at the men about him. They were massively muscled and looked to be in superb health and training. As Bart watched them, one of the four who was in the group that was talking glanced over and saw him watching them.

"Ho!" said the man. He was dark-haired and dusky skinned with what Bart would have ordinarily guessed as the features of someone from one of the Algonquian Indian tribes; but he spoke in English and his accent was, if anything, Scandinavian. "He's awake. One of you go tell Chandt."

"You tell him, Ozzard," said one of the others. "You're the one who saw he was awake."

The one called Ozzard gave the other a long, level look.

"Someday," he said.

"Any time," said the other. "But you better not waste time telling Chandt, now."

Ozzard got up and came down the room, watching Bart. He went past and out a door that was only a few feet from the foot of Bart's bed. The other three who had been talking went back to their conversation without paying any further attention to Bart. Bart thought of getting up and going over to them. Then he decided to wait for this Chandt, whoever he might be. In unknown situations, his father had said, the first to make a move gives away free information to any possible opponent.

After only three or four minutes, Ozzard returned, following behind a shorter and slimmer, but an even wider-shouldered man in at least his mid-thirties.

Like all the rest, he was clean-shaven, shirtless and his trousers were black, upheld by a wide, black leather-looking belt.

The skin of his face, like that of his upper body, had a yellowish tint to it; and there were heavy Oriental folds above his eyelids that gave his gaze a catlike look. His face as a whole was triangular and ageless, with the only lines being two deep parentheses that curved down from the sides of his nose around the corners of his mouth. His eyes, slitted under the heavy lids, were like the rest of his face—expressionless.

His upper body was strange. It did not vee-in dramatically to his waist as did those of Ozzard and the other men upright in the room. The shorter man's waist was scarcely narrower than his chest. But at the same time it was the most muscular torso Bart had ever seen. The abnormally broad shoulders sloped downward at a decided angle from a long, corded neck. But the shoulders themselves were minimized by the thickness of the body below them; so that the impression was of an unnatural length of arm, though Chandt's arms were, Bart saw, actually not out of proportion to the rest of him at all. His legs in their black trousers were slightly bowed.

Unthinkingly, Bart got to his feet as this man approached; and having done so was astonished to find his muscles responding so smoothly and competently after whatever long time had passed since he had fallen through the end of the main tunnel in the mine. He had unthinkingly been prepared to find himself stiff or weakened, as if from a long illness requiring much time in bed. Either his body had been exercised regularly during the periods when he was unconscious, in some manner he had forgotten, or . . . he could not think of any other way he could have been kept in condition over that period of time, at least a good share of which it would seem that he had been bedridden.

Not that he was not changed. He could see the thick callosities upon his ankles below the bottom of the trousers, where the leg-irons had been. His arms were shrunken with the weight he had lost in the mine, making the muscles upon them stand out unnaturally. But he was apparently rested and able to move like someone who had never been off his feet except for nighttime rest.

The shorter man, who must be Chandt, had come to a halt facing Bart; and, this close up, Bart was even more impressed than he had been at first glance over the other. Bart, since he had come into his full growth, had seldom met another man whom he had much doubt he could handle physically, without weapons and hand to hand. But now, for the first time, he looked at someone he had to doubt he could master.

Chandt, in spite of his relative slimness and shortness, gave an impression of invincibility. Bart, used himself to being underestimated by others, did not make the mistake of underestimating the man he looked at now. Some of that mass in Chandt were unusually thick bones, but the rest was simply muscle, muscle like sculptured stone.

In this body Chandt moved as lightly as a boy of twelve. He carried his considerable weight as if it were nothing; and there was a strange, flowing grace to his movements, which made Bart watch him with added interest. Bart's father had taught him a number of physical fighting movements that Lionel had called simply "tricks." But Bart, young as he was, had noticed that they all made use of a turning, flowing movement of the body; and it was exactly that sort of movement that Chandt showed as he came toward Bart's bed—and which had brought Bart unthinkingly to his own feet, so that he was upright and balanced by the time Chandt reached him.

He thought now, watching the other man, that Chandt in his turn had noticed the way Bart moved. But the other said nothing about it.

"You're awake. Good," was all Chandt said. He turned and left the room again. Ozzard and Bart were left standing face to face; and Ozzard grinned at Bart.

"You know?" said Ozzard. "Your breath stinks. Come to think of it, all of you stinks. You better go take a bath."

His grin persisted, and the look on his face said that he expected Bart to do no such thing. Bart did not grin back. He had no real fear of this man; but it had been only a few minutes since he had come fully awake in a strange place, and he did not feel like fighting at the moment.

At the same time, the situation was clearly like that of a lone wolf who joins a strange pack. The other men who were awake had already gotten up from their beds and were drifting down toward Ozzard and himself, with interest on their faces.

Ozzard took a step toward Bart, but also to one side, toward the center of the aisle space between the two rows of beds. There were about fifteen feet of clear space between the feet of the opposing beds and all the length of the room, if necessary. As Ozzard stepped aside, his forearms alone raised, his hands palm up and spread a little outward, almost as if he was about to beckon Bart toward him. Bart stepped forward and at an angle also, closing the distance between them, but his own arms raised until his hands were level with his eyes, the left slightly in front of the right.

They were now only a little more than an arm's length apart. Ozzard moved forward abruptly, one quick step that had come without any tensing of his body by way of warning. The big right hand of the bronze-skinned man closed crushingly on Bart's left wrist and the weight of Ozzard's body shifted onto his own right leg.

But before he could make the throw he clearly intended, Bart's hand below his held wrist had turned and glided up and over the wrist of Ozzard's holding hand, so that the power of Bart's arm as a whole came against the muscles of Ozzard's thumb. The thumb released and Bart's arm was free.

As Ozzard blinked, dumbfounded, Bart hit the other man quickly with his own free right hand, bringing his fist into Ozzard's neck. The blow had been aimed at Ozzard's Adam's apple and would have crushed it and possibly killed him if it had connected squarely; but Bart had deliberately aimed just slightly off-target. Still, the fist took Ozzard in the throat hard enough to make him take one long step back, choking. Bart closed with him, throwing his arms around the other's waist, burying his chin in the hollow between Ozzard's neck and collarbone. He locked his arms together behind Ozzard's back, clasping his right hand around his left wrist, and began to squeeze the barrel of the other man's body.

Ozzard's hands pummeled Bart's back in the area of his kidneys, but the angle was wrong for him to get any force into the blows. Failing at this, he shot his legs forward between Bart's, so as to bring them both to the floor, where the shock of landing might give him a chance to break loose, or to use his legs against Bart's body. But Bart stayed on his feet, literally holding Ozzard up off the floor and tightening his grip. Bart felt Ozzard's spine beginning to curve inward under the increasing pressure on it as he brought that pressure to bear. If he kept this up, in a very little while that spine would break—

"Give up?" said Bart. But the other kept up his struggling and did not answer.

A massive blow struck Bart suddenly between his own spine and right shoulder blade . . . and at once the strength went out of his right arm. His right hand lost its grip on his left wrist and the two fell apart. In the same moment, Chandt was between him and Ozzard, pushing them apart.

Ozzard let himself be pushed, his face staring at Bart with an unbelieving look on it. Bart felt his own now limp and helpless right arm taken by Chandt, who towed him away through the group of men who had gathered to watch the fight; and continued to pull him along until they were out of the room and in a corridor that ran past its entrance.

Chandt let go of his arm. Life was coming back into it, in tingling, pins-and-needles fashion from the shoulder down. Bart, on the basis of what his father had taught him with his "tricks," had no doubt that the other man had paralyzed his arm by hitting a nerve center. Which raised a question that eventually might become important in this place where men picked fights like children in a schoolyard. The question was how many nerve centers and which ones Chandt could be effective against? Bart himself had been taught an elbow pinch that would do to another's lower arm what Chandt had just done to his whole limb; plus half a dozen other nerve points that could be struck effectively when the opponent was in the proper position, so that the attacked nerve center was not at that moment covered by muscle.

He suspected that Chandt knew more nerve center points to attack than he did, possibly considerably more. It might be a good idea if he could figure out some way of finding out all the other knew and learn it, himself.

Chandt was looking at him earnestly.

"Sometimes, a little fighting is all right," said Chandt. "But only at the right times, and only a certain amount of fighting. You understand?"

Bart nodded.

"Come with me," said Chandt.

Bart went with him. Chandt took him along the corridor, stopping now and then to show him, wordlessly and with a single wave of his hand from the entrances to them, a gymnasium with running track, a swimming pool, and a room with straight chairs and small square tables, at each of which perhaps four men could sit, with a bar along one wall, and bottles racked behind it.

"Here, you can drink," said Chandt, breaking his silence for once, "but only when you've been told you can."

Bart nodded again. It occurred to him that the last drink he had taken had been the one after his nighttime encounter with the two cougars. Except at unusual times like that he was indifferent to alcohol and a little contemptuous of it—possibly because he had found he needed to drink more than other men if he really wanted to feel any effects from it. But it was also true that he did not care all that much for those effects.

Chandt led him on. There was a room rather like the surgery of a medical doctor, but with only a few strange instruments around a sort of reclining chair, rather than the usual array of medicine bottles and surgical instruments. No framed degree hung on a wall.

Finally, Chandt brought him to a room with long tables served by wooden benches.

"Sit," said Chandt, indicating the end of one of the benches.

Bart obeyed. Chandt clapped his hands once and sat down beside him. They waited. After several minutes a small, very ordinary man wearing a long white apron below a white shirt, and who would have made Arthur Robeson look robust by comparison, came out of a farther door in the room, carrying a wooden bowl and spoon, which, at a gesture from Chandt, he set down in front of Bart. He said nothing but directed a glance at Chandt that was almost one of fear. Chandt nodded and the man went back out by the same doorway through which he had come.

"Eat," said Chandt to Bart, pointing at the bowl.

Instinctively, Bart was tempted to refuse such an abrupt command—the kind of order one might have given to an animal. But the bowl was filled with some sort of stew that sent up an appetizing odor; and he found, suddenly, that he was very hungry indeed. He remembered that he had weight to gain back, and he picked up the spoon to taste what had been served.

It was what it looked like, a meaty stew—not just with meat flavor in the gravy of it, but with large chunks of what seemed to taste like goat meat, although the dish had been so spiced with cinnamon that it was hard to be certain. In any case, it tasted good, and he got to work on it.

"I am Chandt," said Chandt.

Bart nodded, for his mouth was full. He swallowed.

"Dybig," he said. He met the other's eyes briefly and then returned to his eating. "I heard the men call you Chandt."

"I don't care if you fight," said Chandt. "But if you do, you mustn't hurt the other men seriously, for then they can't work for the Lords. Learn to fight so that you win; but do not harm them much. Here you cannot die, but you can be not-well; and anyone who's not-well deprives some Head of his services until he's well again. And that is bad."

Bart stopped eating to look at the other man.

"I know I'm below the mine," he said. "There's no windows anywhere around here." He looked up at the lights over their heads which made the room as bright as day. There had been similar lights in all the rooms he had seen so far. They were round globes that radiated illumination. Bart had at first assumed without thinking that the globes enclosed gas lamps, but now, examining them more closely he could see nothing inside them but brightness that he could not examine closely.

Chandt had not replied.

"Where am I, then?" he asked Chandt.

"There is no special name for it," said Chandt. "It is away from ordinary Earth and Time. Some call it Hell, but its proper name is the Inner World."

"Hell?" Bart stared at him. The chained men in the mine had called that Hell, but with obvious bitterness and hatred. Chandt, on the other hand, now pronounced the word almost worshipfully, as if he had said not *"Hell"* but *"Heaven."*

"All the new ones ask where they are." Chandt looked away from him, at the wall—no, through the wall. There was a look in his eyes that was thoughtful and sad. "All of them wonder why some call this Hell. It's because they don't understand, at first."

"What don't we new ones understand?"

Chandt looked back at him, into Bart's eyes.

"You died," he said. "Just as all of us here did. Probably you can remember, if you think hard enough about it, exactly how you died. But whether you remember or not, now you are with the rest of us in Hell for eternity; and here you will spend all your days from now on serving the Heads."

He stopped speaking, and sat watching Bart. Bart sat in silence himself for a moment, thinking.

"I don't believe I died," he said, finally.

Chandt continued to look at him. The expression of thoughtfulness mixed with something sad was there in his eyes again, but now directed at Bart.

"It doesn't matter whether you remember or not," said Chandt. "Most of us here in the end remember how they died, but not all. It makes no difference. Those who call it Hell mean the word with no discourtesy. We use it because to the Lords "Heaven" is a special place from which they, alone, came; and which brute beasts like ourselves have never known and can never know. The closest we can come to Heaven is to exist to serve the Lordly class. There are also the Hybrids, who are the children of those who take human concubines; but you'll learn more about them later.''

"Who are 'Lords'?" asked Bart. He had almost finished the bowl of stew. "Can I have some more of this?"

"Clap your hands," said Chandt absently. "One clap for one bowl. If there are more of you, one clap for every bowl you want. Would you like something to drink with it? You can have water or beer.''

Bart clapped his hands once, then turned back to Chandt.

"Beer," said Bart. At least it would have more taste than water. "The Lords?" he reminded the other. Chandt looked through him with that sad and distant look that had been in the shorter man's eyes since Bart had asked where this place was.

"In a minute," he said.

They sat in silence until the white-aproned man brought Bart another full bowl and spoon and took away the utensils he had brought the first time.

"Beer. One," said Chandt to the serving man, who went off without a word and was back shortly with one of the largest drinking glasses Bart had ever seen, filled with a brown liquid that fizzed and held a head of foam above it. As the man left, Bart tasted the liquid. It was sweet, more like a nonalcoholic root beer than ordinary beer; but since he did not care whether it was alcoholic or not, that made no difference.

He put the glass down and turned to Chandt, ready to remind the other man again about his question. But Chandt spoke before Bart could.

"Who and what the Lords are, you'll find out for yourself," Chandt said. "I'll tell you this much. They are an Elder Race, older than we who call ourselves men. They have many strange powers. My people had known of the Lords for many generations before I came to serve them; but the world you live in is one of the Lords hate, with good reason.''

"Your people?" said Bart. "Who are your people?"

"They live far from this place. On the plains to the west of Cathay. Whether they're still there I don't know. It may be the world has killed them off, otherwise they would have conquered it. I come from a race of conquerors. At one time we had conquered all but a few small pieces of the world.''

"When was this?" Bart had stopped eating to stare at him.

"A very long time ago. I was one of them, then. We rode west, and farther west yet, conquering as we went. I told you most remember their deaths, in time. I remember mine. It was at a bend in the river. We were only a small part of Ogotai's force and the Germans trapped us there, many to our one. In the bend where we were, it was all marsh and our horses' legs sank deep in the muck, so that they were hampered. On his horse, any one of us was unconquerable, but without his horse a Mongol is only half a Mongol. Still, we slew most of them before they killed us. They had to kill us all to stop us; and so we died and I came to be a servant of the Lords. In other places, then here, in the Inner World.''

''When did you and the Lords come here?'' Bart watched the other carefully.

Chandt shrugged.

''Who can tell time in Hell? Here we are beyond time. But I have worn out fourteen belts serving the Heads.''

Bart looked down at the broad band of black leather that encircled the tree-trunklike waist of the other man. How quickly would something like that wear thin? In any case he did not believe what Chandt was telling him.

''You were one of the Mongols who fought at the time of Ghengis Khan?'' he asked.

''I fought under the Great Khan, yes,'' said Chandt.

Ghengis Khan, Bart remembered from the history books he had devoured in his father's study, was a Mongol chieftain who had lived in the twelfth century. He had pulled together the multitude of tribes of Mongols into one force, with which he conquered India, China and as far west as eastern Europe. he had lived.
There were historians who felt that he would undoubtedly also have conquered Europe if he had lived.

It was unthinkable that Chandt had lived that long. As unthinkable as that the Lords, whose group must include the three big-skulled, thin-limbed individuals he remembered seeing briefly during an interlude in his unconsciousness, could be an Elder Race of the sort Chandt described.

''You mean you've lived since the time of the Great Khan and never grown old?'' Bart said.

''Yes,'' said Chandt. ''There is no change here; and no one ever dies unless killed. The Heads have taken us beyond ordinary death. And now you, too.''

At that moment a tiny, very sweet bell chimed on the air. It chimed again; and Bart traced the sound to Chandt's belt, to which were clipped five small metal clips, each with a different colored jewel. It was impossible to say which jewel had made the sound, or how.

"I had forgotten, in all this talk," said Chandt.

He reached down and took from his belt a clip with a yellow, cat's-eye colored jewel. It ceased sounding the moment he touched it.

He handed it to Bart.

"Fasten this to your belt and always answer when it sounds, no matter what you are doing at the time. Say '*I hear.*' Say it now."

"I hear," echoed Bart, feeling foolish, speaking to the empty air.

"And now we will go," said Chandt, rising. "For you are called. I had not thought it would be this quickly."

chapter
six

BART FOLLOWED CHANDT out of the room. Within himself he had abruptly become alive. His goal, here as it had been in the mine, was to escape—except that the purpose was doubly imperative, because he would not be escaping alone. He would be taking Emma with him—because the only reasonable deduction was that Emma was in this place also. She and her brother would not have been in the mine as mere sightseers. They had to have been headed toward the end of the tunnel that had dumped him in the underground river. Although for Emma's party there must have been some way to activate a bridge over that river.

So she must be here, and somehow he would bring her out of this place with him when he went. Of course, by the same line of reasoning her brother must be here as well. But whether she would insist on Arthur's being taken along also was a bridge Bart would cross when he came to it.

First things first. And the first thing he needed to know was all there was to be learned about this place connected with the mine. Particularly, he must make himself a mental map here as he had in the mine; the memory system of counted steps and turns that he had developed while wearing the leg-irons could be used here in the light as well as in the dark of the mine tunnels.

So it was he began his mental map with his first turn to the right as they left the eating room, counting his first step up the corridor. He continued as they went on past the other rooms Chandt had shown him. They went for some distance and eventually came to the end of the tunnel—or corridor would be a better name for it, the bright lights and the light-colored walls gave more an impression of being inside a building above ground than buried deep in the earth.

In that end wall was set a tall door of metal with its surface carved in bas-relief to show undersized children being whipped or otherwise tortured and made to dance or do balancing tricks. Bart stared at the figures with astonishment.

"Can you blame the Lords that they call us brute beasts?" said Chandt as he opened the door.

He pushed Bart inside; and Bart found himself in a small, square room with smoothly finished walls, floor and ceiling, but otherwise either cut from the surrounding rock or panelled with slabs of it. Four very large men in gray, knee-length tunics, belted at the waist, and short boots of dark brown leather—men larger than himself and those he had seen in the dormitory, and muscled in proportion—took hold of him; and he elected not to struggle as they put on him a tough, thick leather jacket of a dun brown.

It was like no garment Bart had ever seen before, for there were no sleeves, in the real sense of that word—only casings within the outer shell into which he was made to put his arms—in effect locking those limbs helplessly in front of him once those dressing him had buckled tight the straps that closed the garment at his back.

None of the four, or Chandt, who stood watching, said a word as this process of encasing Bart went on. Once he was completely fastened within it, one of the men took hold of a leather cord which depended from the middle of the chest area of the garment and pulled Bart after him, out a farther door of the room and into a completely different scene. Another of the men followed after Bart, silently. Behind him came Chandt.

Bart was once more in a corridor, but here thick carpets cushioned the floor beneath the soles of the light, moccasinlike shoes they had furnished him at whatever time they had dressed him in the trousers in which he had awakened. The walls of the corridor were panelled in dark wood which shone under softer light from the globes overhead in a ceiling that was twice as high as the ones Bart had seen up until now.

The corridor led them out into a very large room indeed, with a ceiling three or four times the height of the corridors back in the area where Bart had awakened. They had come out into it by one of a number of doors that pierced one wall under an overhead, open gallery that ran the full length of the wall over their heads. Opposite it was what seemed to be a great stained-glass window, easily twelve feet high and twice that in width, lit from behind so that the figures it showed glowed in the same quiet lighting that had illuminated the carpeted corridor that had gotten them here.

Alerted by Chandt's question earlier, Bart now noticed that all the children depicted had enlarged heads—not so abnormally enlarged as those of the three figures at his bedside in the episode he remembered from a break in his earlier unconsciousness, but larger than they should be. He had not recognized this difference in them at first, the starved scrawniness of their bodies and the things pictured being done to them having too overwhelmed his attention to give him a chance to pick out fine details.

They came out through the pillared archways that upheld the gallery overhead, into the carpeted open spaces of the room. A profusion of low, upholstered seats and tables, clumped into islands that made a series of scattered lounges, seemed to fill the vast space; and yet there was a great deal of open space between those islands. They crossed between them and went to a pair of great metal doors, that were again carved much as had been the metal door Bart had seen earlier.

His escorts pressed a metal stud that was mounted on the doorframe to the left of the doors. The doors swung inward, away from him; and he found himself looking down yet another carpeted corridor.

Standing in the center of this corridor, just inside the doorway, was a middle-aged man. Unlike most of those Bart had so far seen in this place, this man was not a particularly well-muscled specimen. In fact, he was no more than ordinary, physically, and he looked thin after the others Bart had so far met in this place—except for the food-server.

This new man wore a short robe or tunic, a knee-length garment belted at the waist, of a light brown color. His legs were naked below this, and on his sockless feet were leather sandals with thin, soft-looking soles.

He looked at Bart, and at the two escorts.

"This one'll do," he said. His voice was soft, tenor, and a little husky, but it reminded Bart of the voice of a singer he had met once in an opera house in Denver some years back.

The escort who held the strap attached to Bart's leather body-casing let it drop. He, his fellow, and Chandt turned away, going without a word back out through the doors. These closed behind them, and Bart turned back from watching them go to find the eyes of the man in the robe watching him with what seemed to be amusement.

His eyes were a bright blue, and the face was slim, almost ascetic. Like all the rest Bart had seen here below, he was clean-shaven; but his hair was brown and thinning back from his forehead. It had been cut short and combed smoothly into place. He smelled of soap.

"That's good," he said now. Like all the rest so far down here, he spoke in English. "You act like you've got some brains. That's very good. But I hope you don't let them carry you away and tempt you to do anything contrary to what you're told. Believe me, if you did you'd only make trouble for yourself—and the rest of us."

He turned and began to walk away down the corridor.

"Follow me." He did not bother to turn his head as he gave the order. "Don't talk."

Bart followed him, shrugging, and staggered a bit, finding that bodily movement such as a shrug could throw him off-balance as long as his arms were held tight against his chest this way. But he got himself back under control and continued to follow.

At the end of the corridor, perhaps a hundred feet or slightly more down the way, were a pair of doors that exactly matched those at the head of the passage. The stranger strode directly up to the doors and pressed the metal button beside them. This time the doors swung open toward Bart and his guide.

Two people were in evidence beyond the doors, both dressed exactly as was Bart's guide; and both well-formed, clean-shaven, middle-aged men. No words were spoken as Bart's guide stepped to the side and motioned Bart to enter ahead of him. Bart did so, and heard the doors close softly behind him. The guide had stayed in that bare passageway, and Bart was alone with the two new strangers.

Bart, in a wry, way, was once more feeling the old stir of rebellion—and he amused himself with it, by checking his first impulse, which was to ask questions. He suspected these men were expecting any newcomer to babble questions; so he deliberately stood silent, once more following his father's precept about making the first move.

The room he had entered was small, with a door at each side wall, to his left and right. Both the middle-aged men were standing near the back wall, which appeared to be of bare but white-washed rock. Each door was of a single wooden panel, again set with bronze fittings. The wood of each door was carved, but Bart could not see the details of that carving.

Bart deliberately looked around him, then returned his attention to the two waiting men, and found them watching him. Still, they

said no word, and Bart remained silent, simply watching them and
waiting. After a moment, one of the two looked away from him
and moved closer to his companion; they did not look at each
other, but it was almost as if they had drawn together for mutual
protection. Bart grinned at them.

Again, he heard the bell-sound that he had heard in the dining
area; this time, however, it seemed to come to his ears out of the
air, from no definite point. Instantly the two faces before him lit
up, and they moved. One went to Bart's right, toward the door on
that side of the room; the other moved to Bart's left, and took a
position near him. This one motioned Bart to turn and follow the
other man, so Bart turned to his right, realizing that this put the
man on his left directly behind him. But there was no point in
worrying about that, he thought; he was already helpless, for the
most part.

The door opened and again he was led through and into a
strange room. Without a word the two men conducted Bart down
another passageway—this one narrower and lower of ceiling than
the preceding one, but with softer, more yellowish lighting and
deep carpeting into which his feet sank.

On the walls, here, heavy tapestries hung from metal fittings set
into the wooden overhead panels, and were so close together that
their separations were hidden in the folds of the hanging cloth.
They were all of a thick cloth like velvet, mostly of a maroon
background color and with detailed scenes of some story seeming
to be worked into them in threads of gold, black, blue, green and
silver. Bart watched with interest as he moved down the passage,
turning his head to try to see both sides, for there seemed to be a
different narrative going on on each side of him.

In fact, now he thought of it, the two sides were vastly different.
On his right, in rich, warm colors, the cloth seemed to be laying
out scenes of life in what he thought were medieval-era palaces—
there were lordly men and beautiful women, eating well, listening
to singers and watching jugglers, riding horses, and doing other
things which seemed to date from the Europe of several centuries
ago. He had no time to investigate these tapestries further, for
those on his left were demanding more and more of his attention.

These tapestries had seemed at first to be of a set with the
others, in style and colors; but as Bart watched them more closely,
he saw that they set out the same sort of scenes of princely
entertainments, but with a difference. The tapestries on that side
showed a variety of cruelties—deer being torn apart by slavering

hounds as mounted lords and ladies watched and laughed; hunchbacks being exhibited in chains for amusement; bears being egged into fighting each other—over and over, it seemed to Bart, the scenes were of handsome, cruelly laughing faces.

He came back to himself with a start. He had become so wrapped up in watching the walls that he had not noticed the end of the passageway approaching. But now they had arrived, the door there had opened, and he was being passed into the custody of yet another ordinary-looking man.

This one was also dressed as the others had been; but he was older, with thinning, gray hair and a wrinkled, pale face. His eyes were brown, standing out darkly under this lighting and against the paleness of his other features. Even as Bart finished noticing this, he heard the door close behind him. The man before him spoke.

"You're new," the man said. "You're strong. But you don't know anything about our ways here. So listen and do what I tell you. Only that."

He paused, watching Bart, his head cocked slightly to his right, the dark brown eyes glinting with the lids half closed upon them. He seemed satisfied with Bart's silence and went on.

"You're never to speak unless ordered to," he said. "Never move until directed. Never laugh here. In your own quarters you can laugh, but nowhere within these doors. Never scratch or fidget. Hold still when your handlers place the chair upon your back, and stand straight so as to keep the Lord as level and still as possible."

He stopped again now, watching Bart closely. For the first time, Bart felt doubt. To continue his silence and impassivity in the face of people was a form of what had been called "dumb insolence." This man was now beginning to recognize that. Now he was deliberately waiting for Bart to acknowledge these instructions in some way—and the rebellion inside Bart wanted to keep on disappointing that expectation.

But perhaps he was not being wise.

He reminded himself that what he needed most was information. And it would be easier come by if his captors thought him duller and weaker than he was. It was much better to sacrifice that bit of pride that was keeping him silent. By asking questions he could appear normal, even dull; and at the same time perhaps pick up some more information. . . .

"Where am I?" he asked; and he knew that only a bare instant had really passed since the other had ceased talking and begun watching him.

"Silence!" The voice of the other was louder and suddenly savage, but satisfied now. "Didn't I just tell you never to speak unless you were told to?" And he raised a hand that now, Bart saw, held a slender rod. Before Bart had time to wonder what the other expected to do with that tiny stick, the other had touched its metal-shod end to Bart's cheek—and it felt as if a very small horse had just kicked Bart in the head.

Bart's head jerked back from the rod, and he heard himself give a grunt, even as he realized that the spot the rod had touched now felt as if it had been touched by red-hot metal, and the area around it tingled as if the nerves had been put to sleep and were just now waking up. He became suddenly aware that he had backed up a step and tried to bring his arms up in front of his face; only, because those arms were still bound before him, the movement had almost thrown him off-balance.

He watched the man in front of him. Yes, the other had wanted that; some excuse to use his rod so that Bart would feel its power. He heard his own breathing rasp in his throat. His eyes had begun to water and his nose to run; and, in spite of his understanding of what had happened, a grim fury had been kindled in him, along with a deep sense of his helplessness.

"I can do that to you any time," the other man said to him.

The man's eyes were wide as he watched Bart. His nose seemed sharper now, and the skin stretched more tightly over his cheekbones. As Bart recovered his own control, he could hear the breathing of the other man, quiet, but deep and rapid. The other either enjoyed the giving of pain, or lived in some deep fear of consequences to himself if Bart should fail to follow these orders.

Bart said nothing and made himself stand utterly still. After nearly a full minute of silence, the other slowly began to relax. His arms came back down to his sides, and the rod was tucked back into some fold of his robe, out of Bart's sight. The man's eyes returned to a more normal width and his head cocked slightly to one side, consideringly.

"That's better," he said.

He turned and pushed a button on the wall behind him, and in a moment a door opened.

Three men came through the door, all dressed in robes like that of the man before him. They were younger than the other, and two of them were carrying some sort of leather-covered device that bore a vague resemblance to a saddle—but a saddle with back and arm rests. The third man closed the door behind him and then stationed himself in front of it, taking a wide-legged stance with his arms folded across his chest. His right hand held a rod like the one that had just been used on Bart. And Bart now saw that the older man had now moved to stand before the other door, by which Bart had earlier entered the room. The other two men paused in front of Bart.

"Turn around," one said. He was the slightest person Bart had yet seen in his place, swarthy of feature and with an accent that Bart could not place. He said nothing further, and Bart turned to face the wall behind him.

He heard movement behind him. In a moment his back was touched. He kept himself still, and felt a weight descend on his shoulders. From the corners of his eyes he could see movements, and he felt straps being tightened around his chest, fitting snugly enough to define and lodge under the elbows of the arms hidden within the leather garment. His shoulders seemed to each be held in a vise that distributed into his body the weight that had settled above his back, seemingly centered behind and above his backbone.

"Turn around," he heard again; the command was punctuated by a light tap on his left temple area; and automatically he swiveled in that direction as he turned. He found himself looking at the four men again.

"Now follow these men," the older one said. "I'll be behind you."

The fourth man opened the door opposite the one the three had come through, and the three preceded Bart through it. On the other side, as it closed, the three moved to the left and vanished through another doorway, while Bart was commanded to move ahead. Following orders from the man behind him, Bart was directed to another door, through it, and down a short hallway, until they came to a high-ceilinged, round room. It had the usual deep carpet and very little by way of furniture; but there was a wide staircase with a heavy balustrade that curved upward to the right. At the height of four feet or so up the staircase was an elevated platform, a kind of landing that had a vertical, unrailinged side in the little alcove that was formed by the curve of the stairs.

They stopped and waited for some time, which Bart used to look about him. The room had a rich, cloth covering glued to the walls, which were themselves curved, giving the room a round, foyer look. There were six sconces topped with lit globes, set into the wall at intervals. They were made of what seemed to be ornately carved metal that was gold or gold-colored, and stood out sharply against the cream and light pink of the wall-covering.

Overhead, the walls curved to come to a point above the center of the room, very high; but the center of the ceiling was obscured by a large, crystal chandelier that seemed to shed no light of its own, but glistened and reflected in a myriad of pinpoints the light that shone from the glass globes in the sconces below and surrounding it.

They stood and waited.

chapter

seven

IN THE MOMENT of rest which had unexpectedly come upon him, Bart took time out to try and put the discomfort of the chair on his back out of his mind and examine the mental map he had been making as far as it had so far developed.

As far as he could judge, now that he had the completed, proportioned line of his journey in his mind's eye to examine, he seemed to have come in along a straight line from the section that held the Steeds' dormitories and other rooms such as the one where the four men had harnessed him; and then he had made a turn, a sharp right angle to another straight-line trip along a section made up entirely of these carpeted rooms and tunnels; these seemed to lie in relation to the line of the first section of rooms as the crossbar lies in relation to the vertical line of the letter *T*—

His thoughts were abruptly interrupted.

From somewhere out of sight on the balcony level above them, that level to which the wide, curving stairway ascended, figures had just appeared. Bart's first reaction was that they were children in elaborate robelike costumes. Then he saw that they were a man and a woman, but both were the size of the three he remembered briefly standing over him and talking. In fact the man of the pair approaching could have been the white-bearded one of the three. He and the woman with him were a good deal less than five feet tall. The man's head was bald except for a tuft of white hair above each ear, and his face, above the narrow shoulders, sported a wispy white beard like that grown by the very old of those human races who normally had little or no facial hair, such as Orientals or the Indians of the Americas. There was something definitely familiar about the man—and in a moment Bart was sure: the one descending the stairs was indeed one of the three who had stood over him in that momentary episode of consciousness before he woke up in the dormitory. He was the one who had pointed out the fact that evidently Bart had been escaping from the mine when he had fallen into their hands—and he had mentioned the fact as if it was a point in Bart's favor.

Bart was suddenly, irrationally, cheered. He might not have fallen among friends, he thought, but perhaps he had fallen in with one of the lesser of his enemies. For, clearly, with the one of the three who had talked of making use of him here, he had simply exchanged one form of slavery for another.

It did not matter, he told himself now. Wherever he was, whoever held him, he would escape. The determination to do that was as much a built-in part of him as his body and mind.

But he had no time to think about that now. He was being fascinated by the other small person who was accompanying the little man down the stairs—not arm-in-arm, but close enough so that the impression of intimacy was almost the same.

The other had seemed to be a beautiful blue-eyed young girl of somewhere between nine and twelve years of age. Now it was plain that she was a mature woman, if still much younger than her companion. And whereas the man wore a rather plain, robelike costume, up close the woman's dress was long and lacy, sweeping the carpet on the stairs behind her as she came down; and her blond hair was put up in an elaborate coiffure high on her head. The effect was rather like that of a young girl dressed up in her mother's best party gown. Like the man the exposed parts of her—arms, neck and face—were white with the whiteness of skin that has not seen the sun in years, if ever.

It was puzzling to Bart to see someone even this young so closely partnered with someone as obviously old as the small man beside her; for their intimacy was rather that of man and wife than grandfather and granddaughter. It was only when they came to the midway point of the stairs, much closer to him, and he saw the faint lines of crow's-feet around the outer corners of her eyes, that all at once he became aware of the cleverly applied makeup on her face, and realized that the high-piled hair on her head helped to hide the fact that her head, also, bulged. Then he began to understand.

Perhaps they were, indeed, husband and wife.

Clearly, the man and the woman with him were what Chandt had called "Lords." But they seemed to Bart to be an almost gentle couple, although that impression was somewhat marred by the slim rod attached to the waist of the clothing of each. For the first time, Bart found himself wondering which of the two he was supposed to carry.

"In there—the alcove."

The whisper came from the man behind Bart, and at the same time Bart felt the end of the other's rod—with no shock to it now—pushing him forward. He moved into the alcove mentioned, a small space of floor semi-enclosed by the curve of the staircase. The landing was just about level with his chest—a small space of flooring larger than one of the steps that interrupted their descent at that point.

"Turn." The whisper again.

He turned, putting his back to the landing.

"Back up." Bart backed until he felt the edge of the landing touch his back, just above his ribs. "Stand still."

Sure of what was coming, Bart braced himself in position.

He barely heard the soft feet of the small man and woman reach the landing and stop.

There was a moment of silence; and then he felt weight settle on his shoulders and back. Either the man or woman was now in the saddle they had fastened upon him.

There came a very light tap upon the top of his head. He heard, however, no verbal order, and so he did nothing—although he noted that unconsciously he had been resettling his body, shifting his stance to compensate for the new weight bearing on it. For the chair and the weight of whoever was in it, small though they might be, was still enough to throw him considerably off-balance backward. There was a tap on the back of his head.

"Forward!" It was the voice of the man who had guided him here.

He took a cautious step forward, and then another. It was going to be difficult until he got used to balancing the weight on him, which threatened to drag him over backward. A touch on his right temple from the rod of his rider.

"Left."

Bart made a ninety-degree turn to his left. The rod tapped him on the left temple—and he was already turning to his right when the whisper to do so came again behind him. Another tap, another turn, another tap, and he ended up facing once more up the stairs. The woman still stood on the landing, watching. It was the man, then, on his back.

But the two successive turns in opposite directions had disturbed his new precarious balance. He swayed—but his sway was halted by the end of the rod of the man behind him digging into his side. This time the rod did not carry the powerful blow he had felt once before; rather, it seemed to have a sharp, pinlike point, which felt as if it sank deep into his side.

A second later that rod was knocked away by the smaller rod of his rider; and out of the corner of his eye, Bart saw the man bowing deeply before the rider.

"*Ne le touche pas plus!*" the words came, unexpectedly, in French from above Bart's head, in the slightly hoarse tenor voice of an old man. Surprise held Bart still for a second. His rider had clearly interfered to save Bart punishment with his order to the man behind Bart not to touch him again.

Once again, as in Bart's first remembered moment with the three standing over him, whoever it was who now rode him had shown a sort of kindness to him.

Small taps of the rider's rod against Bart's right temple turned him once more with his back to the staircase. He moved, wavering only slightly, and completed the turn with much more control than he had shown in that sort of movement before. His guide was still in view.

"*Va t'en!*" came the rider's voice.

Bowing repeatedly, the guide came around from behind Bart and then backed away toward the door until he had reached it. Then he turned and went out, closing the door behind him. Bart felt the weight of his rider shift on his back—he moved his own feet, widening his stance to compensate—and then the rider's voice, speaking again in that odd, almost understandable tongue he remembered from his moment of consciousness. The pronunciation was off, he told himself, that was most of his trouble with it. If he could just hear the words spoken a little differently . . .

The woman answered, from the staircase behind them.

A light tap of the rider's rod against the back of his skull started Bart moving. He went forward, toward the door by which he had entered and through which the man who had ordered him about had just left. As he approached, it opened in front of him. There was another tap on the back of Bart's head, and he continued his movement along the corridor stretching before him. He was learning that the only way he could balance his rider properly was to move in a semi-hunched position that threw their mutual center of gravity forward over his legs. It was an awkward and unnatural position in which to walk, but it was the only way that would work.

As he went, however, Bart found himself growing more familiar with the needs of his burden. He found his steps picking up a smoothness and ease that he had not thought would come to him this quickly.

The corridor led them into a series of rooms, through which Bart's rider steered him. Bart noticed that one of the differences of this section was that all the rooms here—which like every place here underground must have been carved out of the rock—were very high-ceilinged, for no conceivable reason except the taste of those who had caused them to be made so. The doorways were also higher than necessity alone would require and their tops arched to high peaks, as in the architecture of Moorish cultures.

For the next three hours, obeying the light rod-taps of his rider, Bart roamed the corridors and rooms of what he came to realize was a vast underground establishment; and the map in his mind grew busily. Very plainly, he was not going to learn the overall layout of a place this size in one day.

Once he had discovered the trick of maintaining his balance with a rider on his back and with his hands secured in front of him, there had seemed no great work to the job of carrying the small old man about. The weight of the Lord, he estimated, could not be more than ninety pounds or so; and the chair contraption strapped onto Bart would add less than five pounds to that.

As a matter of weight to be carried, therefore, it should be nothing to someone his size. Nonetheless, as the time he spent moving around under these conditions went on, the task grew harder, the burden he bore seemed to become heavier and heavier. After all, perhaps it was as Chandt had suggested and this was really Hell.

By the end of the three hours the muscles of his shoulders and the area of his neck felt as if they were clamped in a vise of hot metal. For the first time he began to fear that the cramping would become unbearable, and he would run amok in a frantic effort to get chair and rider off him. He could feel his neck and face growing red and hot, and was unable to do anything about the sweat that occasionally trickled into an eye. More and more he longed to be able to move his arms about, to windmill them and stretch his shoulder muscles—but after these hours it was a question whether he would be able to move his arms at all when they were finally freed.

But, in spite of the growing agony of his neck and back, at all times he kept up his observation of the places through which he was directed.

These caverns seemed to extend over a sizable volume of the rock underground—much more than the extent of the mine had been. The mine that now must be either off to one side or overhead of this place where he now trudged—for unlike the mine, this place seemed to possess a number of levels.

The other people Bart and his rider encountered seemed to fall into three classes. Most of them seemed to be servants—or slaves. Invariably these were dressed either in short tunics or—if they seemed to have some authority among their own kind—somewhat longer robes. Always these robes were of solid colors, brown, gray or blue. Occasionally, they encountered a man or woman dressed in what Bart thought of as 'city clothes,' the kind of clothing he always thought of the people in large, eastern cities as wearing. This was the only familiar form of dress he saw; and those who wore it were treated with great respect by those of the tunic classes. In return, the city-dressed ignored those in tunics, but were polite and respectful to all the small people they met, whether they were riding a Steed like Bart, or on foot.

Like the servant or slave class, they addressed any small man or woman they encountered as "Lord" or "Lady."

As for the Lords and Ladies, themselves, whom Bart saw busily occupied at incomprehensible tasks in a number of rooms filled with strange devices with which they tinkered, these were apparently a law unto themselves as far as clothing went. They dressed in all sorts of fashions, although the togalike garment worn by Bart's Lord was the type most commonly seen.

Toward the end of the third hour, when Bart was beginning to think he could not last much longer, they passed briefly through a room that had to be entered past two guards holding what looked like oddly lumpy rifles—but who stood aside at the sight of Bart's rider.

It was a strange room. To begin with, they crossed only one end of it; and it was much longer than it was wide. This distance was almost filled by great pipes, as cleanly white as if they had been freshly painted, running lengthwise through the room. Some of these pipes radiated a fierce heat, others an equal aura of icy coldness. The length of the great room was such that the farther ends of the pipes were almost out of sight. Their nearer ends, which Bart and his rider passed, plunged into the stone floor and wherever they went was also out of sight. The room must have been painstakingly carved out of the rock, itself; and all of the exposed stone surface of the walls was highly polished, as was the floor. The stone was of a pale pink color here, except for a wide vein of a darker gray material that, at this end of the room, ran down one wall, across the floor and up the other side wall.

In the far distance Bart could barely see that the pipes turned downward there as well, disappearing into the floor of the room; and somewhere beyond that point was something that caught the eye and dominated the farther wall, a thick, metallic pillar rising vertically from out of sight below, to out of sight above in a room that must be both higher and deeper than this one.

Whatever explanation there was for all this, the labor involved in what Bart now saw must have been incredible. At the direction of his rider, he passed through a farther door in the near end of the long chamber, and a short distance down another corridor found himself suddenly in the midst of a large, book-crammed library.

A tap on the left side of his head directed him down the carpeted floor between two floor-to-ceiling walls of laden bookshelves, and to a door which opened before them.

They stepped through into what was obviously a spacious office with a desk and chair scaled to the height of one of the little people. Furniture of comparable height was about the room. A man wearing city clothes—a suit of dark brown and a white shirt with brown vertical striping under a black bow tie—turned from the room's large desk, upon which he had been arranging some papers, and came to stand before them.

A tap, for the first time, came directly on top of Bart's head.

For a moment, he did not understand; and the tap came again. Then, he understood. His eyes darted quickly about the room and settled on a small wooden landing stage at the right side of the room. He moved toward it and turned, backing carefully into position before it; and gratefully, with a gratitude as deep as he had ever experienced in his life, he felt the weight of his rider leave the saddle on his back. There was only one more thing he could want. The man in city clothes went around to the back of Bart and took care of that.

A second later, the weight of the chair itself disappeared from Bart's back; and Bart straightened up to the sudden shooting agony of pains in his shoulder and back muscles, but with a blissful sense, at last, of the freedom to stand straight.

chapter
eight

BEHIND HIM, BART heard the Lord speak in the strange tongue. Again, Bart felt he almost understood it. It was something about not needing Bart any further.

The man before Bart nodded and looked at Bart almost commiseratingly.

"The Librarian says you are now to leave this office of his and return to the Steeds' dormitory from where you came," he said in stiff, accented English. He toed the saddle and the thick cloth used to bind Bart's arms in front of him. "I send one of the stack workers back with these and another one to show you how to get to the dormitory."

"Merci," said Bart unthinkingly, for the accent had been eastern Canadian. Behind him, the Lord spoke again; and once more Bart felt something stir in him at the words. But this time, soggy with weariness that seemed to be building up in him rapidly now that the load was off his back, he did not gather even a sense of the message behind the words.

"English only is spoken, in the work place, by those who are not Lords or Ladies," said the man in the brown suit, still in English. "In the home, is always French."

"Thank you," said Bart again, numbly.

"Good. Come with me," said the man, and led Bart out of the room into the main body of the Library again.

Beyond the ranks of bookcases, there was an open space with tables and chairs of both ordinary size and smaller. The ordinary chairs consisted of upright wooden pieces of furniture, some unpadded, but most, though much the same sort of chairs, padded and with angled backs to be more comfortable. There were also a few chairs, the smaller ones, that were luxuriously padded, and closer to the floor. Some of these were in use by Lords who were sitting in them reading.

Similarly, the padded regular chairs were some of them occupied by men or women in "city" clothes, and two of the completely unpadded chairs held women in gray short tunics. All were reading. In the center of all these chairs was an area enclosed by a circular counter, within which were several desks, at each of which tunic-clad people were working; and one other such was presently standing at the inside edge of the counter, answering in English an inquiry from a man in a dark blue suit on the outside.

"I am the Assistant Librarian," said the man with Bart, who, perhaps because of his movements, was beginning a little to come out of his fog of weariness. "My name is Charles Mordaunt. I'm in charge of the Library here—under the Lord Guettrig's supervision, of course."

He pointed.

"The stacks are numbered," the Assistant Librarian said, "beginning with number One at that end. If you go down between stacks numbers One and Two, at the end you'll find a red door. You may have been told about these rooms with red doors before; but in any case, that's the one for the Library. It's a withdrawing room for slaves, with all necessary appurtenances for bodily comfort and relief. You understand?"

"The latrine," said Bart.

"Not just that!" Mordaunt seemed very nearly offended. "There are beds and chairs in there as well . . . you'll see. In fact, you may find yourself spending much time there, if you're going to be bringing the Librarian to work here often—and waiting to take him home."

"I see," said Bart.

"Never enter a room with a gray door—that is for Hybrids, like myself. And absolutely never even pay attention to a black door, which would be for the Lords and Ladies alone."

Bart nodded.

They had reached the circular counter now. Mordaunt leaned across it and spoke to a tunic-clad man at one of the desks.

"Find me two stack-workers," he said.

"Yes, sir."

The man got up from his desk, went out through an opening in the counter and disappeared down the aisle between stacks One and Two.

A few minutes later, Bart was being guided back to the dormitory he had left nearly four hours earlier. The stack-worker, a slave named Jon Swenson, took a different route back to the dormitories than the one by which Bart had come to the Library. It was also, Bart was interested to note from the growing map in his mind, only about a fifth of the distance Bart had carried the Librarian, and it took only about fifteen minutes to cover it.

From Swenson, a black-haired, white-skinned young man of about twenty, who held what was apparently a common attitude among the tunic-clad workers—that the Steeds lived lives of luxury compared to themselves—Bart was able to learn a good deal.

The Librarian's full name was Pier Guettrig, although no Steed or ordinary slave would dare address him or refer to him other than as "Lord." Guettrig's wife's first name was Marta. Mordaunt, or a Hybrid who was related, might on rare occasions be permitted to call Guettrig by his name alone, rather than his title; but only by special permission and in private.

"And what's a Hybrid?" Bart asked.

"You a Steed and not know that?" Swenson looked at him in astonishment.

"I'm a very new Steed." said Bart drily.

"Oh." Swenson nodded. "Just new from the dead, is that it? You do have a lot to learn, then. But you ought to be able to guess what a Hybrid is. It's a man or woman who's a child of one of the Lords and a slave concubine. If a Hybrid passes the inspection when he or she's eleven years old, and another test at seventeen, they get to be officers and supervisors over the rest of us. Sometimes a Lord even invites one of them into his home for a visit. Usually, in that case, of course, the Lord's either the father or mother of the Hybrid."

"Do Steeds," asked Bart, "ever get invited to a Lord's home?"

Jon looked at him with wide eyes.

"Of course not!" said the stack-worker. "You're slaves, just like the rest of us, after all!"

"Out of luck, then," said Bart. "I see."

"Oh, no—we're very lucky, all of us; not only to have been raised again from death in the first place, but because the Lords will be destroying our own accursed race almost any time now; and only those of us who were brought back to life to be their slaves down here will be left alive to serve them."

Bart stared at the slight young man; but obviously he was completely serious.

"Don't talk like a crazy," said Bart. "No one, no bunch of people can destroy the human race. It's impossible. For one thing, you'd have to destroy the world to do it."

"But that's just what the Lords are going to do!" said Jon triumphantly. "Destroy the world—the surface world, that is— just like that!"

He snapped his fingers.

"And how do they think they're going to do that?" Bart asked.

Jon, it seemed, was not quite sure. He talked a lot about mountains falling and seas drying up, and seemed to have the impression that when the moment came all the Lords would gather in a circle around a great, magical device they had called the Tectonal and, holding hands, order that the world be destroyed. Once they had done this, Jon was confident the Inner World where he, Bart and all the rest were now, would cease to be Hell. Hell would become the surface of the world; and everything alive on it would be destroyed.

Bart made a mental note to find out what kind of basis there was for Jon's wild belief. It was ridiculous, of course, but there just might be something real behind it—on a much lesser scale, of course. After all, the Scottites had advocated an armed takeover of the Canadian government, and since their mine somehow connected with this place—perhaps these people were involved with those plans, too. There might be some kind of a plan to attack a number of governments, or some such thing.

But for the moment, he put it out of his mind; and it turned out just as well he did. Because the moment he stepped back into the dormitory, he found a new challenge waiting for him.

The dormitory was full of Steeds. More were present than Bart had seen there at any time before. Not only that, but just by the way their faces all turned to watch him as he came in, he could guess that it was his return that was the cause of their presence.

No, he corrected himself—it was not him alone they watched.

A short—as Steeds went, which made him still at least five feet eight—but very broad man, with straight black hair cut short on a round skull, turned as the others looked to the doorway. Seeing Bart, he came striding down the center aisle between the beds to stop an arm's length away.

Of necessity, Bart stopped also. He looked into a square, hard, face with a scythe of a nose, and a chin and jaw the olive-colored skin of which was darkened even further by the roots of a close-shaved, but very black, beard. For the first time it struck Bart that he had seen no one but Lords wearing any facial hair here in this place they called the "Inner World."

"I'm Paolo Collini," said the broad man in a flat bass voice, "and I run this dormitory. That means I run you, too. If I tell you to do something, you jump! You understand? Or do you need instruction?"

Inside himself, Bart sighed. He was still less than his usual strength and weight from the mines, on top of that exhausted from his first day's chair-carrying; and this Paolo Collini, who seemed to be the head man of the dormitory, seemed determined to settle his authority here and now.

"Suppose I just agree to that," said Bart. "Can we let it go like that, then?"

Paolo frowned.

"What's the matter? You don't look like the sort of man'd run from a fight. No!" he said. "If you don't fight me you fight Michael Bolt, who runs things here, after me."

He took a half step closer to Bart and peered up into his face, suddenly frowning.

"What's happened to you?" he demanded. "They take you out for your first day of carrying one of the Lords, today—and you're just back from that?"

Bart nodded.

Paolo made a disgusted noise, as if he was about to spit.

"It's not on for now, then," said Paolo. "It wouldn't prove a thing to lick you in the shape you're in now. In fact . . ." He surveyed Bart from head to foot. "I think you've probably got less than the usual meat on your bones, anyway. We can settle it later. Where were you before they brought you back to life?"

"I was a slave in a mine that connects with this place," answered Bart.

"That settles it, then!" Paolo swung around to speak to the others watching in the dormitory. "I know that mine. Some of the rest of you do, too. Hear this, all of you! This man has no rank. You hear that? When he's well enough he can try me out, if he's got the guts. Until then, the rest of you leave him alone! You'd probably be wise to, anyway. You hear me? Everyone leave him be!"

His voice had raised on the last two sentences. There was a general reluctant growled mutter of acknowledgment.

Bart found himself strangely touched. He was numb with physical exhaustion; but through that numbness something about Paolo's words reached to the core of him, where the loneliness was. That loneliness which only Emma, for some strange reason, had been able to banish from him. What Paolo had just said had not altered that feeling in him, as Emma's mere presence could, but it had held an echo of his own solitary sorrow—why, Bart could not say.

But even as he felt this, Paolo was turning back to face him.

"Right," the head Steed was saying to him, "now you—you come with me."

He led Bart away from the dormitory and to, not the usual eating and drinking area of the Steeds, but the general slave social center, where they wedged themselves into a corner box consisting of a table and high-backed benches.

"Talk more privately here," grunted Paolo, once they were seated. "I know, you'd rather be catching some sleep on your bed right now; but I think we better have a talk without any more wasted time."

A male slave waiter came and took their orders. Paolo's was for some of the light-alcohol slave beer and a side glass of the raw, almost pure alcohol that was also available here in the social center. Bart, since he guessed the other would be offended if he did not, took the same thing.

He waited for the other to begin the conversation. Here, he hoped, was his chance to begin getting some idea of the place he and Emma now had to escape from. He continued to wait, however, for Paolo to give some indication of how the talk would go.

Paolo, however, said nothing. They sat in silence until the waiter had brought the drinks and left them once more alone. Then the dormitory leader took the small glass of alcohol in one swallow, drank a large portion of the beer in another, and stared hard at Bart. Their faces were so close together across the small table of the corner booth that Bart could see one long black hair curling out from Paolo's left nostril. Bart stared at it in fascination. It had a curve like the tusk of a boar; and, rather than making the other man look unsightly, gave him a boarlike appearance of innate fierceness.

"Look you, Bart—it's Bart that's you name, isn't it? That's what they said back in the dormitory—"

"Bart Dybig," said Bart.

"All right, Bart. You want to be in another dormitory? One where the Leader'll be easy for you to whip; but a good, solid dormitory, with no real crazy men or wood-heads in it? I can fix it."

Bart stared at the other, startled, suddenly, so that he found himself coming out of a fog of weariness that he hadn't fully realized. He knew he had not, indeed, regained the strength the mine had taken from him. But Paolo was a heaven-sent opportunity.

"Why'd I want to be in another dormitory?"

Paolo held up one finger, signaling their waiter, who was standing across the room, watching. The waiter went off and Paolo drank deeply from his tall glass of beer, almost finishing it.

"I'll tell you the truth," he said, banging the near-empty glass down on the tabletop and wiping his mouth on the back of a thick hand. "I—no, wait."

The waiter was returning with two new orders of beer and alcohol. Bart hastily emptied his own two glasses, the large and the small, and was suddenly sorry he had not done so earlier. He had no fears of being outdrunk by Paolo, who seemed in a friendly mood, anyway; and the alcohol now inside Bart would act as an anesthetic for the aches and pains from the day's unusual effort.

Paolo waited until the waiter was again across the room, watching them and ready to serve, but out of earshot.

"I'll tell you the truth," said Paolo again, "I can whip you. Particularly the way you are now; and even when you get rested and fleshed up again. I know I can whip you."

He stopped and drank his second alcohol and some beer.

"But I'm not like those wood-heads back in the dormitory." He tapped the right side of his forehead with one thick finger. "I can smell things. My mother was a *strega*—a witch; and I can smell something on you. Something I smell says not to fight you. A smell like that—it's never wrong."

He stopped speaking and stared at Bart as if waiting for an answer. Bart only looked back. Even weary as he was now, and worn down as his time in the mine had left him, he thought he had a good chance of defeating Paolo. Of making him unconscious or even killing him, if necessary.

But he could be wrong, and he would much rather have the dormitory Leader as a friend than a defeated rival. "Same time," Paolo spoke up again suddenly, after another drink of beer, "there's something about you I like. But if you stay in our dormitory, I'm going to have to whip you. And I won't take no chances, because of what I smell in you. That means it'll be bad for you. You got to understand. It means a lot to me, being Leader. It's the biggest job I ever had. Even if the Lords end up someday having me killed, I've still been Leader. You understand?"

"Yes," said Bart.

And he did. He heard the words that the other said—and something more as well. Under the harsh voice of Paolo there was a note of appeal.

"You want me to move to someplace else, so we don't have to fight," Bart said, half to himself.

"That's right," said Paolo. "I can fix it. Some things I can fix. It'll take time."

Bart nodded.

"You'll still have to fight whoever's Leader there for first place," Paolo said, "but he won't try to kill you if he sees he can't win any other way. I will—and believe me, Bart, after being in the dormitories twelve years, I know how to do it before you can guess what's coming."

Bart sat, thinking. But not from fear of Paolo killing him. He hesitated because he wanted to think about the possible advantages of this attitude of Paolo's. There might be some way it could help him get Emma out of here. Equally, there might be disadvantages. The problem was that he did not know enough yet about this place in which they were trapped to make a decision.

He decided a decision was best put off for the moment.

"I don't know—," he began. But Paolo had already evidently guessed his reaction.

"Think it over, if you want to," said the Leader. "Or, hell! Ask me anything you want, to help you make up your mind. We've got until you've got your proper weight back anyway. That's two, three months, maybe more. And as I say, not counting the fact I'm not going to let you take my Leadership from me, I like you. Drink up; and let's talk a bit."

Bart nodded.

"I'll take you up on that," he said. "I'll think about it."

"Tell me as soon as you know," said Paolo. "Remember getting you transferred to another dormitory'll take arranging; and that'll take time."

"I will," said Bart. "Meanwhile, as you say, let's talk. I need to know about this place. Has it got a name?"

"It's got lots of names," Paolo smiled, and his smile was as savage as the hair curling from his left nostril, "depending on who you talk to and what's happened to him—or her. But its real name is the Inner World. That's the name the Lords gave it."

The expression on his face changed to one of curiosity.

"How's it you don't know that?" he said. "Whenever anyone's

reborn from the dead here, they come back knowing all about the Inner World, the Lords and the Hybrids.''

"I don't," said Bart.

Now it was Paolo who shook his head.

"Doesn't make sense, man," he said. "Let's take it from the beginning. You remember dying, don't you?"

"No," said Bart

Paolo sat for a long second, simply staring at him.

"Here!" he said. "You lying to me?"

"No," said Bart. "I remember being in the mine. I remember getting loose from the work crew I was chained to, when we were put away to sleep, one night. I'd counted my steps in the tunnels and so I managed to find my way to where I'd seen some of those on the mine staff, and some other people, going. I came to a hidden door, I found my way through it—and I fell. Into some sort of underground river. Where I fell in there was room above the water to breathe; but the river carried me on to where the rock overhead came right down to the water and I had to swim holding my breath, hoping to make it to where there was air above me.''

He paused.

"That's all I remember until I woke up—" Caution made him hold back the memory of the three Heads standing over him and talking in their strange, but in that moment oddly comprehensible, language, "—woke up in the dormitory.''

"All right," said Paolo. "There's nothing crazy in that. You must have drowned in the river. The Lords brought you back to life. You try—you'll remember what it was like dying." He shuddered. "No one forgets that!''

"There's nothing I remember about either dying or being brought back to life," said Bart. "Maybe I was next to drowning, enough so I was unconscious—but that's all.''

"You couldn't have been just unconscious," said Paolo emphatically. "The Lords'd never let anyone into the Inner World—let any human in, that is—who's alive.''

"Why not?"

"Why, because of what people—us humans—did to them—" Paolo's intensely black, busy eyebrows drew together over his eyes. "You really saying you don't remember that? Everyone here's reborn knowing that—why the Lords wouldn't never let a human being come alive, here in their own, personal world.''

"Everybody but me," said Bart patiently.

"All right. I'll tell you—but if you're joking me . . . ," said

Paolo, then checked himself. "But you're not. I can tell. All right, then, you ought to know that the Lords, they aren't like us. I mean, they're not real people. They came here from another world."

"A what?" said Bart.

"Another world—a world, just like this here world of ours; but another one, someplace else."

"Someplace else? Where?"

"So far away . . ." Paolo's voice failed at trying to make the description. "Look, you know you stand at the foot of a mountain and look up at the moon; then you climb that mountain and look at the moon again—I mean, same time of night, same time of year—right away?"

"Yes," said Bart.

"Right. Now, the moon—does it look any closer from the top of the mountain—any bigger—than it looked from the bottom?"

"No," said Bart. "Of course not."

"All right," said Paolo. "Well, that world the Lords come from, it's beyond the moon, they say. So of course you can't see it, it's so far off."

"How'd they get here, then?"

Paolo lowered his voice.

"That's their secret—one of their secrets; and they've got lots of them. But they got here; and then what happened?"

"You're the one who's telling me what happened."

"You know what I mean," said Paolo impatiently. "I was just saying it that way to get you ready for what you're going to hear. When the Lords landed here, the first humans that saw them took them for some kind of little freaks, all of them. That was thousands of years ago, when they had kings and courts. The kings dressed the Lords up in clown suits and made them do tricks for the court, and used them that way. Hell, you must have seen the carvings on doors and paintings on walls, and such!"

Bart stared at him.

"You see?" Paolo said. "Now you see why they'd never let any one of us in here, alive? Man, they hate us—I mean they hate the humans we were before we died. Since they raised us from the dead, they don't hate us as much."

"If that's so," said Bart slowly, "how'd they get from those courts to this Inner World?"

"They snuck away from the courts—thousands of years ago, like I said," Paolo answered. "And they began raising dead humans to work for them and they built this place—thousands of years ago."

Bart nodded. There were holes in this story you could drive a freight wagon through. Even granted that it must have taken a very great amount of human labor to build this place . . .

A new idea interrupted his train of thought. Come to think of it, the labor would have been a lot less if most of this underground area had been a series of natural caves that merely needed to be connected, cleaned out and finished inside . . . .

But that was beside the point. The one thing that had to be patently false was that the Inner World had been built thousands of years ago. Thousands of years ago the kings and courts of the world knew nothing about North America—let alone about this particular part of it. Even if they had . . . Bart had seen enough already to know that this place was heavily dependent on supplies from the outside world. Supplies which could only come in here by way of the railroads and ocean-going vessels of a modern or near-modern world.

It was not merely their clothes and furniture, the carpets, the lighting, and a thousand other items that were obviously not manufactured here, below ground. It was the edibles; the foods and drinks that had to come from outside. There were no farms, no domestic food animals, and no distilleries under the earth. Such items as food and drink, along with many other things, would have to be shipped in through some nearby port and brought by wagon to the mine for delivery here below ground.

That port could only be the town of New Westminster, which was the capital of the Canadian coastal colony of British Columbia; and which was probably not more than a couple of weeks of wagon-travel time away from the mine.

A thought kindled in his mind. It was that when he finally managed to get Emma and himself free from this place, the port of New Westminster and a ship to somewhere else might well be the destination they should seek.

"Tell me about the Hybrids," he said to Paolo. "The slave from the Library who guided me back to the dormitory just now said they were the result these little people—"

"*Lords!*" hissed Paolo, leaning toward him. "Call them Lords, here. We're out where people can see us and maybe read your lips!"

"All right, 'Lords' then," said Bart. "Tell me about the Hybrids. What's their part in the scheme of things around here? There was one at the Library who said he was the Assistant Librarian and I saw people wearing fancy eastcoast clothes who were supposed to be other Hybrids. What's their rank and what jobs do they do? I get the idea they're something like foremen over the slaves. Or do they just sit around like the Lords and enjoy life?''

''You got a lot to learn,'' said Paolo heavily, leaning back in his seat of the booth and signaling the waiter for refills. ''You really got a lot to learn.''

The dormitory Leader waited until the waiter had brought freshly filled glasses and gone again before leaning once more toward Bart.

''Sure, you could say they're like foremen,'' Paolo said. ''They do some of the in-between jobs, where someone has to give orders to a whole bunch of slaves every day. But most of them do work even the Lords aren't able to do, in the laboratories—''

''Laboratories?''

''You don't know about those, either?''

''I carried one of the Lords through some of them, today,'' said Bart. ''But I don't know what they're working on, or anything else about them.''

''Stick to the Hybrids for now. The point is, they work at all kinds of things. And get something else clear—'' Paolo paused for a moment as if gathering himself. ''Here in the Inner World everybody works, including the Lords. Any of them who isn't a worker isn't let grow up.''

Bart frowned. He sat with two full glasses of alcohol and one and a half of beer before him, almost untouched. Paolo seemed to have ceased to pay attention to the fact that Bart was not drinking as heavily as he was himself.

''Isn't let grow up?'' echoed Bart.

''Right! The only children let live down here are Lord or Hybrid young ones; and they get checked when they're eleven and again when they're seventeen years old, to see if they're fit to grow up. If they're not, even the young Lords, they're killed.''

''The Lords kill their own children?''

''You believe it!'' said Paolo. ''It's true. And it's not just because they might not want to work hard. They've got to be just so smart and just so healthy and so strong, and all that; or else, down they go!''

''Strong?''

Paolo laughed. For the first time the effect of the liquor he had poured down showed on him.

''You think the Lords ride us because they're too weak to walk?'' Paolo spluttered again into his drink. ''They may be little—and I don't say one of them's a patch on you or me, or any Steed for that matter—or even any good-sized, healthy man in the slave dormitories. But they practice all the time—''

He leaned forward farther, suddenly and urgently.

"Now, don't go talking about that," he said in a whisper. "The regular slaves, most of them, don't know it. Just a few special ones, including us because we get to be part of some of their ceremonies. But we're not supposed to let the ordinary slaves know. Anyway, you'd be surprised how strong some of those little—'' He paused, blinked, and then went on. ''—are—even the Lady Lords. By the way, you remember that, too. That's what you call their womenfolk —not the Hybrids, but the full-blooded ones. 'Ladies.' ''

Bart nodded, hiding the grin that the name "Lady Lords" had triggered off inside him.

"I'll remember. Ladies," he said.

"That's right; and you take my advice," continued Paolo, leaning back and belching almost inaudibly. "You get in the habit of calling them 'Lords' all the time. Bad enough when one of the ordinary slaves is caught calling them anything else, let alone one of us. Why're you so interested in Hybrids, anyway?"

He leaned forward again, peering at Bart curiously.

"You know," he said, "you could be one of them. You've got that sort of look about you. The way your forehead sticks out over your eyes, almost the way a Head's does."

chapter
nine

PAOLO'S FACE HAD become hard and his voice was suddenly clear of any trace of drunkenness. For a moment he merely stared at Bart; but then the tension went out of him and his voice returned to having the slightly alcoholic blur it had held a moment before.

"No," he said, "of course you aren't. I know every Hybrid in the Inner World who's anywhere near your age and they don't let even their own people out into the surface world until they're a good ten years older than you are. Besides, why would they go to all the trouble of setting up a Hybrid spy among the Steeds just to trap someone like me? Even for the Lords, that doesn't make sense. I'm not that important."

After a moment he added—

"Besides, I kind of like you. You ain't the type."

He took a deep drink from his latest glass of beer and sat back in the booth.

"Go on," he said, "tell me. I asked you why you were so interested in the Hybrids, anyway?"

"It's just that I don't see their place in the scheme of things, here," answered Bart. But his mind was already off and galloping down a new line of thought. If he could pass for a Hybrid, that fact might open up a whole new world of possibilities. "What do you mean, the Lords don't even let their own people out until they're older than I am now? Out, for what?"

Paolo frowned.

"How would I know what for? Some Lord business that means one of them has to go above ground to do it. All I know is, there's some Lords who suddenly just aren't here anymore, and later on word comes they left. Most of them come back in a few months. But some don't come back at all—or don't come back for longer than it's been since I was brought back to life."

"It could be some of them never come back because some accident kills them—or something like that," Bart said, as much to himself as to Paolo.

"Not likely. I suppose it could happen, though," said Paolo. "What do you want to know that for?"

"I just wondered why nobody above ground I met ever seemed to have heard of anyone like a Lord. Some ordinary people must know about them. They have to be seen sometimes by people who don't know them."

"They don't look that different from ordinary people," said Paolo. "Just small, that's all."

But Bart's real reason for the question had been entirely different. He was thinking now that without even wandering too far from the truth, he might be able to make the Lords believe that he was the son of a Lord who had gone out into the ordinary world and sired a child by an ordinary woman. A son who had never known the truth about his father until he had seen other Lords down here.

His father had been small enough to be a Lord—a somewhat large one, but a Lord; although from what Bart had seen of the rulers of this underground kingdom, Lionel Dybig could never have been one of them. His father's character had been too free-thinking and honest to let him belong to a society like this one.

Bart felt a twinge of guilt, remembering how in spite of the language, literature and science that his father had tutored him in, he had been more drawn by the almost lawless life of the métis fur traders in the open woods. He had hidden the attraction he felt for that part of his life from his father; but he was not sure that the older man had not sensed it in him, after all. His attention came back to Paolo, who was talking.

". . . but maybe some do die up there," Paolo was saying. "What's that to do with anything? Anyway, whatever they do above ground's no business of slaves like us, even if we are Steeds. You'll do better to leave the Lords to their own business. Yes, and the Hybrids, too . . ."

He went on. The effect of the alcohol on him was now plain and he was not shamming. He ran on, and Bart let him run for a while, before bringing him back to their dormitory.

Paolo seemed, thereafter, to have decided that Bart was his particular friend; and he sought Bart out at times for a drinking companion—not minding that Bart generally only went through the motions with his glasses.

Several nights later, Bart, at the end of an easy evening, brought up the other subject that was always in his mind.

"There's a female slave down here who's an old friend, since we were children together," Bart said to the dormitory Leader. "How would I go about finding her?"

"Finding her?" Paolo squinted at him. "Female slave? Your woman when you were alive?"

"No," said Bart. "Just a very old friend. I'd like to find her. How do I go about it?"

Paolo frowned at him for a second, then turned to beckon the waiter.

"Lorena here?" Paolo asked.

"I don't know." The waiter's manner was apologetic.

"Go look."

The waiter went off.

"Who's Lorena?" Bart asked.

"Slave I know," grunted Paolo.

It was only a few minutes before the waiter came back with a tall, thin young woman who looked as if a little more flesh and a good deal more happiness might have turned her into someone more than usually pretty. But as it was, she looked gaunt, harried and weary.

"Did you want me, Paolo?" she asked, coming up to the booth. The waiter faded away behind her to his position across the room.

"Sit down," said Paolo. She slid onto the seat of the booth beside him. "Lorena, this is one of my dormitory—his name's Bart Dybig."

Lorena smiled at Bart. It was a mechanical, almost pathetic smile that expected anything but had no hope that whatever it might be would be anything she would welcome.

"Hello, Lorena," said Bart.

His own voice was automatically gentle, as it might have been to some small, wild animal trapped by accident. Lorena's smile changed and became, while still wary, genuine.

"Bart wants to find one of the female slaves," Paolo said. "She'll be new reborn, like he is. Tell Lorena what this woman of yours looks like, Bart."

"Her name's Emma Robeson," said Bart. "She's Scot by breeding, just a few inches over five feet tall, with straight blond hair, white skin and blue eyes. She's got a . . ." He searched for the proper word. ". . . a very peaceful face. Once you see her, you'll always recognize her again; because that face of hers looks as if nothing could ever touch her."

Paolo grunted.

"Death did," he said.

"Death—" Bart checked the angry answer that sprang up in him. This was no time to argue with Paolo, or with anyone else, that he did not in the least believe they had ever died and been brought back to life by the Lords.

"If you can find her," he went on to Lorena, "tell her Bart Dybig's down here, too; and I want to see her. Here, would be a good place for her to meet me, wouldn't it?"

He turned to put the last sentence as a question to Paolo.

"Sure. Here's the place to meet anyone," said Paolo. "Any slave, that is."

He laughed shortly, and not happily.

"Hybrids and Lords—those you don't need to meet anyway," he said. "They've got their own places and they call you to them. They don't meet with slaves."

It occurred to Bart that, considering the fact that Arthur Robeson had been working with the Scottites, his activities might have given not only him but his sister some form of preference here in the Inner World—depending on exactly what the Scottites had to do with all this—so that they might be classed with the Hybrids, rather than as slaves—

For a moment a wild new thought crossed his mind. But then he shook his head, mentally dismissing it. Neither Emma nor Arthur could possibly be born Hybrids. There was nothing about them in the way of physical characteristics that would identify them as progeny of this race that called itself Lords. Besides, what he and his father had known of their parents' history above ground—no, it was impossible that they were Hybrids. But maybe it was possible to be given something like a courtesy ranking as a Hybrid.

He hesitated, on the brink of asking Paolo if such courtesy rankings existed. Then he decided not to ask. The caution built up in him by his childhood, the years of the Rebellion, and everything that had happened to him since, checked him. It was always wise to give away as little information about yourself and your interests as possible, no matter with whom you were dealing.

"How are you going to go about finding her?" he asked Lorena.

"I'll just start asking around," said Lorena. "Sooner or later word'll get back to me of someone who's seen somebody like that."

"Don't mention my name," said Paolo suddenly. "Or his. I don't want anything personal like this connected with the dormitory. You never know how the Lords and the Hybrids'll act, if they hear one of us is looking for some particular one of their slaves.

They may want to know why; and maybe even figure something they don't like is going on.''

He looked at Bart almost suspiciously.

"There's nothing special about this Emma Robeson?'' he asked.

Bart met his eyes squarely.

"She's just a childhood friend. Just what I told you,'' he said. "I like her and want to be sure she's all right. That's all.''

"How'd she end up down here?''

"I don't know,'' said Bart. It was only a half-lie. "All I know is, I saw her being taken down the tunnel of the mine toward the entrance to the Inner World. She didn't see me. No one with her did. They had light, but I was a good ways off from them and in the dark.''

"How'd you get around in that mine in the dark?'' Paolo asked.

"I counted steps and turnings while I was being taken to and from work with the gang I was chained in,'' answered Bart. "Bit by bit, I got to know most of the mine.''

Paolo stared at him, more than a little drunkenly.

"You must be pretty good with your sense of direction,'' he said. "I was in that mine too, for a few weeks, like I said; but I never could've found my way about it without a light.''

"I grew up finding my way through the woods on dark nights,'' said Bart. Their eyes locked again for a moment before Paolo looked away.

"Well . . . ,'' he said. He turned to Lorena, reached out and patted her clumsily on the head.

"You're a good woman,'' he muttered.

Lorena flashed a smile at him; and this time, Bart saw, it was a smile of pure affection. Then she got up from the booth.

"I'll go start asking,'' Lorena said. "Don't worry. I'll just sneak it into the talk; and I'll say it's me that wants her, that she owes me something from the time we were both alive together; and now that I've got her down here, I just want to make sure she pays up.''

"How could someone pay a debt down here?'' Bart asked as he watched her retreating back. "There's no money, is there?''

"No, all that ends when you die, right?'' The other laughed a bit grimly. "No, down here you pay off with favors, taking duties if that's allowed—like that.'' He was watching Lorena leave, too.

She went out of the room, and through the space she had vacated Bart now saw, near the doorway, the unmistakable figure of Chandt, standing gracefully balanced on the balls of his feet, his hands on his hips, looking over those in the booths and at the tables of this particular cranny of the slaves' recreational area. Like all the Steeds, including Bart and Paolo, he was now wearing a shirt; but his manner made it clear who he was.

"Wonder how long he's been there?" Paolo muttered. At the same time he was waving his arm over his head to attract Chandt's attention. Chandt's head turned. His eyes looked at them and he started in their direction, moving fluidly.

"That's one you'd better never try to whip, Bart," said Paolo under his breath, as the Leader of All the Steeds made his winding way among the tables intervening, toward them. "He's got devil-tricks I think the Lords must have taught him, so that no one could ever push him aside as the Master of us all. No one stands a chance against Chandt."

Chandt had reached them. He sat down on Paolo's side of the booth without waiting to be asked. His black eyes focused on Bart.

"You're ordered to the home of the Lord Librarian," he said. "Now. Immediately."

"Now? But I just got back a little bit ago—"

"That's the way it is, boy," Paolo interrupted him. "Twenty-four hours a day we're on call, all of us, by our riders."

The dormitory head looked at Chandt, however.

"Did they send someone to guide him over there?"

"There's a slave from the Lord Librarian's household waiting out at the front entrance," Chandt said. "He told me he guided you back to the dormitory a few days ago, Bart Dybig, and you'd recognize him. I left him there, because our Steeds have a reputation to live up to. If you'd been drunk, I'd have had to sober you up before I let you go to him."

"You'll never need to sober me up," said Bart—and felt Paolo's knee press suddenly, warningly against his under the table. Ignoring the pressure, Bart kept his eyes fixed directly on Chandt's.

"So much the better," said Chandt. His expression had not changed. "Leave your shirt here. Go, now."

Bart stood up, took off his shirt, and left, leaving the other two behind him. At the entrance to the slave's recreation area, he found Jon Swenson, now wearing a different sort of short toga, belted at the waist, of gold and silver cloth.

"Oh, there you are!" said Jon on catching sight of Bart. "Are you all right?"

"Right? Of course I'm all right," said Bart.

Jon came close and stuck his face up toward Bart's.

"You do smell of alcohol," he said, "but not too much. You say you're not drunk?"

"I'm not drunk," said Bart. "Or anywhere near it."

"Do you drink heavily on occasion?" asked Jon. "You might as well tell me now, if you do. That's the sort of question the Lord and the Lord Lady are going to be asking you when we get there."

Bart set aside in his mind a few occasions at gatherings of the fur traders and holidays. These had been during times of his youth. He would not be doing that again.

"Never," he said.

"I hope you're telling the truth—for your sake," said Jon. "Let's go."

They moved off together down one of the long underground corridors.

"And why do you hope for my sake I'm telling the truth?" asked Bart, looking down at the younger man, who seemed to have put on an aura of importance with his gold and silver toga.

"Well, because the standards for a house slave's so much higher than the standards for a work place one," said Jon. "I'm both, you see."

It seemed to Bart that the younger man strutted a little.

"Yes," said Bart.

"The Lord and his Lady want you to be able to run errands between the Library and their home, sometimes when the Lord's in his office at the Library," said Jon. "So, of course they want to look you over and decide if you'll do for the house end of things."

"I see," said Bart. It had not occurred to him before that a higher standard might be set on those slaves that had duties in the homes of the Heads. But it made sense. Theoretically, their little overlords could be more vulnerable to those who had the freedom of their living quarters than to those who simply had the freedom of the area in which the upper class worked.

He filed the information in his memory. His father had been fond of saying that any piece of information would be useful sooner or later; and Bart had found the statement true many times over.

He thought again about Lords leaving the Inner World for times of various lengths; and the chance that he might be able to get away with passing himself off as a Hybrid.

As he had been thinking since his talk with Paolo a few days ago, Lionel Dybig had been small enough, certainly intelligent enough, and different enough from ordinary men that he ought to be picturable as a Lord. Bart would simply have to claim that he had barely met his father before the older man's death, so that his memory of him was limited and hazy.

All the rest of Bart's life story, including his Cree mother and his growing under the conditions of the Riel rebellion, could be acceptable as the story of a young Hybrid who had grown up thinking himself an ordinary human.

But it would still be wise to go carefully with the story. The Lords must have records, let alone memories of those of their own kind who had gone out into the upper world and never returned. Bart could claim ignorance of his father's true identity; but he would be wise if he could, to discover the identity of some actual Lord who had gone out and never come back; and whose character, appearance and time of going could be fitted in with Bart's sketchy "memory" of his father.

Where to get such information?

The Lords themselves were not likely simply to answer questions from him. One or more of the Hybrids might know; but as a slave he was no more in a position to chat with Hybrids than he was with Lords.

And the slaves would not know. The Lords would have made sure that the slaves did not know; if necessary changing those on duty near the exit point into the mine, or even—from what he had seen of this place, and the mine before it—killing them off to make sure they would never suspect what they should not know, or tell what they had seen.

So, there was no person who could tell him the name of some Lord who had gone away into the upper world and never returned, and was almost undoubtedly dead by this time. A Lord who not only fulfilled those requirements, but had gone out at a time that would precede the time of Bart's own birth, and possibly match the place of it.

There remained the Library. He would be taking Pier Guettrig there daily. The Lords must keep records—where more likely for those records to be kept than in the Library?

But it would probably not be easy to find the records he wanted. The Lords would hardly advertise their location by making their keeping place easily visible and identifiable. Probably the best way for Bart to discover where they were kept would be to wait until one of the Lords came in who wanted to consult them; and by following him or her, to find out where that was. There was no way to tell how often such might come about.

Moreover, it would hardly be possible, let alone practical, for him to follow every Lord who came into the Library. What he needed was some way of recognizing a Lord who was there for the purpose of dealing with the records Bart wanted to find. Offhand, he could not think of one.

He felt frustrated.

If he could only really understand that private language of theirs, it would be a simple matter of listening when the Lords came in and spoke to the slaves on duty at the desk. The kind of records Bart was looking for would probably require at least the permission of Charles Mordaunt, the Hybrid who was Assistant Librarian, to be looked at. They might require even the permission of Pier Guettrig, himself, and if Bart could only overhear and understand the conversation between the visiting Lord or Lady and Guettrig, he would find out where to look, or at least learn enough to follow the visitor to the place where the records were kept.

It would undoubtedly be a safe place, possibly a hidden one . . . .

Meanwhile, Jon had brought him to the Guettrig home and a staircase-dominated room he recognized. The man who was always here and in charge when Bart was brought to his Master was not present this time, and Jon led the way up his stairs with as much aplomb as if he, himself, was a Lord.

The top of the stairs gave on to a balcony under the high ceiling of the same room, and a number of corridors led back off through the wall behind the balcony. Jon took the second corridor to his right and led Bart down a carpeted and panelled corridor, past a number of closed doors made of some heavy, dark wood, to one which sat squarely in the wall that closed the far end of the corridor.

At this door he stopped and scratched on its surface lightly with his fingernail.

They waited.

Bart had just about reached the point of suggesting to Jon that he scratch again, when the door opened itself before them. They went through it, and the door closed again behind them—once more, apparently by itself.

They stood in a large, square room with very thick and soft carpet underfoot, and tapestries on the walls. Overhead in the ceiling, the mechanical lights that were all about the Inner World glowed in their warm, sunlight color. Along the base of the walls, panels also glowed—but redly, since they seemed to be composed of bars of heated metal which raised the temperature of the room close to the point where Bart would have found it actively uncomfortable. A scent like that of spring flowers mingled with the faint smells of carpet and hot metal, not hiding the two latter odors, but in a sense excusing them.

The room was furnished with chairs and couches, all heavily padded and overstuffed and all built to the size of the small people who ruled this underground country.

In two of these chairs—brown upholstered, high-backed pieces of furniture—facing each other across a small table that held something like a chess board, sat Pier Guettrig and the tiny, young-appearing woman who had been on the stairs with the Librarian the first time Bart had seen him.

The two were now ignoring the game that had evidently been in progress between them; their eyes were fastened on Bart.

"Lord and Lady," said Jon in French, "here is the slave you ordered me to bring you."

"Yes. Wait outside, Jon," answered the rusty voice of Pier in the same tongue. "You'll be needed to take him back to his dormitory, after we've talked to him."

"Yes, Lord."

Jon backed toward the door, which opened to let him out and then closed again after he had passed through it.

"Come here," said Pier to Bart.

Bart walked forward until he stood a step from their chairs, towering over them as they sat looking up at him.

"He'd better sit," said the woman. Her voice was as young as her superficial appearance, and had a touch of humor in it. "I'm going to get a stiff neck looking up at him."

"Sit down, Bart," said Pier. His own voice was not unkindly. "You can sit cross-legged on the rug, there."

Bart lowered himself into the sitting position suggested. From that position he looked upward at the two and they looked down at him almost benignly, like elderly relatives.

"Bart," said Pier, "this is my Lady. You will address her as such, but in case some other Lord should need to ask you or speak to you about her, her name is the Lady Marta Guettrig. I am the Lord Pier Guettrig, in case no one has already told you."

"I understand, Lord," said Bart.

Pier nodded almost enthusiastically.

"Exactly!" he said. "Of course—you're quick to learn, Bart. But now we have to learn about you."

"Where were you born, Bart?" asked Marta.

Bart had not expected to have to give any of the story about his personal background until he had had a chance to reconcile it with what was known about Lords who had gone out into the upper world and never returned. Now, he was faced with the danger of saying something that might later trip him up. Also, he had expected Pier to do the questioning; and Marta had caught him off guard—so that in spite of himself, he hesitated for just a moment before answering.

"I don't know exactly," he said. "At a Cree camp, somewhere near the Red River, not far from Assiniboia."

"In métis country," said Pier.

"I am a métis," said Bart.

"And your father was a man named Lionel Dybig?"

"How did you know that?" Bart turned his gaze on the old man.

"You won't remember it, but you were questioned at the time you were revived," said Pier. "That's done with all who're brought in here . . ."

"What was your mother's name?" Marta asked, leaning forward.

"It was—in French it would translate into 'Listens to Trees,'" answered Bart. "Both she and her mother were said to understand the language the trees speak when the wind blows."

"Marta—," began Pier.

"Allow me, Pier," she interrupted him. "I want to hear these things from Bart himself. Bart—what was she like?"

"She died of a coughing sickness the winter I was five years old," said Bart. "I hardly remember her."

It was true, he hardly remembered what she had looked like, how she had walked and talked. But he remembered vividly a presence that had been hers, a presence, warm and large, that had surrounded his whole life up until the time she died.

"After she was dead, I was sent to my father," Bart went on, remembering as he spoke. "I knew who he was, because he'd visited our camp from time to time. I liked him; but if it had been up to me, then, I'd have stayed with the camp rather than have gone to him."

"Tell us about him," said Pier.

"He wasn't much bigger than you, Lord," said Bart. "His arms were long for his size and he was much stronger than he looked. He lived with the métis—in fact, he was close to Louis Riel, and Riel sometimes acted on his advice. He was a small, dark man, very intense. People who didn't know him sometimes began by taking him too lightly, at first—''

"Ah!" said Marta unexpectedly.

Bart looked at her.

"Go on," she said.

"As I say, they'd begin by taking him lightly but once they got to know him, they found out quickly he was somebody they had to respect, either as friend or enemy. He was so much smarter than those around him, that he was almost like a man living with a pack of animals. He taught me how to speak French with several different accents. Also, other languages, and a lot about the world that the métis and the Indians didn't know.''

As with his mother, talking about his father had brought back to Bart the feeling of his father's presence.

Only, in the case of his father, Bart had sharp visual memories to go with that feeling. The one that came most often to him was the image of Lionel seated across the cabin from him, writing at a table under the bright white light of a parafin lamp in the evening as Bart sat at his own studies with another lamp at another table.

His father's face in that image was carved into Bart's memories. It had been a lean, narrow face under long, straight black hair. A face with brilliant eyes, quick to expression; so unlike Bart's own square, nearly expressionless features, that Bart had hated his own image when he saw it in the cabin mirror, thinking of himself as incredibly ugly—just as his father, to him, was the handsomest of men.

"Tell us," Marta was saying to him, "what life was like for you as a boy, growing up among the métis?"

It was an odd question, Bart thought, under the present circumstances; but Pier's wife—if ''wife'' had the same meaning here in the Inner World, among the Lords—seemed to be indulging some private interest; and it seemed her husband was sitting back and letting her do so.

Bart tried, therefore, to tell them. But it was hard to pick what they might want to hear and what might not bind him too tightly to a history that could stand in the way of his claiming Hybrid birth later on.

As a result, he told them—told Marta, actually—about little things. Like the schoolhouse, which he had attended because his father said that he must not seem too different; although the teacher dealt only with simple things Bart had learned early in his time with his father. In any case the other students there sensed a difference in Bart, anyway, and most of them kept their distance from him—all of them, that was, except Emma. The others did not dare pick on him because, like his father, he was strong for his size and the Indian camp had taught him early not to be afraid of a fight. But they made no effort to be close to him.

It was the learning sessions he had had with his father that were most important in his memory. His father told him fascinating stories of a world far beyond these north woods; told him of people, places and things, taught him different languages and customs and a different historical background to the time they were now in than even Louis Riel seemed to know.

Listening to Lionel's words, Bart had eagerly absorbed fascinating details about Europe and North Africa, Persia and China; and also about something called the Ottoman Empire. The overall picture his father's words built for him was of a human race made up of many different kinds of men and women, struggling, always struggling, upward toward some better form of life that they could hardly define themselves but which led them over the centuries to build and invent tools to give them dominance over the earth and even to change the face of it.

None of these latter memories were in the account he gave Marta and Pier—and, still, he had an uneasy feeling that the two of them were reading some of his private thoughts through the bare account he gave them of his father's life and death; and his own life after that, when he had left Riel down in the United States and made his own way here.

Bart was first puzzled, then wary, about the wealth of detail they wanted to hear, both about himself and his life with his father. Pier, it seemed, was interested mostly in what Bart and Lionel had done and talked of, and where they had gone. Marta's interest fastened on other elements: on how they had felt toward each other and the people around them. She seemed more interested in their joys and sorrows.

It occurred to Bart, suddenly, that just possibly he had tapped a vein of intense curiosity in this race of strange little people who owned and spent their lives in this Inner World. A curiosity about the world of open air and sunlight above them, and curiosity about the ordinary humans who lived there. Nothing else, thought Bart, could explain the exhaustiveness of the interest Pier and Marta were showing in every detail of Bart's former life.

When it came to the point of his mentioning Emma and her brother, Bart touched on them only lightly. He did not want to reveal either the importance of Emma to him, or his knowledge of her presence here, until he knew more about whether it was safe to do so. He wondered uneasily whether they already knew that about him, too; but he had no choice but to put the best face he could on it all.

Fortunately, their questions all stopped with Bart's capture at Shunthead; and eventually—Bart was beginning to feel harried and wary—there came a slight pause. Once more Pier and Marta looked at each other.

"Whatever you wish, my Lord," said Marta out loud, in the French they had been speaking, with a demureness completely unlike the way she had been speaking so far to her husband. Bart gazed at her with curiosity and more of his earlier suspicion.

"And now, Bart," said Pier, also still in French, "stay as you are and wait. I'll talk to the Lady privately for a moment."

He turned to Marta and began to speak in that oddly familiar-sounding, but barely unintelligible, private language that the Lordly class and Hybrids, sometimes, seemed to use among themselves.

Bart sat motionless, cross-legged, with his face impassive as always; but with resentment warming inside him. He had never found it pleasant to be in a group where all the other members were speaking and understanding a language he did not understand. The suspicion that they were talking about him—aloud and in front of him but in such a way that he could not catch them at it, was emotionally inescapable. It was doubled when—as now—he actually knew himself to be the subject of the indecipherable conversation.

. . . And yet the language they were speaking was so tantalizingly close to something he knew. Not French, not German, not Italian . . .

Then, without warning, he suddenly found himself understanding. All at once, he could follow more than enough of the words Pier and Marta were saying—for by now the two were in animated discussion—to recognize it as a twisted version of something he had once learned. Only, these people spoke it with a totally different pronunciation, some difference of form, and a number of unknown words.

Pier and Marta were speaking Latin.

But it was not the classical Latin his father had painstakingly taught him. It was a Latin in which the words were mispronounced and sometimes used to mean something largely different from the meaning his father had taught him.

Recognizing the language at last, Bart abruptly remembered something buried so deeply that it had been forgotten over the years. His father had put a great deal of emphasis on the fact that the correct speaking of a language, or the correct accent for a regional version of a language, was all-important. Latin, he had told his son, being a dead language, should never be mispronounced or misused—and if ever Bart ornamented his conversation by so much as a Latin phrase he must be sure to pronounce the words of it as they had in classical times.

He had even, Bart remembered now, made the boy promise that he would never commit the vulgarity of speaking Latin, of all languages, incorrectly.

". . . but we must go very slowly and carefully," Pier was saying to Marta at this moment. "Very slowly and carefully. The evidence must be beyond all argument before we even accept it ourselves, let alone think of showing it to others."

"But I hate to think of him—," said Marta.

"We have no choice, my love. No choice," Pier answered. "Even as Librarian, I'm not free to do anything that might be construed as violating the Compact. . . ."

These words he was listening to and now understanding, Bart thought, should have been obvious to him from the start as a dialect of the Latin his father had taught him.

But there was no time for remembering now. At the moment all of his attention was needed, trying to follow the unfamiliar forms and words of the conversation about himself going on between Pier and Marta.

"Well, I'm not that concerned about the Compact!" said Marta. "And I'm not afraid to say what I think. He's not the usual type of slave at all! You can't deny that after hearing what he's been telling us—"

What caused Bart to gamble at this point, he was never afterward able to decide. Perhaps the impulse was the result of a kindliness he seemed to feel in Pier and Marta; or perhaps it was simply that his own instincts cued him when logic would not. His original intention as far as the language spoken by the Lords was concerned had been to master it sooner or later; but he had never even speculated on the possibility of trying to speak it until he should be certain that he could use it with a fluency equal to the little people's own, such as would astound them with his knowledge.

He knew that in speaking now, he would be risking his plan to pass for a Hybrid. But it was as if a spark from Marta's emotion kindled the decision in him. In his mind, he built the phrase he wished to say in classical Latin—with difficulty, for his knowledge of it had been rather a reading than a speaking knowledge—then made such changes in the pronunciation as he thought he had heard when Pier and Marta spoke it just now. He knew that it would take more than a few changes to make him sound fluent, or even completely understandable. The grammar was much simpler and words were so often used with a somewhat different meaning than they had held in the classical form. But, hopefully, Pier and Marta would follow what he was trying to say.

Stumblingly, he spoke.

"Give me pardon, Lordly Ones," he said, choosing the closest terms he could think of to those he had heard, "is it pleasing or not to you to know that knowledge some of language yours I have?"

He was careful to speak slowly and clearly and make the changes in pronunciation. Having done so, he waited for their response.

It was not until after the words were out of his mouth, and Pier and Marta had abandoned their own conversation to turn and stare wordlessly at him, that he realized the true proportions of his gamble—that by speaking out in this manner, if he failed to make the proper impression on the two before him, then he might very well have signed his death warrant, as a slave who knew something he should not.

chapter

ten

THE SILENCE STRETCHED out. Pier and Marta continued to stare at him, and it occurred to Bart suddenly that perhaps his attempt to speak their dialect might have been so bad that they had not understood him.

What he had constructed in his own mind had been, in classical Latin, the simplest form of what he wished to say; since the dialect he had been listening to seemed simpler and more direct in its grammar than classical Latin as he had been taught it by his father. Written, the words would have been *"Veniam date, dominatores. Placeatne vobis cognoscere quote congnitionem aliquam linguae vestra habeo?"*

The changes in pronunciation he had picked up and used from the Lords' dialect had primarily been the pronunciation of "w" sounds as "v" and the "c" sound before open vowels as a soft "c"—in other words, like "s" rather than like "k."

Accordingly, the phrase, which he would ordinarily have pronounced as "Weniam dahtay, domeenatorays. Plakeeatnay wobis kognoscoray kwoad kogneeteeownem ahleequam lingueye westreye hahbayo . . ."

. . . he had spoken instead as "vayneeam dahtay domeenatorays. Plasayatnay vobis kognoscoray kwoad kogneeseeownem ahleequam leenguay vestray hahbayo?"

Something very much like a panic stirred in him now. He searched his mind hastily for lines that they must recognize, even if the pronunciation was not what they were used to; and his memory came up with the opening lines of the *Aeneid*, by Virgil: *"Arma verumque cano Troiae . . ."*

"Owdeetay," he said hastily. "Arma veerumquay kano troyay . . ."

"You mean, I think," interrupted Pier in Latin, almost coldly, "Owdeetay: Arma weerumquay kano Troyeye."

It was not exactly the classic pronunciation of that first line of Latin verse as Bart had learned it from his father, but it was so similar that the differences in pronunciation were negligible.

"Where did you learn to speak classical Latin?" Pier went on to ask in French.

"From my father," answered Bart; also, with relief, in French.

"Ah!" said Marta, in a universal tongue, looking at her husband.

"He spoke a number of languages," added Bart hurriedly, "and he taught me a lot. There was no one else to learn from, except the teacher at a little school that really only tried to teach writing and basic arithmetic to the local children."

"What other barbarian tongues do you speak?" asked Pier.

"German, Italian—French and English, of course—Cree, some bits of other Indian languages and a little of other European languages."

"And you learned all these from your father?" Marta demanded.

"All but the Indian languages," said Bart. "We only had each other; and the only thing he had to give me was what he knew—about languages and things like that—"

He broke off.

"Go on," said Pier.

"I was going to say, about the world and people," answered Bart.

"What people?" The question came like a bullet from Pier.

"People in general. The history of those in Europe eastward into China, and southward into Africa . . ." Bart hesitated, then took the bull by the horns. "He never told me about any place like this one, however, or any people like yours, Lord and Lady."

Marta and Pier once more exchanged glances. It occurred to Bart that they hardly needed the Latin dialect in which to communicate privately. Like many people who have lived closely together for a long time, with the help of a glance or the ghost of a facial expression one to the other, they could practically converse in silence.

"Leave it up to Bart," said Marta unexpectedly. "Bart, how much have you guessed about yourself from what we've all said here?"

"I don't know what you mean, Lady—with submission," said Bart.

"Yes, you do," said Marta. "You're just afraid that you may get yourself in trouble by being completely open with us. While what I think," she turned to her husband, "is that either too little or too much has been said already."

She turned back to Bart.

"Pier and I promise you, Bart," she said, "whatever you have to say to us, we'll keep to ourselves. We won't tell anyone of anything you say; and of course, we trust you to do the same with what we tell you. Isn't that right, Pier?"

She looked at her husband again. Pier sighed.

"Yes. Yes . . . ," he said. "Bart, honor is a great thing to those of us who are Lords. I give you my word of honor that whatever you may tell me about yourself will not be told by me to anyone else. I'll also promise that I'll not act upon what I hear from you, in my official capacity as one of the Three and under my responsibilities as a Lord."

Bart's thoughts were tumbling over each other in his mind. He felt at once a great elation and a great wariness. What he was hearing was far more than he had ever expected to hear and almost more than he could trust. He had found himself coming to like Pier and Marta. But there was no guarantee in that which meant he could trust them. And while their attitude seemed to bode well for his ideas, he still had no idea just what they were themselves seeking.

Not yet, said his inner, cautious soul. *Not completely, yet. Perhaps eventually.*

"Are you satisfied, Bart?" Marta asked.

"Yes," he said, knowing that his naturally expressionless face would not give away the lie.

"Then, I'll ask you again. How much about yourself have you guessed from what's been said here?"

"I've guessed," said Bart, "that the Lord and the Lady are more interested in me than they might be if they were only concerned with me as a possible house servant."

"Vincent, all over again," murmured Marta. "Bart, you've got to do better than that. I want you to tell me the most you've guessed, not the least."

She had him cornered.

"My greatest guess," he said slowly, "is that for some reason you seem to be interested more in me, as me, than as one of your slaves, in any possible slave capacity."

"Of course," said Marta. "Tell him, Pier."

"Tell him what, my dear?"

"Tell him everything."

"No," said Pier slowly, and his voice deepened. His dark eyes were steady on Bart under the gray, straggly eyebrows. "I'm sorry, my love, but not everything, yet. He still has to prove himself to the world we live in. He's only one person, and healthy. We're two, and no longer young. He might live anywhere. Here is the only place we can survive; and we have a right to defend the safety of our position here. You'll have to wait—wait a little, Marta.''

"At least tell him—"

"I'll decide what to tell him," said Pier. "I'm one of the Three; and I know things I've not even told you, who are closest to my heart—things I've not told any living soul. There are things that have to wait for the proper moment for their telling; and a lot that you'd like to have me tell Bart hasn't yet come to its moment.''

He stopped, still looking at Bart, then went on.

"I think Bart understands. I think, too, he's got his own matters about which he waits for the proper moment for telling us. Am I right, Bart?''

"Yes," said Bart. He felt an admiration for the small, old man before him. "I have. I trust you, Lord and Lady, but there are things I can't say because they involve others besides me.''

"But—," began Marta, then checked herself. Once more she looked at Pier.

"Bart's hesitation to be completely open with us, and ours to be completely open with him, needn't stop us from going ahead with what you and I planned for this moment,'' Pier said to her. "After all, this is only our first talk. He doesn't know us yet; as we don't fully know him. But we do know enough to tell him some things and do what we had decided to do for him first.''

Bart's inner ears pricked up at the "for him." He was tempted to bring up the subject of Emma, but reason told him not to push his luck until he knew more of what these two extraordinary people had in mind.

"Then it's all right," said Marta, "to let him go on just the way he has so far? If he goes on without knowing any more than he does now it'll be cruel to him and shameful for us.''

"Sometimes cruelty and shame can't be avoided," said Pier. "But you're right. Bart, listen to me.''

"Yes, Lord.''

"Many things I'm not going to explain to you now. For now, it's enough for you to know that Marta and I once took an interest in the young man who later became your father. Because of that interest we—while we were still careful not to break any of the laws of our Inner World, here—were able to help him considerably. Because you're your father's son, and if you continue to show you deserve it, we'll try to help you in the same way.''

"I see. Thank you, Lord and Lady.''

"You don't have to thank us—'' Marta checked herself. "You'll be giving us something in return.''

"What, Lady?''

She smiled.

"Nothing, I think, you'll hesitate about giving,'' Marta said. "But I should let Pier handle this part of it. Go on, dear.''

"Bart,'' said Pier, "you're a slave. Even as one of the Three Who Command, I can't change that. There are only three classes here in the Inner World. Ourselves, who are born to be its rightful rulers, the Hybrids, who are born with a part of our bloodline but in whom the slave blood of one parent bars them forever from being Lords—and all else, who are slaves as you are.''

Bart nodded.

"Yes,'' said Pier, "I'd assumed you'd understood that much. I just wanted to make it very clear that there are limits to what my Lady and I can do for you—but, at the same time, what we can do is considerable. There are slaves and slaves.''

"Like Chandt?'' said Bart.

Pier frowned.

"You should never speak to me or any other Lord or Lady without being spoken to first,'' he said.

But then he, too, smiled.

"However,'' he went on, "here in the privacy of our own home, you're absolved from that rule. Yes, like Chandt. Chandt's a special kind of slave, and specially favored because only one of that kind is needed. Also he's required to be in a position of authority over a large number of other slaves.''

"Including me,'' said Bart.

"Yes,'' said Pier. "But I'll speak to him. After that, he'll still have the authority, but he'll use it with restraint, in your case.''

"Thank you, Lord,'' said Bart.

"You're not a Steed by accident, you know, or by reason of your size and strength alone,'' Pier went on. "There're advantages to being a Steed, as you'll find out. For one thing, you'll get more respect and obedience from other slaves than you would in any other position you could hold among them. Part of this is because they believe—with some reason—that the Steeds are specially favored by us Lords. But there are other advantages that'll be useful to you as well as to my Lady and myself. You'll find out about those, as occasions involving them come up.''

He broke suddenly into a warm smile.

"And while I'm on the subject," he said, "forgive me if you can for having ridden you such a distance that first day. It's not that I'm not aware of the effort and discomfort of carrying one of us in a chair. The original intent was frankly punitive: one more way to make humans suffer as they'd made our ancestors suffer. Later it became a way of showing off, as it were . . ."

He interrupted himself.

"But that's beside the point, now," he said. "The important thing is that I knew what I was doing to you and wouldn't have done it if it hadn't been necessary. I had to show you off all over the Inner World, the way any one of us with a new Steed would have shown him off; and also I had to show that I was indifferent to the pain and effort you felt as a result; so that no one should suspect I intend to favor you—as they'll see me doing later on."

"I understand," said Bart.

"I thought you would," answered Pier. "And you'll understand, consequently, if in public—for no apparent reason you can see or understand—I seem to treat you with deliberate harshness for a while, yet. The reason will always be the same; to avert suspicion of any favoritism toward you by me or my Lady."

"You don't understand what's meant when my Lord speaks of himself as one of the Three Who Command, do you?" put in Marta to Bart.

"No, Lady." Bart shook his head.

"Here in the Inner World, we rule," said Marta. "But we've got out own rulers. From among ourselves we elect, for life, Three Who Command us generally. Sitting as a body, they resolve disputes and make all the decisions that affect the Inner World as a whole. The Three are the Emperor, who is in authority even over the two who Command with him—the Regent, and the Librarian. Pier's the Librarian. As such, he has some powers and freedoms even the Emperor doesn't have—particularly so far as the Library's concerned. So, what'd be only a minor bit of favoritism for the average Lord or Lady would be scandalous in his case."

"Oh," said Bart.

"I want you to understand that, because I want you to understand how much he's risking to give you the help you'll be given," she said. "He's doing this not only for your own sake, but for me, because he knows how much it means to me to help you. So, if he's hurt by it, both you and I are going to have to share the blame—not that that'll help, because he'll have to face the other Lords as if the responsibility was his alone.''

''I see,'' said Bart.

He looked at both of them.

''I appreciate what you want to do for me,'' he said slowly. ''I don't understand, but I'm grateful. Only, I'd like to know more about why you're doing it.''

''You'll find out soon enough,'' said Pier. ''Just as soon as it's safe to tell you. Meanwhile, I'll tell you this much. You're a Steed because, as I said, it's a useful job for you to have. But, also as I said, I'll be talking to Chandt and making sure he understands that while you're still one of his corps, your primary duty is going to be to wait on my pleasure here; or go back and forth between me and my Lady with messages and perhaps other things. Now, you'll remember all this, what I'm telling you now?''

''I've got a good memory, Lord,'' said Bart.

''I'd expected as much.'' Pier nodded. ''All right, your duties, then, are going to leave you free to move about the Library and even the Inner World in general, if necessary. If questioned you can always tell whoever's questioning you that you've been sent on some errand by me. Refer them to me. I'll take care of it from that point on.''

He paused to stare piercingly at Bart. Bart nodded.

''Good. Now, in the Library itself, I want to give you as much opportunity as possible to take advantage of what's there. If you're the sort of person we think you are, you won't waste any time making use of that. Slaves who work in the Library and slaves of supervisory rank—like Chandt—are allowed to make some limited use of the Library facilities. If I were to create some excuse to grant you that kind of privilege, it'd attract attention. Steeds aren't thought of as the type of human who's interested in books.''

Bart could believe that.

''So we need an excuse to give you the freedom of the stacks and the freedom to carry off for reading any book you want. There's a way. You can have been sent by me to pick out a book and bring it to me in my office. Also we need a place of privacy for you where you can read without people knowing you're doing that. It won't do to have you sitting down in the rest quarters for slaves and have the other slaves who come in while you're there find you reading all the time. So, to answer both problems, I've ordered a small alcove partitioned off in my office, on the excuse that I need you at my beck and call to run errands for me. It should be finished by now.''

Bart stared at the small, old man. Pier's authority evidently was considerable, and a good deal more than Bart had assumed before. He had been in that same office only a few hours past, when he had, as ordered, picked up Pier and carried him home; and there had been no sign of an alcove, then, or preparations to build one.

"My official reason for the alcove is that I don't wish to be reminded of your presence all the time, but I do want you at hand. It'll be assumed that you don't understand our true language, so anyone of rank visiting me in the office will believe they can speak freely." Pier frowned again. "We'll have to guard the fact you do understand. I think you can imagine how my guests would feel, having some of their more private utterances overheard and understood by a slave."

"Yes," said Bart—and was careful to keep out the note of irony that threatened to creep into his voice.

"So," said Pier, looking for a moment at Marta. "I think that's all for now. Jon, outside, will show you around our quarters here, so you'll have some idea of how they're laid out. Then he'll show you the route from your Steed quarters to both here and to the Library."

Bart did not offer to explain that he already knew at least two routes to the dormitory and was fairly confident, from what he had seen so far of the Inner World, that he could find a more or less direct route from here back to the Library by himself—even though in his trips with Pier he had been led on roundabout inspection tours—using the map he had built in his head from his earlier movements around the Inner World. But Jon might have things to show him he had not suspected; and in any case there were a great many questions about the Library and the Inner World in general he still wished to ask the young man—not the least being some queries dealing with Pier's status among his fellow Lords.

"Yes, Lord," he said. "Was there anything in particular you wanted me to study, using the books in the Library?"

Pier raised his eyebrows.

"Don't be ungrateful, Bart," said Marta. "We assumed you'd want to read the books in the stacks at the Library. Pier's simply making it safe and easy for you to do so."

"You might start out, of course," said Pier, "by looking at maps of the Inner World, so as to familiarize yourself with the ways around in it."

Bart did not see him move. But the other must have made some kind of signal, for with the last of his words the door opened and Jon stepped in.

"My Lord and Lady?" he asked. "You called?"

"You can take Bart away, now," said Pier. "Show him around this home of ours, and the direct routes from the Library to here, as well as from the dormitory to the Library. Tell him anything he needs—or wants—to know."

"Yes, Lord," said Jon.

He stood aside and Bart moved past him toward and through the entrance. He noticed that the door stayed open behind him; and so, once he was through it and outside the room, he turned to look back at Pier and Marta.

"Thank you, Lord and Lady," he said.

Neither of the small people responded. The door closed.

chapter
eleven

"PAOLO DOESN'T WANT to fight you," said Chandt. He spoke with careful articulation, for the drink was already beginning to affect him.

For two weeks after speaking to Pier and Marta, Bart had seen nothing of the Master of the Steeds, beyond an occasional glimpse of him going about his duties in the domain of the Steeds. Then abruptly he had appeared in Bart's dormitory when Bart had just returned there from the Library and taken Bart off with him. Now, they were sitting in the private eating and drinking area of the Steeds, with tall glasses of the sweet, weak local beer in front of them. As with the first time Chandt had brought Bart here, they had the place to themselves. Bart wondered whether this was because of the times that Chandt picked to bring him here, or whether some sort of message that he was coming had cleared ordinary Steeds out of the room.

In either case, they had been alone here except for the serving man for three glasses now, and surprisingly, already Chandt was beginning to show the effects of alcohol. Bart noted the slightly slurred speech, the short-focused gaze, with suspicion. It did not seem possible that someone of Chandt's size, let alone in Chandt's magnificent physical condition, could be honestly affected by drink so strongly and so quickly. It was true, he had known some men who were hit hard and quick by alcohol—but never this quickly, nor had they been someone like Chandt.

Nonetheless, Chandt was indeed beginning to look and sound drunk, to the point that the statement he had just made had a faintly challenging note to it, a near-pugnaciousness of the sort a drunk might show.

"Oh, I don't think so," said Bart.

Chandt's black eyes bored into him.

"You think I don't know when a man does not want to fight—particularly one of my own men?" he said, and drank. His gaze wandered off toward another part of the room. There was a pause before he went on, almost to a change of subject.

"Paolo's all right," he said. "Some of the dormitory Leaders . . . they think of fighting anyone. Even me."

He laughed, shortly and harshly; and drank again.

"Some have tried," he said. "Yes, some tried to fight me. Not many, but some."

His mind seemed to wander.

"Some . . ." he said again. His eyes focused once more on Bart. "You would try, maybe."

Bart shook his head.

"I don't want to fight anyone," he answered.

It was a small disappointment. He had somehow expected Chandt to understand, even where others did not. But the other man's attitude had been no different from that of most people Bart had encountered.

It was strange, Bart thought, how people—essentially men, but some women too—could not think of unusual strength as being otherwise than a blessing. It never seemed to strike them that it could be a curse as well. There was no pleasure in winning when you knew that the dice were loaded in your favor by nature. Strength that had been earned by some great labor might be different; but Bart's had simply been visited on him from birth and he had never been able to take any particular pride in it.

But Chandt was talking again.

"You know," he was saying, his dark eyes squinting a little as if to keep Bart in focus, "you may be telling me the truth. There are some who'd not care to be even Master of the Steeds. There are those like Paolo—but you're not like Paolo."

Chandt shook his head as if to shake shadows clear of it.

"Never mind," he said. "What you are is specially favored; and that is something you and I have got to come to an understanding on. You're not the first Steed, you know, for whom someone more than a slave has come to me and wanted me to give that Steed special privileges. In the centuries I've been what I am, there've been a number who asked."

He stopped and stared for a moment across the table at Bart.

"When those who asked were agreeable to me, I agreed," he said, "—provided there was nothing unnatural involved. They can have their men or their women, whichever they prefer; as can my Steeds. I don't interfere ordinarily. But a fighting man is not to be made a toy of, to be put on soft cushions and cozied up to and made love to. It spoils him for what he should be. And my Steeds are not for spoiling. In those cases, where I did not like what was asked, I went to the Emperor—and the Emperor always understood, because he knows what the Steeds are for.''

Chandt paused to drink and look again at Bart.

"You know what the Steeds are for?" he asked.

"No," said Bart.

"They are for the protection of three things," said Chandt. "For the protection of the Inner World, if that should ever become necessary. But more important than that, they are for the protection of the Lords against all else, such as a rising of the slaves; and beyond that they are for the protection of the Three Who Command. But last and most of all, and beyond those three things—above all else—they are for the Emperor, whoever he may be.''

"The Emperor?" Bart said. "You mean, even against the other Lords?"

"I mean even against the other two of the Three Who Command, if necessary," said Chandt. "The Emperor holds in his living body the spirit of him who ruled aboard that which brought them to this Earth from beyond the moon. Most Steeds know this but don't understand it. If the time comes, they will have to understand, then. But someone like you, whom I've been asked to treat as only partly one of the Emperor's Steeds, needs to understand it from this moment.''

He paused. Bart said nothing.

"The Emperor is your final responsibility," Chandt said. "In the end, only your loyalty to the Emperor counts. Do you understand that?"

"Yes," said Bart. "I understand that."

"If necessary, for the Emperor, you will do anything. You will kill anyone. You will kill me, you will kill the one who has asked for special favors for you, if you are ordered by the Emperor or in the Emperor's name. You understand that? No matter what you owe anyone else, no matter who you care for, as long as you are a Steed, you belong only to the Emperor.''

"Yes," said Bart.

"And you accept that—that duty, that honor, that obligation," said Chandt. "You agree to and understand and accept?"

"You don't need to keep hammering it home," said Bart. "I understand what you're trying to tell me—that I'm the Emperor's man first and foremost, no matter what.''

"Good," said Chandt.

He sat back in the booth, reached for his glass and drank deeply, almost draining it.

"Good," he said again.

He pushed the glass away. The signals were plain that the Master of the Steeds was through drinking and about to get to his feet. But Bart had questions of his own.

"Who are the Three Who Command?" Bart asked. He had already been told by Marta, of course, but Chandt had no way to know that Bart knew, and it was a natural question to follow what the Master of the Steeds had just said. And it might be a good lead-in to get him more information about who stood where, down here.

Chandt stared at him for a moment, as if testing the question for sarcasm or insult.

"The Three Who Command," he said, "are the Emperor, the Regent and the Librarian. As one of them dies, a new one is elected by the Lords, for life. Until now it's never been one of the Three who asked me for special use of one of my Steeds. Do not think because it is the Librarian who speaks up for you that it makes any difference. You are still a slave and one of my Steeds, that is all."

"What I am, I am," said Bart, meeting the other's gaze.

Chandt stared at him again for a long moment.

"That was a good answer," he said. "Almost a Mongol could have said that. But there are no Mongols anymore."

"There are a great many Mongols in central Asia," said Bart.

Chandt's face did not change, but his eyes narrowed between their lids until they were mere slits of darkness in his round face.

"You are a liar!" he said; and though his voice got no louder, it was blurred by a fury that overrode the drink in him. "They are dead, all dead—like me! If they were not dead, they would have conquered the world, long since. Yes, even this Inner World they would have found and conquered. They are dead!"

Bart had spent nearly all of one of the days since he had become an inhabitant of the Librarian's territory learning his way around the Library. In the process he had run across a book in English, titled *The Life of Jenghiz Khan,* Translated from the Chinese by a Robert Kennaway Douglas. He had put aside his general search of his surroundings to read that book and learn more about what Chandt claimed to be. His mind was full of its facts now.

The only battle that came close to fitting what Chandt had said before about his death had been the Battle of Mohi, fought April 11, 1241, on the banks of the River Sajo in Hungary. The international Christian army had been made up of Hungarians, Germans, Croats and five hundred French Knights Templar.

That Christian army, as in all other conflicts between the West and the Mongols, had been routed. But it had been a remarkably bloody battle in which many Mongols perished, which was not the usual case. The Mongol expedition that engaged in that battle had been commanded by Ghengis's grandson Batu (who was later to establish the Golden Horde in Russia); and Batu had been assisted by an experienced general.

That general was Subotai, who was famous in his own right. He had commanded under Ghengis himself; and he was an "Orlock" or "Eagle"—one of nine chief princes created by Ghengis. But in spite of Subotai's help and Batu's own budding genius as a commander, the battle was one that gave the Mongols their accustomed victory only at a heavy price in Mongol lives.

"Do you know the name of the place where you were killed?" Bart asked now.

"The name?" Chandt swayed a little where he sat. "What difference does a name make? It was by a river in the West. What mattered was that Mongols died. I died."

"Why do you suppose," said Bart, "that of all people the Lords decided to revive you to be Master of their Steeds?"

"Who else?" Chandt growled. "I was of the tribe of the great Khan himself. How could they do better than to bring back to life Chandt, who was first a Mongol and second, knew more about steeds, beast or human, than anyone?"

"Yes," said Bart, "that tribe that both you and the Great Khan belonged to. What was the name of it?"

Chandt's eyes wandered away from Bart, to rest on a far wall of the room.

"The name of the tribe? My tribe?" he said. "The name of my tribe is sacred to Heaven. I don't tell Steeds the name of my tribe."

"Was it 'Borjigin'?" asked Bart.

"Perhaps . . ." Chandt still watched the distant wall.

"It was Borjigin—'the Gray-eyed Ones'—that was the name of the tribe in which the Great Khan was born. And his name 'Ghengis Khan' was Chinese for 'Perfect Warrior,' isn't that true?"

"Perhaps," said Chandt, almost to himself.

"What was the real name, the tribal name of the Great Khan? Can you remember that?"

Chandt looked back at him.

"Do you think I don't know the name of him who was of my tribe and the greatest warrior the world has ever seen? Of course I know his real name. It was Temuchin."

"Of course it was," said Bart. "But tell me, then, what was the word for 'arrow' in your language? Certainly no Mongol, a people of the bow, would ever forget the word for arrow."

Chandt's head had sunk on his chest.

"Some other time," he muttered. "Some other time I'll tell you that."

"There was a former enemy of the Great Khan whom the Great Khan renamed after the Great Khan conquered him," Bart went on unyieldingly. "The Great Khan renamed him 'Jebei' so that later he became 'Jebei Noyon,' which would mean 'Prince Arrow.' Could 'jebei' be the word for 'arrow' in your native tongue?"

Chandt lifted his head slowly and stared at Bart. He got heavily to his feet.

"Why do you ask me questions like this?" he said thickly. "Has someone put you up to this, seeking to attack me? Is it that you seek to weaken my loyalty to the Emperor, by reminding me of those who once held my loyalty? Of my clan? My people? How could you know all this? Have you been with those free-thinkers among the young Lords who have always clustered about the Library? Well, it won't work."

"No one put me to anything," said Bart, looking up at the other man swaying above the table.

"I am drunk," said Chandt, "yes. But your purpose has not escaped me. I see how you try to make me doubt what I know to be true." He paused for only the shortest of times, as if gathering himself for a leap. "If you could prove to me—if, I say," he said thickly but quickly, "you could prove I had been lied to—if my people were not dead, and I not dead, and the Lords not what they say they are—then I would pull these walls down around them. But there is no way they can have lied. What I know is the truth. Talk to me no more like this—and remember, if I call on you in the Emperor's name, you abandon any loyalty you have to anyone else and answer immediately like the Steed you are—to me."

Bart watched the other man's broad back weave its way between the square tables and out of the room. His probing for information had certainly hit a sensitive spot in Chandt; but he had not intended quite as much as the other had implied, at the end. And certainly it looked to be a dangerous avenue to seek information on. But what was this about free-thinking young Lords and the Library? It was certainly another thing to find out about, if he could only find some avenue to the information.

Jon Swenson, he had discovered after leaving that first private interview with Pier and Marta, was useless as a source of important information. He knew nothing of any slave in the Guettrig household who had resembled Bart's father—hardly surprising, since Bart's father must have left the Inner World long before Swenson came into it. The very fact Lionel had once been in the Inner World and gotten away—perhaps with the help of Pier and Marta—however, hinted that there was some secret way out.

A slave would hardly be allowed to depart by the way of the mine; unless he had been under the control of a trusted Lord or Lady who was also going into the outer world—and maybe not even that was allowed.

In fact, generally speaking, Swenson had nothing to offer Bart at all by way of information except a knowledge of the geography of the Inner World, plus an acquaintance with the general workings of the Library and the household of Pier and Marta. He was more than willing to talk, but as far as having anything to say that Bart could find useful, the young slave's conversation was a waste of time.

Chandt, on the other hand, obviously had a great deal he could tell. Equally obviously, he had no intention of doing so. Not yet, to Bart, at least.

That left the Library itself as a source of information; and other slaves who might be more knowledgeable than Jon and more communicative than Chandt.

Bart got to his feet and left the Steeds' Recreation Center himself. He headed for the general Recreation Center, the one for all slaves, to which Paolo had taken him for their earlier talk. Paolo had promised to be there this evening, and Bart had made it a promise on his part, not expecting Chandt to show up and demand his time as he had; but then, the time had not been all that long, and chances were that Paolo was still there—he liked his evenings in the Recreation Center.

So there should be plenty of time to find Paolo and, more to the point, Lorena, with word of Emma.

When he got to the Center, he passed in through the doorway and stepped to the side, out of the traffic and watching the crowd. The place seemed to be swarming with slaves, and Bart saw now a number of faces that he recognized from having seen them during his time here in the Inner World. He had put in several hours every day carrying Pier about the working areas of the Inner World, and he supposed that in those rounds he would eventually see almost everyone in the total population of the place.

He really knew none of them to speak to—slaves spoke only on their Masters' business, outside of their free time and living spaces—and it seemed that most slaves avoided Steeds when they could, anyway. Besides, he had made no effort to strike up an acquaintance with any of them; that would only make him more conspicuous—something he wanted to avoid if at all possible.

He was grateful for the special luck that had made him a favorite of, and the property of, Pier Guettrig. The Librarian, unlike many of his fellow Lords and Ladies, was not afflicted with the fancy to dress up his personal Steed in some sort of flashy uniform or livery. A Steed usually stood out from the other slaves in any case, being usually shirtless unless on some special duty, or off-duty altogether —but even then they often stood out; but livery would ensure that anyone noticing Bart doing something unusual would be able to identify exactly which Steed had aroused his notice.

On Bart's right wrist now, secured there by a leather band stained black, was a device with a face something like that of a very small clock, except that instead of a ring of numbers, its visible surface was covered with dots of some material like glass, which, on a signal sent by the Steed's Lord, could glow with an assortment of different colors. Each color was a signal to the Steed—and at the very top of the face was a single isolated bulb which simply ordered the Steed to report to his owner for orders.

With this, his size and his shirtlessness to identify him as a Steed, Bart made his way easily through the crowd of slaves in the room—no one of them would be eager to impede his way, or that of any Steed. And although the yellow lights in this room were rather dim, it seemed that no one had any trouble telling what he was. No one seemed to recognize him individually, though, which he supposed was the best he could hope for.

Paolo had enlightened him on the social layers of the slave world; and it was a fact that the presence of any Steed in these rooms was somewhat unusual, and attracted attention. Other slaves seemed to share the assumption that the Steeds had other, much more luxurious recreation rooms of their own—so a Steed in this place *was* at least noticed. But there was no help for that; Paolo liked it here, and it *was* the only place where a Steed could associate with a non-Steed slave.

It was in the third of the three dining rooms he investigated that he spotted Paolo's bulk—as dormitory Leader, Paolo had some specific hours off, during which he was often to be found here, wearing other clothes than the rather simple uniform his owner required him to wear during work. This was convenient not only for Paolo but for Bart in this moment. Paolo was sitting in one side of a corner booth against the wall, with Lorena sitting facing him. Paolo had his back to the room, but Lorena saw and recognized Bart by the time he had crossed half the width of the room on his way toward the booth.

Bart saw, but because of the noise of the crowd, did not hear what Lorena said as she leaned forward and spoke to Paolo. In any case, Paolo did not turn his head in Bart's direction until Bart reached the booth. Then, at last, he turned it enough to look up into Bart's face.

"Lorena thought you might come by tonight," Paolo said. It seemed that he almost grunted the words.

"Oh? Why?" asked Bart.

Paolo had not asked him to sit down and Bart's constant alertness to possible danger made him suspicious now that there might be some reason for the invitation being withheld.

"Lovers' instinct," said Paolo, still not moving; and laughed heavily.

"Don't let him torment you, Bart," said a familiar voice, and Emma's face appeared as she leaned forward and looked around Paolo's thick body at Bart. She had been sitting back in the corner and the position of the booth, plus Paolo's size, had effectively been hiding her from the sight of everyone else in the room, including Bart.

"Emma!" he said happily. He cupped his hand about the point of Paolo's shoulder, with his thumb pressing into the nerve in the middle and at the very top of the arm.

"Up," he said, "and let me sit down."

Paolo rose suddenly, swearing softly under his breath; and Bart took off the pressure of his thumb.

"Damn you," said Paolo between his teeth. "Where did you learn a trick like that?"

He rubbed the area of the nerve point.

"You've been taking lessons from that devil Chandt!" he said as he sat down on the opposite seat of the booth, beside Lorena.

"No." Bart slipped into the space the other had vacated, sitting down beside Emma. "From a much better man than that and a long time ago. Emma—you're all right!"

"Of course I'm all right," said Emma. "But Bart, how are you ever going to forgive me?"

"Forgive you?" Bart stared at her. "Forgive you for what?"

"For getting you into this awful place!"

"You didn't get me here," Bart said, puzzled. "I came here on my own."

"But only because you trusted me!" said Emma. "And I promised you something that wasn't true. You remember you asked me if Arthur had anything to do with the Scottites, and I told you he didn't—but he did. And because you trusted me, you've ended up here."

"Don't be ridiculous!" growled Bart. "I was coming this way looking for my relatives, remember? I would have followed any lead. Besides, I'm always cautious, just as cautious as if I'd known that mine was run by Scottites—and it didn't save me. They caught me in a net nobody could have dodged and chained me up anyway. Now, this is one thing you're not going to take on yourself. I was caught in spite of myself, and I was trying to escape when I fell into an underground river and it brought me to the Inner World. So, that's all there is to it."

"Perhaps," said Emma, gazing at him. "Anyway, you look all right—in fact, you're much better looking without your beard."

"I couldn't have one down here if I wanted it, evidently," Bart said. "Beards are for Lords alone. But it's marvelous to see you. You look just the same as ever."

"Why should I look different?" said Emma. She leaned toward him and raised a soft, small hand to touch him, fleetingly, on his right cheek. But indeed he was right. The slave tunic she wore was the only difference, shorter in the skirt and sleeves, cut lower in the neck than anything he had ever seen on her before. But the dress had no power to change her. Her blond hair was drawn back as always into a bun, her round face was as calm and unchanged as ever, except that now it was lit up by her warm smile.

She looked, thought Bart, as if not she, but everything else around her was unreal and out of place.

"No," he said, "you wouldn't."

It took all his willpower, as always, to keep from putting his arms around her. Only the knowledge that she would not want him to do so, here and now, made him keep them still at his side.

"Of course, you wouldn't be," he repeated. "I should have known."

"What the Lord has made me," said Emma, "is what I am.

Nothing on Earth has power to change that. Bart, you've lost weight.''

"I'm gaining it back," said Bart. "Anyway, that's not important. What's important is you—"

He had been speaking to her automatically in her native English. Now out of the corner of his eye, he saw Paolo and Lorena, watching and listening.

"Come on with me," he said, taking her hand and starting to get up. "We'll go some place we can talk privately."

"That's right, be an idiot!" said Paolo. Bart stopped and looked at the other man.

"Don't you know," Paolo went on, "if you two go out across that floor, hand in hand like that there, the fact that the both of you make a pair is going to be something half the slaves in the Inner World can learn at any time by asking about either one of you. Slaves watch slaves. Anything there's to know about some other slave may be worth selling to someone at one time or another. But go ahead, if you want to."

"They already know we're together here in this booth," said Bart.

"You think so?" said Paolo. "Think again. Your Emma there came in by herself and sat down in this booth and had something to eat. Before she was done, Lorena happened by and sat down opposite her—just like for a chat. Your Emma was sitting back in the booth there, on her side of it, out of sight of everyone outside unless they came right up to it and looked in. Nobody did, because I came in about then and sat down opposite Lorena. Most of those out there know who I am and that I'm a Steed. They wouldn't come calling on a booth where I sat without being invited, let alone on one where I was sitting with a woman. Since Emma first came in to eat, this place has filled up. Only the server on this table knows she's here; but he knows me, too, well enough not to go talking about me and anyone with me to somebody else."

He paused.

"Well?" he said. "I thought you two were leaving."

"You're right," said Bart, settling back. "And thanks. And forgive me for moving you out of the booth that way. I owe you both a lot for finding Emma and bringing her here for me."

"That's better," said Paolo. Then he grinned. "But it's all right. Any time. I like you and Lorena likes this one of yours. You got to show me what you did to my shoulder, though."

"I'll do that," said Bart. "And a few more such tricks, if you want. But right now—forgive me—I want to talk privately to Emma; and since we have to do our talking right here, we're going to have to do it differently than I first thought."

He turned to Emma.

"Emma," he said in a tongue he was more than ordinarily sure neither Paolo nor Lorena could understand, "remember when we were children?"

When they had been young, in the settlement with the little school where they had met, they had concocted a need for a private language between them. One that they could expect most of their classmates and many of the adults around them could not understand. So he had taught Emma the Algonquian Cree tongue that he had learned in his first years of life with his mother's people. Emma was intelligent and young, quick to learn, and—in a settlement dominated by métis—she had already picked up a word or two of the Indian tongues heard locally. She was soon almost as fluent in Cree as he was; and to further confuse listeners who might know the language, they gave fanciful names to the places and people they talked about. The school teacher was 'Woodpecker' for his sharp nose; Bart's father was 'Owl' for his wisdom and mysterious powers—and so forth.

"Yes—," she began in that language; but he was already going on in it, himself.

"You're really all right, though?" he was demanding. "They haven't done anything to you?"

"What would they be likely to do to me, except put me to work?" she answered. "They've done that. Don't look so fierce. It's not a bad job, at all."

"Oh? What is it?"

"If you give me a chance, I'll tell you. Bart, my dear, I really am all right; and the job they've given me is a perfectly ordinary one. Arthur must have told them I kept the books at the store, because they've given me a sort of bookkeeper job. I check all kinds of figures sent in from various—I'll have to say it in English— 'departments' of the Inner World. Statements of things used or needed, supplies—matters of that sort. It's really just like being back in the store, except I do it all day long, instead of in my spare time. Poor Arthur, though."

Somehow, Bart had known that the problem of Arthur's difficulties would find its way into the conversation.

"What have they done to Arthur?" he asked.

"I suppose because they know he was a storekeeper, they've put him to work in their supply department. He has to keep track of certain expendables, estimate how much they'll need in time to order it shipped in before they run out, and make out the orders. He's terribly afraid he'll make a mistake of some kind because the other workers there have told him he could be beaten or even killed if he was wrong and the Inner World ran short of something because of his errors.''

''He's a slave like all the rest of us, then?''

''Yes. And he was sure they were going to put him in some supervisory position. Of course, like everyone else in the upper world, even among the Scottites, he didn't have any idea the Inner World existed, much less what it was like here. If he'd known he was going to be a slave he'd never have come. He thought he was getting a promotion to the Scottite headquarters.''

''Yes,'' said Bart, ''I can see how he wouldn't like being a slave. But to bring you along with him into the same beartrap . . .''

''Be fair, Bart. He didn't know. And he could hardly leave his sister behind, alone and defenseless—''

''Defenseless!'' exploded Bart. ''You've taken care of him, instead of the other way around, ever since your baby legs were strong enough to toddle after him!''

''In some ways, perhaps,'' said Emma. ''But you know what I mean—a young unmarried woman living alone out here in the woods. If I didn't get married almost immediately in self-defense, none of the decent women would have anything to do with me. Besides, it does take a man's strength to do a certain amount of the work, running a store.''

''I suppose so,'' said Bart grudgingly; he had to admit she was right on both points. An unmarried woman, living alone, and even if not particularly young anymore, had no proper place in frontier civilization. A widow, or even a wife with a husband who was away from home on long trips nearly all the time—almost anything but that immediately suspect entity, a single woman—was acceptable. But Emma, living alone, and in spite of the many people who liked her and would stand by her in face of the inevitable gossip, would not have been. Her situation would have made it difficult for her to successfully run a store, which was the only means of respectable self-support open to her. Also, she was right about there being a certain amount of fairly heavy physical labor required even in storekeeping; and Emma, though strong for her size, was small-framed.

''Anyway,'' said Bart, ''the point is, you're here now. I'm going to find a way to get the two of us out of here."

"And Arthur."

"And Arthur. Of course."

"But what've they got you doing, Bart?"

"I'm a Steed. You've been down here long enough to know what that is?"

Emma laughed, then sobered.

"Yes," she said. "I'm sorry I laughed, Bart. It was just the thought of one of those funny little men perched up on your shoulders like a child with a beard."

"I suppose it does make a funny picture," said Bart.

"No, it doesn't at all," said Emma. "It was wrong of me to laugh. Carrying someone, bent over like that with the weight of the man and the chair together, has to be painful. How you see where you're going, I've no idea."

"It's a little hard the first day," said Bart. "But after that it's not bad. I've got to talk to you in more privacy than this, though. It turns out my rider-owner's the Librarian, one of the three elected officials among the Lords. So we may be lucky. But how do I go about seeing you alone?"

Emma frowned.

"I don't know if you should try," she said. "We were talking about this, Lorena, Paolo and I, before you got here. It's dangerous."

"Dangerous? In what way?"

Emma turned to look across the table at the other man and switched back to English.

"Paolo, you tell Bart why it'd be dangerous for him and me to try to see each other privately."

Paolo grunted.

"Maybe," he said. "First, who's this Arthur?"

"My brother," answered Emma. "You see—"

"Look," Bart interrupted, speaking to the dormitory Leader. "I know it's uncomfortable having people talking in front of you in a language you don't understand. But believe me, what we were talking about had nothing to do with—we didn't say a word about you two. We were only talking about ourselves."

"This Arthur," said Paolo. "I want to know what he's got to do with everything. I did you a favor because we had an agreement, you and I. So that brought Emma here into it. Now, all of a sudden, there's somebody called Arthur in it, too. I've managed to live all these years down here by not being a fool and I want to be sure I'm not making a fool of myself now.''

"I promise you," said Bart, turning to look a message at Emma, "and Emma here will promise you, too, that her brother's not going to be told a thing about any of us, by any of us.''

"Emma?" Paolo looked at her.

"If Bart thinks we shouldn't say anything to Arthur, then we won't," she said.

But her glance at Bart emphasized the fact that Arthur was not to be left out of their plans in the long run.

chapter
twelve

"JUST TO PUT your mind at rest," said Bart to Paolo, "what Emma and I talked about was what had happened to the two of us down here. I told her I was a Steed and she told me she was a bookkeeper. She also told me her brother's been put to work in Supply, wherever or whatever that is."

"If it was just that," said Paolo, "why didn't you say it in plain English or plain French?"

"Paolo!" said Lorena. "Can't you understand? No you can't, can you? Because you've never been in love. People in love who haven't seen each other for some time sometimes want to say a few things without the whole world knowing."

Paolo grunted, plainly not convinced, but willing to let the argument go, for the present.

"Now," said Bart, "let me ask you something. What makes you think it'd be important to anyone that Emma and I make a pair?"

"One hell of a lot of experience down here, that's what makes me think it!" said Paolo. "You came in and landed in some kind of soft spot—just being made one of the Steeds was luck enough; but you seem to have something else going for you. I don't know what yet, but Chandt says I'm to let you go from any exercise hour or dormitory duty you want off, when you tell me you need to be someplace else. You've got some line to something and I'll find out sooner or later what it is."

"The Librarian likes me," said Bart. "Why, I'm not really sure myself. But he does; and he seems to have a lot of power."

"He's got that, all right," said Paolo. "So that's what's making you so special! The Emperor's word rides over anything else; but there's talk the Librarian knows things no one else does and even the Emperor has to listen to him on some things. But you're maybe going to find it's not all gravy being a favorite of someone with that much power. Little people like us here at this table can get crushed real easy between a couple of large stones like two of the Three Who Command."

"If the Emperor rules and the Librarian keeps the Library and knows things not even the Emperor knows, what does the Regent do?" Bart asked.

Paolo gave a short, snorted laugh.

"Nothing," he said, "but stands there waiting to step into the Emperor's place if anything happens to the Emperor and there's no one else elected yet to take his place."

He stared at Bart.

"Don't let that make you forget not to walk softly around him, too," Paolo said. "He's still one of the Three Who Command and only the Emperor and the Librarian don't have to do what he tells them."

Bart nodded.

"All right," he said. "Back to what I asked you before. What makes you take it so seriously that somebody might ask if Emma and I make a pair, and that someone else might tell them we do?"

"Man," said Paolo, "it's easy to see you haven't been reborn for more than a few days. You're going to find out how things really are, here."

"Tell me, then," said Bart, "how are they?"

"I will. Count up," said Paolo, holding up three thick fingers. "There are about three thousand full-blooded Lords and Lady Lords, counting from the youngest baby to the oldest of them. There's maybe fifteen hundred Hybrids, because they only keep the best of the half-breeds, and of those, many work outside; and five hundred Steeds. Call it a round five thousand. But there's fifteen thousand slaves. You got to be crazy to think the Lords never worry about the slaves making a revolt, when the slaves outnumber everyone else, including the Steeds, put together, three to one."

Bart nodded. To himself he had to admit that he had been singularly blind. Of course, a governing class like the Lords would have to worry about their slaves, no matter how well the two classes seemed to get along on the surface.

"So?" said Paolo. "So that means they try to keep watch for any signs of something that might lead to trouble from the slaves, all the time. And it's not easy. They can put those magic boxes that they talk over and listen over and see each other on all over the place; but slaves can still whisper to each other where they can't be heard, and make plans. So what do the Lords do? You tell me?"

"I've got no notion," said Bart.

"What they'd like to do," said Paolo, "of course, is send spies in among the slaves. But down here everybody knows everybody else. Sure, they could produce a fresh slave saying he's just newborn and the slave could really be a spy for them; but where're they going to get the spy they can trust? The only one they could trust would be a Hybrid; but everybody knows every Hybrid from the time they're born on up—if they're let live. So, what do they do?"

"I just said I didn't have any notion," answered Bart.

"They just don't take chances, that's what they do," Paolo said. "Any suspicion—any suspicion at all that a slave's a potential troublemaker—any reason for suspecting anything— and that slave's gone. I mean dead. Dead and gone down that river they pulled you out of and brought you back to life."

"Are you trying to tell me," said Bart, "that the simple fact that people think Emma and I are close would be reason enough for the Lords to have us killed—or do they do their own killing?"

"Sometimes," said Paolo. "Mostly we do it for them, we Steeds. It's part of our job. You're going to find there's a lot of things we do you'd never suspect. But you're right. That's exactly what I've been trying to tell you. Now, suppose you're a slave who wants something from the Lords, or who's about to be in trouble with them himself, or is in trouble with them, already?"

"You mean a slave like that could buy himself out of trouble or get what he wants just by saying Emma and I are getting together to plan a revolt, whether it was true or not?"

"If you were a Lord, and slaves as easy to get as they are, would you take the chance of waiting around to see, or checking?" said Paolo.

"Probably not," said Bart.

"Bart!" said Emma. "Of course you'd check first before you did anything to anyone. You can't tell me that about yourself."

"If I was a Lord, I might not," said Bart. "Paolo's right. Or, maybe not. Paolo, if just being seen together's good enough to accuse somebody of planning a revolt, how's it happen you and Lorena are still around?"

"We've been here long enough so that we've each been given permission," said Paolo. "Seems like the Lords have some way of deciding you're not the kind to start a revolt—and I'm not. Neither's Lorena. Anyway, we've both been told, a long time ago, we could make friends or whatever. Not that it'd be exactly safe for even us if we started suddenly meeting with a gang of about a dozen other old hands and whispering to each other so nobody else around could hear.''

''Who do you get permission from?'' asked Bart.

''You get it from your Lord, because when he gives it, he takes on the responsibility of you going bad,'' said Paolo. ''Matter of fact, what happened to me was Chandt put in a good word for me to somebody and it went up and around and came back down to me from my own Lord. Maybe you can deal direct with the Lord Librarian; but you'd better wait awhile. It's not just him. He's got to convince the other Two Who Command that it's a safe bet.''

''All right,'' said Bart. But he was thinking that very probably he would not be waiting anywhere near as long a time as Paolo had in mind.

''So,'' he said, ''how do I go about seeing Emma? Only when you two are able to act as chaperones?''

''What's a chaperone?'' asked Paolo. ''Never mind, I figure I know what you mean. That's right, pretty much so for the first few months. Then you can start meeting with just one of us there, and finally, maybe, you can ask your Lord and get permission to meet by yourselves.''

''Hmm,'' said Bart.

Emma put a small hand on his arm.

''If we have to be patient, Bart . . .'' she said.

He looked sideways and down at her. His heart seemed to move in him, looking at her. She was so small, to be here in this unnatural place. They could not know it—Lords, Hybrids and slaves alike—but any of them who tried to take advantage of that smallness would find Bart's own hands, which were anything but small, to deal with. After which they would never try to take advantage of anyone or anything again.

''Don't worry,'' he said to her gently, ''I'll go slowly and carefully. Even if it keeps us apart, I won't rush things.''

''I know you won't,'' said Emma, patting his arm momentarily, like an adult approving a child who had just promised to be good. He smiled at her and she smiled back.

In the end the four of them decided that they would meet on a signal passed by Bart to Paolo, or from Emma to Lorena; and from Lorena to Paolo or vice versa. It was a clumsy arrangement, but even Bart had to admit it was about the only one that could be made under the present circumstances.

Bart looked across the room at the clock again.

''I've got to get back to the Library,'' he said.

Emma also thought it was time she was leaving and Lorena started to go with her. Paolo, however, wanted to sit and drink for some time yet. His particular Lord was a late riser in the morning, even on those mornings when he did call for Paolo to carry him; and these had grown infrequent as that Lord—who was a good deal older even than Pier—spent more and more of his time in his own quarters. But Paolo did not want to drink alone. With a small sigh, Lorena sat back down in the booth.

"Better go out separately," Paolo told Bart and Emma. "You first, Bart."

Bart got up regretfully.

"Be careful, Emma," he said. "Good night."

"I will. You too. Goodnight, dear," said Emma.

Bart got up from the booth, but just as he was about to turn, a question occurred to him.

"By the way," he asked. "Lorena, what work do you do?"

"Her?" Paolo answered for her, even as he was looking across the room to flag down the server for another drink. "She scrubs floors—things like that."

"I'll see you by tomorrow evening," said Bart and left the Recreation Center.

In the past few days of exploring during the free daytime hours his work for Pier afforded him, he had been able to fill out his mental map of the Inner World. The place consisted, he now knew, of an outer ring of excavations or caverns which were, as one went around in a circle, living quarters for slaves, Hybrids, and finally for the Lordly class itself.

Within that ring were the recreational centers for the various classes, storerooms, offices, machine shops and other working areas, which in turn surrounded a core area of special workrooms, which seemed populated almost exclusively by Hybrids, Lords and Ladies at incomprehensible work in what seemed to be laboratories and workrooms.

This last area, because he had seen so few slaves in it, he had barely penetrated. Since slaves were so scarce there, he had suspected that his own presence might be particularly noticeable. But the urge to explore it further itched in him; and he reasoned that, at this time of the evening, when the corridors around him were filled with slaves, Hybrids and even Lords out on recreational purposes, he should find the labs and workrooms fairly deserted.

Also, his most direct route back to the Library would lie right through the center of this core area.

He gave in to the impulse and headed down the corridor toward it, automatically giving way to the Hybrids and Lords he encountered, and hardly noticing that most of the other slaves who were not Steeds gave way to him.

However, when he reached the core area, he was surprised to find the workrooms apprently nearly as full of busy people as they had been in the daytime. It was finally beginning to sink into him that, whatever else the Hybrids, Lords and Ladies might be, they were not idle. Having committed himself to explore, however, he continued down the corridors, which all seemed like the spokes of a wheel radiating from some central spot in the core area.

It was an exploration with all of his nerves alert for any contingency. More than a few of those he passed in the corridors, or near the open doors of the workrooms, glanced at him. Still, as long as Bart kept walking down the corridors with a reasonable speed and a purposeful air, no one offered to question what he was doing there. He had purposely not donned a shirt for his evening with Paolo in the Recreational Center, and so he was now dressed as was appropriate for a Steed on some duty.

But as soon as he slowed and tried to get a longer look in some doorway or other, someone in that room was almost certain to turn and look at him inquisitively. Little by little, he was moving toward the exact center of the core—the center of the Inner World itself.

Up until now, he had neither been questioned nor stopped. But he came at last to the end of a final corridor, which was almost taken up by a pair of very large doors, wide enough to let six people through abreast. The doors were closed, however, and before them stood a man who was obviously a Steed, though not one of Bart's dormitory. He was wearing a uniform-like red jacket and kilt. He had obviously been chosen in part for his size and impressiveness; for he stood close to six and a half feet in height, at Bart's estimate. And he was carrying a weapon.

This armed guard stood before the doors, barring entrance with something that looked rather like a lumpy rifle, with a miniature half-moon-shaped axehead affixed at its muzzle end where a bayonet might have been fitted on a military long gun.

The impression was reinforced when, as he got closer, the man swung the object down into horizontal position, aimed at Bart; for the small axehead glinted like silver in the overhead lights of the corridor. Bart stopped with what was clearly a razor-sharp end-edge as well as bottom edge a foot from his chest.

"I'm Bart Dybig, slave to the Lord Librarian," he said to the man. "I've got an imperative message to him from his Lady."

The weapon, however, stayed pointed at him. The guard frowned.

"You can't go in here," he said. "No human passes this door unless one of the Lords takes him in. Who'd you say you were?"

"A slave of the Lord Librarian," repeated Bart. He was beginning to feel the first twinges of regret that he had identified himself so readily. Still, Pier had said Bart should use the Librarian's name as a passport and Pier was one of the Three Who Command. "Let me through or I'll have to report you to my Lord."

"Report all you want!" said the big man. His voice, surprisingly, was a reedy harsh tenor that seemed at once threatening and too small for the rest of him. "My orders are my orders and you can't go through here without a Lord taking you."

"All right," said Bart. He was just as glad to make his escape without further trouble. He turned and started back the way he had come.

"Wait a minute!" called the guard. "Wait, I say!"

Bart, however, reasoning that part of the man's orders must be that he was not to leave his post at the door under any circumstances, merely increased his speed, and soon lost himself among the people passing to and fro from the other rooms and the intersecting corridors, farther out.

He turned left at the first cross tunnel encountered, heading back toward the Library.

As he went, he tried to puzzle out what lay behind the doors the guard had stopped him from passing. His one point of reference was his mental map of the Inner World—that, at least, should give him some idea of the size of the room behind those great double doors.

Checking his memory now, he suddenly realized that the space beyond the double doors could only occupy the space at the end of the room, one end of which he had carried Pier through on that first day Bart had worn the chair—the room with the pipes running its length from the even farther end of the room where the great shiny column had risen from some lower level.

There could be no doubt about this, since he and Pier had stepped almost directly from that pipe-filled room into the Library; and from where he had faced the guard just now the Library was on a direct line—ignoring stone walls and other obstacles—no more than three hundred feet away. His way to it now was longer than that only because he had to take a circuitous route to it through the corridors.

But of course, he remembered, the pipe-filled room was one level up from the general level of the Inner World, since the ordinary main floor of the Library, on which Pier had his office back to the side of stacks, was also one level up. That meant the Library stacks must share the wall behind them with the great chamber where the massive column had been visible—that room the guard would not let him into just now.

He was abruptly reminded of how the slaves talked about some great weapon with which the Lordly class was intending to destroy the surface world and all of humankind. He still could not believe in such a weapon; but he had been impressed in spite of himself by the lighting and the ventilation down here, the means of talking, listening and sending animated pictures of themselves back and forth over distances, used by the Lords and Hybrids—as well as a host of other things that as far as Bart knew were unknown in the world above.

The weapon talk had to be nonsense—but something had to be going on here that explained the very existence of such a place.

He began to climb the stairs leading to the main entrance of the Library.

The first maxim his father had impressed on Bart's young mind, from the moment Bart had come to live with Lionel after leaving the Cree encampment on his mother's death, had been "find the reason!"

There was, Lionel had explained, always a reason behind every situation and every human action. Look for it, find it, he had told Bart; and you'll find you have a better grasp of the problem than those who're themselves involved in it and who've studied it hard and long for a solution.

The most difficult part of finding the reason, his father had explained to Bart, was to find the right question to ask oneself. Once that much was done, often the answer came quickly.

In this case, Bart already had the question formulated in his mind. It was—why should something such as this Inner World exist in the first place? Its existence made no sense; and the explanations he had been given for its creation were flatly unbelievable. So—why the Lords, why the Hybrids, why the slaves and the organization of the community to which they belonged? If he could uncover the answer to that *Why?* he felt he would be more than halfway to understanding the whole situation he and Emma faced.

The Lords, themselves, Bart thought, must know the true answer. But, on second thought, if they did, how could a community like this endure this long, develop these kinds of mechanical marvels, and make this kind of progress, without some Lord, in one of the generations that must have gone by since the community was begun, giving away the secret?

Was it possible that the Lords themselves were the dupes of a plan made many generations before this present one?

But that could not be. No such secret plan could exist without someone along the descending stairs of the generations breaking the code of silence and letting the secret out into the world at large. Whether they had come from some world beyond the moon—and he did not for a moment believe such a wild story—or not, they were human enough to make children with human partners; and in other ways human enough so that the secret would have been bound to be given away by some one of them for personal or other reasons.

All right, he said to himself, trying to think as his father had taught him to think—if they can't but they do, there has to be a third choice, somewhere. There had to be a secret. Who would know it? Perhaps only some of them knew—perhaps only one in each generation?

Of course—the Emperor. He would be the one to know; and his position and power would depend upon his keeping the secret . . . .

Maybe.

It was not beyond the bounds of possibility that somewhere along the line an altruistic Emperor would be elected, who would refuse to carry on with the lie.

On the other hand, it was not impossible that no such Emperor had cropped up—at least, yet.

But now he was guessing. And guessing was not the way to solve problems—another maxim of his father's.

Nonetheless, he had come up with a third alternative; and it was one that showed more possibilities than the self-canceling other two possibilities he had been going back and forth between, a moment before.

Someone, or some several ones—but in the case of secret-keeping it was usually better the smaller number who knew, so one was the most likely possibility—in the Inner World must know the reason this place was created and to what end it was aimed. A hiding place for small people was too simple an answer; particularly when you considered that the small people were mechanical wizards and must control enormous wealth, piled up over a period of generations.

He had reached the Library's main entrance. Now, he made his way back through the stacks to the door of Pier's office. Putting the key Pier had given him into the lock, he turned it halfway. Immediately, a small panel above it glowed with an amber light. That would be a signal that Pier was in there, but that he had no objection to Bart entering at this time.

Bart turned his key the rest of the way and opened the door. Pier was seated at his desk, immersed in what looked like the pages of an enormous ledger. He paid no attention to Bart. Closing the door softly behind him, Bart made his way silently across the carpet into his own alcove. Pier's head did not lift to look at him as he passed.

Bart sat down in his chair before the desk. Facing the walls on three sides of him, it was possible to feel himself private and apart. The silence in which Pier worked reinforced that feeling. Bart frowned at the corner ahead of his desk where the two original walls of Pier's office came together.

When one mystery is joined by another mystery in the same place and time, he told himself, the chance the two are connected rises considerably . . . .

His thoughts were interrupted by the sound of the door to Pier's office opening. He turned his head—he was wary of actually turning about in his chair and being discovered trying to find out who had entered—but the angle of the wall set up to make his alcove blocked his view of the door. He heard voices speaking in the Latin tongue of the Lords and a moment later his curiosity had satisfaction thrust upon it.

"Bart!"

It was Pier's voice calling him. The Librarian, Bart had learned, was known for his polite and gentle treatment of his slaves; but there was in his voice now a distant, impersonal note that offset the use of Bart's first name and in which Bart read a warning that now was not the time for him to betray any special relationship with the other.

He rose immediately and stepped into the room. Two other Lords were there, and Bart felt a sudden recognition on seeing them, though he could not remember where he might have seen them before. The two looked at him with a disquietingly penetrating interest, as if they, too, remembered him from some previous meeting.

"Bart," said Pier again, as Bart made his appearance, "I won't be needing you to carry me home this evening. You're free until tomorrow, when I'll want to see you at my home."

"Yes, Lord," said Bart.

The words he had heard were all too obviously a dismissal. He backed away, on his best slave manners, toward the door, which opened behind him to let him out and then closed once more automatically. He took two steps toward the front of the Library and the corridor beyond that would take him out into the public ways of the Inner City again—and stopped.

He had just remembered where he had seen the two before. They had been the two who had been with Pier in that moment of consciousness Bart remembered after his blacking out in the underground river and before he had waked in the Steed dormitory.

They had to be the Emperor and the Regent. He had no proof, but he was sure of that. The Three Who Command were now joined together in conference.

chapter
thirteen

HE WENT ON out of the Library so wound up in his thoughts he almost blundered into a Lord on foot, with a female Hybrid for companion, who were on their way in through the entrance. Bart woke in time and stepped aside. The near collision made him realize that in spite of his determination to remain cool-headed about all this, emotion had crept into the matter. In the office a moment past, he had not been able to avoid thinking of Pier as someone who was to be defended against the other two as attackers. The image of all three Lords was burned in his memory, now, as he went away down the stairs to the main level corridor.

There was a certain unconscious arrogance about all the Lordly class, even those as ordinarily gentle and considerate as Pier and Marta. It had been with something more than that, however, it seemed to him now, that those other two had glanced at Bart.

Both were considerably younger than Pier. Neither, thought Bart, was more than ten years older than himself. In fact their youthfulness, in contrast with the age of Pier, had been striking. These were men in the full vigor of their lives.

Also, they had something additional in common besides their age. They were dressed in the same style, though not in the same colors and fabrics, wearing jacket and skin-tight leg coverings which could have been either stockings or trousers, so that they looked like something out of a Renaissance painting. Though the colors of their clothes differed, all they wore was dark, and the fabrics were adorned and decorated with jewels to the point of ostentation. It seemed to Bart very nearly as if they had deliberately dressed so, to make Pier in his long, unadorned office robe seem drab and insignificant by comparison.

But when Bart had glanced from the newcomers to his Lord, he had seen a surprising thing. For Pier, standing behind his desk, had straightened up. His wisp of white beard barely brushed the high collar of his robe in front instead of having its hairs splayed

out by the collar's upper edge. Far from being dominated by
comparison with the other two, Pier in the floor-length robe of
earth-brown made the others seem gaudy and juvenile by comparison.

There was one thing more Bart had noticed, and which the
shorter of the two incoming Lords had to a greater degree than any
of their kind Bart had seen before. It was an attitude Bart
recognized, for he had seen it often enough in the years when
Louis Riel had been active and Bart's father close to him.

It was the air of accustomed authority. An authority on the part
of the shorter of the two newcomers that was arrogant to the point
where it almost—but not quite—seemed ready to dare try
commanding Pier. Aside from this, so strong was the similarity in
appearance and attitude between the two entering that they could
have seemed brothers; and yet, physically they were different
enough.

The taller one did not radiate the impression of power that the
shorter one had. Which was strange, for physically, the taller one
had been impressive, as Lords went. Almost tall enough that,
except for his clothing and his small chinbeard—in this place
where beards were only allowed on the Lordly class—he could
have been taken for a Hybrid. His hair was slightly curly and
reddish-gold. Below it his face was handsome, in a fine-boned
way, with a straight nose, blue eyes that were almost feverishly
bright and two even rows of very white, regular teeth that attracted
attention when he smiled.

The shorter and more impressive one was normal height for a
Lord—several inches short of five feet, perhaps—but had disproportionately wide shoulders. Other than that, he was slim, almost
to the point of being starved-looking, with straight black hair,
black eyebrows, and a narrow face, the olive skin of which seemed
stretched tight over the bones. He had not smiled at any time while
Bart was watching him; and did not look as if he was likely to,
often. His glance was as aware as the glance of a hunting cat.

The two had already come to a stop in the office when Bart had
first seen them, so Bart did not know if they had walked side by
side, or in file; although they were together in the room, the
dark-haired one was a little in advance of the other. The position
may have been as unconscious as the arrogance of the individual;
but it was not accidental. This one was the leader, the superior of
the two.

This, said Bart's woods-born instinct, sniffing at the memory of the dark-haired man like a wild animal, was the one to fear. There was only one person he could be. The Emperor. The taller, curly-haired one with him would be the Regent. Bart felt the need to know more about both of them; and not only about them, but about their whole structure of authority.

Somehow, he told himself, he must find some channel of access to more information; not only about the Lords, but also about that room he had been stopped from entering, a short while ago. From what he had encountered so far, the slaves were all about as useless in this respect as Jon Swenson had been. Their stories were wild and the details of them did not confirm each other. Obviously they were the result of hearsay repeated over and over and embroidered upon until it approached the level of legend.

It was not legend Bart wanted, but facts. Chandt probably could give these to him, but almost certainly would not. The only other possibility was Paolo.

Reaching the slave Recreation Center, Bart went in and began to search for his dormitory Leader. The last he had seen of the other, Paolo had been determined to do some serious drinking. The time that had gone by since then was too short for Paolo to have gotten drunk enough for bed, but perhaps long enough for the dormitory Leader to have become a little less cautious in how he answered Bart's questions. Asking Paolo for the information Bart wanted was not an ideal situation; but there was no one else he could trust to any extent—not that he could trust him that much—and who also might know some of the answers he needed.

Paolo was no longer in the corner booth where Bart had left him with Emma and Lorena. He found the other finally in the innermost room of the Recreation Center. It was a room constructed to look something like a frontier tavern with trestle tables and benches. Time and the custom of the world aboveground had evidently made it essentially an all-male enclave. Paolo was with half a dozen other men, all of them drunk enough so that their talk made little sense and they roared with laughter at simple-minded jokes they would have sneered at, sober.

Bart tapped Paolo on the shoulder. Paolo ignored the tap until Bart thumped his shoulder with enough force to have roused the other man's anger if he had not been full of drink.

"Hey!" shouted Paolo, looking up to him. "It's Bart! Sit down and have a drink, Bart! Hey, server—"

He threw a thick arm around Bart's waist and pulled him to the edge of the round table around which the party was seated.

"Listen, all of you!" shouted Paolo, jerking Bart against his shoulder in a one-armed bear hug. "I want you all to meet Bart, here! He's a *cetriol*, but I like him!"

The talk and laughter died for a moment around the table as all eyes there focused on Bart, then broke out again.

"Hey, *cetriol!*" called a young, white-blond-haired man at the table. The word, Bart knew—he had a small knowledge of Italian from his father and had also heard that particular word used in this manner by a fellow track-hand during a short period in which he had worked with a railway road gang—meant "cucumber" in English, and implied stupidity, among other things. Paolo, however, had used it jokingly, not the way this man was using it. "Buy us all a drink, *cetriol!*" It was a verbal sneer, since money was not used in the Inner World.

"Hey!"

Paolo leaned his weight forward on the table with his thick forearms among the glasses. The talk and laughter slowly died as the others stared at the sudden absence of humor from his face.

"I said I like him!" said Paolo slowly. "I like him better than I like anyone at this table."

His gaze went around, deliberately to each one of them. One by one, they avoided his eye.

"I call my friend *cetriol*," said Paolo, still in that slow, distinct voice. "That's me. Don't none of you call my friend *cetriol*."

The silence around the table was absolute.

"Paolo," said Bart, speaking quietly into the round ear beside him with the thick, stiff tiny spears of black hair sprouting here and there in it, "I need to talk to you by yourself, for a moment."

"Sure. Let's go." Paolo stood up suddenly and drunkenly, blundering against the edge of the table. Glasses rocked and drink splashed out, here and there; but still none of the others moved or spoke. "I don't like it so much around here, anymore."

He let Bart lead him to a small, empty and isolated table across the room. The server Paolo had called had followed them over.

"I'll have beer," Bart told the white-aproned male slave, in his late sixties to judge from the lines in his cadaverous face. "Give Paolo whatever he's drinking."

"You better have something more than beer, you going to drink with me," grunted Paolo.

The server had already gone off to fill Bart's order. "Beer will do," said Bart. "I have to wait on the Lord Librarian early tomorrow."

Neither man said anything more until the aproned slave had brought their orders and left. Then Bart spoke again.

"Paolo, I need to know some things."

"You want to know too much, that's your trouble," growled Paolo, slurping at his small glass. It was a loud slurp, but Bart noted the level of liquid in the glass had fallen only slightly when Paolo put it down again.

"Go on," Paolo added, "you're the one who's talking."

"I need to know how to get to people around here," Bart said. "What I need right now is some Hybrid I can sit down and ask some questions of. Tell me, how do I get in touch with a Hybrid?"

"Hybrid?"

Paolo stared at him.

"You're crazy." Paolo started to get up, then sank back on his seat again. "All right, maybe you're not crazy, just ignorant. What do you want to talk to a Hybrid for?"

"Because maybe a Hybrid can tell me some things no slave can," said Bart. "Somewhere in this Inner World there's got to be a Hybrid who can tell me what I want to know. If the Hybrid you put me in touch with can't answer me, maybe he can steer me to another Hybrid who can."

Paolo nodded, sitting back in the booth.

"You're ignorant, as I say," he said. "Not crazy, then. Listen to me, Bart. I can't put you in touch with a Hybrid like that. Nobody can."

"After all the years you told me you've been here?" Bart said. "You seem to get in touch with anyone else you need to."

"There's one thing I don't need to be in touch with, and that's any Hybrid," said Paolo. "You got to understand, Bart. They're just like Lords to you and me. What you're asking is like asking me to find you a Lord you can sit down and talk to. Bart, no Hybrid's going to sit and talk to a slave!"

"Maybe not where other people can see," said Bart, "but there's got to be—wait a minute. How about those Hybrids who take a fancy to some particular slave? There's got to be talk going on between Hybrid and slave when they're in bed together!"

"Not anything important any of us'd hear tell about. Not the kind of getting answers you've got in mind. You want me to point you out some of the men or women Hybrids who'd like to take a Steed home with them? I can do it, if that's the kind of thing you want."

"You know that's not what I mean," said Bart. "When I said I wanted to talk, I didn't mean by being taken up as some kind of bedroom pet. You really mean to tell me that there's not one Hybrid in the Inner World who'd be willing to talk one-on-one with a slave?''

"If there was, I'd have heard about it by now," said Paolo. "This here's a little place, when you get to know it. Nothing goes on everybody doesn't get to know about, sooner or later. There's no secrets here.''

He paused a split-second and focused on Bart again, more strongly. "And remember what I told you awhile ago—any slave wanting to ask questions will look suspicious. Slaves shouldn't be asking about things.''

"That's so?" said Bart. "Then maybe you can answer all my questions. To start off with, there's a part of this Inner World that has the doors to it guarded by Steeds. What's inside those doors?''

"How'd I know?" said Paolo. "Those are Lords' secrets.''

"I was looking for my own Lord," Bart went on, ignoring his answer, "when I came across one of those doors. The Steed guarding it wasn't from our dorm. He said no slave could go in unless a Lord took the slave in. That's got to mean some slaves have gone in there; and they're got to've seen and know what's there. So how is it you don't know?''

"Did that Steed say anything to you about a slave ever coming back out?" retorted Paolo. "You're right about one thing. If one ever did come out again, by now I'd know what he'd seen. All that means is that any slave that goes in there doesn't come back— ever.''

Bart stared at the other.

"You don't believe that!" he said.

"Sure, I believe it. You're the one doesn't," said Paolo, "and you know why? Because you're so new and ignorant down here, you still think things got to be like they were in the upper world. Well, what I got to tell you is, you'll learn. You'll learn the difference. We're all dead down here to begin with. You think it matters to the Lords that they put one or a lot of us back where they got us from?''

"All right," said Bart. Inwardly, he began to despair about learning what he needed from Paolo. "But I still think you know more about what's in the room behind those doors than you're telling me.''

He stared Paolo in the face.

"And you can't change my mind on that," he added.

Paolo's face contorted. He jerked up one fist as if to slam it down on the tabletop between them. But the fist checked and wavered in midair and then sank quietly down to the wooden surface below.

"So you got to know what's in the room behind those doors?" he said in a fierce, strained whisper, his face leaning close toward Bart's. "You got to know, do you? All right, I'll tell you what's there—the Old Man himself."

"Old man?" Bart found himself whispering in response.

"The Old Man himself, I tell you," whispered Paolo. "Old al-Kebir himself, all his thousands of years old, showing the rest of them how to build the thing that's going to destroy the upper, living world and everything on it! You never heard of anything like that, I suppose? You never heard talk of anything to kill the world and everyone on it, but us down here?"

"The slaves talk," said Bart, "but they don't make much sense. Al-Kebir, who's he?"

"He was the one who brought them all here, thousands of years ago. Some king or other treated them all bad, and al-Kebir swore he'd smash the world, smash all the human people like you and me. He brought himself and the rest out of slavery, one by one. He started the Inner World; and he's been all these years showing the Lords how to build the thing to destroy the whole Earth with. He and that thing, that's what's behind those guards and those doors; and keep your voice down. Because I already told you enough to get you killed."

Bart stared at him.

"You can't believe that, Paolo—about someone thousands of years old being still alive and telling people how to build something that can destroy the Earth!"

"I tell you it's the truth!" whispered Paolo. "Is it any more for you to believe than your being raised from the dead to work down here?"

"I don't believe I was raised from the dead," said Bart.

Paolo sat staring at him for a long moment. Then he sighed heavily and straightened up, sitting back a table's width across from Bart now. He spoke, no longer in whispers, but in a low voice.

"I might've known," he said heavily. "Bart, I've done for you more than I ever done for anyone in my life. That's because you're a loner, like me. You're my *paisan*. I never had one before, in all my life. But—I told you my mother was a witch—I can smell what you are. That's all I ever had, being able to smell what's in people. That and these—"

He laid out his stubby, heavy fists on the table, side by side.

"We could have had a lot of good years down here," he went on, "even the way this place is; and you'd've had your Emma and I got Lorena. But you're bound to bust it all up. You're bound to try doing something that can't be done and get yourself killed. Maybe get me and others killed with you. I wouldn't do that to you."

"I won't get you killed," said Bart, feeling guilty in spite of the fact his mind told him he was guilty of nothing. "I promise you—"

"Don't make me no promises," said Paolo. "I tell you I can smell it. I know. Chandt's been talking to you about me, hasn't he? He say I was afraid to fight you?"

Bart would willingly have lied to make the situation better, but with Paolo staring at him as he was and speaking in such a voice, he could not.

"Yes," he said.

"It ain't true," said Paolo, still in that low voice that was so unusual for him. "I'm not afraid to fight any man there is. I'm not even afraid of him, Chandt, in spite of knowing he'll kill me. I can smell that, too. The day I go up against him, he'll kill me. Bare hands against bare hands, he'll kill me. But still I ain't afraid of him. He knows that. But he can't let himself think I'm not afraid because of that Mongol way of looking at things he has. He's got to feel there's no one in the surface world or in the Inner World who wouldn't be afraid of him. Else he couldn't live with himself. He thinks he's the last Mongol there is; so he's got to be what all the Mongols were to everybody else."

"You don't like him," said Bart.

"No," said Paolo. "I don't like him. He likes you, though. He'd like you for a paisano, just the way I do, but I can have you for one and he can't; because being the only one of his kind the way he is, he ain't allowed no friends."

Paolo looked across the table at Bart, strangely.

"That's why he'll kill you, too, at last, just like he'll kill me. Because you don't fit the world the way he has to have it."

Paolo reached out for his glass almost blindly, lifted it, and drank from it—a full swallow this time. He set the glass back down on the table and sat staring at it.

"I done my best to save you," he said, his eyes still on the glass.

He stayed as he was, staring at the glass. It was almost as if he had forgotten Bart was there. Bart pushed back his chair and got to his feet; but still Paolo did not look up.

"I promise you," Bart said to him, "neither you nor Lorena, nor Emma nor anyone else is going to be hurt because of what I do."

He put a hand on one of the thick shoulders, but it was like touching a stone statue. Bart left him.

He went back to the dormitory. He had a name now—al-Kebir or el-Kabir. It sounded Arabic; and somewhere in the Library, thanks to Pier and the freedom he had given Bart, he ought to be able to run down something on that.

chapter
fourteen

THE OUTER ROOM of the Library was lit and open twenty-four hours a day. Bart had picked an evening several days after his encounter with the Emperor, here, to begin his search of the Library itself. Though there were still people about, they were fewer than during the days.

A stack slave slept in a chair behind the desk, but the rest of the room was empty of life. At the moment Bart stepped onto the interior carpet, he heard footfalls approaching through the stacks, with their uncarpeted floors; and a moment later there came into view three Hybrids.

Two of them were unremarkable, dark-suited men in their thirties, one with thinning brown hair, one with a mop of faded blond above a round face. But the third, walking between the other two, was a narrow-waisted, broad-shouldered man with a swarthy skin, a sharp nose and astonishingly bright blue eyes.

Bart had never seen this particular Hybrid before, to his knowledge; but something about him riveted Bart's attention. In spite of the fact Bart did not know him, there was something familiar about him. It was as if Bart felt he should recognize him. As if he had known him, even though Bart knew he had not.

At the same time Bart became conscious that he had halted directly in front of the doorway, toward which the three were headed.

Hastily, he stepped aside. The two Hybrids on either side of the one who had attracted Bart's attention merely glanced at Bart as they approached and passed. But Bart became suddenly aware that the third man's bright blue eyes were concentrating on him with an intensity that made him uncomfortable. Here was not a man, like Chandt, who was responding as someone with an authority to maintain. The feeling that reached Bart was merely one of curiosity. But it was a curiosity as blinding as a mirror with the full sun reflected in it, and as sharp as the end of a needle.

Then the three passed him, and the one with the blue eyes took his gaze off Bart and looked ahead, putting a hand on one shoulder of each of his companions. He herded them before him, out the door. Bart felt a strange desire to follow, to find out more about him. Then he remembered what he was here to do, put the feeling from him, and continued on past the circular desk area with its sleeping slave, on into the stacks.

In the time that had passed since Pier had given him the freedom of the Library, Bart had been using some of his free time to explore it. He had had vague notions of trying to find information that might help him to escape from this Inner World, but had really had little idea of exactly what to look for. But now, a few days ago, Paolo had given him a name. That, combined with the dead end he had seemingly come up against in his physical exploration of the corridors, had led him back here. It might be that it would be his mind rather than his body that got them out of here.

What he needed was something that would tell him of the history of the Lords, and of the Inner World itself. The name of this legendary al-Kebir might be the key his researches needed.

At first he had been baffled, for while the Library held a considerable section of histories of the world and its various peoples, in various languages, all of these were perfectly straightforward accounts of the past as he had learned about it from his father and his own reading. The Lords seemed to work hard at bringing copies of as many of the world's books as they could reach to their own Library, but none of them seemed to reference the Lords or their World. Still, he scanned the pages of those histories he had never read before, in search of some reference, however slight, to any people like the Lords, or to a vessel that might have brought them here from somewhere "beyond the moon," but found nothing.

He could not believe it. It was not possible that a race or group like the Lords, who were so capable, rich and well-organized that they could produce something like this Inner World, would not have some sort of written history, or books that at least referred to that history. If nothing else, there would have been records for as vast an undertaking as the building of the Inner World. Not to speak of all the devices that they had come up with, using electromagnetic forces or whatever—he checked himself in midthought.

Of course. Records. Somewhere here in the Library there had to be records of work done, money spent, and probably as well of people born and buried during the time of this Inner World. Records that would at least put him on the track of how this place with its three classes had come to be, unknown to the outside world and buried underground off in a part of the world which most of the world's peoples took to be howling wilderness.

In fact—and his hopes shot skyward for a moment—it was even possible that in finding such records he would find architectural plans of the Inner World itself, complete with some lightly guarded secret exit.

He checked the wishful thinking. A find like that would be almost too good to be true. He would be content to get any kind of a handle on the mystery that surrounded him, any kind of lead to the understanding that would point him to where he could learn more.

So he had begun his search for the records section of the Library. He could, of course, have asked someone there, from Pier on down to one of the stack slaves whose duty was fetching books for those who did not go back after them. But it could be dangerous to let anyone else know that he was interested in such a section, even if such a question turned out to be harmless.

Which it could hardly be, he had thought, remembering that none of the Hybrids or Lords he had listened to or followed had asked for that particular section in all the time he had been here.

So it had been a matter of his starting at the lowest floor of the Library at its farthest back corner, and simply searching each level completely as he moved up through them, until he might come to the section where such records were kept.

It had been a slow job so far, made slower by the temptation to stop and look into interesting books or papers as he went—books and papers which plainly were not what he was looking for, but which might tell him things he might need to know. Moreover, he had been infected by the pleasure of reading early in life, and he found it difficult to shake that off now.

His father had been a constant supplier of books. Lionel had made a habit of asking anyone with whom he made friends to buy books for him, whenever that person got to a place where books were sold. The result for young Bart had been that it seemed that every day brought some newcomer to their door to deliver one or more books that Lionel had asked him to get.

The result was that Bart had come to mirror his father's appetite for the written word. It was an odd addiction for a woods-born, mixed-blood man to have, on the wild western frontier of Canada in the middle years of the nineteenth century; it was not that people did not like to read, but that few of them ever learned how, and those who did learn had only infrequent access to reading materials.

Moreover, Bart had seen first-hand the effect his father's habit of burying himself away with his books had had on the man's reputation; and so he had tried to draw as little attention as possible to his own reading. That fit, anyway, with his desires not to stand out from the crowd.

Pier had been kinder to him than the old Lord had realized, in giving him the run of the stacks.

So he had persevered in his search with occasional hesitations, as he gave in to the temptation to look into some book with a particularly interesting-sounding title. In spite of these interruptions, however, he had continued to make his way up the levels of the stacks, until now he was on the main level of the Library where the main desk and Pier's office was. This night he began about halfway back through the stacks on that level, and he had only been searching for about an hour and a half when he finally found the section he had been seeking all along.

It was in a side room off the main area of that floor's stacks, a side room he had never before known existed. The nearer shelves were stacked with piles of books and papers almost haphazardly; and his first assumption was that these were Library materials stored temporarily, pending collation and assignment to their proper position on the shelves.

He began by examining the papers near the entrance. They were, as he had half suspected from the look of them, loose records of all kinds—memos, orders, supply lists. All kinds and sorts of different paperwork, tied with string into bundles about four inches thick. When he went farther in, however, the bundles of paper gave way to bound volumes; and, opening these, he found that they were merely collections of the same sort of business papers that made up the bundles he had just passed, but of an earlier date.

He could see the end of the side room, now, only a dozen feet from him, putting a limit to the shelves and their contents. All bound books, almost undoubtedly more bound records. There might be information here he could use, but it would take days of searching through the papers to find it. He could start that search tonight; but it was getting to the time for him to head back to the dormitory if he wanted anything like a full night's sleep. Probably there was no point in looking any farther into the matter for now.

So he told himself; but a small devil of persistence that had been part of him as long as he could remember prodded him on to the very end of the room; and this time it paid off. For he came upon the last six feet of shelves, which, from floor to ceiling, were filled with what seemed to be identical copies of a single title. He was looking at several hundred of them. They were bound in soft, dark leather, with covers so oversize that their open ends almost flopped together in spite of the thickness of the volume they enclosed. On each front cover where a title might ordinarily be, there was only a strange sort of scrawl in gold that baffled him for a minute before he recognized it as Arabic script:

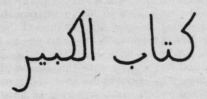

Bart's father had been interested, among other things, in the writings of the twelfth century Jewish philosopher, Moses Maimonides and had secured a copy of Maimonides' *Book of Commandments,* written in the original Arabic. As a young boy, fresh from the Cree camp, Bart had been fascinated by the Arabic script and his father had taken the time to show him how to spell out a few short, common words. The Library, Bart knew, had a large supply of foreign dictionaries, but the temptation to puzzle this out on his own made him search his memory until he began to make sense of it.

The first part read "Kinaab"—no, it was "Kitaab"—which meant, in English, simply "Book." The second part was even easier—it began with the article *"el,"* or *"al"*—which was joined to the beginning of the noun it modified. That noun . . . for a moment it frustrated him; and then he had it, feeling fortunate that it contained two of the same letters as the first word he had spelled out—that made it easier to recognize. It was a common word, which was why he could recognize it at all. It read *Kebir,* which meant "Large" or perhaps, "the Large One." Or "the Great."

So the whole thing read "Book The Large One." And he knew well enough how foreign grammars could differ from that of English or French—he must be missing something, some rule of the language, that would tell him how to add something more to the phrase, to make more sense of it. He could guess that a more proper translation would read, "THE LARGE BOOK"—or, wait—"The Book of The Large One" was also a possible reading.

But for the moment it was not the exercise in translation that transfixed him, but the fact that "al-Kebir" had been the name Paolo had whispered to him, that evening not long ago.

He took one of the copies from a middle shelf and opened it to its first page—it began with its text immediately, without flyleaves or title pages, and despite the Arabic text on the cover, it was written—apparently handwritten—in clean, clear script of a late medieval Latin.

"De origine et via qua adhunc mundum advenimus nihil dicabo . . . ," the first sentence began.

"Of our origin and the means by which we came to this world, as well as the fate of many of us in the moment of our arrival," his mind translated into English, *"I will say nothing, lest the information turn out to be of use to those who should not know such things.*

"Suffice it to say that a number of us were left scattered and helpless upon a part of this earth called Sicily, where we one and all fell into the hands of various local inhabitants of the lowest origin, brutish by nature and lacking in all but the simplest intelligence. Inhabitants, moreover, who were incapable of recognizing in us the superior beings we were, but instead took us under their control and treated each of us as if we were little better than the beasts they fed on or forced to work their fields; for without exception they were peasants of the lowest order . . ."

Bart forced himself to tear his eyes from the text and close the book. It was plainly an autobiography written by that same unbelievable character Paolo had whispered about as being in the great guarded central room of the Inner World—the man supposed to be in charge there and thousands of years old.

Well, the book was written in medieval Latin, which, if it was the original language in which the story was told, effectively disposed of the idea that al-Kebir was thousands of years old. Bart frowned briefly in thought. Since al-Kebir seemed to be the name of this person, and this was his autobiography, it followed that the Arabic title was best translated as "Al-Kebir's Book," or perhaps "The Book of Al-Kebir."

Thoughtfully Bart took the book back to Pier's office, not forgetting to watch lest someone notice him with it, and unlocked the door. The lights within went on automatically as the door opened to his key. The signal light had told him that Pier was not here.

He went into his alcove; sat down, opened the book again and started reading. . . .

It was some hours later that he roused himself with a start from the book, his reading of it still unfinished. He got up and stepped out of the alcove to check the clock on the wall of Pier's office.

It was almost four in the morning; and Bart suddenly realized that he was almost snow-blind from staring at the pages, and dead tired.

The full story of he who had called himself al-Kebir was yet to be read by Bart; but the time in which he had at least begun his existence was now certain. It had been in the thirteenth century; and he had lived mainly at the Sicilian court of Frederick the Second, Holy Roman Emperor. More than that, he had been four feet two, or thereabouts, a dwarf with a misshapen head, a genius and very possibly also a madman; with a black and boiling hatred in him for the Emperor who owned him and for everyone else in the human race who was not undersized like himself.

Also, there was no doubt that he was among the first of the Lords, if not himself the first, on Earth.

But the final words of what he had to say about himself would have to wait for some later time. Bart had two hours in which to try and get some sleep before the dormitory was roused. He returned the book to its place on the shelf from which he had taken it and took himself off to bed.

The next morning he was barely roused by the voices around the schedule pinned to the door. He rolled over and went back to sleep so successfully that he did not wake again until nearly noon. He sat up in alarm, then sank back in relief as he remembered that, luckily, the day before, Pier had told him that he planned to work at home today. He did, however, have to come to Pier's home in the afternoon, if only to wait on his pleasure.

He brightened up, remembering that this was an evening when he was to meet Emma, Paolo and Lorena in the slaves' Recreation Center. They had already met on two occasions, this way. He found the three of them now, as usual, in Paolo's favorite corner booth.

"Just once," said Paolo, as Bart slid into the booth beside Emma and across from the other two, "I'd like to get here and find you waiting for the rest of us."

It was a growl, but a friendly growl. In fact that was the only way

Paolo seemed to know how to speak—in a growl. It was the way he talked to the Steeds in his dormitory. He even growled his acknowledgment of commands from the Lordly class, Hybrids and other superiors, like Chandt.

"Sorry," said Bart. "I was kept late at the Librarian's."

"Oh, the Library!" Paolo's harsh voice disposed of any possibility that anything in the Library could be interesting to anyone but an individual with strange tastes, like Bart. The upper classes naturally all had such tastes, but a slave who liked books was grotesque to the point of being funny to Paolo. He excused this oddity of Bart's only because he liked him, but he prodded him about it.

"I'll tell you about it in a minute," said Bart to Emma, in Cree. She smiled back at him.

"Oh, for hell's sake!" said Paolo. "Are you going to start that jibber-jabber right off the minute you get here? Have a drink and talk some human French or English for a few minutes first!"

He turned to Lorena beside him.

"Don't you ever start talking crazy languages around me."

"Oh, I wouldn't!" said Lorena, then looked hastily at Bart and Emma, then as hastily looked down at the tabletop between them.

"Don't let it bother you, Lorena," said Emma to the other woman. "It's natural for anyone not to like sitting and wondering if you're being discussed in front of your face, in a tongue you can't understand. I know how you feel. But Bart and I haven't any choice. The only way we can get together is with you two, according to Paolo here; and we don't want to make you listen to things from us that'd force you to choose between reporting us to the authorities or getting into trouble for not reporting us. If you don't understand us, then no one can blame you."

"They'd lump us in with you anyway—the Hybrids would, anyhow—," growled Paolo.

"Nonsense!" said Emma. "We can prove you don't understand us. Chances are there aren't any Hybrids or Lords or Ladies who could, either. And don't pick on Lorena, Paolo. She tries too hard to please you, as it is."

It was typical of Emma, thought Bart, that she was already protecting Lorena. The newcomer had taken the experienced old hand under her wing, instead of the other way around. But given the characters of the two women it could hardly have been otherwise.

Lorena, Emma had told Bart in Cree at one of the earlier meetings, had had a sheltered, if not a pampered, childhood. She had been born into a family in the southern United States; and the

Civil War had put an end to the kind of life she had been raised to expect while she was still a teenager.

It had also stripped her of all her close relatives and what little wealth she might otherwise have had. She was an indifferent cook and seamstress, but spoke educated French. She had a sort of pale, fragile, brown-haired beauty and a true singing voice with good range but little power. These were the only tools her upbringing had provided her to survive in the world alone.

That same upbringing and her nature had also imprinted her firmly with the notion that men would behave like gentlemen toward her if only she behaved like a lady toward them. Valiantly, she tried to do so, turning first for help to some distant cousins who, to get her off their hands, pushed her into an affair with a man who lived more by his wits than by any other means. This man had been impressed at first by her manners and her almost desperate desire to please him; but both attractions wore thin for him after a while, since both were foreign to his own selfish way of thinking.

He had pushed her off on a friend. Sold her, as a matter of fact—but she did not learn this until later, when the friend accused her of not being worth the price he had paid for her. From then on she drifted from one man to another in a generally northwesterly direction, as her companions became poorer and cruder and more inclined to try their luck farther west on the frontier regions.

She had been killed, so she believed, by robbers who held up a stagecoach in which she was traveling with her latest gentleman. The holdup man had decided to shoot all those on and in the coach to cover their tracks. She had come back to life here—still the same person with her unshakable belief that somewhere there was a man who would care for her and protect her if only she could figure out the proper way of pleasing him.

Consequently, she had been played with—those were Emma's words for what had happened to her and Bart thought that they were probably as close to the truth as any could be—by a number of fellow slaves here in the Inner World. She lacked the intellectual capacity to attract the attention of Hybrids or Lords. Not that members from either of the upper classes would necessarily have turned out to be much kinder to her if they had taken an interest in her.

The fact was, she was a waif on anyone's doorstep; and she loved Paolo simply because Paolo had his own rough standards of right and wrong, and applied them to her as well as to everyone else. The result was that the other men who still took her up from time to time were constrained in their handling of her by the knowledge that a Steed named Paolo wanted Lorena—when he chose to want her—in good physical shape and reasonably happy. Since the dormitory Leader was a formidable person and known as such, she had been well-treated in the past few years by her other gentlemen.

Emma believed that Paolo, without knowing it, was in love with Lorena. Bart privately reserved judgment on that.

In any case, the result was startling. When she and Emma were together in public, it was Lorena who caught the eye; but Emma dominated the attention of anyone who ventured close to the two of them. Even smaller than Lorena, she had an absolute lack of fear and a perfectly clear perception of the fact that not all people were angels, matched with the determination that they could and would behave themselves if they wished to stay anywhere close around her; Emma cowed most of those who otherwise would have taken almost instant advantage of someone like Lorena.

—And just as well, too, thought Bart grimly to himself. If it came down to it, he believed he would be a good deal more capable of defending Emma than Paolo was of Lorena. However, Emma being who she was, the need had so far never arisen.

"I don't pick on her!" Paolo was protesting.

"You do," said Emma calmly. "You're just so used to doing it that you don't know when you're about it."

Paolo stared at her, baffled into silence.

"Sorry, Paolo," said Bart. "Just let us get our jabber out of the way first; and then we can talk any human language you want for the rest of the time we have."

"Italian," said Paolo.

"All right," said Bart, with a glance at Emma and Lorena, neither of which understood a word of Italian as far as he knew. "If you insist, we'll talk Italian."

"You only know a couple of words," said Paolo gruffly, "and no one else here but me knows it at all. Get the hell on with it, will you?"

"All right," said Bart, "we'll make it as fast as possible."

He turned to Emma and began to talk to her in Cree, telling her of what he had found in the side room of the Library stacks and particularly the book apparently written by al-Kebir about himself and the history of the early Lords and Ladies. He was more than a little disappointed that she took the discovery as much less than the remarkable stroke of luck he had been considering it.

"Don't you realize?" he said to her almost angrily, "what this could lead to? It could lead to a way out of here; and it practically fell into my hands!''

"How could that book lead to you getting us out of here?" she asked.

"I can use the fact that I know about it to back up my story," he said.

"What story?"

"I'm going to talk to Pier and claim I'm a lost Hybrid, the son of a Lord who died above ground after fathering me with an Indian woman."

He did not want to use the recognizable word "Hybrid," so he rendered the word in Cree as man-with-small-god-for-father. Emma looked sideways and up at him, her round face concerned.

"Why do you think you can get away with anything like that?" she asked.

"It all depends on whether I've dug out the right picture of how this place works," he said. "If I have, then, it'll be up to them to prove I'm lying; and the only way they can do that is either by proving no Lord was where I came from, at the right time to be my father—and from what I can learn, there's no way they can do that—or by asking me questions until I trip myself up by contradicting myself. Which I won't do."

"Let's take this one question at a time," said Emma. "To begin with, what makes you think they can't look at their records—and they keep very good records, I can testify to that after seeing their bookkeeping here—and find that there was no Lord anywhere around at the place and time you must have been started?"

"Because I'm not going to tell them enough to let them do a close enough job of checking," said Bart. "All I know, I'll say, is that I was born into an Indian tribe that was always on the move, and when I got old enough to understand, my mother told me a small, ugly white man had been my father, but that she had heard since that he had died somewhere farther west. Meanwhile, down here I've realized that the way she described my father makes it seem certain that he was a Lord."

"And what if they haven't had any Lords at all above ground in western Canada?"

"I think they've had to have," said Bart. "It's like a pack of wolves protecting their territory. They'll have wanted to steer people away from the whole area where this Inner World is underground; and that job's too important to leave to Hybrids alone. My estimate is they must have had at least several Lords up on the surface west of Toronto about the time I was born, helping to influence the directions in which settlers—and particularly the railroad—moved west.''

''All right,'' she said, ''for now, I'll take that answer. How about the other question? What makes you so sure they can't trip you up when one of your answers doesn't match with another you've given them?''

''Because all my answers will match. I'm only going to tell them one story from the wind,'' he said, using their old childish personal euphemism for the word ''lie,'' so that even if they were being overheard after all, and by someone who understood Cree to boot, his meaning would be hidden. ''I'll tell them the absolute truth: how I was adopted by another white man who said I was too bright to grow up to do nothing but hunting and fishing. I'll tell them exactly how it was from then on until I ended up on a chain in Shunthead mine.''

She stared almost grimly at him. He knew that she knew, but would not say anything aloud for fear of the possible unseen listener. Unlike most of the people in the métis territory where they have lived, for whom ''adopted'' was generally taken to be a polite way of explaining the presence of a natural child by another mother than the one with which the father was living or to whom he was married, she knew that Lionel was Bart's true parent.

Also, unlike her brother she had visited Bart's home often, gotten to know his father, and been told by Lionel flatly that Bart was his actual son. In fact, Lionel had asked the little mite that she was then to take care of Bart if anything happened to him. The man had spoken in all seriousness, and since the conversation had taken place in front of Bart, the boy he was then had been both shocked and angry. If anybody was going to take care of anybody, he thought, it would be him caring for Emma, instead of the other way around.

But Lionel had asked in all apparent seriousness, and Emma had answered just as seriously.

That conversation had caused Bart a secret worry that did not fade for a number of years. It was whether Emma really loved him. Now, grown up, he had long since been sure she did. Only her damnable insistence on seeing her brother taken care of first had stood in the way of their being married long since. But back then, as a boy, he had been afraid for some time that she was just, with that implacable will of hers, acting out her promise to be a substitute for his father—even though Lionel was still alive—much as she substituted, later, for her mother on behalf of the rest of her family.

Now, over the lunch table, Bart launched into a picture of the Inner World as the living result of the vision of al Kebir. He told Emma all about the *Kitaab al-Kebir* and his hope that it might lead him to the information he needed for his imposture.

He wound up with his image of the Inner World as a creation supported by a worldwide system of investments pyramided since the thirteenth century and overseen by a number of Lords, Ladies and Hybrids sent above ground for that purpose.

Emma listened to him without interrupting until he was through. Then she mentioned the one thing he had avoided talking about.

"You actually believe, then," she said, "that there's something here in the Inner World which can destroy the world above and it's going to be used soon?"

"Not really," he said. "I can't believe it. It's too farfetched. But there's a large area down here that only members of the Lordly class and Hybrids can get into and out of again alive. Also, all the Hybrids seem to believe in such a weapon and what it can do; and they're not a stupid bunch."

Emma looked thoughtful. He took advantage of her moment of silence to do some eating, having been too busy talking to do so until now; and she had finished her own dinner sometime since as she sat there listening to him.

"It's true that in bookkeeping we've been warned to get ready to start an entirely new set of books in the near future," she said thoughtfully. "But shouldn't you make absolutely sure that there really is such a machine before you go acting on the premise that the whole upper world might be destroyed?"

"That's what I'm about to do," Bart said. "This is what it's all about, this business of establishing myself as a Hybrid. As a slave, I'd never be able to find out about this weapon, or whatever it is. But as a Hybrid, I'll either find my way into the guarded area, or get access to literature that describes what's there."

"You'd better not expect too much," said Emma. "You've only read this al-Kebir's book part-way, and you said that in the beginning he wrote himself that he wouldn't tell anything that might be useful to people not entitled to know it. It seems to me if he has anything to say that would help us, that book's going to be very careful not to show it."

"You don't understand," said Bart. "He may not give away anything he thinks of as a valuable secret, but there's still all sorts of things I can learn from its pages about how this place and its people came to be.''

''How do you know that what he's written down is true at all?'' said Emma.

''I don't, of course. Maybe it isn't. But even a string of lies can tell me things once I start to get the pattern of them. Remember, I can check what he says against the real histories of whatever time he's writing about. He called the island where they're supposed to have come to Earth 'Sicily.' Now, that puts a limit right there as to how far back in time he was writing it. I'll just have to read the book all the way through and study it—but I'll bet you I come up with a whole fistful of information that can lead me on to wherever the things I want to know actually are written down.''

''And meanwhile,'' said Emma, ''you'll be taking a chance doing something that may get you killed.''

Bart gave up. He had learned years ago that if Emma was determined not to be convinced about something, you could talk to her until you fell over sideways from exhaustion and still find her coming up with solid arguments against it.

''We'll see,'' he said.

''Which means you're going to do it anyway,'' said Emma. ''Bart, I love you, but you're the most stubborn man I ever knew in all my born days!''

Bart refrained from saying anything about the stubbornness of other people who might be present at the moment.

''But never mind that now,'' Emma was saying, still in Cree. ''There's something else I want to talk to you about, Bart. It's Arthur.''

''Yes?'' said Bart warily. Experience had taught him that when Emma started out this way, what she had to talk about was something he would not like.

''You asked me not to tell him you were down here, or say anything about my having seen you since you came through town and stayed with us that night in the store. So I haven't. But Bart—''

Bart braced himself.

''You couldn't help feeling sorry for Arthur if you saw him, nowadays,'' Emma said. ''He's so cast down. He expected so much from the move down here; and not only did it turn out it was some of the other Scotties' way of getting rid of him, but he's a *slave*, Bart! To someone like Arthur who was brought up to think of himself as being a gentleman and the son of a gentleman, the fact that he's now called a slave, and treated like one, is almost more than he can bear. And the job he's in! The others working there in Stores tell him stories of how people who make mistakes get flogged, or put to some horrible kind of death if they make a mistake; and he's frightened to death.''

"They're exaggerating," said Bart. "Office-trained slaves can't be that easy to come by. I haven't seen any evidence of brutality. Not that that guarantees there isn't any; but it just isn't all that common, or that easy to trigger off, obviously.''

"But Arthur doesn't know that; and he worries—you know how he is. He's worrying himself into a sickbed," said Emma. "He's lost weight and you ought to see his face. Bart, it could mean so much to him if he just had some reason to hope; if he only just knew you were down here, too, and working to get us all out!''

Bart sat, trying to think of how best to answer her, so that he could be convincing without giving away the fact he thought Arthur's feelings were of little importance concerned with the chance of all three of them escaping. But to give away that would directly attack Emma's sense of protection for her brother.

Emma stopped talking. There was a pause that showed its uncomfortableness so plainly, that Paolo and Lorena, even without understanding, were obviously disturbed.

"Emma, I can't," said Bart at last. "You know Arthur. What he knows he's likely to tell someone—somewhere, sometime. And I can't take the risk of him talking about me to the wrong person. It's not just that he might tell them I was looking for a way out of here. It's the fact he knows too much about me, from when we were children.''

"You mean, what you can do?" said Emma.

She was talking about his capabilities. No one but Emma knew how he was stronger than he looked and how sharply his mind worked when he felt himself cornered. Last of all, she knew how he wished that he would never have to use these abilities, which secretly he feared to display. Attacked, he became a different sort of person with different limits; and it was what those limits might allow him to do that frightened him. He did not know what they were. He had never really been driven to the sort of extremes that would have forced him to find out.

Arthur did not have Emma's sensitive perception of him. But Arthur did remember him from when they had all been children together, before Bart had begun to realize that to get along with other people and not be thought some sort of freak, he would have to shadow the capabilities of his mind and body.

"It's not only that," he told her now, "but Arthur knows about my father and what sort of man he was and how he gave me special training in many ways. I want to keep that information to myself until I see the best moment to use it. . . ."

For a moment he was tempted to tell her how dangerous his plan was—but what he was planning was the sort of gamble that could only cause her to worry about what might happen to him, if she truly realized that danger. What Arthur had been hearing from his fellow-workers had only echoed what people like Paolo had told Bart himself. There might not be much more of the sort of thing than made a good horror story to tell a new slave; but there was undoubtedly some of it; if the situation required it in the eyes of the Hybrids and the Lords.

"Just awhile longer," he said to her. "Please, don't tell him, don't tell anyone you ever knew me before you came here—"

A question he had been meaning to ask her came back to him suddenly.

"Tell me," he said, "do either you or Arthur think you died before you came down here—that you were brought back to life by the Lords?"

"Of course not," said Emma. "Nothing like that ever happened to us. Though the Scotties warned Arthur, and Arthur told me, that most of the people down here would believe some such thing about themselves and we'd be best off if we pretended we believed it, too."

So, thought Bart, the illusion of being raised from the dead to serve the Lords was not universal among the slave class, after all; though it certainly seemed to be among the Steeds. He had yet to meet a Steed who did not believe it; and even Chandt, himself . . .

"All right, then," Emma was saying sadly. "If you really think it's not safe to tell him, I won't. It's just so terrible to see him the way he is."

"I promise you, Emma," said Bart, "the minute it's possible for him to know, I'll tell you and you can pass the word to him."

"All right," said Emma; and, to the relief of Paolo and Lorena, they went back to talking in English.

chapter
fifteen

THE USUAL SIX in the morning buzz of talk about the orders, just posted for the day on the dormitory door, woke Bart. He lay there for a moment, listening. There were to be a couple of formations. The latter one was listed simply as "court" with a 2:00 P.M. assembly in the main gym of all dormitories. It was probably some formal affair in which the Steeds would be part of the decorations —Bart dismissed it from his mind. But the earlier one was the one being talking about by those at the door; and the more Bart heard, the less he liked the sound of what he was hearing.

This earlier formation was simply listed as "Clinic." What had brought Bart sharply awake and set him to listening closely to what was being said by those around the door was not so much the words he heard but a definite uneasiness in the voices uttering them.

Curiously, it was an uneasiness that the Steeds radiating it seemed to wish to pretend was not there. It was this desire to gloss over their reaction that convinced Bart most strongly that the wise thing for him to do would be to skip this particular formation himself until he had time to learn more about it.

It was something of a shock, consequently, to hear Paolo's answer, when he told the dormitory Leader he had an early duty for the Librarian and would not be going with the others to this "Clinic."

Paolo had grinned. He was wearing a livery tunic at the moment, for reasons Bart did not know; but it, in face of the shirtlessness that was normal duty attire for Steeds, had the effect of putting a little formal distance between him and Bart. Alone, or with Emma and Lenora, Paolo was one kind of person; now he seemed someone different.

"This one you don't miss, Bart," he said. "There's no excuse lets you out of Clinic. The Lords know that, and if they forget and schedule a Steed to a duty at that time, and he doesn't show up, it's not his fault."

Bart felt the caution kindled in him by the atmosphere around the door become a hard decision that he must get out of this somehow.

"You know, Paolo," he said slowly, trying to adopt the same formality of manner without being offensive, "my Lord's one of the Three Who Command. I think you or somebody—Chandt, if it has to be—had better check with him before I'm kept from the duty my Lord had in mind for me."

Paolo grinned again—a little uneasily, it seemed to Bart—and shook his head. "Not necessary this time. The rules are clear and there's no time to check."

He slapped Bart on the shoulder.

"Don't let it get you down, Bart," he said. "It's not all that bad! Anyway, the rules are clear and there's no time to check."

He went off, leaving Bart wondering.

There were times when argument was of value—and times when it was useless. Bart could read in Paolo's voice and attitude that this time was one of the latter. He found that Steeds were not allowed to eat or drink before Clinic; and there was only a short wait before he fell in line with the rest of the Steeds in his dormitory, as far toward the tail of the formation as he thought he could safely fit in without drawing too much attention to the fact that he was delaying his involvement with the Clinic as long as possible.

They were conducted in a long line—"marched" would have been too noble a word for their straggling progress—down various corridors and around several turns to the entrance of a large room with several attendants. These were males, to judge by the depth of their voices, and of ordinary adult size; but whether slaves or Hybrids it was impossible to say, for they were completely cloaked and hooded in white with tinted glasslike face plates in the hood to see out of, but which prevented anyone from seeing in.

The Steeds were ordered to strip. Naked, they filed into the next room which seemed a sort of shower room, its ceiling equipped with spray heads that rained down water on the Steeds. The water smelled of something like eucalyptus, a medicinal smell. Then the shower heads ceased spouting; and, four at a time, the Steeds were admitted through a farther door to some room beyond.

Bart had meanwhile been exercising his wits for a reason to get away from the formation. He snarled at himself internally now for being foolish enough to take off his clothes along with the rest. Their clothes, their shoes and everything else they had been carrying had been immediately gathered up by hooded figures and carried away out of the disrobing room. Now, without clothes, he could hardly fail to attract attention even if he could find an excuse to leave.

He was still struggling with the problem when one of the hooded figures in the shower room, his apparently waterproof white gown glistening with moisture as if it had been embroidered with diamonds, gathered Bart in with three others. They were chosen apparently at random, and herded together through the farther door.

The room they entered was little more than an anteroom. Entrances in its opposite wall gave glimpses of a separate room, each with what looked like a couple of white-sheeted, padded tables. The hooded man who had brought them this far left them and went back to the shower room. For a moment they were alone, the four of them.

"What happens here?" Bart took advantage of the temporary privacy to ask one of the other Steeds, named Staggers.

"Nothing," answered Staggers.

He was a heavy-bodied, brown-haired young man with an oval face that looked like it needed a shave only twice a week. But either he had gotten a heavier dousing from the sprinkler heads than the rest of them, or he was sweating; and his face was pale. "They just put you half asleep and check you over to see if there's anything a doctor's got to do to you. It hurts a little, some of it; but not much because you're half asleep. It's something like being drunk. You don't feel things so much."

"Then why does everyone here act like they're not going to like it, if that's all it is?" asked Bart.

"Well, hell!" said Staggers. "Nobody likes people poking around their insides—even if the worst parts're something you don't remember too well, because of being half asleep that way."

"You're sure you're only half asleep—," Bart was beginning to ask when he was interrupted by another hooded figure coming up to them with a board in his hand, to the top surface of which a piece of paper had been attached. Bart caught a glimpse of what looked like a list of names written on the paper; and the look was confirmed a moment later by the hooded man himself.

"Names?" he demanded. Staggers and the other two gave their names without hesitation. Bart was last. After a moment's hesitation, in which he had been tempted to refuse to give his name but invoke the authority of Pier, to back up a demand he be exempted from everything that seemed to be going on here, he complied.

The man with the list did not seem to notice the hesitation. He was busy checking off the names of the other three, repeating them aloud as he came to them on his sheet of paper and directing whoever he had just mentioned to one of the farther entrances.

Having done this, however, he fell silent, scanning through the entire list. He went through it a second time, also without saying anything aloud. Then he looked up at Bart accusingly.

"What'd you say your name was?" he said.

"Bart Dybig."

"Spell it!"

Bart spelled it; and the man went through the list one more time. Then he turned and called to one of the other hooded figures in the room.

"Jules!"

The other figure turned a face plate toward him.

"What is it, Will?" The voice of the man named Jules was deeper than that of the man with the list, deeper and more musical.

"This one's not here."

"What do you mean, not here?" said Jules, coming up. "I can see him, right there, standing in front of you."

There was a chuckle in his deep voice. Will did not seem amused.

"He's not on the list. Nowhere on the list."

"Are you sure?" Jules's voice was curious now.

"I've been through it five times."

A slight exaggeration, thought Bart, but Jules did not question it.

"Some mistake," he said lightly.

"You're sure?"

"Bound to be."

"And what if it isn't?" said Will. "What if there's some reason he's not supposed to be here?"

"Talk sense," said Jules easily. "How could a Steed not be supposed to be here, on a Clinic day for his dormitory?"

"I don't know," said Will. "But maybe there's a reason you and I aren't supposed to know."

"He was in the formation," said Jules.

Bart was tempted to speak up in that moment, to make his demand that he be exempted from whatever was to be, on the basis that he was a special slave of one of the Three Who Command and had a duty elsewhere. An instinct told him to wait. If it should be decided to put him through the procedure here, after all, he could still come up with his argument later. Meanwhile, the conversation between Will and Jules might take a turn that would offer an even better moment for invoking the name of the Librarian.

"That could be a mistake," said Will.

"Ask one of the physicians."

"And I do," said Will, "then if he's supposed to be here, I'll get told off for bothering the physician when I ought to be able to decide things like this for myself. But if he's not supposed to be here, then I'll get blamed for letting him get this far when his name wasn't even on the list for today."

Jules laughed.

"I don't see you've got any choice," said Jules. "If you don't want to send him on through you can't just turn him loose on your own authority."

"Here," said Will, shoving the board with its paper at the other hooded figure. "How'd you like to do it?"

Jules turned and went off.

"Got to get back to my own job," his voice floated back as he went.

Will swore after him and turned. He went away from Bart and the other three, through the entrance to one of the farther rooms with operating tables, all but one of them occupied by the recumbent body of a Steed. Through that same entrance Bart could see him talking to another figure, white-gowned and hooded just as all the personnel here seemed to be, but with an air of deference that suggested the other was someone in authority—possibly one of the "physicians" Will had spoken of to Jules.

The discussion was being held beside the one empty operating table visible in any of the rooms. As it continued, the occupant of the other table in that particular room was helped to sit up. He stepped down onto his feet and one of the gowned figures led him away, walking a little unsteadily. First one and then another of the white-clad figures also in the room gathered together with Will and the one he was talking to, and the conversation became general.

Sight alone only allowed Bart to guess at how the conversation was going. But it was an almost certain guess that the conversation was about his name not being on the list, and this gave him hope.

After several minutes, Will returned with one of the gowned figures. The two stopped in front of Bart and the other gowned figure held up a small white cube Bart had not noticed he was carrying. Unexpectedly Bart's head was enveloped by a cloud of sickeningly sweet-smelling spray. He tried to hold his breath, but it was already too late.

Almost instantly, his mind seemed to blur. He felt vaguely uncomfortable but at the same time overpowered by a lassitude that made it too much trouble to concern himself about how he was feeling. He felt his hand taken by Will and without resistance let himself be led forward into the operating room with the two now-empty tables. He was led to the nearest one and ordered to climb up on it and lie down on his back.

He did so. Somewhere in the back of his mind was the feeling that there was something he should be saying to all these white-dressed people around him; but it was too much trouble to remember what that was. He was in a curious state, at once relaxed and at the same time apprehensive—of what he had no idea. But then there was an interruption. One more gowned figure, with what must be a very tall and thin man in the anonymous garment, shouldered his way into the crowd around the table upon which Bart lay.

"Take him back!" said the newcomer.

The words were spoken in the Latin of the Lordly class and the tones of the voice were the tones of ultimate authority. Bart was pulled off the table onto his feet, by Will, and led in his near dream-state off through a door he had not passed through before, into a room filled with fresh-smelling stacks of Steed trousers.

With the assistance of Will and another man apparently stationed in this room, he was gotten into trousers and shoes. They were just like the ones he had taken off, but apparently brand new. The help was needed, for whenever he was not in the process of obeying a direct order, his mind wandered off and he merely stood there. It ended with Will taking him back to the dormitory and making him lie down on his own bed. The other Steeds were not there.

"Now, you're to stay here," Will told him. "You understand? Say 'yes,' if you understand me!"

"Yes," said Bart.

"You'll begin to feel just like you always do in about half an hour," Will went on. "Until then, don't try to do anything, or go any place. I mean that! Don't move from here, no matter what happens. You have to piss, you piss in your bed. You understand me?"

"Yes," answered Bart, with great effort. It was hard to keep concentrating on what the other man was saying. "I stay here half an hour."

"That's right. Every time you start to think of getting up, remember you're supposed to stay here until you feel better. I'm going now, but you remember that. You'll remember?''

"I'll remember," said Bart.

He watched the cloaked and hooded figure of Will leave the dormitory. He lay there alone in the empty room, and a curiosity came to him to look at himself in a mirror and see if he looked any different, since he felt so different. Particularly he would like to see his face and eyes for some reason he could not pin down just at the moment. He was beginning to get up and go to the wall-wide mirror that was above the washstands in the latrine in the adjoining room when he remembered he was not supposed to leave his bed.

He lay back again.

He tried to think, but his mind would not track. It kept wandering off like the mind of someone just on the verge of sleep. And so, vaguely bemused at what had happened to him, but only vaguely, because the problem was too much for his mind to grapple with in its present state, he did indeed fall asleep.

He woke with a guilty start. But a look at the dormitory clock, large and round in the wall above the entrance door, showed that he had only been asleep two hours at most. Hastily, he got up, went to the latrine to splash cold water on his face, then hurried to the Library.

To his intense relief, no one seemed to have noticed that he had not been there earlier; and Pier was not using his office at the moment, so that Bart's small alcove was doubly private. Seated in his chair, there, before his small desk surface, he tried to make sense out of what had happened to him earlier.

The question of what the Clinic visits were really intended to accomplish could wait for the moment. Bart's guess was that they were in some way for the purpose of reinforcing the illusion that the slaves had died before being brought here and returned to life by the Lords. Perhaps also, the loyalty of the Steeds was reinforced at the same time, creating reasons in the false memories the Steed was given, so that he would feel that he had no choice but to live and die to protect the Lordly class—and in particular, its commanders.

But that was a question the answer to which he could track down later. The immediate mystery was why Bart's name had not been on that list and why he had been let go without the treatment the others had been given.

He had an odd feeling in the back of his head that he had been through something like this before. The memory would not crystallize in his mind, however. All that came back clearly when he tried to remember such a thing was the brief moment in which he had awakened to see Pier and the two others—whom he now recognized as having been the Regent and the Emperor—standing over him. Now that he had called the scene up again out of the warehouse of his memory, he was all but convinced that at that time, also, the surface he had been lying on had been a cloth-padded smooth tabletop like the one they had ordered him onto this morning.

Somehow, all these questions, like the answers to all the other questions that concerned him and the possibility of his escape with Emma, must eventually tie together. He had a feeling in his bones that this would be so—at that moment there came the sound of the door to the office opening. It had to be Pier, he thought; and he came to his feet and out of his alcove, so that he was respectfully standing in the alcove doorway when the door swung closed behind the Librarian.

"Ah, Bart, there you are!" the little old man said; and Bart thought there was a definite overtone of relief in the slightly scratchy voice.

The older man moved forward and deposited some papers on his own desk, then looked over at Bart once more. "How are you feeling?" he asked.

"Very well, Lord," Bart answered quietly; then he smiled. "But it was a close thing."

"So I understand," Pier said. "My apologies. Someone misunderstood his instructions. Do you know what almost happened?"

"I have an idea, Lord."

"I thought you might," Pier answered. "Someday I'll explain in detail, if you like. For now I must not."

"I understand, Lord," Bart said. "For the same reason you cannot explain some other things, as you said before."

Pier nodded, looked away, and moved to sit behind his desk, facing the door through which he had entered. He busied himself for a moment straightening the papers he had just put down on the desk, then looked back up at Bart.

"I didn't expect to see you here at all today, Bart," he said, "with Court scheduled for this afternoon. In fact, I half expected that by this time Chandt would have you all in formation and marching to the courtroom."

He spoke in French, the language generally reserved for use only under home surroundings, which gave the conversation an air of intimacy that was usually missing from the work place where all talk was in English. "You want to get back into your alcove, do you?"

"Not just at the moment, Lord," said Bart. "As you say, I'll have to get back to the dormitory quickly. But I had a request to make of you, if I might. I thought I'd come to the Library and see if you had time to let me speak to you."

"There will be times," said Pier, smiling benignly, "when affairs will keep me too concerned to give you time, but not often. What is it you wanted to request?"

"I was just going to ask, Lord—," said Bart. He tried to think back to the way Paolo had phrased it. "—is it permissible that I make acquaintances and meet with them privately as well as publicly?"

"Strange," said Pier thoughtfully. "I'd completely forgotten that I'd never specifically given you that privilege. Of course you can, Bart. There's only a couple of people who might object to my granting it to you—"

His face suddenly developed a stern look that Bart had never seen on it before. The kindly old Librarian was abruptly replaced by an individual of authority.

"—and I'm under no obligation to take their views into consideration in this case."

He smiled at Bart, and the stern look was gone.

"I assume you have someone in mind you wish to meet?" he asked.

There was no point in hiding the fact.

"Yes, Lord," answered Bart. "It's a female slave that I used to know in the upper world."

Pier's eyebrows raised slightly.

"Indeed," he said. "You know, it occurs to me, Bart, that you might come to my home tomorrow evening, after Marta and I have had dinner."

"I—I would be honored, Lord," said Bart; the invitation— albeit in the form of a command—was, as far as Bart had been given to understand, completely unprecedented to come from a Lord to one of his slaves; that much Bart had already learned about Inner World society.

"Do you know where this female slave works?" Pier asked.

"Somewhere in bookkeeping, I understand, Lord," said Bart. "I'm sorry I—"

"Never mind." Pier fished a piece of blank paper toward himself across the desk top and wrote on it with one of those pens used in the Inner World that carried its own supply of ink. "My Lordmark is on the paper, here, and I've just written a short note saying that I'd appreciate anyone in charge where the slave—what's her name?"

"Emma Robeson, Lord."

"Emma . . . the last name? Spell it for me."

Bart spelled it.

"Good," said Pier, finishing his penmanship. "I've written that— '. . . where the slave Emma Robeson is kept, that they give her over for the moment to the slave carrying this, who is my Steed; and under my authority as Librarian I order anyone so in charge of Emma Robeson to acquiesce and aid my Steed in anything he wishes to do with Emma Robeson. Which is by my command,' " wound up Pier.

He handed the note to Bart.

"Oh," said Pier, as Bart backed toward the door, "and you might bring this friend of yours along, too, so that Marta and I can get a look at her."

He smiled at Bart again—very nearly an impish smile.

"Yes, Lord. Thank you, Lord. It will be an honor for her, too," was all Bart could think of to say.

He went out, and the door to Pier's office closed behind him. His head was whirling. Among the thoughts jostling about it was that it might be of great use to the future plans of Emma and himself, if Pier and Marta took a liking to her. On the other hand, perhaps it was dangerous to draw her to the attention of any of the Lordly class, even ones as apparently kindly as Pier and Marta.

He had not failed to remember that concubines were a prerogative of both sexes of the Lordly class, and of Hybrids, as well—this Inner World seemed to have strong Near East social elements. If a Lord should look at Emma and want her for his own sexual use, there would be little Bart could do about it down here, even at the cost of his life.

On the other hand, as far as he knew, Pier and Marta were unusual among their fellow Lords and Lord Ladies for never having had any concubines; and his advanced age should suggest that the possibility of Pier's wanting Emma for himself was not too likely.

Then Bart remembered how briskly he had seen the old man move on occasion, and his fear of a possible personal interest by Pier in Emma rose again.

chapter
sixteen

BART WENT FORWARD enough in the stacks to see the large clock on the wall by the main desk of the Library. It showed only eleven minutes after eleven. Pier had been anticipating when he had imagined that Chandt would already be getting the Steeds into order for attendance at the Court—whatever sort of occasion it might be. Bart estimated that with a fourteen hundred hours— 2:00 P.M.—assembly time on the schedule, he had at least two hours of free time before he was due back at the dormitory, even leaving him time to make whatever changes in clothing were required.

He glanced at the open outer area of the Library. It was all but deserted. There was one Hybrid seated there, reading in one of the chairs, and within the circle of the desk sat Mordaunt and a single stack slave. Possibly because of this afternoon's affair, visitors to the Library seemed to be few; and that meant the stacks should be all but deserted.

It would be an ideal time for him to get his hands on a copy of the Book of al-Kebir again and finish reading it. Moreover, if the Court ran late, he would have no chance to finish reading it later in the day before he would be due to take Emma to the Guettrigs', where they should probably be by about 7:00 P.M., that being when his Lord and Lady usually finished their dinner. That lack of time would be crucial, since he had decided that this should be the night in which he tried the scheme that had been in his mind for some time, and which a full knowledge of the Book would help support him in the story which he hoped to make Pier and Marta believe.

He turned, went back through the stacks to the small room where the copies of the Book were shelved, and took one. As he had suspected, he saw no sign of anyone else in the stacks, in the process—not Lord, Hybrid or slave.

With the copy of the Book, he returned to Pier's office, on the chance that the Lord might already have left it. If Pier was to be at the Court, he would undoubtedly need to change robes and pick up Marta, in which case he might already have left, so as to get these things done and also have some time for lunch before they set out.

Bart's estimate was correct. The little light above the scratching panel on the door that signaled that Pier was within and whether he was available to visitors or not was dark. Taking from his tunic pocket the key Pier had given him, Bart unlocked the door, let himself in and relocked the door behind him. The automatic lighting had evidently been turned down, and only a dim nightlight burned in the room.

By this illumination he went to his own private alcove, turned on the working light there, and sat down, opening the book before him. The clean Latin script of the first page looked up at him, once again.

"O, Fratres mei—," it began.

"De origine et via qua adhunc mundum advenimus nihil dicabo . . ."

Automatically, his mind translated the words in Latin script before him into English.

"Of our origin and the means by which we came to this world, as well as the fate of many of us in the moment of our arrival, I will say nothing, lest the information turn out to be of use to those who should not know such things.

"Suffice it to say that a number of us were left scattered and helpless upon a part of this earth called Sicily, where we one and all fell into the hands of various local inhabitants of the lowest origin, brutish by nature and lacking in all but the simplest intelligence. Inhabitants, moreover, who were incapable of recognizing in us the superior beings we were, but instead took us under their control and treated each of us as if we were little better than the beasts they fed on or forced to work their fields, for without exception they were peasants of the lowest order. . . .

"But in time the superior intelligence of our people attracted the attention of those who were in authority over our peasant masters, and these—seeing value in us—took us for themselves; and this process was repeated in time by those who were in authority over these others; and so on, with our masters rising in rank until we all became slaves of natives of large power in the land.

"Of all of these, there was only one who was far more powerful than any of the rest, being no less than the ruler of an empire, known as the Holy Roman Empire, and reaching from the north of Europe

*to this island of Sicily. It was this island, however, that was the
favorite seat of this particular emperor, whose name was Frederick,
after the name of the Emperor his grandfather, who had been known
as Barbarossa by reason of his red beard. . . ."*

Bart read on, fascinated.

After this preamble, the writer had gone back to relate in greater
detail the atrocities committed upon his fellows by the humans they
had encountered, in greater detail. According to the writer, he had
been only seven years old when, with his parents and their traveling
companions, he had arrived on the soil of Sicily. In the breakup of
the group that followed, as one by one the adults were parcelled out
among the neighborhood natives, his mother's desparate desire to
keep him with her had impressed at least one of the locals. They
two were taken as a pair—his father had been killed by one of the
first few locals to come investigating them—as the narrator
believed they would all have been killed, if it had not been for one
peasant, somewhat more intelligent than the rest, who saw that live
slaves would be more valuable than dead bodies, and equally
harmless if kept apart from each other.

So he and his mother were taken, the writer went on, by a man
with no wife or family. A man who lived off among the rocks, who
clearly had chosen the writer's mother to be a servant who could
also serve a sexual purpose. For, that night, in the man's small,
windowless hut, with no light but that from the fire under a hole in
the thatch overhead, he dragged her into the hut's one small,
odiferous bed with him, shoving the boy away so hard he went
sprawling.

The boy's mother called out to him in their own language not to
make their new owner angry, but find someplace else to sleep.
Filled with fury toward the man, but, as always, obedient to his
mother, the boy had searched around the hut and finally raked
together a pile of rags to make himself a bed on the dirt floor. On
this, he fell asleep. Later on, when the fire had died down to
embers, so that the hut was barely lit, a cry of pain from his mother
woke him. He jumped to his feet and rushed over to where she and
the man lay, and tried to pull his mother out of the bed. The man
leaped up in a rage and seized him.

"*. . . I was strong,*" Bart read, "*as all our people are strong.
More than that, I had always been half again as powerful as any of
our own people who were my age and size. But still I was only seven;
and he was a large, grown man. Though I fought back ferociously,
he dragged me across the hut, opened the door, threw me out into*

the cold night, and closed the door again. When I tried to get back in, I found that he had barred the door from the inside. The night was chill and a strong wind blew icily about me. The only way I could avoid dying of the cold was to keep walking all night long. Once I realized that this was necessary, I faced the rest of the dark hours with determination. I would live at least until morning, if only to pay the man back for what he had done to my mother and myself. In that same instant I remembered all our people who were now virtual slaves of these creatures who called themselves humans; and the beginning of my hatred was born—a hatred that will in time see them all swept from the face of this earth of theirs.

"It is because of that hatred that I now write this letter to you whom I have helped into positions of safety and comfort; so that you will never forget what we owe these creatures; and so that you will build and cause your children to keep building toward the day when we can destroy them utterly.

"For to that end I have accumulated wealth and power, here at the court of the Sultan in Fez. It is for this reason that I have adopted their religion of the man named Mohammed; and learned to play at their way of life, so that they think me only interested in riches and luxuries.

"But it is for no such real reason that I have actually done what I have done. I shall teach you how to grow even wealthier and more powerful; how to band together and build, apart and hidden, a place of our own that humans do not know of. There, you will rediscover the skills and arts of our people and create a weapon that will end the human race. I have pledged myself to this, and now I pledge all of you, whether you will or not. In the absence of any other, and because by strength of mind and body I am best fitted to lead you, I have taken on myself the responsibilities of Commander of us all; and as Commander I order you, your children and your children's children, now and in the future, to do always as I shall tell you, in this letter and at later times.

"But to return to my own story, which you must learn by heart, for it is the source from which you will draw into yourselves that same strength of my hatred, to sustain you, when necessary . . ."

At this point the writer began, in Bart's opinion, to come as close as it was possible to foaming at the mouth in words written on paper.

". . . for I tell you that nothing has the power of a great hatred, particularly when that hatred has been justified over and over again. With a hatred such as mine you can move mountains, you can dry up

*the sea and cause the very earth to vanish in flame. And this is why
you must keep this letter of mine so that you may read and reread it;
and make sure your children do likewise . . ."*

Bart checked himself. Fascinated by the autobiography of this
strange individual, he had started to reread the Book completely,
once more from the beginning. But now an inner alarm warned him
time was passing. He leaned back in his chair and glanced outside
his alcove at the clock in the wall of Pier's office. It stood at seven
minutes past 1200 hours, seven minutes after 12:00 P.M. He had
probably another forty minutes to read safely if he wanted to have
adequate time to return the Book, get himself to the dormitory
and take care of any preparations that would be needed for the
Court formation.

He turned hastily back to the pages, skimming forward through
those he had already read, which continued to detail the need for
hatred of the humans; then settled down to a regular reading of
what was left. He finished the book with four minutes to go of his
self-allotted time. A number of blank pages had been bound into
the end of it, and this had made it possible for him to finish his
task quicker even than he had expected.

He rose, turned out his light and left. After putting the copy
back on its shelf, he headed toward the dormitory, his head full of
the Book and its meanings. They were not easy to extract, those
meanings, for what he had just finished reading was almost as full
of wild stories as Gallard's translation of the *Thousand and One
Nights*.

Whatever else al-Kebir had been, he had been a stupendous
egotist and capable of the most outrageous exaggerations and lies.
The difficulty was that he was also clearly almost as intelligent and
capable as he claimed to be. Certainly, some of the things he
reported himself as doing or experiencing could not be true; but
some, at least, of them must have been fact, or else the present day
Inner World surrounding Bart could not exist, let alone remain
dedicated to this man's furious idea of a revenge against the whole
human race.

Al-Kebir's mother had soon died under the rigors of the life
forced on them by the ignorant brute that was their master, who was
apparently part owner of a small herd of goats and part anything
else at all that might gain him money or goods. Shortly thereafter,
al-Kebir was taken from this man by another of superior standing in
the area; and so began a succession of changes through the hands of
a number of owners, each of them better off, or more powerful,

than the previous; until at last he who was to become al-Kebir—but was at this time known by the name of Bebe, with which his first owner had christened him—ended up in the hands of the ruler of the island of Sicily.

Of this ruler, Bebe at first had hopes.

". . . *though,*" he wrote in his book at this point, "*even for a human, in body he was ugly and useless-appearing. He was short, as these gangling humans go. He was also fat, even for the young man he was when I first made his acquaintance, and already beginning to lose his hair. His eyes were green and apparently frightening to other humans—I, myself, merely found them to reinforce his general ill-favored appearance.*

"*But even before I met him in person I had heard of his wisdom and seeking mind; and I had some expectation consequently of at last finding a human who would realize the naturally superior endowments of our great race and in particular my own remarkable superiority even in that context.*

"*Alas, he turned out to be only partly what I had hoped. It was true he had a good mind—for a human. It was also true that he had a truly scientific curiosity and the boldness to attempt to satisfy it. Even before I met him, I had heard of experiments he had conducted to discover more about how the body, mind, and that thing humans call 'soul,' function.*

"*During the time I was his slave and his servant, for example, he conducted an experiment in which he fed two prisoners a large, identical meal and sent one to sleep, the other upon an arduous hunt. Afterwards, he had both men killed and cut open to find out which had done the best job of digesting the meal each had eaten. It was, of course, as I had already deduced, the one who had slept.*

"*But he also had the intelligent idea of sealing a man in a large keg which was already placed upon a set of scales so that it could be weighed with the man in it. The man, of course, soon suffocated. Having died, it was to be presumed that he had now lost his living soul, which would have taken flight from his body; and this master of mine was eager to obtain proof of the weight of that soul, about which so many of these humans talk.*

"*But, again, as I might have told him, there was no change in the weight indicated on the scales at all, which went a good ways toward proving that such a thing as a 'soul' had no existence in reality. I could go on, listing many such experiments that he made, but there is no point in wasting paper further. There was only one of his experiments that was of importance to you and me, O my brothers—*

and of that, more later.

"*It is important, however, that you all understand what sort of human he was. He was gifted with intelligence, high intelligence as his race knew it; but aside from this he was like a naive child, merely tinkering with the world around him in whatever direction his current fancy took him. I had hoped that, since he had such a mind, I might at last have found a human who would listen to me and understand the great gift that had been given him by having such as me dropped in his lap, as it were.*

"*But this was not to be—and the fault was in his basic character. That he was lecherous and gluttonous to a remarkable degree was beside the point. He was not self-indulgent in matters requiring work and application; but he was blinded by his own conceit. He was of royal extraction, but he had grown up poor and disregarded, running loose on the waterfront of Palermo, Sicily's main port. This situation continued until a series of inheritances brought him, first, the Kingship of Sicily, then ultimately the authority of Emperor over the Holy Roman Empire, that at this time consisted of Germany and much of Europe.*

"*As Emperor, he challenged the Pope of the Christian Church, in Rome, and showed his indifference to the Pope's excommunicating him by going on a Crusade and concluding a treaty with the Saracen leader, Sultan al-Kamil; under which there was proclaimed a ten-year truce, ceding Bethlehem, Jerusalem, and Nazareth to the Christians, along with a corridor from Jerusalem to the sea, while giving the Moslems full rights to keep their homes and mosques in Jerusalem.*

"*This was the more remarkable in that he had done all this without a single battle. The Pope was furious at such a bloodless achievement of what past Crusades had fought and died for. But there was little he could do about it; and after a time he had no real choice but to revoke the excommunication.*

"*All this I relate was to this man's credit, as proof of a mind with which I might have done much. But it added up to nothing and less than nothing because of the man's character. He was completely self-centered, believing no one in the universe could be so wise and discerning as himself; and, when he encountered my own superior intellect, he simply refused to acknowledge it and treated me like nothing more than a clever beast, who was perhaps of some use with accounts and planning, but was essentially little more than a funny human animal to be entertained by, laughed at, and lent out to other sovereigns from whom he wished something in return. It is hard to believe that a greater egotist ever existed."*

That description, Bart thought to himself now as he hurried to the dormitory, might as well have pictured Bebe himself as well as the Emperor. The man Bebe had been writing about was Frederick II, the grandson of Holy Roman Emperor Frederick I, otherwise known as Barbarrosa—"Redbeard"—and had made six expeditions into Italy in his lifetime, in an attempt to dominate the Italian peninsula.

Frederick Roger—Frederick II—himself, Bart had discovered from other books in the Library—was indeed a remarkable, if not a particularly lovable, person. He dug deeply into mathematics and science, entertaining himself with people like Michael Scot, the scientist-adventurer-philosopher-astrologer and dabbler in magic. Frederick was fascinated by questions such as the ones behind the experiments Bebe had recounted; and with others such as whether children raised without ever hearing human speech would speak naturally the tongue that was spoken by Adam and Eve in Eden.

He also concerned himself with questions as to why a stick pushed into the water appeared to have its section below the water bent at an angle with the part above. He wrote a book on falconry, and ornithology in general. He founded the University of Naples; and himself spoke a number of languages, including Arabic. Like his grandfather Barbarrosa, he spent his lifetime fighting the papal establishment with the hope of uniting Italy and creating an actual, unitary, functioning, Holy Roman Empire stretching from Sicily to the Baltic.

In the meantime, he provided the base on which Bebe built his own heights of wealth and power and united those like him in what was to end in this Inner World.

". . . *Of all of Frederick's experiments, the most detestable,"* Bart read, *"was a farm or nursery which Frederick set up in order to breed human curiosities. As he considered me to be one of these I was forced to leave his court from time to time to attempt to breed with distorted specimens of the humanity on this farm of his, in the hope of producing even more grotesque individuals. Such was his influence and power that he had gathered together individuals of that classification from all over Europe and North Africa, as another man might collect women or jewels.*

"You cannot imagine how repugnant it was for me to interact sexually with the sort of hideous females that were assembled there and continually added to. But, at the same time, unknown to Frederick, a great end was served by sending me there. For it was

*there I met those of our people who had also managed to survive.
They consisted of only six Ladies and twenty-three Lords; but they
were now where I could keep an eye on them, provide means to make
their life easier—secretly and whenever possible—and continue to
maintain my knowledge of their whereabouts when they were given
or lent by Frederick to other rulers and like individuals. . . .''*

There was clearly, and no one ever denied it, thought Bart now
as he hurried toward the dormitory, a very practical side to
Frederick. He kept the most interesting of the ''Naturals,'' as those
like Bebe were called—Bart almost paused, but then resumed his
movement toward his dormitory; he had just realized that at no time
in his book did Bebe—al-Kebir—say just what exactly it was about
himself that put him in the category of the kind of freaks that
Frederick was interested in.

True, the man was obviously very short; but that did not seem to
be the whole story. There must, Bart thought, have been some
other—and severe—abnormality about him; something unsightly
enough to excite the admiration and envy of the world, including
visitors of note. Whatever it might have been, Frederick had made
good use of it, and in effect created a market for such human
oddities—which he then offered to satisfy with the products of his
freak farm, giving away or selling the less promising children of the
sexual unions he had forced there and those adult members who
had failed to prove interesting, either because of natural disabilities
or because they had not proved of value as breeders.

To those of sufficient importance to be supplied with something
better than a baby human grotesque, Frederick balked at selling or
giving, but was occasionally willing to lend for a short term some
of those on display at his court. In this way, Bebe found himself
several times lent out to other masters, with most of whom he did
well by adapting himself to their personal tastes. There was one,
however, he was unable to satisfy and hated above all others; so that
a good twenty pages of his book was filled with anecdotes and
diatribes against that individual. This was a Sir Hubert de Gar, a
German knight and lay-member (as all the knights were of that
order) in the Knights Templar.

According to Bebe's account, he had been lent to such an
insignificant individual because Frederick had some tortuous de-
signs that involved intrigue with the Mongols, who were just then
beginning to invade Europe; and he needed a spy on the activities of
the martial religious orders—and particularly the Knights Templar
—who were the only organization fit and ready to be the spearhead

of Christianity's defense against them.

Intelligent and educated for his time, Frederick had been, Bart thought; but like the Europeans of his day in general, he had obviously vastly underestimated the superiority of the Mongol armies over anything Europe would be able to put in their way. If it had not been for the death of Genghis Khan himself, which caused the recall of all the generals of his blood to choose a successor to lead them, Europe—and Sicily along with it—would almost undoubtedly have fallen to the Mongols.

The day came, however, when lending out Bebe for brief periods was no longer equal to the situation that had arisen. Finally, and perhaps even with some slight sense of relief, since Bebe, if useful, could probably be wearing on the nerves, Frederick made an outright gift of him to the Sultan in Fez, whose kingdom lay to the west, inland along the North African coast of the Mediterranean.

It was the sort of move Bebe was looking for. The year in the Christian calendar was twelve hundred and forty-six and Frederick was beginning to show his age. Bebe had already prospered as a slave of Frederick's. Under Moslem law he had rights, even as a slave, to accumulate property and gain power. He did so; and, when the time was appropriate, adopted the Moslem religion, with the Dey's drunken consent, one night when the ruler was celebrating. As a Moslem he could no longer be held as a slave by a fellow Moslem. Therefore he was now able to free himself and improve his position even more.

He grew wealthy; and, as slowly and quietly as possible, he began to buy, steal, or otherwise free the other members of those he called his own race; and establish them in positions where they could in turn gain wealth and power.

He also drew a blueprint for their future actions, and the actions of the generations that should follow them. The last third of the book was given almost entirely to this.

He told them that they must build toward the construction of an Inner Kingdom, secret and hidden from the rest of the world. To do this, they must learn everything new that humans were discovering and strive to get ahead of them in studies of their own. They must strive to raise children—full-blooded if possible, but half-breeds from their unions with humans, if nothing else was possible. In any case, whatever children were produced in each generation must be trained almost from the cradle and severely tested, at age eleven and again at age seventeen; and those who did not, on being tested, show evidence of unusual mental abilities should be destroyed.

Those who survived must mate with each other and with humans of the highest possible intelligence. Lords and Ladies of the true race should in turn mate with the half-breed progeny of other Lordly individuals, those who showed promise. So that in every way a community should be produced of unusually brilliant individuals who would work toward knowledge beyond that of the humans. From that knowledge they would then derive a means to destroy the humans and their world, in payment for the cruel treatment the true race had received from them—

Bart's mind left the subject of the Book of al-Kebir with a jolt, as he finally stepped through the door of the dormitory, on reaching it. The clock on the wall within read still twenty-eight minutes before the hour at which the Court formation had been set. But the dormitory was deserted. On one bed, only—his own—lay a scarlet tunic and a pair of scarlet sandals.

chapter
seventeen

DRESSED IN SCARLET and out of breath, Bart plunged through the wide open, huge double doors of the Court Room and checked to a panting halt just a few steps short of Chandt, who was standing with his back to the entrance, talking to the dormitory Leaders, Paolo among them. Catching Bart's eye behind Chandt's back, as the Master of the Steeds slowly turned around at the sound of Bart's sandals on the polished floor behind, Paolo made a grimace of warning.

Beyond Chandt and the Leaders, the Steeds of all the dormitories were lined up in formation. The clock on the soaring ivory-colored wall to Bart's right read two minutes to the appointed formation time of fourteen hundred hours. Bart gulped for breath. He had literally run most of the way after finding the main gym of the Steeds empty. A grinning janitorial slave there had told him how the rest had marched out of the gym fifteen minutes before to go to the Court Room—and had given Bart directions on how to find it.

Now he gulped air so as to speak before Chandt could.

"I was held up on an errand for my Lord—," he began.

"I gave him permission. To come as soon as he could," said the growling voice of Paolo. Paolo had come forward out of the group of other Leaders and now stepped level with Chandt, who turned his gaze on Bart's immediate superior.

The two pairs of eyes, the Master's and the Leader's, locked on each other. Both sets of eyes were dark, but Chandt's were mountain pebbles in shadow, while Paolo's held in their black depths a sullen fire. Chandt said nothing and the two men continued to look at and into each other.

"Very well," said Chandt finally, without removing his gaze from Paolo's, "put him in ranks."

Paolo was forced to look away at Bart, and the moment was ended.

"Into your place, damn you!" he said.

Bart went hastily to the lineup of men from his own dormitory, while Chandt and Paolo once more rejoined the other dormitory Leaders and Chandt began speaking quietly to them all again, as if there had never been those seconds of confrontation between himself and Paolo.

Bart had expected under-the-breath gibes from the Steeds around him as he pushed himself into his usual place in the formation. But this time those he joined looked stiffly ahead, ignoring him and each other, not moving—on the best behavior he had seen among them since he had first waked up as one of them.

Left with a minute in which to catch his breath, Bart for the first time took a look at his Court Room to which they had all been summoned.

It was a high-ceilinged, expansive chamber, with false windows having cathedral tops. These were carved into the ivory-colored material of the upreaching walls on all four sides of the room; and what would have been their openings on an outside surface world were filled with paintings of the kind of gardens found in tropical or semi-tropical latitudes. Curtains of sky blue, reaching to the ceiling, were tied back in graceful folds at each side of each of these windows.

This much about the room was pleasant enough. But the ceiling overhead was carved into gargoyles and death's-heads; and at the far end of the room was a dais raised off the floor and covered, top and sides, with glaringly scarlet cloth of the same color as the tunics the Steeds were now wearing. On this sat three high-backed chairs of dark wood, like thrones. They were carved all over and their armrests ended in lion's heads. Half a dozen feet in front of them stood something that was a sort of mixture of pulpit and lectern with a platform on which a speaker's notes might rest, at a convenient reading height for one of the Lordly class.

But now, as Bart watched, Chandt finished speaking to the dormitory Leaders. They went back to the heads of the formations and Chandt moved over to stand facing all the waiting men. He was dressed in what would have seemed a slave's simple, short tunic if it had not been made of glittering, gold cloth, trimmed with black fur around the edges of the skirt and armholes; and he waited with an almost ominous patience until the Leaders were back in position. When, at last, all was still and silent in the room he spoke.

"All right!" he said. He faced them all, legs spread apart, hands locked together behind him. The muscles stood out on his brown arms. Under the remarkable acoustics of the room, he did not seem to raise his voice, but it came strongly and clearly to the ears of all of them.

"Listen to me now, all of you; and listen closely! There will be no mistakes by any one of you today. None. You will all do what I'm now going to tell you to do, nothing more, nothing less.

"You understand?"

Apparently, Bart concluded, there was no answer expected to this; for no one among the Steeds made any.

"Shortly," went on Chandt, "this room—" His extended arm swept right and left at shoulder height before him, to indicate its expanse. "—will be filled with Lords and Ladies. Later on, for a short while, a few Hybrids will be allowed in, but that's unimportant. As far as you're concerned, there will be only Lords and Ladies here. Understand me? Answer me!"

This time, everybody around Bart muttered "yes," so Bart muttered along with them.

"Those of you who've never been to a Court before are going to see the Lords—not the Ladies and the Lords, but the Lords alone—doing some things that may seem strange to you. Remember, no matter what they do, you're not to show you're seeing anything out of the ordinary. You'll be given small whips. If a Lord comes within reasonable reach of you, swing your whip at him. I don't have to tell anyone here, I think—"

Chandt's eyes raked back and forth across the mass of them.

"—not to let the lash of the whip actually touch a Lord, unless you've been actually told or signaled by a Lord to do that. Even then, remember it should be as light a touch as possible. Some of you may find yourselves faced by Lords who want you to strike them harder than that. In that case, I leave the matter up to your judgment, how hard the Lord actually wishes you to hit him; and you'd better pray your judgment is right."

He paused. "Now, the slaves will pass out the whips and you'll spread yourself around the walls of this room as if you were soldiers standing on guard—ceremonial guard at a Court. Dormitory Leaders, place your Steeds!''

Bart found himself positioned beside a blue curtain flanking one of the false windows. He felt ridiculous with the small, toylike whip that a slave placed in his hand; and the began to feel more ridiculous as the room began to fill with members of the Lordly class. But the embarrassment he felt was lost in wonder at what he saw. The Lord Ladies were dressed in ornate, frilly gowns, their faces painted—no, overpainted was the only proper word for the makeup they wore. The Lords, on the other hand, were either in rags or wore clothing that was expensive but cut to grotesquely exaggerate their shortness of body and limbs. Some had artificial hunchbacks built into their garb, or other deformities created in them by padding in their clothing.

About twenty minutes or so after the room had started to fill with these members of the Lordly class, there was a final arrival. Three figures wearing identical, floor-length black gowns, but with differing, heavy neckchains in which cloth, gold, silver and jewels were all wound together, swept into the room. One of them was Pier. The other two were the Emperor and the Regent.

They walked together rapidly to the dais, ignoring all of those around them. Moving almost in unison, they mounted the dais. Each took off his neckchain and laid it on the seat of one of the chairs. Then they returned to the edge of the dais, stepped down, and moved apart, out among the crowd on the main floor of the room.

Immediately, things began to happen. The small men and women who had been scattered thickly about the floor of the room, talking with each other, split into two groups. The Ladies went to and mounted the dais, looking out over the room. The Lords themselves became active. They began to—*cavort*, was the only word that Bart could feel literally fitted their actions.

It was as if they had all become clowns and tumblers. They pretended to knock each other down; and the one knocked down flipped end-over-end backward as if he had been struck by a giant's blow. They leap-frogged over each other and walked about on their hands. A small group made a living pyramid, four individuals on the bottom, three standing on their shoulders, and one on the shoulders of these. A bronze tray, a gracefully long-necked glass container with what looked like red wine in it, and three wine glasses, were handed up to the man on top. He arranged the vessels on the tray, filled the glasses from the container, then did a flip off the pyramid downward to the floor, landing with the vessels in place and the wine, even in the open glasses, unspilled.

There were none of the Lords there, old or young, who did not busy themselves with some contortion or exercise; and the Ladies up on the dais pointed and giggled, some of them waving fans they had produced from pockets in their gowns.

The whole scene would have been utterly ridiculous if it had not been for the actual, remarkable physical skill with which all of the Lords performed, which lent an air of grim purpose to the whole procedure. Acts such as Bart saw being performed now were not done, he knew, so skillfully and correctly without long and arduous training. The very perfection of them pointed to a higher purpose than a simple showing off by the performers.

The Steeds about the room flourished their little whips in the air at any Lord who came close to them, the lashes whistling through the air at a safe distance from the potential target—except in a few rare cases, when the Lord in question moved in close and evidently gave some order. Even then, the Steed with the whip seemed careful to strike very lightly indeed.

But there were some rare exceptions, who evidently wanted the real thing. One of these was the Emperor, who stopped, not once, but several times in front of Steeds—and in each instance, Bart noticed two things. One was that the Steeds he stopped in front of were older than the average, which might have indicated that they had complied at earlier Courts with the Emperor's desires. The second was that, far from holding back, they were striking with as much force as they could produce without moving their body from its position.

Bart was puzzling over this and continuing to follow the Emperor with his gaze—as were a great many in the room—when the sight of another Lord drew Bart's attention away. The one he had just caught sight of was Pier; and, to his astonishment, the aged Librarian had just done two back-somersaults in midair; a very good trick for a much younger man.

Too good. Bart was still astonished not merely at the skill these members of the Lordly class were all showing, but the actual physical strength many of them were revealing, when the maneuvers they executed obviously required more than ordinary power of leg, arm, or body. These people might be small, but they were also deceptively strong, for all that they did not ordinarily let that fact show in everyday life.

But at the moment he was not concerned with this. His attention was all following Pier. The Librarian had walked away from his two somersaults with brisk and competent steps, as if removing himself for others' way by moving to the wall. But now that he had finished his demonstration, Bart noticed that when the old man reached the wall he leaned against it with one shoulder. It could be merely a casual pose; but if so, it was one much more suited to a younger man. Bart suspected that the two violent physical executions had taken more out of Pier than Pier wished to have known. Pier was clear across the wide room from him, too far for Bart to make out such a small detail, but Bart could almost believe he could see Pier's chest heaving under his robe.

A sudden, powerful impulse stirred in Bart, to go to the old man; but leaving the place where he had been stationed was clearly impossible. He could only hope that Pier had known what he was doing; and that his body was able to stand the strain he had just put on it.

Bart woke suddenly to the fact that he might be staring too openly at Pier. His fixed concentration of gaze could bring attention on the Librarian that the old man might not want. A Steed was supposed to be concentrating on waving his whip at any of the Lords who came close enough. He brought his awareness back to that part of the room directly in front of him; and, as he did, he realized something that he was suddenly angry with himself for not noticing earlier.

Alone among the Steeds around the room, he had not had a single Lord come close enough to him to invite even the pretense of his using his whip.

It could be sheer chance, of course; but Bart had learned to distrust chance as a reason. However, if it was not chance that had caused him to be left alone this way—he could think of no possible other cause. It was preposterous to suppose that all the Lords, from the Emperor on down, had gotten together and agreed to avoid him. Even if he could entertain such a wild possibility, what would the reason for such avoidance be? No, it had to be chance.

Luckily, he did not have to worry about this at any length, because already the actions on the floor were coming to a close; and very shortly there were no Lords who were doing anything but standing, as if waiting. They had all turned toward the dais; and the Ladies were now descending from it.

As soon as it was clear, Pier, the Emperor and the Regent mounted the large half-disk of scarlet space.

Solemnly, they picked up and put on their neckchains; then turned and seated themselves each in one of the chairs, the Emperor in the middle with Pier on his right hand, the Regent on his left. They stared at the crowd on the floor before them with expressionless faces.

"Come closer!"

The voice of the Emperor echoed through the silence of the room. The Lords and Ladies crowded together, close to the dais. The emotional tension in the room had been growing steadily all through the Lords' performances, even among the ring of Steeds surrounding, for all that they could not understand the shouts and comments in Latin. Now it sang even higher around them. It seemed to Bart they were all enclosed by a feeling like that of people locked in some small place and knowing that an explosion there was imminent.

The smell of male sweat was thick in the room.

chapter
eighteen

WHEN THEY WERE all as close as they could get, the Emperor abruptly stood up.

"Look!" he said, speaking in Latin.

He turned his back on the audience. Pier and the Regent rose also. Each seized a handful of cloth at the side of the Emperor's robe and pulled. The back of the robe split down the middle as they pulled it apart, revealing the Emperor's surprisingly muscled, naked back. A small mutter ran through the crowd; and even Bart felt the emotional reaction that moved them. The little whips might be toylike in appearance; but they were evidently effective enough when used seriously. The red lines of lash-marks could be clearly seen, crisscrossing the exposed back.

The Emperor stood for a moment, then turned again to face them. Pier and the Regent had already reseated themselves; and now the Emperor did so as well. His eyes glared at the audience.

"You see!" he said. "This—this and worse—our forefathers endured daily at the hands of those animals that call themselves humans! What you all have just done for a little while, a few moments since, they did daily, and all day long; making a show and parody of themselves in order to stay alive and in the good graces of these humans!"

The last word came out with such fury, saliva flew from the corners of his mouth. He was up on his feet again, suddenly; and he came forward in two long strides, half the way from his chair to the front edge of the dais.

"This," he said, "this fool-playing and pain might still be your lot if it had not been for those who went before us; and particularly Him, He who spent his life freeing Himself and others, setting us all on the only conceivable path that honor allows us—the pathway to power and revenge. That is why, at times chosen by your Emperor, we relive what was once our lot—in remembrance of him. What was his name? Tell me!" He paused.

"Al-Kebir!" said the crowd.

"Again!" he commanded.

"Al-Kebir!"

The crowd shouted the name, this time, back at him.

"Al-Kebir!"

"Again!"

The crowd roared.

A quiver ran down Bart's spine. He glanced at the Steed to his right and saw the man, from some other dormitory, standing rigid. There were large, circular dark areas on the cloth of his tunic under his armpits. He looked left at a Steed from his own dormitory, and that man was also rigid, and also showing large circles of dampness under his arms. They, he, all of them, Lords and Steeds alike, were caught up in the emotion of the moment and the Emperor's oratory.

"He cut our bonds and shackles from our limbs," the Emperor went on now. "He, and He alone, first of all, gathered the seeds of the wealth we have grown and tended to its present fruit, that bears His name, the weapon that will end the days of this race that calls itself human. My brothers and sisters—we, His children, have done as He commanded; and all has come to us in time, as He predicted; and that time is now. *Now!*"

The crowd roared again, and this time it kept roaring for some moments. He waited until the last sound had died away, and then he spoke again, once more in ordinary, almost gentle tones, as if he reasoned with children.

"I know," he said, "there have been times when some of you've doubted. I know that faintness of heart that can come over you when you think of what will be, what we shall all need to do. I know because I've felt it myself. I don't blame you for it. I don't even blame myself. We—none of us—are forged of that immortal metal which was in al-Kebir. It's natural for us to wonder at times and hesitate, after six centuries, facing the final result of what's been that long in the building."

He paused and deliberately ran his gaze back and forth over all of those standing bunched together below the dais.

"We all have weakness," he went on, "and from some one of those weaknesses, into the back of our minds, occasionally the thought will come . . . *why?* Why? We already own this world. We pull the strings of wealth and power, and nations move as we wish. Subtly and invisibly, we move them. So why don't we simply come forward and claim what's already ours, and enjoy what an undestroyed world and its full native race for our servants can provide?"

He stopped speaking. This time the pause was a long one. When he spoke again, a faint, hard edge had crept into his voice.

"I'll remind you all why," he said. "There are two reasons, as al-Kebir warned us. One is that while we may control nations, and societies, and even groups—we can never be completely sure of controlling individuals. And there are, even after these thirty generations, only the few thousand of us to control the millions of individuals who go on two legs as we do, but call themselves human. Only after their numbers have been reduced to a helpless handful from what they are now, is it going to be safe for us to openly take control of those who're left. Those who've survived our just wrath and our revenge—al-Kebir's revenge!"

The crowd shouted, but less loudly than it had a couple of times so far.

"So we have to take the slow but certain pace such a massive undertaking needs," he went on. "Soon now, we'll take the first, irreversible step, from the consequences of which there'll be no turning back. That first step of activating the device developed here in the Inner World from the work of Morton Cadiz, over a hundred years ago. That weapon with al-Kebir's spirit in it, that we call by His name.

"Soon now, we'll be setting that great creation to its work, generating the first of the electromagnetic power input into the magma below us, on which float the tectonic plates which bear the surface of this world. Slowly, reinforcing itself, the buildup of that continuous power input during the next eighty to a hundred and twenty years will finally produce wavelike tensions within the magma. Tensions that will eventually destroy the always fragile balance that presently exists in the plates. Those forces will build to the point where eventually the thin shell of this planet can contain them no longer. It will begin to crack and let through the forces held within. With the first breakup of the plates, the balance of inner forces will begin their shifting, increasing the rising and falling of the great plates themselves, as the edges of each of them slide up and over or under the plate adjoining."

The Emperor paused.

"You all know this," he said. "But now the time has come to begin it."

He looked at them and smiled.

"Up until now, the moment of starting that great engine we call by the great name of al-Kebir, our private doubts and wonderings have been tolerated; as were the private doubts and wonderings of those generations who stood between Him and those of us in this room now. But from the moment of starting the engine that is He, there'll be no more room for anything but a wholehearted devotion to the end we will then have made inevitable."

He smiled again, and, turning, began to pace back and forth before them on the stage, stopping after a moment once more at the lectern. With no smile at all.

"*He* did His part!" the Emperor cried out suddenly, "long ago! Now the time's come for us to do ours! It's time to unleash what we have chosen to call by His name. Unleash it, so it can do its part in the century to come. And there's still much for us to do. We must make sure that what past generations of our people have worked for succeeds. If al-Kebir, the machine, is to set the plates in action at the moment of its starting, the resultant drowning of continents, and uplifting of seabeds, the volcanoes and the killing weather— even all of these—will be well enough, but not alone enough to produce the ends we want.

"You know why? All of you know why. But, once again your silence asks me to say it again, even though all of you already know the answer. The answer is that the world is still too full of self-reliant societies and individuals. Close to us, on the surface surrounding the entrance to this Inner World, are people who can too easily live off the land about them and endure hardship. There are too many like them, from the vast areas of Asia, Africa and South America, to say nothing of those I mentioned above us here.

"Before the time of cataclysm comes, that self-reliance must be drained out of them. As we preserved our strength for six hundred years, so they must lose theirs in the next hundred and twenty years; and we have the means to make them do it."

He paused.

"Wealth," he said, holding up two fingers, "wealth and science—but most of all science! We must prepare the fruit for picking. We must crowd them into cities, soften them with the luxuries science makes possible.

"Then, all will be ready; and the moment will come, the hour will strike! Somewhere, at one of the vulnerable points that have been stable for millions of years, a plate will rupture; and its two new halves be forced apart by the upwelling of the hot, inner material from below. Then the disorder will begin to spread as massive tectonic forces are subtracted from or added to—not just in the area of a few hundred square miles, but all around the world.

"The sea will rush northward from the present Gulf of Mexico as far as Nebraska. To our north—but safely away from our Inner World, here, the volcanoes will explode upward through the Alaskan ice and snowfields. The lower east and west coasts of this continent will be drowned in the sea, as will England, as will Japan. Volcanic ash will darken the sky. Tornadic winds will blow. The world of humans will be destroyed.

"But that destruction must strike a humanity changed from the one we know even now. By the time al-Kebir bears fruit, much of the human race must be gathered together in millions by their own desires, like beasts penned for the slaughter, in great cities where the light, the heat, the food, all such things are brought from great distances—even from other continents.

"Suddenly, then, with the cataclysm, those things will no longer be available. The land and the atmosphere will have destroyed the two great carriers on which the present and future depend—the railways and the steamships. In their millions the humans will die of starvation and disease, those that have survived the land-shocks and the in-flooding seas and the hurricanes.

"Then, finally, they will be ripe for harvesting by our armies, which now exist in embryo throughout the world. These come from tribes and small ethnic groups which we have cultivated through intermediaries. Once al-Kebir has been set to work we will begin the building of the great city-traps, using the bait of what science can offer those who come to live in them. At the same time, we will start the building of a military tradition in our proto-armies, furnishing them with weapons and money, raising in them the dream of conquest and power and loot. In every way we will prepare them for the time of conquest, when we, ourselves will officer them."

He smiled, almost wildly it seemed to Bart, at the crowd.

"We will lead them, armed and prepared, to swoop down on the humans that are left after the catastrophe, and enslave them. And this will be done until the whole world is in our control; and then, except for a necessary handful of the most faithful of them—with their job done, these soldiers of ours will begin to die. They will die quietly, and individually, of the slowly accumulating poison we will have been mixing with their food over a long period of time. For in spite of their service for us they share the guilt toward us that is in all humans, by the very fact of their humanity. In the end, we alone will be left with a few cowed human creatures at our feet."

He drew a deep breath and opened his arms wide as if, symbolically, he would embrace the whole crowd beyond the dais.

"So, my brothers and sisters," he said, on one great exhalation of breath, "we will come at last to the time of our revenge—that holy duty placed upon us by Him of whom I have been speaking. He has written it down for us to read and learn—'. . . *as we have learned to hate them, they must learn to hate us. They must taste that hate in their mouths, and know their helplessness to do anything about it, as we have learned to do something about our hate. For as many centuries as we have waited for revenge, they must wait. Then, when the period of their penance has been covered, we will be free at last to build the ships that will take us homeward, leaving not one of them behind alive.*'"

He stopped, dropping his hands to his sides.

"And so," he said, "the will of Him, of al-Kebir, which is our will, will finally be accomplished."

He stepped back and sat down again in his chair between Pier and the Regent. It was curious, thought Bart. This was a time for applause, when a speech had at last ended. In the world above there would certainly have been applause; if only polite applause, or applause from a few in the audience.

But here there was no such thing. Instead, from the crowd before the dais there was something that was like a sigh—as of tension released, as of a difficult job done. It seemed to him that he saw a relaxation in the grotesquely costumed figures who turned now to each other, spreading out a little as a group.

"And now," said the Emperor, both his forearms laid out along the arms of his chair, his sinewy hands laxly enclosing the lions' heads at their ends, "we let in the champions among our nephews, to show us what they can do."

The crowd began to draw back to the walls, leaving the wide center area of the room open. Apparently some signal had been given which Bart had not seen; for the space had barely been created when four men ran in, wearing black trousers and white shirts, ruffled and open at the neck. Bart recognized only one of them, the brilliantly blue-eyed Hybrid he had encountered at the Library. This man was by far the largest of the four, the three with him being between five feet and five feet four inches in height. As a result, the other stood out from the rest of them like a giant, though he was certainly no taller than Bart, and perhaps slightly shorter. Also, because he was wearing a shirt without a jacket, Bart could see that the unusual width of the blue-eyed man's shoulders was natural and not a product of his tailor's art.

The four reached the center of the open space, formed a line, and bowed to those on the dais.

The Emperor waved a hand.

The Hybrid on the far right end of the line, as they faced the dais, bowed again. The other three withdrew to the same side of the room on which Bart stood, but a dozen yards farther up toward the dais. Meanwhile, the one who remained in the middle of the floor—he was a short, physically trim man in his early twenties and with straight brown hair worn at shoulder length—had turned about.

Without further warning, he launched himself in a series of flips down the room away from the dais until he had almost reached the doorway by which he and the other three had entered.

Then, equally without warning, he began a series of back-flips that brought him back to his original position before the dais, except that on the last flip he twisted his body about in midair and landed lightly on his feet, facing the dais.

Again, oddly to Bart's ears, there was no applause, only the sigh of breath among the audience. The man who had done the flips bowed once more to the dais and went to the side of the room, from which the man who had stood next to him advanced to the room's center.

This Hybrid launched himself into the air and made a double-somersault before landing once more on his feet. He stood a moment, his chest expanding rythmically and widely, then launched himself upward once more in a spring. This time he made two somersaults—and almost completed a third, but was not quite able to make it. He was off balance backward as he landed and though he struggled to stand upright, he ended by falling backward.

He rose, bowed to the dais and retreated to the side of the room. This time there was no sigh from the audience.

The third man came out and successfully leaped several times in succession through the hoop made by his arms when the fingers of his two hands were interlaced. He was rewarded with a small sighing.

Last of all came the Hybrid Bart had seen before. There was nothing which could with certainty be called a swagger to his walk as he left the wall for the center of the open floor; but the lightness of his step and the length and certainty of his stride had a sort of inborn arrogance about them.

To Bart's surprise, all this confident-seeming man did was a simple handstand. He stood there, upside down, head between his arms, arms themselves neatly parallel, legs together and the toes of his shoes extended and touching each other.

A faint sigh came from the crowd.

Baffled as to the reason for any version of applause, Bart stared at the man for a long moment before he suddenly realized that the other was no longer resting on the palms of his hands. Instead he now held himself in the same upside-down position—but supported only on the extended tips of his ten fingers.

Now Bart, for the first time, began to keep his gaze closely on those splayed and rigid fingers with an unusual interest. This much he had once, as a boy, been able to do himself. It was what further the blue-eyed Hybrid might do that fascinated him now. He watched closely; and his watching was rewarded.

Another sigh from the watching crowd signaled the further action of the performing Hybrid. Still keeping his upheld body motionless he had withdrawn the little fingers of both hands from the floor, so that he now upheld himself only on eight digits.

And as Bart watched, the other man withdrew one more finger from supporting each hand, lifting the ones next to the little fingers. He stood upright on six fingers; thumbs, first and second fingers of each hand.

The crowd sighed again. Bart sighed with them. It would be most natural now for the other man to drop to the floor and stand up to receive the Inner World applause he had certainly earned. Apparently the crowd felt the same, for he heard the beginnings of the most recent sigh from the crowd cut off abruptly.

The performer had moved. In fact, he was still moving. Deliberately, finger by finger, he was shifting position. Literally, he was walking across the floor on the six fingertips on which he stood.

Understanding hit Bart in the pit of his stomach. What this man was now doing was something that Bart himself could never do, even if he trained for months or years. It was simply impossible for even someone with his strength to support his full body weight as the other was doing, on the unequal support of three fingers on one hand and only two of the other, during the moment in which his body weight was being shifted forward.

But the blue-eyed Hybrid, having finger-walked perhaps sixteen inches of floor distance, had now dropped back onto the palms of his hands and raised himself to his feet. His face was darkened by the congestion of blood in it, but otherwise he showed no sign of the terrific physical effort he had just made.

He bowed to the dais. The sighing of the crowd around the walls was loud in the room.

"Once again," said the Emperor, smiling, "Michel Saberut has proved himself most Lordly among our nephews. A reward will be sent to your home, Michel; and we honor the memory of your father." Michel Saberut bowed once more and all three of those seated on the dais inclined their heads in return.

"And now," said the Emperor, rising, with Pier and the Regent standing up also on either side of him, "Court is over."

The Lords and Ladies were already crowding toward the far entrance of the room. Pier, the Emperor and the Regent followed them, caught up with them, and had a way made for them through the mass of bodies. When all were gone, Chandt walked out from the far wall to stand in the center of the floor.

"Dormitory Leaders," he said; and his voice seemed to echo strangely in the new emptiness of the large room, "take your Steeds back to their proper places."

chapter
nineteen

MORE THAN A little out of breath, Bart entered through the double doors of the main entrance to the Library once more. It was just after sixteen hundred hours—4:00 P.M. The whole Court session had taken less than an hour and a half; and less than another half hour was all it had taken to march back to the dormitory and be released. Along the route, Bart had gathered from his fellow Steeds that tonight would be in the nature of a celebratory occasion. After a Court, only those absolutely required to be on duty, were so.

The rest of them—slaves, Hybrids and those Lords who were up to it—would be engaged in revels, parties or social get-togethers of one sort or another; and his fellow Steeds were already planning their fun.

This fact, and the several hours that remained until he would need to pick up Emma—at about seven o'clock, he estimated—were by way of a gift from heaven, in Bart's view.

The events which had just taken place in front of his eyes in the Court Room had gone a long way toward answering many of the questions he had still been asking himself about the Lords and their Inner World. He had intended to use his invitation to visit Pier and Marta this evening to confront them with his fabricated story of being the son of a lost Lord himself. And while he had been worried about falling victim to holes in that story, he had decided that it was necessary to use it quickly and hope for some luck—or even help from the Guettrigs.

But the Court—not only the words of the Emperor, but what he, Bart, had seen there—had changed all that; in a way, it had changed his whole world.

It was now necessary to try to locate whatever records he could find on the Hybrid Michel Saberut. He had not yet located any such records in his explorations of the Library, but he had a few hours in which to look.

Entering the Library, he found it as deserted as it had been on any of his late-night visits. A stack slave he did not recognize dozed behind the main desk—either sleeping off the previous night's entertainment, or resting himself in preparation for tonight's.

The slave did not wake up as Bart silently passed him and entered the stacks. Three levels down, he turned from the stairs in the direction of the section he hoped to find a way to enter—and checked himself suddenly, aware of faint sounds among the farther stacks.

These were quiet enough so that he could easily have missed them altogether; but now that he paused and gave all his attention to listening, he recognized them for the distant murmur of conversation.

Quietly he moved through the aisles of the stacks on that level, toward the sound—not directly toward it, but in a roundabout way that would not let someone look down an aisle from the place ahead of him, and see him. Still the sounds grew plainer as he approached their source.

Shortly the murmur resolved itself into voices, pitched low, at the very back of the level. What was there, he already knew.

It was an iron-fenced area, with its only entrance a locked door, which held within it the particularly valuable and special books of the Library's collection. Even Lords did not simply walk in here unsupervised.

Normally, withdrawing one of these special books required summoning Pier, who himself unlocked the door and went through it either alone or with a stack slave to carry whatever was to be brought out, and which the Lord in question had justified his need to see. Hybrids were not allowed to have books from this area at all, and only two others besides the Librarian had keys to the door. These were the Emperor and the Regent.

They two, Pier had told him, could visit the special area when they wished without permission from Pier himself. No one else was so allowed.

So the special collection—the "X" collection, it was called by the Library's workers—was inviolate.

But before it, and separating it from the ordinary shelves of books in the stacks occupying the rest of this level, was a small open space with half a dozen chairs, interspersed with little side tables, all built to the physical dimensions of Lords alone. In this area, those permitted to have a book brought out by the Librarian might sit and read it—carrying one of the volumes away was not permitted even to Lords—before sending a waiting stack slave for Pier; and, when he arrived, handing it back to him to be replaced in security.

Now, however, when Bart moved quietly close enough to not only hear, but see, who was there, he did not see one or more single Lords reading, with waiting slaves at their elbows. Now all the chairs were occupied, rather uncomfortably, by the almost full-sized bodies of adult Hybrids; and in addition there were at least half a dozen other such Hybrids standing amongst the chairs; all of them in earnest discussion.

Bart was about to congratulate himself on his luck in stumbling on such a gathering when he realized they were only doing what he, himself, was doing—taking advantage of the Library's emptiness after Court. Among them, he recognized now, with a certain sense of shock, was one man who had never been completely out of Bart's mind since he had seen the other's act in the Court Room.

It was the Hybrid the Emperor had called Michel Saberut—the one who had walked on the tips of his fingers. Now, wide-shouldered, black-haired and piercingly blue-eyed as ever, he lounged in one of the little chairs, listening to the others talk—in conversations that mixed French and English.

Alone among all those there, he seemed to find it possible to drape himself comfortably and casually in the undersized chair in which he sat at an angle. He still wore only the black trousers and ruffled white shirt he had dressed in to perform. The simpleness of his garb and the brilliant glance of his eyes at each individual as he or she spoke gave him a challenging, almost piratical look, sharply in contrast to those around him, who, for the most part, were still dressed in their ordinary working costumes—sober-colored suits on the men and long, elaborate dresses on the women.

Michel sat, looking as strikingly different from the others as a falcon in a flock of ducks. He was draped with one leg over a little side table, his head a trifle on one side and his teeth showing very whitely in the gentle smile on his swarthy face. He swung his leg slightly, listening. So removed, he seemed, from all the rest, that for a long moment, as he watched, Bart had thought that he might be here more as a spectator than a participant.

But then, unexpectedly, Michel interrupted the standing Hy-

brid who was speaking, a tall thin young man with straight brown
hair on a round skull above a round and somewhat sulky-looking
face.

"What was it Marcus Tullus Cicero told us?" Michel broke in
on the other's rather strident tirade. *"There is nothing so
ridiculous but some philosopher has said it—"*

"Descartes said that," reinterrupted the man who had just been
speaking.

"Only about sixteen hundred years after Cicero had, Jorg," said
Michel. "In any case, the point is that you've all been chewing the
same old cud. The names we use for ourselves may be 'Liberal' or
'Textualist'—"

"The Lords and Ladies call themselves by those names, too,"
Jorg broke in again.

"But not as publicly as we do," went on Michel patiently, "and
with about as much truth. Scratch a Liberal or Textualist—
including all of us in this select little company, gathered secretly
here while everyone else is getting on their party clothes—and
you'll find a particular self-interest that makes him or her adopt the
label. Nothing is ever going to get done by any of us until we face
that fact."

"I don't know what you're driving at, Michel," said one of the
women, a slight blond in a large, flowery dress—the only one of
her sex who was seated.

"I'm driving, Yna," he turned to her, "at the fact that we're like
those insects of the upper world, who emerge from their chrysalis to
fly one summer's day, but with no mouth parts because they won't
be around long enough to feed, and who have only one purpose in
life—to breed and die. Except that unlike them, unlike slaves, and
unlike our Lords and Ladies, we Hybrids can't even reproduce
ourselves. Each one of us is a dead end in a generational sense. Our
progeny, if we have them by anyone else than one of the Lords or
Ladies, go back down among the slave class. To be quarter-Hybrid
is to be nothing. All this being so, what have we got to live for any
more than those insects—the one brief day of our own lives? And
so to clothe our self-interest in talk of the past and future is
meaningless."

"Speak for yourself, cousin Michel," said Jorg. "I, and some of
the rest of us here, are able to speak in larger terms than the kind of
self-interest you talk about."

Michel yawned politely behind the fingers of one hand.

"Good for you," he said. "I'm only pointing out the pointlessness of generations of unrelated Hybrids getting together in secret conclave like this, and under considerable danger, to talk, and do nothing. Who knows but what we're being monitored right now, by a spy in our midst?''

There was an uneasy stir among the gathering. More than one glanced at the person closest to him or her.

''If there was such a one,'' said Michel, still smiling and looking at Jorg, ''wouldn't it be to his best interests in protecting himself from discovery, that he advance only foolish ideas, so that no one else there would think him clever enough to be a danger?''

''Michel!'' Jorg's face reddened. ''If you mean me, come right out and say it. I'm not afraid of you! I'm willing to meet you any time, with any weapon, or even without, even though I know you're better than me with almost every one of them!''

''Calm yourself, calm yourself, Cousin Jorg,'' said Michel. ''No one, and me least of all, doubts your sincerity. I'm only reminding us of one of many dangers in this sort of meeting. And when those dangers are undertaken only to produce a lot of what's been said many times over before, it becomes ridiculous.''

''How can you call it ridiculous?'' said a short, bulky man, who was one of the ones seated, ''when al-Kebir's ready to be activated within weeks? And after that, irretrievably though far off in time, the upper world's civilization'll be under three hundred feet of sea water or buried in volcanic ash—and it'll be too late for anyone to do anything after only a few more days.''

''Yes,'' said a tall, thin young man standing behind the last speaker, whose long neck accommodated a remarkably high, upstanding collar, ''and the Lords will inherit the Earth—what's left of it. While we, who could have put it to good use, won't even be needed anymore. In fact, it's been we Hybrids who've been putting it to good use for centuries, managing the investments and ownerships up there—except the Lords are the ones who get the benefit from them.''

''Exactly,'' said Michel. He looked at the stocky man who had spoken first. ''I assume when you talk about al-Kebir being activated, you're referring to the Tectonal, Cousin Paullen, not the ghost of our revered ancestor. Well, if we've met here to talk about what to do about that, let's have at it—instead of rehearsing old grievances.''

''You're so clever, Michel!'' said Jorg. ''You tell us what you think we ought to do.''

''No, no. By all means,'' said Michel with a courteous wave of his hand. "Let's have what the rest of you've got in mind. I'll listen."

"So," said Jorg contemptuously, "you're quick enough to make demands, but you haven't got anything more in the way of a solution than the rest of us."

"I don't think so, Jorg," said Yna. "When Cousin Michel talks like this it's precisely because he has some idea of his own up his sleeve. Only he enjoys baiting us all with our own lack of a solution first. Aren't I right, Michel?"

"You may not always be right, Yna," said Michel, managing a sort of bow to her in spite of his seated position, "but you're never wrong. Which is to say, in this case, you're half right. I don't say I have a solution, only a suggestion. Most of us want the upper world for our playground, undestroyed; and our freedom from our revered uncles and aunts. Very well, let's start thinking of solutions in proportion to the problem. For example, how about destroying al-Kebir—and I, Cousin Paullen, am speaking about the Tectonal, not the original ghost."

A complete, dead silence followed his words. Not only that, but Bart noticed no one moved for a few seconds, and when they finally did, it was only to stare wordlessly at each other.

The silence went on to the point where Jorg evidently decided that it was his responsibility to end it.

"Michel—," he said, and his voice cracked. Michel looked courteously at him. Jorg tried again. "Michel, are you joking—or simply insane? Hundreds of years of work, the Lords' very reason for existence, and you talk about destroying it?"

"Why, yes," said Michel calmly. "And as for hundreds of years of work, nonsense! Morton Cadiz may have been a genius—who knows, maybe as much of a genius in his own way as the original al-Kebir was in his—but his work was purely theoretical and he belonged to the eighteenth century. It promised nothing until we—and 'we' includes we Hybrids—got to work on it with more modern methods, after this place was created eighty years ago, at the beginning of the present century."

He shifted comfortably in his undersized chair.

"And what if its destruction *would* amount to the destruction of a hundreds-of-years-old dream!" he went on. "Al-Kebir's ancient dream was of personal revenge, but I don't think even the Lordly class took the idea seriously—until our development of electromagnetic power made it possible for us to actually reach down and play games with the electro-gravitic currents in the magma of this planet. This whole idea is really fairly new, after all.

"Besides, you want to do something to convince the Textualists among the Lords we're serious about not wanting to destroy human civilization, and want chunks of its wealth and luxuries for our own use above ground, isn't that right? Or was I mistaken in the reason this meeting was called for—a meeting of those of us considered to be activists among the Hybrid Liberals?"

And he looked around at the faces staring at him, as if waiting for an answer.

"Michel," said Yna, "you know better than this. There may be twice the unadmitted Liberals among the Lordly class that there are Textualists there. But the Lordly Textualists believe in a book—the Book of our ancestor—and those who'd rather not wreck the world above don't dare stand up and say so. What you suggest would force all the Lords to stand together against us. While, as it is, we're able to talk Liberalism as much as we do only because of that hidden majority, up top."

Michel shook his head.

"I don't see that it'd matter if all the Lords combined against us—us and the slaves," he said. "And the Steeds are a joke, really. Oh, Chandt is dangerous enough. But most of those muscle-bound oafs he commands stand to gain as much as us Hybrids and the rest of the slaves by standing against the Lords as we have. I think that could be pointed out to them—most of them, anyway. In any case, I also don't agree that the Lords would immediately combine against us. I think that large, hidden majority you talk about, Yna, would most of them heave a sigh of relief—quietly, of course—on hearing the Tectonal had been put out of action."

"That's a wild thought!" said Jorg angrily.

"Jorg, Jorg," said Michel, and for the first time Bart heard a note of impatience in his voice, "everyone always assumes that his or her enemies are monolithic in their attitudes. Actually, what they always have been, and always will be, right down to the moment when battle lines are drawn, are as individually different from each other and everybody else as the one facing them."

"The Tectonal is the promise of the Book of al-Kebir come true!" said Jorg stubbornly. "Without the Book, what're the Lords? What's their justification for existence? To prove to themselves what they are, they have to follow their Book!"

"Ah, yes," said Michel. "But what Book is that? It was the Book of al-Kebir only to al-Kebir himself. The mistake you make,

Jorg—and the rest of you, too—,'' he added, looking around at them, ''is in assuming there's only one Book; and that's the Book you know yourself. Have you ever sat down and talked about that book to your closest friend? If you do, you'll end up finding that he or she seems to have read a volume that's totally different from the one you read. The more you go on comparing notes, the more you'll find you two disagree about specific passages and interpretations of those passages—and about what al-Kebir actually meant, when he wrote it.''

''Michel!'' said Paullen. ''How can you say that?''

''Because it's fact, you dunderheads!'' said Michel. ''There's only one Book for every person alive—the Book we write for ourselves, or would write for ourselves if we sat down with pen and paper, the way old al-Kebir did! And that's a book we make up out of our own beliefs and fears and experiences—that book which defines for us what we will do and what we won't, what we'll die for and what we won't die for. It's a book that may be flavored by one or more other books we've read, but whatever they were to the writer, to each of us they've been bent to fit our individual picture of things; and when the chips are down, we follow our own text—no one else's. And you'll find that'll be true for each Lord and Lady if you ever get the courage up to put an end to the Tectonal! Look into yourself and see how you'd act, if word came the thing had been smashed. Then ask yourself if any other human below here would react in any other way except according to his or her own, inner way of looking at both worlds—the Inner and the surface ones!''

''But you can't deny,'' said Paullen, ''that the destruction of the Tectonal would destroy the Lords' rights to consider themselves Lords.''

''Oh, Cousin!'' said Michel. ''Do you think that being Lords and Ladies is all that attractive to most of them—aside from the fact that they, too, see the advantage in not destroying a world of which we already own a considerable chunk? Certainly, there're some of them who revel in their power and authority; or at least rate it highly enough so that it means more to them than anything else. But the great majority of them . . . the surface world nowadays doesn't enslave and torture the small or deformed, or treat them like living toys. What wealth and power will buy in the upper world for you and me would also buy it for the Lords and Ladies. Here, like us, they work from the cradle to the grave. Just as it is with our Hybrid children, theirs are taken from them and killed, not merely if they aren't bright enough, but if they're growing too big to be considered one of their special, little race. And on top of all this, unlike us, they have to conform to dietary laws that help ensure that they and their children are undernourished and so likely to grow up undersized.''

He looked around at them.

"All they really have by way of a reward down here, from the Book and the Tectonal and the ghost of al-Kebir, is their honor and their pride, which they wear like the medieval knight wore his armor or the religious penitent his hair shirt. How many of them, do you think, wouldn't give a private sigh of relief to be free to come out into the upper world as ordinary, if undersized, people, again?''

Jorg half turned from the circle of people, throwing his hands wide in a gesture of helplessness.

"This is nonsense!'' he said. "And it's getting us no place!''

"The rest of you feel like Jorg?'' Michel asked, looking around at them.

For a moment no one answered.

"I don't know what to think,'' said Paullen. "What you suggest—it's too much all at once, Michel.''

"Well!'' said Yna, in brisk, businesslike tones, "whatever anyone else feels, I think there's no more point in sitting around here. Michel's either given us an answer to the situation, or put us all in an impossible position. I, for one, want to get away and think it over.''

She got to her feet. Slowly the others who had been seated followed her example. Michel was last up.

"Leave separately—and in the order we came—that's the rule!'' said Jorg hastily.

He glanced at Michel.

"That means you're last—it's what you get for always coming late.''

"Not at all.'' Michel waved a hand and sat down again. "I'll be glad to be last out. The rest of you go ahead.''

The others began to leave, at intervals of about two minutes. They took the direct route down the aisles to the stairs, leaving Bart, who was now standing off to the side and behind a double stack, in no danger of discovery.

Jorg, Bart noticed, was one of the first; and an idea which he had not conceived until he had heard that Michel would be the last to leave began to build in him, like tension as a bomb ticks down toward its moment of explosion.

The heavy-bodied Paullen was next to the last to leave. As soon as his boots had ceased to sound on the bare, polished wood floor of the stack level, Bart came forward and through one of the openings that were spaced along each stack to allow passage from one aisle to another. He stepped into the area before the bars protecting the "X" collection, and stood looking down at Michel in his chair.

"So," said Michel in French, laying the magazine he had been glancing through down on the small table beside him, and smiling up at Bart. "There was a spy after all. I'm afraid it won't do you any good, though, all your listening. The Emperor and the Regent already know all about my attitudes and beliefs—that's why I can't get assignment up to the surface world. But I'm too popular among my cousins for His Majesty to take any action against me; and the work wouldn't get done if the Hybrids refused to help. So as long as all I do is talk, I'm left alone."

His smile sobered a little as he examined Bart more closely.

"You're Pier's Steed, aren't you?" he said. "I'm surprised to find you at something like this. Pier's one of us—in his own Lordly way. I wouldn't think he'd set his Steed to spy on us, even if he knew—which I've been sure he has, for some time—that we hold our little secret meetings here. Or was this all your own idea for some reason? Tell me, slave!"

"I will," said Bart. "You're right, this was all my own idea, this listening. It was accidental, but it turned out more important than I expected when I heard you were to leave last. As you'd expect, I was in the Court Room with the other Steeds earlier today and saw your performance; and I think it was more interesting to me than to anyone else in the same room. You see, it's possible we have the same father."

Michel got to his feet very quickly. He checked himself just short of hitting out at Bart.

Bart had not moved. He had half expected the blow and thought he should be able to move enough, in time, to let it slip by him. If not—if Michel was too quick for him—he was prepared to take it, rather than move or change the expression of his face; and now Michel's face was so close to his own that he could feel the warm puffs of the other's breath against his skin.

"By God, man!" said Michel softly. "I could have sworn there was nothing you could say to me that would make me lose my self-control. But you almost did, then! Tell me quickly—and tell

me straight, for your life's sake—what gave you the notion to say a
wild thing like that? Vincent Saberut was a great and noble man.
The idea that he'd be the father of someone like you is laughable!"

"You aren't laughing," said Bart.

Michel smiled.

"I am now," he answered, "and what've you got to say to that,
my friend?"

"I say," said Bart, "that it's impossible for any living adult man
of your weight to walk on six fingers alone."

"And what," said Michel with continued softness, "has that to
do with my father? What do you know about walking on six
fingers—or my weight for that matter—which I don't believe you
could guess correctly if you wanted to?"

"I know about the finger-walking from the same source you
learned it," said Bart. "Our mutual father, whom I've seen do it.
In fact he taught me the trick and I could do it myself as a
youngster; but as I grew up I got heavier and gave up practicing, or
possibly I could still do it yet, as you do. Though I doubt it, because
I'm heavier than you."

Michel's smile broadened.

"I doubt it. Tell me, O sapient slave, how much I weigh?"

Bart looked him over.

"We're alike enough in height and general build," he said, "but
your frame's a little lighter than mine. I'd say two hundred and
forty pounds, Canadian."

The smile was suddenly gone from Michel's face.

"So?" he said, on a softly indrawn breath. "You'd make me out
that heavy, would you? I'll admit you guess weights better than I'd
have thought. And how much do you weigh yourself, then, my
friend?"

"I lost a lot of weight working in a mine the last year," said
Bart, "and I'm just now getting it back. But two-sixty would be a
good weight for me when I'm in shape . . . perhaps up to
two-eighty."

"Vincent Saberut," said Michel softly, "weighed—"

"A little over a hundred and forty pounds," said Bart swiftly.
"He was four feet, ten inches tall; wide-shouldered—you have his
shoulders—but otherwise he looked no more than wiry."

Michel stood, staring at him. After a long moment, he spoke.

"You could have looked that up," he said.

"In here?" Bart waved his hand at the shelves about them.
"Believe me, I tried. Could you have?"

Michel did not answer for a long moment.

"No," he said at last, "I don't believe I could have."

"It's curious," said Bart. "Do you know I was going to claim to be a Hybrid, and I'd built up all sorts of information in my head to make the imposture work; and here it turns out I actually am a Hybrid."

The breath went in between Michel's even, gleaming teeth in a slight hiss.

"Are you?" he said. "Suppose you tell me a little more about yourself first, before you start counting on the fact. You said it was impossible for anyone to walk on his six fingers alone. Why?"

"Unless the person's got no legs, so his weight's reduced. Or he's a freak," said Bart, "with nothing but skin and bones, and hands like shovels having fingers to match. It's not possible even for massively boned people like you and me, not even possible for our father—"

"We'll call him Vincent Saberut until you've convinced me you've the right to call him something closer, if you don't mind," said Michel.

Bart shrugged.

"If you want," he said. "I knew him as Lionel Dybig. What'll convince you I know what I'm talking about?"

"You called what I did in the Court Room earlier today a trick," said Michel. "You still haven't explained that word, except to say what I did can't be done. How was it then I did it?"

"As I say, with a trick," said Bart. "You only appeared to do it. By the time you were up on the tips of all your fingers in a finger-stand, you had the audience wanting to believe you could do anything. So when you seemed to move forward on the fingers of one hand, no one was watching your other hand—which was carrying most of your weight with the heel of the palm flat on the floor. Even those who might have noticed it, would have ignored it. What you were doing was marvelous enough, anyway. Besides, where are the rules written that say you can't rest your weight on your right hand while pretending to move forward on the fingers of your left?"

Michel watched him with those blue eyes of his, saying nothing.

"What more do you want me to say?" Bart shrugged. "In practice, everyone watching would go away ready to tell other people that you'd not only walked on your fingers alone, but on perhaps two of them from each hand, instead of three. That'd make the story even better. But, as I say, to actually do it only with three fingers on each hand is impossible. My finger joints used to ache for a day or two after I'd stood on them—and that was when I was still young, with a boy's quickness to get over damage and sickness. My father told me that he was already getting too old to do it and he only did it on special occasions when it was absolutely necessary to impress people who looked down on him because of his size. But he told me once he was already beginning to suffer arthritis in those joints from doing it even that little.''

It was Bart's turn to smile at the other man.

"How about it?" he said. "Aren't your finger joints aching right now? Don't they usually ache for several days after you do the act?"

Michel nodded—the movement of his head was slight and slow, but it was a nod.

"You know a great deal," he said, "and you weren't so greatly wrong about my weight. Most people guess me forty or more pounds less than that. What made you pick the weight you did?"

"You heard me doing it," said Bart. "I estimated your weight from mine, knowing we'd share the dense bone structure of our father."

"So you're that sure that we're half-brothers? How can you be so sure?"

"Your mother's name," said Bart. "It wouldn't have been Didi, by any chance?"

Michel stared at him for a long moment.

"No," he said tonelessly; then, "it was Diana."

Bart blinked—then understood.

"Perhaps I phrased the question wrongly," he said. "Perhaps I ought to have asked if Vincent Saberut ever called your mother Didi?"

"Yes!" The word came out explosively at last between Michel's teeth. "No one but he ever called her that. No one living except me knows he did."

"He mentioned her name only at the end, a number of times as he lay dying," said Bart gently. "He was in delirium most of the time from the infection of the bullet wound that killed him."

Michel said nothing.

"I was convinced when I saw you—and your act—at the Court, that you were my half-brother," Bart said finally. "What do you need to convince you? As far as I'm concerned it's not just these things that prove our relationship. There's a hundred others—small things. I see things about you that're like the things I saw in him. In some of the ways you move and look. As I say, you're more like him than I am. I see him in you.''

Michel breathed out softly. His shoulders sagged and the tightness went out of his body.

"And you," he said, "are more of a gentleman than I am. You're right. I acknowledge the relationship. It's just the shock of finding family after being alone all my life. My mother died when I was still a boy; and my—our—father had already left for the surface by that time."

He extended his hand. Bart took it. Instinctively, they both gripped hard, then both smiled.

"No, no," said Michel, "no more tests."

They let go.

"But you'll forgive me, won't you," said Michel, "if I can't bring myself to call you 'brother' right away? I've been alone in the world too long."

His voice changed.

"And as I say, I barely knew Vincent," he said. "I was just old enough to remember what he looked like, when he went out on a mission to the surface world. I was only six years old then; and those six years were as much as I remember of him. You had more of him than I ever did, my friend."

"The father I knew would have approved of your present self, I think," said Bart.

"Enough!" Michel shook his head. "I've admitted you're the gentleman of the—of the family."

He took a step back and looked Bart up and down.

"We've got to get you out of those slave clothes," he said.

"I was hoping to do that but not this soon," said Bart. "You see, I'm supposed to see Pier and Marta tonight . . ."

He told Michel of Pier's invitation. Michel's eyes flashed as Bart finished.

"But excellent!" Michel said. "I'll join you on that visit, tonight. That is—you go ahead with it as you planned, you and this, this . . ."

"Emma Robeson," said Bart slowly, "and if I'm a gentleman, she's a lady."

Michel nodded.

"You and this lady—small *l*, of course—," he said, "the two of you keep your appointment as ordered. I'll invite myself to the Guettrig's unexpectedly while you're there." His teeth showed themselves in a momentary smile. "We'll arrange to meet at the door; and let me be the one to announce to Pier your relationship. It'll be more believable, coming from me. Now, let's both of us get out of here."

He started to leave the stacks.

"Just a minute," said Bart, following him. "There's things you need to know."

chapter
twenty

BART CAUGHT UP with the other and grasped him by one elbow.

"Hold on," he said. "Didn't you hear me? Before you talk to Pier about me and for me, you'd better understand how I feel about things, myself. I'm not just looking forward to being a Hybrid recovered to the fold. That whole masquerade I had in mind was only a step toward what I really want; and that's to get out of here, taking Emma Robeson along with me."

Michel had halted at the touch of Bart's fingers on his elbow. Now he turned to meet Bart's eyes.

"Ah," he said, "and this Emma Robeson—another slave, I assume?"

Bart nodded.

"She must mean a great deal to you."

"Yes," said Bart. They stood looking at each other, and Michel smiled.

"Then cheer up, Brother," he said, pulling his elbow from Bart's relaxed fingers and clapping the shoulder above them with one hand, "because that's my goal, too, to get up into the surface world; and I think, with what's been done to you we can all manage it. But you'll have to trust me how to go about it, because there's more at work down here than I could teach you in several months, and we don't have that sort of time."

"You've got time to tell me a few things I need to know, though," said Bart, "and you can answer a couple of quick questions to begin with. Most of the slaves here seem to believe they've been raised from the dead; and I've been with the Steeds when they reported to something called a Clinic. I don't believe anyone can be raised from the dead; but I'm ready to believe these Clinic visits have something to do with their believing it. Am I right?"

"Absolutely," answered Michel. "Drugs and mesmerism—hypnosis, if you want the proper word," said Michel. "What's the other question?"

"From what I've heard even you Hybrids seem to believe that something you have down here can destroy the Earth. That I can't believe, either, any more than I can believe in people raised from the dead. Don't tell me that's true!"

"That, I'm afraid, is," said Michel, "though again, it's a long story. Why don't you let me tell you about it when we've got some time to kill."

Bart stopped him again as Michel started once more to turn away.

"Sorry," Bart said, "but if there is such a thing, I've got to see it for myself. If it's actually there, Emma's not going to agree to leave here until we've put it out of action; and I won't go without her."

Michel gazed at him.

"You'd shame the devil himself!" he said softly. "Don't tell her then. Even if the Tectonal reached Action Point in the next few weeks, it would take scores of years before the geologic changes on the surface actually begin. Meanwhile, those can be good years for us, up in the surface world."

In the other's words Bart heard strange echos of what Paolo had said to him the last time he had seen the dormitory Leader—

"*We could have had a lot of good years down here,*" Paolo had said, sober with sadness in spite of the alcohol in him at the slaves' Recreational Center, "*even with the way this place is; and you'd've had your Emma and I got Lorena. But you're bound to bust it all up. . . .*"

Bart shook off the memory.

"No," he answered. "But you've already said this thing actually exists and can do what I've heard said it can. I'll have to tell Emma that much, when she asks—and she's bound to ask. Once she hears she'll never agree to leave without putting it out of action. And I won't go without her. Besides, I thought you suggested awhile ago to the other Hybrids, here in the stacks, doing just that?"

"Yes, but that was with their agreement and a number of them helping," said Michel. "For you and your Emma, even adding me into it, to try it by ourselves—"

He broke off.

"Perhaps you're more like our father than you look," he said. "You'd better see the Tectonal for yourself. Want to? I'll show it to you."

"I just said I did," said Bart. "How?"

"Well, first we fit you out with some proper Hybrid clothing."

He examined Bart from head to foot. "Some of my clothes won't fit too badly on you. Come on."

He led off again, and this time Bart was satisfied to follow.

Thirty minutes later, dressed in a bottle-green suit outlining one of the shirts with a ruffled collar—all in all more flamboyant than Bart would have chosen himself—he waited impatiently outside a closed but impressively carved, large door, in a corridor down which he had never been before.

"What do we want here?" he had asked as Michel had left him to go inside alone.

"Yna Sicorro," answered Michel. "She's the only one that can provide credentials for you. You saw her at the meeting, and I think she came back here. If anyone comes along—Hybrid or Lord or Lady—and asks you questions while I'm inside there, you never heard of me. Give them your surface name and tell them you just came down from spending most of your life up above and aren't allowed to say anything about it—or about yourself, yet."

Bart had nodded, and watched the other vanish through the doorway with misgivings. The corridor about him was a well-traveled one. He felt his half-brother could have found a safer place for him to wait than in this exposed and public location. He sweated under the bottle-green jacket every time a Hybrid or Lord passed by; but thankfully, none of them seemed to have the time or curiosity to stop and question him.

After what seemed an intolerably long period, but was probably less than twenty minutes, Michel suddenly re-emerged, jerked his head at Bart and headed off down the corridor. Bart took several long strides and caught up with him.

"What—," Bart began.

"Wait until we're around the corner," said Michel. A moment later, he turned into a small side corridor that was clear of traffic except for a couple of figures going away in the distance. Michel stopped, pulled Bart back against a wall and reached into one of the pockets of his waistcoat. He came out with a three-by-two inch square of bright green cardboard, encased in a frame of light-colored, varnished wood. The name *Michel Saberut* was printed on the cardboard in this black letters less than an inch in height; and he pinned it to the wide lapel of his own dark gray suit.

"And now, one for you," he said, producing a second card and handing it to Bart. "Pin it on."

Bart stared at it, for this card also read *Michel Saberut*. In fact, it was identical to the one Michel had just pinned on himself.

"But it's the same!" said Bart.

"And lucky we are to have it," said Michel. "Yna can be a handful; but she's a good person to have on your side. Still, there're limits. I told her I'd mislaid my own card. According to the rules, there's not supposed to be a new one issued until a special team has searched everything and either found the original, or has proof it's been destroyed. Yna stretched a point and gave me a duplicate on my word that I knew I'd just set it down somewhere in my apartments and I'd be able to find it when I had a moment to search—but I needed to get in right now for a piece I've got to get finished."

Seeing Bart's blank stare, he explained.

"I'm an archivist. That's my job. I told her I was working on a piece about our present moment in history, as we archivists do all the time. Everything was to be noted down and kept track of—one of al-Kebir's more sensible commandments. The only trouble is, once I'm done with a paper, it vanishes behind the lock and bars of the 'X' collection in the Library, and I'm not even allowed to reread my own work. Of course, like all of us in my department, I keep identical copies for my own files; though that's technically against the rules. But so is issuing a duplicate badge without first searching for the original."

"But if we go past one of those door guards together—," Bart was beginning.

"He'll never notice anything but the shape and color of the badge," said Michel. "People don't look, you know, ninety per cent of the time. Of course, some people, and there's more of those among us and the Lordly class, look more than others. But one of your Steeds? Ha!"

He led the way back into the busier main corridor they had left a moment before, to put on the badges. Bart caught up with him. Together they went some distance, and made several turns, until they came at last into a corridor empty except for the door with its armed guard at its dead end.

"I'll talk to him, when we reach him," said Michel quietly to Bart, while they were still some yards away. "You pay no attention and simply walk straight in. He won't have the nerve to call you back, particularly since he's seen you wearing the proper shape and color of badge. . . ."

The doorway they approached was not the doorway where Bart had been denied entrance once before, nor was the guard on duty there the one who had denied it to him. Nonetheless, the differences were too small to matter. Only, this time the guard stepped aside and saluted with his odd weapon as they approached.

"Sirs!" he said, as the door opened before them.

"Ah, yes," said Michel, stopping and turning to face the man as he and Bart reached the door. Behind the shield of his back, Bart walked through it and kept going.

"Your name's Ebbett, isn't it?" he heard Michel's voice diminishing in volume behind him as he moved away from it, "—oh, no? Marquez! Of course, how could I have forgotten? I knew I'd seen you on duty here before; and it's a relief to know it's someone like you on guard here. Not that anyone but some demented slave might try . . ."

Bart stopped. He was already out of effective earshot and he did not want to make the mistake of going where he should not go inside the door until he had Michel to guide him. To cover his pause, he made a point of frowning extravagantly and turning around as if just discovering Michel was not with him.

To his relief, he saw his half-brother just turning away from a section of the workbench just inside the entrance. Michel came toward him, one hand stuck into a side pocket of his suit coat, and the pocket bulging more than even Michel's bunched fist should make it do. Now, having an excuse to wait, Bart also had a quite reasonable excuse to look around him.

The room he had entered was too big to take in at one glance. In the center of it was a huge device, which must be the Tectonal that Michel had talked about. At first glance, it seemed to consist of a round shape—effectively, a doughnut shape—with its bottom edge some two or three feet off the floor. It was in motion, rotating about the central column, a massive round shaft that rose high from the center of the round shape. This was clearly the same shaft he had glimpsed from a distance on the first day as a Steed, when he had carried Pier through one end of an upper room opening on this one. The shaft mounted to and through the ceiling far overhead. Around the four walls of the room ran a continuous series of workbenches like the one he had seen Michel coming from. Benches at which white-coated men and women seemed to be busy with picture screens, other desk-mounted devices and various smaller bits of machinery or material. But these seemed almost unimportant.

Indeed, the room was truly enormous. It was several stories high and had several acres of open floor. Bart, thinking of the interior of factories and steamships as they had been described to him in the past, had expected the space to be crammed with machinery. Instead, it seemed almost empty, although there must be close to a hundred people in white coats busy at the benches.

The walls and the ceiling, and even the floor, were simply polished, faintly pink, rock. But it was the Tectonal, in the center of the open space, that denied the room any real claim to emptiness.

It was simple but gigantic. The turning doughnut-shape itself was perhaps eighty feet in diameter, raised from the floor by the vertical shaft to which it seemed to be attached, although there might have been more underneath than Bart could see from here.

This shaft shone like polished steel, and probably was, to carry such a weight. It was a good ten feet in diameter itself; and stretched upward until it either touched, or penetrated, the ceiling far overhead.

Now that he looked more closely at the doughnut shape, he saw that a milky, semi-transparent surface covered its visible portion, through which he could barely make out what seemed to be an endless number of fins, or sheets of shiny metal, separated from each other by a foot or so. And the whole thing was turning about the shaft at a speed that barely allowed the fins of metal to be seen as separate parts, rather than one blurred mass.

Michel led Bart up to the doughnut shape and put out his hand above the rotating milky shield enclosing the fins.

"Listen," he said—but Bart was already aware of a low-pitched hum coming from the shield. "If it wasn't for the fact that we've got this protecting us, you and I and everybody else in this room would have lost their hearing by now."

He pointed to a rock wall nearly a hundred feet away across the room.

"That'll be coming out in the next few days," he said, "so as to make seating room for the ceremony. The whole Lordly class—you didn't see all of them at Court—would have trouble fitting into this room, big as it is, unless we add the lounge beyond—you know it, the one with the big stained-glass window. So the wall comes out. Then we'll have room for not only Lords and Ladies, but us Hybrids as well. The slaves, of course, are going to have to make do with standing in the corridors leading to here and watching the proceedings on electroscreens."

"What ceremony?" asked Bart.

Michel looked at him with unusually intent eyes.

"You don't know?" he answered. "The Commencement. The

Breakout. The beginning of the world's end. Don't tell me even the slaves haven't been talking about that?''

''I've heard of it,'' said Bart. ''But it doesn't mean anything to me. This thing's already running. What's going to commence?''

''Right. It's running, and it has been, for nearly eighteen years now,'' said Michel. ''But it's taken that many years just to prime the pump, so to speak.''

''I suppose,'' said Bart, ''somewhere along the way now you're going to explain all this you're telling me about?''

''That's what we're here for,'' said Michel. He gestured at the turning doughnut-shape. ''That, Brother Bart, is the heart of the Tectonal, at least the visible part of it. It goes up, as you see, and down as well, but to get to what's beyond the ceiling and under the floor below would require some dismantling upstairs and some rather incredible excavation. So you'll have to make do with what you see here.''

''I see some sort of fan. Or is it a spinning top of some kind?'' said Bart.

''Neither,'' said Michel. ''It's a technological stirring rod for roiling up the electromagnetic currents in the magma of the central part of this world; and tangling them into an electric storm that'll end up by breaking the magma out through the crust of the continents and sea floors—''

He was interrupted by one of the white-clad workers in the room, who had come up to them without either of them noticing. The newcomer was a thin, sharp-faced Hybrid in his mid-forties, with an air of authority about him.

''You're not thinking of taking this person underneath?'' the thin man said to Michel.

''Of course,'' said Michel soothingly. ''Cousin Merk, this is Cousin Bart Saberut, who grew up away from us all in the wilds of the upper world; and only now's returned to take his rightful place among us. Bart, this is our cousin Merk Jocelyn, assistant Superintendent in the Main Machine Group and probably the ranking person on duty here this shift. Yes, Merk, I've been ordered to tutor Bart because he's been up on the surface nearly all his life; and so we're just about to crawl under so I can show him the machine's underside.''

''You can't do that. We can't be responsible for what might happen—to the machine, or him. I'm sorry, I'll have to forbid it.''

''I'll write your forbiddance into the records, dear cousin,'' said

Michel. ''But as you can see, Yna Sicorro has already issued him a badge—'' Bart had forgotten about the badge he wore, and now turned himself slightly to make it harder for Jocelyn to read the name on it.

''Him—badged!'' exploded Merk. ''When he's hardly more than a surface savage? Are you going to keep him out from under, or do I have to call Yna and insist that she order you personally to do that?''

''Best of cousins,'' said Michel, draping an arm over the thin man's shoulders, which the other angrily shrugged off, ''now, you and I both know you're running a bluff on us, aren't you? So, why don't you trot back to your work and let us get on about ours?''

''You think so?'' snapped Merk. ''You'll see! I'm calling Yna.'' He turned and stalked off, white coat flapping around his rapidly moving legs. Michel shook his head sadly.

''Sounds like our time here may be shorter than I thought,'' he said to Bart.

''Then you'd better give me a quick look under that thing, right now, hadn't you?'' said Bart. He was not sure just why he wanted to look under the rotating apparatus, but since he had come this far . . . he looked at the machine shape. The whirling metal flanges were completely enclosed in the milkily transparent cover, and in spite of what he had just said, there was a strong, instinctive, exciting feeling of danger that spread along to his nerve-ends at the idea of crawling in underneath it. He pushed the feeling aside. ''There's time enough for that, still, isn't there?''

Michel nodded.

''I think so,'' he answered soberly. ''Come on, then.'' He took his fist out of his pocket, producing what looked to Bart like two pairs of oversized earmuffs with a slim, carved piece coming around from one of the ear-parts of each pair. The earmuffs seemed to be made of some hard material, rather than soft; and they bulged out like the bottoms of teacups. Each of these pairs was connected to the other pair by some eight feet of flexible cord that felt—when Bart picked it up between his fingers—like something smoother than ordinary cord or leather, but with some kind of hard core within, though that was also flexible.

''Put them on,'' said Michel, demonstrating. ''Cover your ears.''

He put on one pair of the devices. The slim piece attached, curved around until its end almost touched his lips. Bart followed his example and was surprised to find that, although they were in no way sticky, the earmufflike parts clung over his ears like iron to a magnet.

"Have you got them on all right? Can you hear me?" Michel spoke to him, thinly but clearly, directly in his covered ears.

"Yes," he said, and his voice, too, sounded thin and strange in his ears as Michel's had done.

"All right, then," said Michel's voice. "Follow me. Keep well down and whatever you do, don't reach up to touch the shield overhead. It ought to be perfectly safe to touch it, but let's not take any chances. And you've got to stay close enough to me for the wire to reach. Ready? Go!"

He got down on his back and began to pull himself with his arms, sliding across the smooth floor, in under the edge of the machine. Bart imitated him and followed. He had expected darkness and had fleetingly wondered how they were to see anything in any detail underneath here in only the light that was reflected from the room outside. But he found the space into which they crawled had its own, if very strange, form of lighting.

There was a good foot and a little of clearance between his upturned face and the same milky, semi-transparent shielding that he had seen covering the spinning, vertical sheets of metal on the sides and above. But down here, above the shielding and below the turning fan blades, once they were more than a few feet in from the rim, was a network—something like a grille—of interconnected, heavy bars that looked like copper but seemed to give off a pale, almost moonlightlike glow.

"What's that light?" he asked Michel.

It was strange to speak into the small end of the curved part touching his lips; even stranger to hear Michel's voice in answer, thin and distant-sounding, but clear and understandable in his ears.

"It's a lot of things," Michel's voice answered him now, "but it's toward the blue end of the spectrum and there's a lot of ultraviolet—that's invisible light which is beyond the color of blue, at the blue end of the spectrum, if Vincent taught you anything about the spectrum of visible light—"

"He did," broke in Bart shortly.

"Ah, well, I'd have thought he might. At any rate, the ultraviolet is so far beyond the visible end you can't see it. It's there, though, as in natural sunlight, too, our researchers tell us. It's what gives you a sunburn and it helps plants grow. It's in our corridor and other lights too, because we try to make our light down here as much like natural light as possible. But there's so much of it right here that you'd get a bad burn on your hands and face if we stayed here half an hour or so.''

"I see," said Bart, mentally filing the fact that whatever Michel had to show him must be something that could be shown in something less than half an hour. Not that they probably had anything like that much time before they were rousted out from under here.

It was only after that thought that the implications of these people being able to produce light beyond the visible spectrum began to impact on Bart. He had taken almost for granted their machines for seeing and talking at a distance over wires, their lighting and ventilating systems and everything else, so far. He had told himself that these things were merely devices he, himself, had not known existed. But the sudden connection between invisible light and what his father had taught him gave him unexpectedly a sort of yardstick by which he could measure the distance of their accomplishments; and he was suddenly shocked to feel how much perhaps these strange cavern people might indeed have learned, that humanity in the upper world did not know.

"All right," Michel's voice in his ears interrupted his thoughts, "we stop here. Look closely at what you see above you."

Bart turned his attention to what hung a foot and a bit above his nose.

The milky shield was the same, but what he stared at now was an intricate interlacing of the light-shedding bars, while connecting them and running between them were small flexible cables each of which seemed to be sheathed in a woven network of silver wire. Above all these, in the few empty spaces he could see, there was only gloom, since the moonlight illumination of the glowing bars seemed to block out further vision. No sign of the moving blades of metal he had seen from the outside was now visible.

Tilting his head back, Bart's eyes focused on the shiny metal surface of a round pillar of shaft—which, he suddenly realized, was turning as the metal blades had turned and which must be the continuation of the metal shaft he had seen reaching up to and through the ceiling. It was about eight or ten feet beyond him, occupying the center of the area under the doughnut shape, and in the luminous light under the doughnut the shaft seemed to be dark in color. The featurelessness of the metal had fooled his eye, he realized, into not seeing the swift rotation of the shaft at first.

"I won't try to explain in any detail how the Tectonal works,"

Michel's voice said in his ears. "For one thing, I'm not an engineer in this area and for another thing it'd take far too long. Briefly— and you'll simply have to take my word for it—the part we're lying under is the motivational part for the shaft farther in—what I saw you looking at just now."

"It goes down, from here?" Bart asked.

"That's right," answered Michel, "a great distance down, but only about a third of the way to the magma that underlies the continental plates—those are the rafts of solid, usable land that the surface world lives on. The plates float on the magma; and every so often one of them jostles up against the one next to it. Then its edge rides over or under the edge of the other plate, and a crack's created that lets magma boil up from the interior of the earth. The results are volcanoes or rising or falling of the plates—so what was under the sea a million years ago is now dry land and what was dry land a like time ago may now be the floor of the seabed."

He paused, looking at Bart.

"You follow me so far?" he said.

"I think so," said Bart.

"Good. Well, then. Thanks to the theory of Morton Cadiz, an eighteenth century Lord who was an early paleologist—that being an elaborate term for a person who goes around dating the age of rock layers by the kinds of fossils he finds in them—and the fact we've later proved he was right, we know there are electromagnetic currents in the magma. These don't exactly move it the way ocean currents move the ocean waters, but they have a somewhat similar effect. To the point that a disturbance in the pattern of these electromagnetic flows can disturb the balance of forces in the magma and lead to one plate trying to climb over another. You're still following me?"

"Again, I think so," said Bart. He looked up at the turning machinery overhead and it seemed to him he could feel the massive forces Michel talked about, stirring, deep beneath him.

"All right," went on Michel. "We consequently theorized, tested, and finally built this device called the Tectonal, which you see around you."

"And it does what to the magma?" asked Bart.

"Well," answered Michel, "the answer to that's a bit complicated. In layman's language, it began by sending pulses of electromagnetic force from the lowest end of the drill, to tap it to one of the currents of like force already down there, suck it up, build it up, and feed it back down again—and continue this. As it continued, it took up and returned larger and larger elements of the force, until now, after a number of years, it's pumping enough force into the flow it touches to change it from a small current to one much larger than it was originally, large enough to disrupt the pattern of force flows. It is just now at about the point where that pattern is going to give."

He paused.

"Then what?" demanded Bart.

"Well," said Michel's voice, "when it does, there'll be a widespread readjustment of the pattern of forces in the magma, and consequent widespread readjustment of the plates above it. In short, the surface world will go through hell—some land subsiding below sea level, other land rising abruptly; and volcanic activity all over the place. Except here, of course, which was carefully chosen because it was in one of the safe places."

Bart tilted his head back and fastened his eyes on the turning, polished shaft.

"How far down does this go below us?" he asked.

"Several miles," answered Michel. "It's not the diameter you see for more than the first few hundred feet down. After that, it begins to narrow every few thousand feet. About half a mile short of the end of its shaft, it's the diameter of the original drillhole— some six inches in diameter. After that last half-mile, it comes to an end. From there on down, the penetration through rock the rest of the way to the magma is immaterial. I don't know enough to explain that part of it to you, if I wanted to; but essentially, we've energized a channel down through the rest of the plate rock into the magma itself."

"And so this electric-whatever force of yours—," began Bart.

"Electromagnetic."

"—Electromagnetic force of yours," Bart went on, "pours down this channel into the magma. What is magma, exactly?"

"It's rock that'd be melted to a liquid if it weren't under so much pressure," Michel said. "When the pressure's taken off; as when it breaks through to the surface—in a volcano, say—it does become liquid. But even under pressure down there, it acts a lot like a liquid. As I say, don't ask me for details. That's not my specialty. The point is, the force does go into the magma, it does act like a current of water flowing into the ocean and mixing with the currents already there, and altering them by the force of its thrust."

"And what you can send down is strong enough to do that?" Bart asked skeptically.

"Of course not!" said Michel. "Not by itself. But for years now, the Tectonal's been drawing up electromagnetic forces and pumping them back in a patterned manner—in such a way that it's finally become strong enough to produce a . . . I don't know quite how to describe it to you. Imagine a sort of whirlpool that keeps growing until it begins to touch and bend around itself the currents it finally reaches, incorporating them, too, into itself. It uses its own strength to just bend, a small amount, the forces already there—and as a result the whole balanced pattern of currents becomes unbalanced."

"All right. The pattern is unbalanced. Then what?" Bart asked.

"Then the magma begins to push differently against the plates of solid rock floating in it, harder than it pushed before in some places, less hard in others. As a result, the plates begin to move. Somewhere, the boundary between two plates breaks, releasing even more pressure and setting the magma below free to boil up to the surface, through a volcano, or just through a crack in the level plate. Or the pressure is drained away from under a section of a plate, and then that section drops—subsides, in geological terms. For example, the whole central plate of North America between the ranges of the Allegheny and the Rocky Mountains is destined to sink, and the waters of the Gulf will rush in northward to cover what once was dry surface land. Like things will happen at other places around the globe."

"Fine," said Bart, squinting overhead at the visible section of the turning shaft. "How do we put it out of action?"

"That's the problem," said Michel. "There's only one way of stopping what's going to take place. That's to stop the patterning of the force being returned to the magma, so that randomness will return to the currents. And there's only one way to do that. It's by stopping the turning of this shaft, jamming it in its drillhole and breaking it off, so that its upper part will have to be withdrawn and they'll have to fish out the broken lower part. The time involved in doing that is time out from the continuous feed that's been kept up for the last eighteen years and, interrupted, it'll fail to supply the whirlpool of force below until it's self-supporting, which it should be in a matter of weeks, now."

"Which will cause what to happen?" asked Bart.

"Which will cause the whirlpool to fall apart, the captured currents will be lost before they're firmly caught and the project will have to start over again. It could cost them anywhere from twenty to fifty years just to build the Tectonal back to the position it had when the breakage happened."

"Then that's what we'll do," said Bart.

"Ha!" Michel's voice came to him over the earphones, thinly derisive. "You think it can be done—just like that? Have you any idea of what you're dealing with, or what it'd take to jam the shaft? It's not just a matter of dropping some explosives down the shaft and triggering them off. Even if everyone in this room—and there's a shift on duty like this twenty-four hours a day—would just stand around and watch. To begin it, it'd take some days of work to get the cover off the shaft, where it enters the floor. Then, since none of us can get into the X Collection, where the plans are, we've got no way of knowing how much space there is to introduce explosives beside the shaft, how much it'd take to break it, how far down to lower them, how to fuse them so that—"

His voice broke off. Bart was not surprised, for at that moment he felt both his ankles grabbed from behind and he was unceremoniously dragged out from under the turning shape of the Tectonal. He saw Michel being pulled out with him.

They were brought out into the bright light of the room, where they scrambled to their feet to face a triumphant Merk, flanked by Yna Sicorro. Michel took off his earphones and Bart followed his example.

"This time," Yna said to Michel, "you've gone too far."

chapter
twenty-one

SHE TURNED HER gaze on Bart and held out a hand, palm up, bent
at that emphatic sharp right angle of the wrist of which women
tend to be more capable than men.

"And you, whoever you are," she said to Bart. "Hand it
over—*now!*"

There could be no doubt what she meant. Almost sheepishly
Bart found himself unpinning his badge and putting it in that slim
demanding palm.

Her fingers closed on it firmly and she turned her glare back on
Michel.

"As I say," she told him, "you've finally gone over the limits.
You know better than to do something like this. I've no choice. I'll
have to tell the Emperor about it."

"To be sure, dear cousin," said Michel with one of his bright
smiles, "and as far as my companion goes, let me introduce you
cousin and my half-brother, Bartholomew Saberut, son of our
mutual father, that remarkable Lord Vincent Saberut who went on
a mission up to the surface many years ago. Bart grew up there
as a consequence; and we're just now introducing him to his heritage."

"That's not going to help either of you with the Emperor!" said
Yna grimly. "Michel, how could you be so stupid as to pull a wild
trick like this? Everybody's always said you'd try one joke too
many some day; and it looks like this is it."

"Oh, as for the Emperor," said Michel, "have no fear, dear
cousin. Bart and I have an appointment to see him first thing
tomorrow morning, anyway. I'll explain it all to him, then."

"It better be some pretty tall explaining," said Yna.

"And if it doesn't satisfy him, then what?" Michel smiled at her
again. "Maybe I'll just disappear and no one will ever see me
again—all because you had to tell him!"

"You know better than that," said Yna. "We'd never stand for
his doing anything like that. If he could do that to you and get away

with it, as if you were a common slave, then he could do it to any of us. But there's plenty of other ways he can make your life miserable.''

She watched them out the door. In the corridor outside, Michel turned to his right and set off at a good pace like a man with no time to lose.

''What was all that about disappearing and the fact they wouldn't stand for it?'' asked Bart in a low voice. ''And who did she mean by 'we'? That group I saw you with in the Library stacks?''

''More than that,'' answered Michel. This time his ready smile was tight-lipped. ''She was talking about the whole Hybrid class. My cousins have an affection for me, god knows why. If I suddenly turned up missing, one of them—probably Yna herself—would request an audience with the Emperor to ask that I be found; and if I was found dead, or couldn't be turned up at all, our Emperor would have a neat little revolution on his hands. He wouldn't dare kill off another Lord without powerful reason; and he can't do away quietly with his loyal nephews and nieces, either.''

''But if you simply weren't to be found—,'' Bart began.

''There's no such thing in the Inner World. We're a tight little closed box here, with only two official holes to elsewhere. One is a trash disposal, that's a crack in the rock going no one knows how far down; but a crew's on duty there twenty-four hours a day, including at least one Lord, slaves, and—of course—some Hybrids. Then there's the bridge into the mine—but there's a twenty-four hour guard and crew on that, too. Of course, there're a couple of secret bolt-holes, undoubtedly—one at least of which I've got high hopes he'll be telling us all about tomorrow morning. But every Hybrid and Lord knows those exist, even if they don't know their exact locations. So, a failure by him to produce me alive and healthy would pretty well prove he'd done away with me.''

Bart nodded. Michel was setting a good pace, as they turned into a wider, more traveled corridor.

''When did we get an appointment to see the Emperor tomorrow morning?'' Bart asked him in a low voice.

''In about twenty minutes,'' said Michel. He flashed Bart a momentary, sideways grin. ''There are two classes of people who can get immediate audiences with the Emperor. Those he likes very much, and those he dislikes tremendously. Count me among the latter number, Brother.''

"Now, I'll tell you what," he went on, but looking once more ahead of him as he went and speaking in a voice as low as Bart's, "actually, what I've got to see is the Emperor's private secretary; and I think I know where to find her. But this is something I do better alone. So I'll leave you here, and meet you at Pier's front door. What time are you supposed to be there?"

"After he and his wife have dinner," answered Bart. "I figured on nineteen hundred hours as an arrival time."

"Good enough. 7:00 P.M. I'll see you and your Emma, then—and remember, when we're finally closeted with Pier and Marta, let me do the talking."

"If you think so," said Bart, with some misgivings. He stopped, and watched Michel walk rapidly away from him, and then vanish around a corner.

In spite of these misgivings, however, 7:00 P.M. found him, with Emma, moving along a corridor pierced by entrances to living quarters of those of more than ordinary consequence among the Lordly class. Bart was back in his Steed's clothing.

All along the wide, tapestried, corridor walls there were, at intervals, pairs of doors. One door was always large, ornately carven and impressive; the other just large enough to admit a good-sized male slave, and with a plain, brown, dark wooden surface.

They came close to the doors to the quarters of the Librarian and his wife; and it had been obvious from some distance that there was no one waiting outside them. Wherever Michel might be, he was not here as he had promised.

Bart was trying to decide whether they should wait a few minutes at least for his Hybrid half-brother, or simply go in and trust to his turning up eventually. He had filled Emma in on his relationship with Michel and the events of the afternoon; and as they approached the entrances, she was now doing the talking. As a matter of interest to them both, she had been taking advantage of her job in the accounting department to try and make some estimates of the financial situation of the Inner World, and its owners, the Lordly class.

". . . I couldn't do much about getting any solid figures on anything—particularly without seeming to be looking for them," said Emma as the two of them walked up the long hall to the door of dark, heavy wood that was the slaves' entrance to the multiple rooms that made up the apartments of Pier and Marta Guettrig, "but maybe there's no need to know exactly. Just a general look at the sort of figures we're handling implies something . . . unbelievable. At a guess, the Lords're so rich the figures hardly make sense. Every one of them has to be a millionaire many, many times over. They could probably give a million to each of the slaves and never know the difference, as far as their general fortunes go."

She paused as they reached the slaves' entrance and he scratched on the panel in it provided for carrying the sound to whoever was on duty beyond.

"Of course, most of that worth is tied up in property and investment," Emma went on, "but it's exactly the profits on that property and investment that pay for the continuous inflow here of all kinds of goods—"

The door swung open and she stopped talking. A tall, erect, gray-haired, rather angular woman, wearing a slave tunic in dark blue, nodded to Bart and looked more than a little contemptuously at Emma.

"They've just finished dinner," the doorkeeper said, speaking to Bart, "earlier than usual. But the Lord told me to say you weren't to feel you've been negligent in not getting here before this."

She led the way; and they followed her through a series of corridors, each more thickly carpeted and paneled than the last, until she stopped and stood to one side of a plain, but tall door of polished maple wood.

"They're having tea here in the dining room's side lounge," she said.

Bart stepped forward and scratched at the door.

"Who?" asked the voice of Pier, from somewhere over their heads, in French.

"Bart Dybig, Lord, with a slave companion named Emma Robeson," answered Bart in the same language.

"Come in, Bart," said the voice of Pier.

Bart opened the door and the two of them entered a room that was so conventional and like all the sitting rooms in well-to-do homes above ground that it suddenly brought back to Bart an aching memory of that single parent he had known and loved. It was a square room, filled with heavy square furniture, standing on thick carpets; and with the many surfaces of its furniture covered with small bits of lace, or cloth with scenes worked into it.

The only unusual touches were the smallness of the furniture, the heavy tapestries covering the walls, which were so common in the rooms of the Lordly class of the Inner World, and the fact that the lamps lighting the room had under their shades a round ball of glass lit by electromagnetic force.

Pier and Marta sat in dark blue, downscaled wingback chairs, partly facing each other but essentially side by side, with a small, lace-covered table between them on which stood a silver tray and a tea service in white and gold china.

"Come in, Bart," repeated Pier as the door closed behind Bart and Emma; and they both halted, as was the custom, a pace inside the door. "Come and sit down with us. You'll find hassocks to sit on, over at the far side of the room."

Bart went and got the hassocks, round leather creations which, when he and Emma were seated before the two in their chairs, put their eyes on a level with those of Pier and Marta. Close up, in the lamplight, the makeup Marta wore was not visible, so that she looked indeed like Pier's granddaughter, or even great-granddaughter. Nonetheless, she took immediate charge of the proceedings.

"You'll have some tea," she said decidedly.

For the first time Bart noticed that there were four, rather than just two, cups on the silver tray. It was a highly unnatural thing, by Inner World standards—that much Bart had discovered for himself already—for Hybrids, let alone those of the Lordly class, to eat with slaves. In fact it was not done even to eat at the same time that slaves were eating, in the same room. But Pier, as he had said occasionally, made his own rules, particularly in his own home.

"Here you are," said Marta, handing a steaming cup on its gold and white saucer to Emma, who seemed at the moment only a bit larger than she was.

"Thank you," said Emma, as politely, but also as calmly as if there was nothing unusual in taking tea with the wife of one of the Three Who Command. She accepted the cup and sipped from it, while Marta handed another cup to Bart. He also sipped at the dark tea in it, but cautiously. All his life he had found that he seemed to be able to burn his tongue on food and drink other people swore were no more than comfortably hot. Emma, on the other hand, could drink tea at practically scalding temperatures.

"Now," said Marta to Emma, "how long have you known Bart?"

"Oh, we grew up together," said Emma. "From the time he was about six years old and his father brought him in from the Indian camp where he'd lived until then. His father insisted he go to the little school where we were; though from that time on, I think, Bart learned more from his father than from the teacher, in all sorts of ways. At the same time, though, he came to understand why his father wanted him to unlearn being an Indian and learn how to get along with civilized folk, instead. His father was right."

"Oh?" Marta smiled encouragingly. "Why do you say that?" Emma laughed.

"You'd have said it yourself, if you'd seen him, those first few weeks. Standing apart from all the other boys and girls, refusing to play any games and scowling at everybody and everything!"

"I didn't scowl!" said Bart, startled.

"You most certainly did. All the girls were fascinated; and all the boys wanted to pick a fight with you, but there was a rumor you'd try to kill them, if they got you started.—It was just as well." Emma turned to the other woman. "Bart was strong for his age and might have actually hurt one of the other boys, or gotten himself hurt. After a few weeks, though, he stopped scowling and he'd play some of the games with the rest of us at recess; but really he always preferred being by himself."

"How interesting," said Marta, putting her cup down carefully. "You and your brother came down here from that revolutionary group we sponsored, didn't you?"

"Not sponsored, my love," Pier said. "We funded and encouraged them to a certain extent—through intermediaries, of course—on the theory that if we did so, they'd actively discourage exploration and exploitation of the area all around us. Actually, we rather believed that they would end up getting themselves killed off, and we did not care one way or the other for their political aspirations. But in the meantime they serve us by keeping civilization from spreading to this part of the continent too quickly. And so they have—along with the terrain, the weather, and other hardships, of course."

"I understand—as well as I understand any of these things—," said Marta with a brilliant smile at Emma, "that some of those revolutionary friends of your brother didn't trust him too well, or else the two of you wouldn't have ended up here with us.''

"Oh, you're very right," said Emma. Her own tones were almost an echo of Marta's and she smiled back. "I never did like what those Scottites stood for; and I didn't realize that Arthur—that's my brother—was working for them. In fact, I don't think he really did much for them—he's really not very effective. But in any case he wouldn't have paid any attention to me, of course."

"Of course," said Marta.

It was almost sickening, thought Bart, the way they could smile at each other that way, as if they were sharing some sort of secret knowledge. He sat back, waiting for his tea to cool and pretending to take sips from it while Marta cross-examined Emma about her background—and Bart's. Emma bore the examination not merely with fortitude, but as if it was an actual pleasure to have such a talk.

From Bart's point of view it was downright dull, if not uncomfortable, to listen to his childhood being rehearsed this way. Apparently Pier must have shared some of his feelings, for the old man interrupted his wife after about ten minutes.

"My love," he said, "why don't you take Emma off to do the rest of your conversation in one of the other lounges? I've just remembered some business to do with the Library I want to talk over with Bart."

"Of course, dear," said Marta, standing up immediately. Emma rose also. "Just leave your cup there, Emma. I'll have fresh tea brought us someplace else. Come along."

They rose to leave; but at that moment there was a scratching at the door.

"What?" asked Pier, raising his voice.

"Your pardon, Lord," said the voice of the woman who had escorted Bart and Emma to the room. "But Mr. Michel Saberut is calling. He says he has business with you concerning your present visitors."

"Hmm?" said Pier. "Marta, my dear, perhaps you and Emma hadn't better leave us just yet."

Marta sat down again in her chair, motioning Emma to her hassock, as Pier raised his voice.

"Let him in!"

The door opened immediately and Michel was ushered in, now wearing a suit of beautifully tailored black evening clothes.

"My Lord, Lady," said Michel, stopping just inside the entrance. He came forward with outstretched hands. "Uncle Pier, Aunt Marta—it's good of you to let me drop in without warning like this."

"You're always welcome here, Michel. You know that," said Pier, as he and Marta each briefly grasped a hand of the younger man. "What've you been up to now?"

"Up to, Uncle? What makes you think I've been up to something?"

"That's usually what brings you here; or else you're about to be up to something—oh, find yourself a hassock and sit down, Michel!" said Pier.

"Seeing you is always reason enough for coming," said Michel solemnly, dragging up a hassock like the ones Bart and Emma were seated on and sitting down himself. "You've always been the closest thing to family I ever had."

"We love you, too, Michel," said Marta, smiling warmly at him. "But what is it this time?"

"Well, you'd hear all about it tomorrow anyway," said Michel. "As a matter of fact, Bart and I have an appointment to see the Emperor at 6:00 A.M. tomorrow morning about it. You see, just this afternoon I took Bart to see the Tectonal; and Yna Sicorro caught me at it. She's probably already passed a message on it to His Majesty."

"You did what?" Pier's head came up sharply and suddenly.

"I took him in to see the Tectonal," repeated Michel. "You see, Bart, whom you know as a slave, is actually a Hybrid. The fact is, he's my half-brother, sired by Vincent Saberut after he went up on a mission to the surface."

The words were out. Pier did not at once respond and Bart had braced himself for any conceivable kind of reaction. But while Marta did not even change expression, the response from Pier was one he could never have expected.

He noticed suddenly a glitter to Pier's eyes and realized with shock that the old man had tears in them.

"Of course," said Pier at last, looking at him. "Of course you are. My boy, we knew it from the first moment we found you!"

The equivalent of the explosion Bart had expected in the old man now took place in Bart, instead. He stared at Pier.

"I don't understand, Lord," was all he could manage to say. He realized that no matter how shaken he felt inside, to his listeners his words had seemed to come out fully controlled. Bart had realized for a long time that he had a tendency to conceal emotion of any kind. Now he only hoped he hadn't sounded so flat as to seem cold or hostile.

"Naturally, you don't. How could you?" The tears were running down Pier's cheeks now along the lines that time had engraved there, into his sparse beard. He wiped them away with an edge of his robe and stared at Bart with a misty smile.

"We Three Who Command," he said, "enforce the laws evolved from the Book of al-Kebir. But, out of necessity, we also enforce rules on ourselves. And these are rules backed by our own sense of honor—which must never be compromised. My honor has compelled me, even privately, to keep from acknowledging you for who you really were—as I would have otherwise. With the other Two it was agreed that you shouldn't be told who you were, until and unless you were able to recognize it for yourself."

Bart was still tumbling mentally from this bombshell of information. The only thing he could think of to say was a repetition of the words he had just said. He put to one side the fantastic puzzle of what about him had convinced Pier and the other Two he was a Hybrid, before he had even been conscious enough to speak.

"I still don't understand, Lord," Michel said slowly. There was a faint, tight smile to the corners of his lips and a glitter to his eyes, in turn, that was not at all emotional but almost malicious. "If all the Three Who Command were convinced Bart was a Hybrid, why was he made a slave in the first place?"

"Oh, Michel, Michel—life's never simple. You'll learn that more and more as you get older. You know we Three have to be unanimous in our decision on all things; except in an emergency, when there's no time for consultation. Then the Emperor's word alone rules over everything else. I agreed with the other Two, although I knew the ruling was unfair; but let me tell you how it all happened."

"Thank you, Lord," said Bart.

"Oh, call me 'Grandfather,' not 'Lord!' Your father called me 'Father' even though he was no child of mine—neither Marta nor

I ever had children . . . but never mind that now. In the privacy of this house, call us Grandfather and Grandmother!''

''If that's what you want . . . Grandfather,'' said Bart, touched; though the word seemed to fit strangely and awkwardly in his mouth.

''You see,'' said Pier, ''the door by which you tried to enter the Inner World from the mine where they had you working—and believe me, I had no idea you were there—no idea you even existed at that time, or I'd never have permitted you to be held there at all—has a bridge which comes into place only if the proper controls in the mine are moved.''

He half lifted a hand as if to reach out and touch Bart, then dropped the thin, veined fingers back into the lap of his brown robe.

''Not knowing those controls were there—and how could you have known? Not knowing they were there, you opened the door, went through, and fell into the underground river that forms part of our protection against unauthorized entrance. It's a fall of some thirty feet; and the river is deep, icy, and very fast-running. It swept you away with it, as it's swept other intruders before you, until it came to a point where the rock around it closes down completely, and there's no air space left at all. It's six minutes before the speed of the current carries anything swept into that water-filled tunnel out the other side, into an area where the overhead rock rises again and there's air above the surface to breathe. At that point we've got a guard post.''

''Guard Post Two,'' put in Michel. ''The bridge is Guard Post One.''

''A Guard Post?'' asked Bart.

''Yes,'' said Pier, ''it's where the rock opens out—actually, it opens out naturally and the opening's been improved by blasting, and cutting out a ledge in the rock along one side of it. At that point we've a net strung across the river to catch anything headed downstream. Downstream—since upstream the river is for practical purposes unreachable without a great expense of tunneling, and it's our fresh water supply. We use the net to keep anything that might foul the water from getting downstream to the point where we pump it out. That includes, of course, the dead bodies of anyone who tried to enter the Inner World from the door in the mine.''

"And after six minutes underwater they're pretty sure to be dead, even if being banged about on the rocks hasn't finished them," said Michel.

"That's right," said Pier, "and they always have been dead—until you came through. Somehow you were still living. Unconscious, but still living."

"I swam with the current, hoping to come to some place where there was air," said Bart.

"You must be a powerful swimmer," said Pier. "At any rate, the foreman of the slaves who pulled you out in the net noticed this and got in touch with the Hybrid in charge of that duty shift. The Hybrid woke the Lord whose responsibility was the work of protecting the cleanliness of the water. That Lord—you may meet him one of these days if you haven't already, his name is Jan Rakar—recognized the possibility that you might have some Hybrid characteristics; and this, together with the fact you'd lived through the six minutes of water tunnel, made you a matter of extraordinary concern.

"Jan went, as was only proper, to the Emperor; who set up a time for we Three Who Command to examine you in strict privacy, the following morning. Until that time you were to be taken care of, but watched and drugged, so that you didn't wake to find out where you were. You were transferred to a private room in the Clinic, under a medication to keep you asleep. More was used when you showed signs of regaining consciousness naturally. Meanwhile, the Head of Clinic, the Lord Doctor Abu Galum, personally examined you."

His voice hoarsened and he stopped. The glint of tears were again in his eyes. Bart waited patiently for him to go on. After a moment the eyes cleared, and when he spoke again, his voice was as under control as usual.

"We Three and Dr. Lord Galum saw you in that private—and guarded—room, early the next morning," he went on, "and one thing had been proven by that time. You definitely had a sufficiency of the physical characteristics that marked the Hybrids among us—traits that could only have been inherited from one of our own Lordly people. But none of us recognized you; and as Librarian I had already searched the records for any mention of you being born to one of our people who was temporarily in the upper world—for of course we knew from the records of the mine, when we looked, what your name was. I testified that I had found no mention of you.''

Once more his voice had hoarsened, but it cleared again immediately as he went on.

"The conclusion was obvious. You were beyond all doubt a Hybrid, but one who had grown up in the upper world, knowing nothing of your heritage. The sores and scars from the ankle irons on you showed that much. If you had known what you were, there were any one of a dozen words you could have said that would have made even those ignorant slave-crew foremen start a process of checking up that would have brought you to our attention; and once we knew who you were you would have been freed immediately.''

Pier shook his head sadly.

"The question, of course, became what to do with you. The simplest solution, which the Regent suggested right away, was simply to eliminate you. I pointed out that this might not be contrary to law, but it certainly was to custom. If you were indeed a Hybrid, whether you knew it or not you were a nephew to all of us and we owed you a certain consideration.''

He hesitated.

"Bart,'' he said, "it's going to take you a little time to understand all this, but there are philosophical, what you might even call political, divisions among us—even us of the Lordly class.''

"I think Bart realizes that already, Uncle,'' said Michel.

"Yes,'' Pier gazed at Bart, "perhaps he does, with you and others to help him. In any case, it exists, Bart, with us as with others. Our people are divided into two groups, Textualists and Liberals. The Textualists tend to believe strongly in the exact words al-Kebir wrote originally in the KITAAB, although he wrote them in a world as it existed six hundred years ago. We Liberals—and you'd guess very quickly, if Michel hasn't told you so already, that Marta and I are of that thinking—believe in adjusting those original precepts in terms not only of a changed world, but in the light of the growth of our own fortunes in that world . . . but I don't want to get involved in telling you all that, now.''

He cleared his throat, and with the effort, his small, wispy beard twitched for a second.

"The important thing is, both the Emperor and the Regent belong to the Textualists; and this, in addition to the difference between their generation and mine, makes us natural opponents in many ways. When you were found, it quickly developed that the problem of what to do with you, now you'd appeared among us, was one of these. There's a natural historical swing in the thinking of all populations between generations. When I was still relatively young and first elected Librarian, Lordly thinking was predominantly Liberal. The generation that followed, the one to which the Emperor and the Regent belong, swung back toward Textualism. Now it's swinging back once more toward Liberalism, if it hasn't already—in fact I think it may have.''

He hesitated.

''I think if a vote was taken today,'' he said, ''we'd find the majority of my class now favor finding a way of living with the outside world the way it is, rather than destroying it and dominating the handful of humans who survive. But there's no certainty; and if I was to call for a popular vote on the subject—for which I'd need a reason, but which as one of the Three I'm empowered to do—and the majority wasn't overwhelmingly in my favor, I could lose most of my authority; because it rests, in practice, on the Emperor's and the Regent's assumption that a large number of the Lords are with me on anything I want to do. So if I called for a vote and failed, then the other Two could practically do what they want with the Command.''

He shook his head as if to clear away from his mind the cobwebs of a dream.

''But that's beside the point right now,'' he said. ''I want to tell you how matters stand with you, so you can understand why you've been treated the way you have. When the Three of us got together beside your anesthetized body in the Clinic—it was quite some time after you'd been fished out; and, left to yourself, you'd have regained consciousness and seen where you were—as I said, the Regent's immediate proposal was to eliminate you. You'd grown up entirely outside the Inner World, you knew nothing of our customs, and could only be a burden and a source of trouble among us, with your essentially human point of view.''

Pier took a deep breath.

''The Emperor agreed with him. I disagreed. You have to understand. As a Hybrid, according to the written word of al-Kebir, you've no more rights than any other human. But over the centuries—since the Hybrids are, after all, our own children—a certain amount of affection on our part . . . well, the result has been for them to acquire a body of essentially unofficial, but still effective, rights.

"I told the other Two that, under those rights, you had to be given a chance to survive among us, who were your family; unless there was a specific reason you shouldn't be given that chance."

Pier shrugged.

"Naturally, from that point on the disagreement progressed along political lines; Liberal versus Textualist thinking. The other two pointed out that by being born and having grown up outside the Inner World, you'd never passed the tests you would normally have had to take at age eleven and seventeen, to prove your right to be here among us. I said that while this was true, there was no reason you should not first be given a chance to learn about us and the Inner World, and then take those tests."

Pier smiled.

"You have to understand," he said, "that this argument put them between the jaws of a nutcracker. The insistence on anyone with at least fifty per cent of our blood being tested for survival—for fear that our Lordly strain should lose itself and be diluted among the mass of humanity—was one of al-Kebir's strongest precepts and as such is venerated by the Textualists, like all his precepts. On the other hand, the mere fact that I had opposed them on the question of your being allowed to live made it a matter of face to them that you be destroyed."

Bart nodded.

"'Let him live, then,'" said the Emperor, "'but if he's worthy of being a Hybrid he'll have to prove himself, without any help at the start from anyone. Let him begin by being a slave; and we'll see if he even recognizes himself as something more than that or just accepts his lot. If he decides to stay a slave for the rest of what life is allowed him, then it'll be plain that's all he's worthy of.'"

"Of course I protested," said Pier. "I argued it was unfair to make anyone of Hybrid blood serve as a slave. I asked how they could expect you could even have the chance to question the fact you were something more, when all our system was set up to leave a slave with no alternative to accepting what he was. Let alone, the regular Clinical drugging and mesmerising to create the illusion in their minds that they had been raised from the dead to be what they were."

Pier smiled again.

"They objected in turn, particularly the Regent, who of course had agreed with the Emperor from the start that the system could not be violated. But they knew they were trapped. You would have to be allowed to bypass the Clinic visits. I pointed out that there were already exceptions, such as certain former politicals and others, like your Emma, here, and her brother, who were excused from them. Such slaves are usually exempted because it might turn out to be useful, once again, to use them above ground. In a nutshell, I was bargaining for what I eventually got, which was a grudging approval from the other Two that I might personally make use of you as my own slave; and, under the restrictions of honor and duty, expose you to the opportunities, only, to discover you were something more than an ordinary human."

He stopped and watched Bart.

"I see," said Bart thoughtfully. "I'm indebted to you, Lord."

"Grandfather."

"I'm indebted to you, Grandfather." Bart was astonished at the deep rush of gratitude in him, in spite of the questions that still were there. He decided to bring the questions out and have done with it. "But you went to a lot of trouble—and probably even some risk—for me. Why should you? Just on your Liberal principles, alone?"

"Oh no, child," said Pier. "You remember I told you your own father called Marta and myself 'Father' and 'Mother' in the privacy of this home. Galum, with his Clinicians and the other Two had recognized you as a Hybrid. But secretly, I had already recognized not only that but something more, from the moment I set eyes on you. I'd recognized you as the son of Vincent Saberut. You're nearly twice his size, you've strong indication of the Indian blood in you. But to my eyes, from the start, you were unmistakably his son; like the grandson Marta and I might have had if it had not been for the KITAAB, and Marta's determination."

chapter
twenty-two

IT WAS THE last three words that caught at Bart's mind and held it. The implications in it were strong enough so that he risked a question even though it might threaten the personal relationship Pier had just set up between them.

"Did you say 'Marta's determination,' Grandfather?" he asked.

"Yes, Grandson," said Pier. "Your Grandmother is a woman of powerful will."

He smiled a little.

"It might even have been interesting, if they'd been members of the same generation, to see her and al-Kebir himself in opposition on some point. But, in any case, much as she's loved me all these years and supported me—so that otherwise I don't know how I'd be alive today, particularly with the present Emperor and Regent—she's always refused to have a child. A child by me or any concubine—not that she's ever taken concubines—"

He turned his smile fondly for a moment on Marta and her smile answered him. For a moment the two of them were alone in the room.

"—Though that was her right as much as mine. But, we have ways of preventing conception that are absolutely certain; and Marta's made certain that not even she and I produced children."

Bart looked at him curiously.

"If I may ask—have you ever taken concubines, Grandfather?"

"I? No," said Pier. "I have to admit that there were a few times, when I was younger, I was tempted. But the temptation was only transient; and those who tempted me fell so far short in any comparison with Marta, that I soon came to realize they'd only be a source of disappointment to me in the end. Besides, as I say, Marta had made up her mind to go childless; and that in itself created a bond between us that shut out any real desire for concubines in me."

He stopped talking and seemed lost in his own thoughts—or memories. Bart gently stirred the conversation back to life.

"I think," he said, "you were about to tell me why Grandmother refused to have any children."

Pier's gaze came back to him from whatever place it had wandered to.

"Yes, I was," he said. "Because I think it's something you ought to know and understand, Bart; in order to understand what your father was like, and how you came, evidently, to be born as you were, to a native human mother. Marta told me from the very beginning of our love that she knew the failings of her own strength."

Bart glanced at Marta. She was seated with her hands clasped in her lap, her face utterly calm, watching her husband.

"As a youngster," Pier went on, returning his wife's steady gaze with an affectionate look, "she'd always wanted children and expected to have them. But as she grew up she came to understand she'd never be able to endure having and loving a child, when there was the slightest danger she might have to give it up. That she might have to hand it over to the Executioners—if for some reason it failed in either of the examinations required of us and the Hybrids at ages eleven and seventeen."

Momentarily, his mouth became a thin, straight line. "In spite of the fact that the Executioners would only be doing their duty," he went on, "and in the gentlest way possible. For we kill these failed children of ours as painlessly, and without their realizing what is happening, as we can. Because we love them, Bart. In spite of this, as I say, she realized she'd never be able to allow such a thing to happen to a child of hers."

He looked suddenly and harshly at Bart.

"Before giving up her child, Marta would see the whole Inner World destroyed; or leave it, and me, to take her child with her into the upper world. Of course, if she had so left, we'd have had to send Executioners out after them both. For al-Kebir's writing is uncompromising on that subject: '. . . *any who shall not qualify, or any who aid them to qualify when they are actually unable, must die.*'"

He paused again, still looking at Bart.

"And she knew," he went on, "that, since I was already one of the Three Who Command when we married—we'd married later in life than most—honor would not let me either leave that post to go with her, or refuse to concur in the orders to send the

Executioners after them. I would have been one of those who killed our own child—and her. For, find her, they almost certainly would. Kill her and the child eventually, they possibly would: for we'd keep sending them out until some of them succeeded. But there's no one like Marta; and she just might have been able to get away safely with our child. Still, it was for the pain she knew it could end in giving me, as well as the pain it would give us both, if we ever realized a child of ours could not pass the tests, that made her decide to never have children.''

He sighed.

''And so,'' prompted Bart again after a long pause, ''you've been childless all your lives.''

Pier smiled gently at him.

''Not childless,'' he said. ''We ended by having your father as a surrogate son; and now you and Emma, as grandson and grand-daughter. Also, we've had Michel and others back to and before your father—though none of them were ever so close to us as Vincent was. When he made his decision and went up to the surface, he left us desolate.''

Bart tried to imagine his father, who had always seemed to him so old and wise, as a young man named Vincent seated at the feet of the smaller and much older figure before him. But his mind found the image hard to form until he remembered his father's love of learning; and the picture became conceivable, but just barely so.

''You see, we had a disagreement, your father and I,'' said Pier slowly. ''A long-standing argument. I believe that the duty of all of us is to work for the Liberal point of view *here,* in the Inner World. He believed that the Textualists of the succeeding generations would never be converted. That they would die rather than change their beliefs. . . .''

Pier shook his head.

''Over the years, many other Liberals have tried as well, to bring me to your father's view; including Michel, here.'' He smiled for a second on Michel, who answered with his sudden flash of his own white, even teeth. ''But I found none of them could really change my mind. To this day I can't believe that there isn't an innate common sense in everyone; and the problem is only that of reaching through to it. I couldn't believe anything else, if I wanted to.''

''The belief does you credit, Uncle,'' said Michel, ''but generation after generation we've had people like the Emperor to deal with.''

''We also have those who, while calling themselves Liberal,'' said Pier, "are as ready to find their solutions in destructive ways as any Textualist. Over the years I've defused more than one plan to wreck our Inner World in the name of saving the surface one. As if two wrongs would make a right! In fact, I think I still have around here one elaborate explosive device that its builders could hardly wait to use; until I talked them out of that—and it. But aren't we getting away from this business of the appointment you and Bart have with the Emperor tomorrow? What you said sounded ominous, Michel. I hope you haven't got Bart into any trouble."

"Not him," said Michel, "he's my half-brother after all, and after being without a family all my life, I'm not going to lose the one I've found. Actually, it's the Emperor who's in trouble."

"Michel, Michel!" said Pier. "What sort of wild thing are you planning?"

"Lord—," began Michel, only to be interrupted by Pier.

"Lord?" The old man's eyes were sharp once more on him. "What happened to 'Uncle'?"

"What I've got to tell you will, I'm afraid, carry us into areas where your official responsibilities lie."

"Oh, Michel!" said Marta unexpectedly. "No!"

"I'm sorry, Aunt," said Michel, looking at her apologetically. "But it has to be."

He turned back to face Pier.

"Lord," he said, "as you know I've always been of the opinion of my father—and Bart's. You've known for some time I wanted to leave the Inner World for the surface, but the Emperor was hardly likely to send me up on mission. He'd like nothing better than my escaping to the surface, if that were possible, so then he could send the Executioners after me. But simply to turn me loose up there might be more dangerous to his plans than keeping me here where he can watch what I'm up to."

"I know all this," said Pier. "And you know how I'd feel about losing you. No one has the influence with the Hybrids that you have. I'd hoped to have your help in bringing our whole Inner World to the point of view I've always worked for. I take it you've concocted some scheme to be sent above? How does it involve Bart?"

"Bart wants to go back to the surface, along with Emma and that brother of hers, who's also a slave down here. I was planning to take them with me when I go."

Pier stared at Bart. He was conscious, also, of Marta's gaze on him, but refused to turn his eyes to her to acknowledge it.

"Is this what you really want?" Pier asked Bart. "Have you thought of what it might be like for you down here as a Hybrid, with Marta and I to assist you?"

"I'm sorry—" Bart had been about to follow Michel's lead and address Pier formally as 'Lord,' but a sudden realization of the pain this would give the old man made him stay with the newer form of address. "—Grandfather, but the Book of al-Kebir isn't in me, as it is in the rest of you. I have to go back; and I have to take Emma back. She doesn't belong here."

There was a long pause, and then Pier breathed in deeply.

"You must do what you feel you should," he said unhappily. "I can hardly have followed that rule all my life and deny it to—to anyone else. But we had hoped, Marta and I, that we could even bring you both into this household of ours, into jobs here that permitted it; and then, when and if children were born to you, we would have great-grandchildren, after all—"

He broke off.

"Forgive me," he said in a flat voice. "Age has made me weak enough to whine. I'm ashamed of myself. Of course, if you wish to go, and there's a means, I'll not only not stand in your way, but help, if I can."

"The help we'll need is something beyond just getting away," said Michel, "but I'll remind you you said that—after I've told you what I plan to say to the Emperor tomorrow morning."

"Yes." Pier turned his attention to the black-clad Hybrid. "What've you planned to say to the Emperor that'll make him let you go?"

"Something, I'm afraid, that'll put you and me on opposite sides of the table, Lord," said Michel, "much as I love you and Marta. But I can't hold the Emperor guilty without, in fact, holding all the Three Who Command guilty."

"Guilty?" Pier frowned, but as much in astonishment as affront. "How can the Emperor or the Three be guilty of anything? The law doesn't allow it."

"It's not law we'll be dealing with in this case," answered Michel, "but custom, justice, and practicality. Above all, practicality, for with all his other faults, the Emperor's a very practical man."

"Michel," said Pier, "give me a straight answer. What is this you're planning to confront the Emperor with, that strikes at all of us Three, including myself?"

"You, Lord," said Michel, "are guiltless. But I know you.

You'll act according to the dictates of your office; that's the only reason you're included in this. In a word, I intend to confront the Emperor with the fact that he had no right to make a slave out of someone he knew to be a Hybrid, as he did with Bart.''

"No right!" Pier's frown had become dangerous.

"No right under the unwritten agreement by which we Hybrids labor all our lives for ends which are the Lords' alone," said Michel. "He violated that unwritten agreement—the Three violated that agreement—but it was his will that made them do so; and unless he makes amends, he'll have to face the consequences.''

"What consequences?"

"My telling all the Hybrids what happened to Bart," answered Michel, "and leaving it up to them to consider that if such a thing could happen to someone like Bart, something like it could happen to any one of them.''

Pier let out the breath which evidently he had been holding all this time. His face was angry now.

"Michel," he said. "You're threatening the Emperor—all of us—with revolution. I warn you, think before you say any such thing. You may believe you and your fellow Hybrids know the full arsenal of our powers. Let me tell you, you don't. Threaten a revolution, try a revolution, even if the slaves would join you in it, and we could still destroy you all.''

"You could—if all the other Lords were really ready to join you in killing their Hybrid sons and daughters. But then?" said Michel. "Then, who'd you use to get done the work that still has to be done, here in the Inner World?"

Pier sat, saying nothing.

"The Emperor," went on Michel, before that pause could become painful, "is, as I say, a very practical man. I think he'll see the wisdom of letting the four of us—myself, Bart, Emma and her brother—go free into the upper world rather than have me say anything to my cousins. Of course, the moment we're gone, he may find some pretext to send the Executioners after us all, or even simply do that secretly without pretext. But we'll take our chances with whoever comes for us, if anyone does.''

There was a long silence in the room. Finally, Pier spoke.

"You're right, Michel," he said. "This does indeed put us on the opposite sides of the table—not only from you but from Bart and Emma, here. But as I couldn't in honor stand in your father's way when he wished to go above, I can't stand in yours. You'll have to do what you've decided to do; and if called upon by the other

Two I may have to vote in any measures that are planned against you as a result of that.''

He dropped his head against the back of his chair for a second and closed his eyes; then opened them and sat up, putting his arms on the arms of the chair.

''And now,'' he said, ''I think that's enough for this one night. Marta and I will excuse you now, so we can get our rest.''

''One moment more, please, Lord,'' said Michel. ''That explosive device you said you still had around the home, here, and which I've heard you mention having before. Would you give it to us and explain how it was to be used? You see, all of us feel we have to at least give the world some breathing space in which people like yourself down here, and we, above ground, can try to bring the Textualists to their senses, or else warn the surface peoples about the disaster that'll otherwise face them, eventually.''

''No,'' said Pier.

''But Lord—,'' Michel began.

''I was against its use in the first place. I'm against it still,'' said Pier. ''My duty is to protect our community, not destroy it.''

''I doubt we could actually destroy the Tectonal, with whatever you've got,'' said Michel. ''Aren't I correct? But to damage it enough to put it out of order for a few months, say by breaking the main shaft and causing it to jam in the drill-hole so that it'd have to be fished out and replaced—that'd give time for the currents already gathered by it in the magma below to disperse, and more time for them to be gathered back up again by a reworking Tectonal. We could gain ten or twenty years, perhaps even thirty; and in that time you and those who came after you could marshal the Lords who are against destroying the surface world and enlist them with the Hybrids in a position to put an end to al-Kebir's ridiculous dream of revenge. Knowing that we're up there and the secret of the Inner World can't be kept much longer, you could lead the way for everyone down here to finally rejoin the real world above.''

''No,'' said Pier.

''Isn't that what you want? What you've always preached should be our goal—reunion with the rest of the human race? I know you don't believe that nonsense in the Book about the Lords being a separate race from somewhere beyond the moon.''

''No, I don't. Nor, I think does any intelligent mind, even those who pretend to believe,'' said Pier. ''But you remind me of some of the Textualists at the time I gave in to the public pressure to advance myself as a candidate for Librarian, one of the Three. I was asked in open debate by one of those Textualists how I'd be able to reconcile my taking of the oath I'd have to take as Librarian with my views as I had announced them for years about the intentions of al-Kebir. How, in short, could I defend the precepts of the Kitaab when my own principles disagreed with it?''

''And how can you?'' Michel's voice held a tone of unusual interest. He stared at the old man.

''I told my questioner,'' said Pier, ''that there was not just one *Book of al-Kebir,* there were as many different books as there were different people who'd read it. For the experience of life and all our teachings combine in each of us to make our own personal Book—that bundle of beliefs by which we live; and the Book that was al-Kebir's in each case had to conform to the individual Book inside each reader if it was to be accepted by that reader. I did not doubt that the *Book of al-Kebir* in him would make it hard, if not impossible, for him to reconcile what he believed he read with what he believed I believed. But in me, there was no conflict between my own and al-Kebir's Book that would prevent me from doing my duty if I was elected.''

''Ah,'' said Michel softly, ''somewhere I must have heard those words repeated. . . .''

He stopped, and Pier looked steadily into his eyes.

''And that,'' the old man said, ''is why I will not give you the means to destroy the Tectonal, even though my heart might be with you in many ways. I am one of the Three and must defend the Tectonal on my honor against the kind of destruction you'd bring on it. Al-Kebir may have been half or more a madman, with his desire to destroy the world; but the end result of what he started has been the development here of the finest scientific work place in the world, and the people to use it. No, I will not give you the means to damage what we have worked for generations to build.''

He got to his feet. Marta rose also; and Bart, along with Emma and Michel, found himself also rising.

''We will say goodnight,'' said Pier formally—then the formality crumbled. He looked almost beseechingly at Bart. ''You and Emma will come by at least one last time before you leave, if leaving is what you end up doing? Can we count on seeing you that one last time?''

''You'll see us,'' said Bart. ''As far as I know, my father never broke a promise and I never have either. I promise you. We'll see you before we go.''

chapter
twenty-three

THE OFFICE IN which the Emperor received Michel and Bart—Emma had come with them but had been separated from them just inside the main entrance and been taken to some separate waiting room from which she had not been called in with them—was large and businesslike. It was also almost devoid of furniture. A thick brown rug was underfoot. The walls and ceiling were panelled wood that was pierced by several massive, closed doors, and Bart realized that he had gotten used to walls hung with tapestries. The desk behind which the most important of the Three Who Command sat was large. It held only an inkwell, a pen, and a single piece of heavy, gray-toned paper, which had been pushed to one side.

Aside from the desk and its chair, the room contained only a handful of padded armchairs built to the physical dimensions of the Lordly race. Clearly visitors of any other rank were expected to stand. Michel led the way to just before the desk and bowed. Bart made himself do likewise, although he was aware that his dislike for doing so made it an awkward gesture on his part.

In any case, the Emperor paid no attention to him, concentrating his gaze instead on Michel.

"Well, Nephew," he said in French, "it seems you've been up to something a little worse than your ordinary tricks?"

"Worse, Majesty?" said Michel innocently.

"Come now," said the Emperor, gesturing at the paper on his desk, "it seems you used illegal means to commit the further illegality of introducing a slave to the room of the Tectonal, without authority. What've you got to say?"

"Why, I hardly know what to say, Majesty," answered Michel. "I don't want to accuse whoever reported this to you of being in error, but I did no such thing."

The Emperor's thin, arching black eyebrows went up in sardonic disbelief.

"You deny this?" he said.

"Why yes," answered Michel. "When was it supposed to have happened, Majesty?"

"Yesterday, as you know very well," said the Emperor. He smiled, and it was a pleasant, if brief, smile; but Bart did not like it, on the handsome, narrow face before him. "Come now, Michel, I hardly thought even you would try to get out of this with a direct lie."

"I assure Your Majesty I would never lie to him," said Michel, "any more than I would ever take a slave into the Tectonal room, unless duly authorized and ordered to do so. In fact, I can't imagine why I would want to do such a thing. I was, indeed, in the Tectonal room yesterday; but only briefly, to give my half-brother and fellow Hybrid, here, Bart Saberut, a glimpse of the Tectonal. Since he grew up on the surface, he'd never had a chance to see such a thing. He was filled with wonder at the sight of it, Majesty."

The Emperor still ignored Bart.

"Now," he said, "what sort of a story is this?"

"Oh, it's the absolute truth, Majesty," said Michel. "A number of Hybrids saw us there, including Yna Sicorro—"

"This report is from Yna Sicorro," said the Emperor, again indicating the paper on his desk, "fully admitting her own fault in letting herself be tricked by you into giving you a copy of your badge, so that the slave could get by the guard."

"What slave, Your Majesty?"

The Emperor stared at him for a long moment, then got to his feet behind his desk.

"Stay!" he commanded. He went out one of the interior doors, closing it firmly behind him.

They waited. Bart had time to worry about Emma. How was she taking all this waiting, he wondered? As he had expected, last night after they had left the Guettrigs', ushered out separately from Michel so that they had had no further chance to talk with Bart's half-brother, Emma had asked him about the Tectonal.

So, he had finally told her. As he had suspected, she had been firm about doing something to stop it. But curiously she had not seemed as concerned as he, himself, about how they could do this, now that Pier had refused to help them.

"The thing is," he had felt he must tell her, "I don't see how we can do anything, now that Pier's set himself against helping us in any way—"

"Don't worry." Unexpectedly she had patted his arm. "We've got some time yet."

Her calmness had puzzled him; but he knew her too well to press her for an answer she was not ready to give. Sooner or later, she would tell him whatever was behind her surprising reaction to something he had known she would feel very strongly about. When she was ready she would tell him.

The Emperor came back in, found another piece of paper magically from below the top of his desk and wrote on it scratchily for a moment, then passed it to Michel. "The date and time are in the upper right hand corner," he said.

Frankly leaning over to read what his half-brother had been given, Bart saw:

We give our imperial word that all recorders have been turned off and all conversation from this moment in this room are held in complete privacy.

It was signed *"Zoltaan—EMPEROR."*

Michel folded the paper and put it slowly into a pocket of his suit.

"Thank you, Majesty," he said.

"Your thanks are beside the point," said the Emperor. "Now, can we get down to what's actually going on, with no more nonsensical answers from you? If you're not here to plead your side of the incident, yesterday, why are you here at all?"

"I'd like Your Majesty's kind orders to send me on mission to the surface, taking along my half-brother, and the slaves Emma and Arthur Robeson."

The Emperor nodded slowly, tilting back in his chair which, to Bart's surprise, obediently changed the angle of its back and arms from the vertical to accommodate him.

"You know, Saberut," he said, "every so often I think about sending you up to the surface instead of keeping you here; up to where you'd be out of sight and hopefully out of the minds of the less reliable of your cousins. I weigh the trouble you can cause me down here with the trouble you might be able to cause me, out of my sight up above, among your cousins there; possibly setting up some procedure for strangling our line of supply from the surface. Each time the answer comes up that I'm safer with you down here where I can watch you. You're aware of all this, no doubt?"

"Why, yes, since Your Majesty asks me," answered Michel mildly. "I'd concluded as much."

"So you're also aware that I'm not likely to send you up on

mission under any circumstances. Yet here you show up, not only with a request for mission, but to be allowed to take along someone who presumably knows other ordinary humans up there who'll believe what he's seen, who has deliberately been given a view of the Tectonal itself. The question arises—why? What makes you think that I'd be likely, particularly in view of what you did yesterday, to suddenly let you have what I long ago decided you'd never have?''

"I'm not surprised Your Majesty's mind finds this question bothersome," said Michel.

"Good," said the Emperor. "Then you'll put it at ease by answering it for me, won't you?"

"I'll be happy to, Majesty," said Michel. "I make this request of you now because it's just occurred to me that you might prefer me up on the surface rather than talking further to my cousins down here—particularly about the case of a Hybrid who, against all custom, was put to duty as a slave instead of being given the rank and position his inheritance entitled him to.''

"Entitled!" exploded the Emperor, suddenly sitting straight up in his obedient chair. But then he caught himself and leaned back again, speaking in the same easy voice he had been speaking in a moment before. "You certainly must understand, Saberut, there can be only one judge of what anyone in the Inner World is entitled to; and that's the single concerted decision of the Three Who Command—whom I lead and direct.''

"Of course, Majesty," said Michel, "just as there can be only one judge of the fear that if a Hybrid has been made into a slave, the same thing might happen to any of them . . . for any reason, or by the decision you spoke of; and the judge of that fear is the concerted opinion of those who do the great majority of skilled and professional work here in the Inner World. We Hybrids, ourselves.''

The silence in the office after Michel finished speaking was so complete it seemed to press down on Bart with a weight of its own. For what seemed several actual minutes, the Emperor neither moved, nor changed expression. Finally, he spoke.

"So," he said quietly, "there we have it at last. You'd blackmail me into letting you go?"

"It was Your Majesty, not I," said Michel, equally quietly, "who used the word 'blackmail.' ''

"Don't split hairs with me, Saberut," said the Emperor, still in his own quiet voice. "We both know what it is."

He sat up in his chair and got to his feet. It was remarkable, Bart thought. The ruler of the Inner World was a full head shorter than either Michel or himself; but for all that, in this moment with his wide shoulders, his slender-faced, bony good looks and burning dark eyes, he seemed to loom as large as either of them. He turned half away from them and, putting his hands together behind his back, began to pace back and forth across the width of the room behind his desk. It was a few seconds before Bart realized that as he walked he was talking to himself, in the same French in which they had been holding their conversation, his voice gradually rising until it became understandable to both his listeners.

". . . a damnable thing!" he was saying, and at that point to Bart's astonishment he began to swear. Bart had not consciously taken note of it until now, but he suddenly realized he had never before heard any of the Lordly class use any religious, profane or obscene word. He realized now that unconsciously he had assumed that with the *Book of al-Kebir* as their bible, they were neither Muslims nor Christians, in spite of al-Kebir's original conversion to the Muslim faith, which, as he remembered from the KITAAB, had been made solely for reasons of personal advantage. It occurred to him now—though it was unimportant at this moment—that others of those who were later to form the Lordly class could have been nominal Christians for the same reason.

He had assumed, in fact, that the Lords and Ladies had, for practical purposes, no religion at all; and somehow associated their lack of expletives with that assumption.

But the Emperor was swearing now, in a rising voice, in a language that gave him scope for highly imaginative profanities and obscenities. It came to Bart abruptly that what he was swearing at, while it was primarily Michel, Bart and everything connected with them, was actually at the Inner and surface worlds as a whole, and anything else that might threaten to frustrate him.

Abruptly he ceased swearing, ceased pacing, and swung about behind his desk to stand facing them; and all at once he was talking directly to them.

"Saberut!" he almost shouted at Michel. "You were the brightest light among your generation of Hybrids, just as no other Lord could touch me for intelligence. You should have been at my side, all along, making yourself useful. Instead, you've fought me every inch of the way, every inch of the way! With all you had, you were a fool like the rest of them. Stupid! Stupid! These things called humans are no more than animals! You, and our kindly old

Guettrig, weeping oceans of tears over the fate of a tribe that's spent its history in murder and in despoiling the world that was given them!"

He gave Michel no chance to answer, and obviously wanted none.

"Murder, wars and dirt—and still, the Liberals cry over them, generation after generation, and pardon them all their crimes and foulnesses. Yes, I know what you think of al-Kebir's claim that we're from a superior place from off this planet—and I don't believe it any more than you do. Tell it in public that I said that and I'll deny it. But I know, and al-Kebir knew, damn well he knew, some such story was needed to hang his plans on."

He gasped, a long, indrawn breath.

"But the plans were necessary, the plans were good. Can't you see that, you soft-minded fool? With that story the others like him swallowed his practical teachings—stay apart, take advantage, accumulate wealth . . . and above all learn, learn more and faster than the ordinary human animals and let only the elite live! That was what he sold them, to one great end—that in the end there would be only the elite, on a world they'd built themselves."

He did pause now, as if waiting for an answer, glaring at Michel and Bart both, now. But Michel clearly had the sense to stay silent, and Bart saw no reason to speak.

"What have they done, from the beginning, but kill and maim each other? Steal from each other, torture and enslave each other, inhumanely—treat each other like the lower animals around them, that they also killed, tortured and maimed? They crowded together in cities and bred filth and disease. They sowed plagues and the greatest names in their histories were the greatest excuse for slaughter of their fellow man. In all the years since al-Kebir began what's now the Inner World, have *we* ever had wars among ourselves? Have we prized stupidity, or sickness, or let disease run unchecked among us? Never! And meanwhile they've been up there on the surface, killing each other by the millions, turning the rivers into sewers, clearing the natural growth from the face of the world—the trees, the grasses, the animals—even poisoning the sea itself."

"And while all this has been going on, what have we been doing? Learning! Studying! Finding out how to control even the massive center of this world—as we'll learn to control the hurricanes and droughts and floods they aren't able to do anything about but die under! And with all this, there are those like you who'd save them by destroying us!"

He stopped. His stare was all on Michel once more, and the glass went out of it.

"Now, Saberut," he said, calm again, "you've heard more from me about me than any other living soul has. Well? No protests? No argument?"

"No, Majesty," said Michel, in a completely expressionless voice. "The Book that is in you is the Book that is in you."

"I didn't think you would have," said the Emperor contemptuously, ignoring Michel's later words. "Let me tell you one thing more, then, to carry off with you. I always knew what I was and what I could do. Long before I was elected Emperor, in fact when I was a child, I made up my mind that whatever it should turn out to be, I'd give my life to doing the greatest thing there was to be done. And I found that greatest thing. It was to deliver this world into the hands of those who could put it to the best use. *That I will do;* and here in the Inner World, or up on the surface, neither you nor anyone else is going to get in my way!"

He stopped talking, went back to sit once more at his desk, producing another piece of paper on which he wrote.

"Names of the slaves?" he asked, still writing.

"Emma and Arthur Robeson," answered Michel.

"You've left out one." The Emperor raised his head and looked directly at Bart. "This one?"

"Bartholomew Saberut," answered Michel.

The Emperor's pen hesitated for a moment, and he wrote again.

"Very well, let it be Saberut," he said.

"A Hybrid."

"Yes, and we'll call him a Hybrid, too, if that's what you want," said the Emperor.

He wrote again and stopped. He handed the paper across to Michel.

"You'll have to make some preparations, I suppose," he said. "But I want you gone as soon as possible." He looked at the timepiece on his wrist.

"It's not yet seven hundred hours. At nine hundred, be in storeroom seven of warehouse twenty-nine. I've noted on that paper, there, that your orders are verbal; and our people above are commanded to accommodate you according to what you tell them. So you can draw on our offices for funds or go to hell in your own way."

"Thank you, Majesty," said Michel.

"Get out!" said the Emperor.

Bart, coached ahead of time by Michel, backed away beside his half-brother until they reached the door; then, hearing it open behind them, they backed on through it and watched it close between themselves and the man behind the desk.

"Now," said Michel, jerking his head to indicate the way out, "we get out, as he said."

But before they went, they had to ask that Emma be produced; and there was a small delay during which it seemed that she could not be found. Then it was discovered that she had been sent off by the Emperor the moment he had been told she was there.

"I hope she went to the Guettrigs'," said Bart, concerned; and they headed for Pier and Marta's home themselves.

But it turned out when they got there that, not only had Emma sensibly come here rather than reporting for her usual work or some other unpredictible destination; but she was in fact having breakfast with Pier and Marta, again an unheard-of thing. As usual, Pier was setting his own rules in his own household. Since neither Michel nor Bart had eaten, they were invited to join the breakfast party—an invitation Bart hungrily accepted but Michel declined.

"We've only got a little over two hours before we're due in that storehouse the Emperor directed us to," he said. "I've got to go get some things from my quarters to take with me—it won't take long. I ought to be back in half to three-quarters of an hour. It's safe enough for me, in any case, here in the Inner World; but Emma's a slave, and Bart's still technically one. I'd appreciate it, Uncle, if you'd keep them under your roof until I get back. The Emperor's in no good temper and what he might do to them is anyone's guess. Particularly if he could catch them wandering around loose."

"True," said Pier, stroking his small beard. "His father, Ymro Radetsky, was a brilliant man but had a very unstable temper; and the boy inherited not only the strength, but the weakness. I'll watch over them."

"Thank you, Uncle," said Michel. Bart, at Marta's urging, sat down at the table on the hassock that had just been brought for him. "Oh, by the way, Emma, where's your brother?"

"He's here," answered Emma.

She offered no further explanation; but a faint, transitory frown on Pier's face was enough to tell Bart that while Emma and Bart might be welcome at his table, that welcome did not include just any slave, Emma's brother or not. Bart wondered fleetingly if

Arthur had already begun exhibiting his usual lack of charms.

"Then, I'll be back shortly and we'll leave as soon as I get here," said Michel. He went off.

Left behind, Bart, between mouthfuls of breakfast, gave Pier and Marta a more detailed account of how the conference with the Emperor had gone; since Michel had only told the older two that permission had been granted for all of them to go to the surface. Breakfast over, Marta took Emma off with her for some last-minute addition to the luggage they would be carrying; and for the few minutes that were left Bart was left alone in the sitting room adjoining the breakfast parlor, with Pier.

"Sit down with me, my boy," said Pier, taking a chair. Bart pulled up a hassock and seated himself. Pier's face was concerned —almost embarrassed in its mingled look of affection and worry.

"Bart," he said with an effort, "there's something I'd like to say to you. There's been such a short time to know you, and particularly Emma; but our hopes were raised rather unusually high, after all these years, and . . . well, what I mean to say is, neither Marta nor I want to lose touch. You will indeed be marrying, once you get up there and off by yourselves, I understand?"

"You can count on it, Grandfather," said Bart almost grimly. The grimness was real enough. He had been telling himself for some time now that he had given in to Emma's wishes all his life; but if they ever got out of this glorified hole in the ground, there was going to be no more nonsense about her responsibility toward her brother standing in their way. It was ridiculous, the best part of their lives slipping away from them . . . .

He was abruptly so caught up in his own emotion that he missed something Pier was saying, and it was something the old man had been trying to tell him in strongly emotional fashion.

". . . if you would stay in touch," Pier was saying. "You see, we're reconciled to never seeing you again; but it'll mean a great deal to us to know when you're finally safe and settled; and particularly about any children, when you have them, and their names and so forth . . ."

Bart would have assured him immediately that they would keep in touch, somehow, but Pier was going on talking, giving him no time to break in.

"At your age, it may seem like a foolish, old-people's whim," he was saying, "but even though we'll never see them, either, it would mean a great deal to us to hear about them. I mean, not only their names and the dates of their birth, but how they do as they grow up . . . and so on.''

"Grandfather," said Bart, finally getting a word in, "I promise you, somehow we'll find a way—''

"Now, that's what I was going to talk about," said Pier, "the means you could use to contact us. What you must do is write us letters, and keep in touch with Michel. Pass them on to him. I promise you, he'll find some way of passing them to Hybrids he knows up on the surface, and they can pass them on from hand to hand, or otherwise see that they're carried back down here and delivered to us. Whoever handles them will just make sure that he does so with a letter from some other Hybrid above who writes that he found the letter in the possession of someone who had been killed—''

"Killed—'' began Bart.

"—The letter will merely say that, only so that any Hybrid found carrying it by someone who shouldn't see it, would have no way of tracing it back to you. What I mean to tell you is, merely write the letters and entrust them to Michel. No one but the Emperor or the Regent would dare open a letter addressed to me personally, in any case. Most people handling it will assume it's a perfectly correct sort of message for them to carry.''

"I see. Of course," said Bart, "we'll write regularly; and if it's possible for you to write us back—''

"Oh, we will if at all possible," said Pier. He coughed. "You won't mind, of course, if the letters seem to be in a number of different hands, and unsigned? You'll know by what they say, who they come from.''

"Of course," said Bart. He was still trying to think of something more to say that would reassure Pier that such a correspondence would be certain, when the door to the sitting room opened behind him without any of the customary preliminary scratching, and Michel strode in, carrying something that looked like a leather suitcase, but with twin straps attached to one side, so that it could possibly be carried like a shoulder pack.

"That's going to rub your shoulders raw in the first mile," said Bart critically, looking at the burden, which Michel was carrying at the moment by a handle in the same position as that on the ordinary suitcase.

"We won't have to walk a mile, or even half a mile," said Michel, putting the suitcase down and opening it, "to get to storeroom seven of warehouse twenty-nine. I've brought some rough clothes of mine for Emma's brother. They'll do until we can find him a regular outdoor outfit. What you're wearing, Bart, ought to do well enough until we run into our first help station. Uncle, would you order Emma's brother brought in here?''

Arthur was duly brought in and outfitted in what seemed a tweedy, knee-breeches and boots outfit like some of the easterner hunting costumes Bart had seen worn on rare occasions by visitors to the frontier, down in Montana.

As soon as Arthur was dressed—so immediately in fact that they could have been suspected of waiting outside the door until he was decently clothed—Marta and Emma appeared. Emma was dressed in a heavy tartan wool skirt, and a thick gray sweater under a leather jacket, clothes of which Bart heartily approved. What he did not approve of was that she and Marta were between them lugging two suitcases which seemed more heavy than light.

"Emma—,'' he began; but she cut his protest short.

"Bart,'' said Emma, "you take the one Marta's been carrying. I can manage this one alone. Now, don't argue. It's not going to be as easy for me to find things to wear—especially personal things—out there, as it would be for you, Arthur and Michel; and from what I gather, I'm not likely to have the time to sit down and make them, even if the makings were available.''

"In any case,'' said Michel, "we've no time to argue. Not only is the time short, but I don't trust the Emperor. He could change his mind at any minute, and we don't want to give him the chance to set up any barriers in our way. Add to that the fact that we're best off if we get where we're headed before most of the day's foot traffic is up in the corridors.''

In fact, Michel hurried them out of the Guettrigs' quarters faster than any of them, particularly Pier and Marta, were ready to see them leave. But Bart had to admit to himself that his half-brother was correct as far as the need not to waste time.

The suitcase Emma had given him to carry—though the larger of the two by a good margin—was a little heavier than he would have expected of one filled with women's clothes, but it was no real burden to carry the short distance Michel had insisted was all they needed to cover. In fact, after a half a hundred steps his conscience began to bother him, and he offered to take the one Emma was carrying, as well.

"Certainly not!'' she said. "This has all my personal and precious things. I wouldn't trust you with it. Besides, it's a lot lighter than it looks—not like yours.''

The route they followed took them by corridors that became progressively more barren of ornamentation in the way of floor and wall coverings and more empty of other human beings; until at last they trudged down ways that held no one but themselves, wide enough for seven or eight people to move abreast, but with plain rock ceiling, floor and walls. They had also come up several levels from the level of the normal day-to-day traffic areas of the Inner World.

The sound of their footfalls was loud in the stillness on the hard surface and their voices were instinctively hushed, so that they said very little at all to each other. Even Arthur, who usually had too much to say for the comfort of his companions, was uncharacteristically silent.

Warehouse twenty-nine, Bart discovered, was not really a warehouse in the above-ground sense at all, but merely a grouping of storerooms. In spite of its relatively high number, it was no farther than Michel had promised it to be. They came to it at last; and to the door marked "STOREROOM SEVEN." It was a solid door, closed by a solid, square brass lock inset in its wooden—thick-looking, by the appearance of it—body below an ordinary brass doorknob. Michel put down his suitcase, which he had carried most of the way by the handle, after all, and took hold of the knob. But when he tried to open the door, it did not budge.

"Locked," observed Bart. He examined the keyhole below the knob. "And the Emperor didn't say anything to us about a key."

"Hmm." Michel looked at his watch. "We're a couple of minutes early, and there could be remote, electric control of that lock. Let's wait for the time he set for us."

They waited. At the end of a hundred and twenty seconds, Michel tried the knob again. This time, it turned and the door swung open before them—not without a small groan, as if such movement was not frequent for it.

Light had gone on inside the room with the opening of the door. But as Bart, the last to enter, stepped over the threshold, there was another faint groan from behind him and they all turned to see the door swinging shut. Bart immediately tried the knob.

"Locked again," he announced.

"I'm not surprised," said Michel. Arthur, however, had gone quite pale; and his pallor was all too obvious in the stark glare from the ceiling globes that shone over them.

"You mean we're trapped?" Arthur demanded.

No one bothered to answer him.

They looked about. The room was utterly bare. Walls, floor and ceiling were all rock; the room, like the corridors outside, had obviously been carved out—whether there had been a natural, smaller cavity here to begin with, which had been later enlarged, or whether every square inch of it had been excavated from the solid stone, was impossible to tell.

"Now what?" said Michel, half to himself. "He can't mean to lock us up in here and simply leave us to die of thirst or starvation. He's too intelligent not to know we'd have to let other people know we were going; and that one at least of them would be Pier, who'll be doing some unobtrusive checking within the next forty-eight hours to make sure we got off safely."

"Pier also knows which room we were sent to," said Bart. "I suppose the Emperor would guess that he'd know that?"

"Yes. Of course!" Michel looked disgusted with himself. "Come to think of it, Pier knows the ways out as well as the Emperor. If there'd been anything unusual about us being sent to this particular place, Pier would have said something at the time he first heard that was where we'd been told to go. This must be all right."

"It doesn't look all right to me," said Arthur.

"Hush, Arthur!" said Emma. "Don't be ridiculous."

"Oh, it's all right for you!" he said, rounding on her. "As long as Bart thinks it's all right, it's all right for—"

"Arthur!" said Emma, the unusual tone of her voice cutting across his and effectively silencing it, "I'd watch my tongue if I were you!"

He stared at her, obviously stunned. It was clear he was not used to hearing such words from her. He gave Bart a sudden quick glance and did not try to speak again.

Bart, meanwhile, had been paying no attention. He was prowling around the empty room, literally sniffing the air from time to time, like an animal. The fact that he could smell the air and yet isolate nothing to quell the tenseness inside him, did nothing to relieve him of his uneasiness.

"What are you up to, Bart?" Michel asked finally. Clearly his nerves were also on edge.

"I'm not sure," said Bart.

There was nothing he could point to as evidence to confirm his inner feeling. But he had trapped enough animals in the woods himself so that their present situation reminded him uncomfortably of a live trap, one designed to capture prey unhurt.

"I haven't any real reason for this," he said finally, "but I can't help feeling there've been other people through here in just the last few minutes before we were let in. As I say, I've no proof; but it's the kind of feeling I'd pay attention to if I was out in the woods alone and got it."

"You must have some reason for thinking something like that," said Michel.

Bart shrugged, still prowling, more by instinct than anything else.

"It could be the air in here has a smell my nose can't quite identify, or something about the floor or ceiling lights. It could be anything—"

He was interrupted by a grating sound. They all turned to its source, the wall in the back of the room, opposite the door by which they had entered. A section of the stone there, about three feet wide and perhaps six inches thick, was dropping downward into the floor to expose a corridor beyond, widening off to the right and lit, but dimly, at long intervals, by the same sort of lighting under which they stood at the moment. A breath of cold damp air blew to them from the opening.

The descending slab disappeared completely into the floor. The corridor beyond was no wider than the door itself. It stood waiting for them.

chapter
twenty-four

"Will you step into my parlor?
Said the spider to the fly . . ."

quoted Emma, putting into words the uneasiness that now affected all of them, whether springing from the same causes as Bart's or brought about in them by his pacing and sniffing. None of them so far had made any move toward the waiting tunnel.

"Nonsense!" burst out Michel in the same English in which Emma had spoken the bit of children's verse—as the silence and motionlessness which had followed it now began to stretch out uncomfortably. "Our friend is capable of anything, of course. But trying anything while we're still safely in the Inner World and where people know we've gone makes no sense. Let's go!"

He led the way, shrugging his arms into the straps of his suitcase, so that he now carried it for the first time like a knapsack, from his shoulders. Bart and Emma followed him and Arthur hurried to get ahead of his sister, whom Bart had let go ahead of him, so that the male Robeson was now a good three places from being at the end of the column.

They went into the tunnel.

As with the door to Storeroom Seven, the stone slab that had descended into the floor to let them into the tunnel began closing again, rising upward the moment Bart was through it, and it continued up with a rumble of noise in the echoing tunnel until it clashed at last into place against the ceiling behind them, and was silent.

Now, there were only the loud echoes raised by their footsteps on the stone floor beneath them as they made their way along the tunnel. As they went, the reason for its meandering progress became apparent. The rock through which it was driven was pierced by fissures; and the tunnel had evidently been made by widening the larger of these which went in the general direction at which it was aimed.

Large cracks were visible in the side walls as they went along; and where the tunnel had been made to follow one of these, the crack ran down the center of the floor under foot, showing a glimpse of darkness that promised to be bottomless, except in those cases where a burbling and murmuring of water could be heard from far below.

After some distance they came upon the first of a series of steps, broad and low, carved out of the stone; and for some distance they alternated between stretches of level tunnel and climbs of six to ten feet.

The air in the tunnel was laden with moisture, presumably from subterranean waters; it stood in beads on the raw stone wall, and slowly began to work its moisture in through the warmth of their clothing.

The tunnel was longer than any of them had expected; and Bart became curious that Michel still wore his suitcase on his shoulders, which must already be rubbed uncomfortably raw by the case. He also noted that Michel was carrying both hands out of sight in front of him; and, struck by a sudden suspicion, he pushed past both Arthur and Emma.

"Stay in line!" he whispered as he passed.

He caught up with Michel, and pushed past him. Now, as he suspected, he could see that Michel's hidden hands were not empty. One held a six-shot revolver, the other a heavy, woodsman's belt knife with no less than an eight-inch blade.

Michel glanced at him. There was no need to do more than exchange looks. Bart pressed himself against the tunnel's wet wall and stood still until Arthur and Emma had passed him again.

"What is it?" asked Arthur, in hushed tones that nonetheless echoed and reechoed along the tunnel.

"Nothing," said Bart out loud. He fell in behind Emma and they continued.

The tunnel was longer than any of them had expected. It came at last, however, to an open stretch which widened at the end to accommodate a door very much like the one at the entrance to Storeroom Seven. As they approached to within some two dozen feet of the door, it swung silently open, outward; folding itself back toward the wall upon which it was hinged, so that they looked out on a ledge perhaps thirty feet in width, as best Bart could judge from the section he could see through the open doorway.

The ledge seemed to be still underground, for despite the morning hour, the space they saw beyond the lighted rock surface was pitch dark. Beyond the ledge there seemed to be a river; it could be seen as a black sheen, moving a little, beyond the ledge. A number of small rowboats and three Indian canoes were moored at that edge, to the left, last one touching the vertical rock wall that came down to mark the end of the ledge.

Bart's first assumption was that they were back at the river into which he had fallen on entering the Inner World from the mine tunnel. Though this was strange, considering that the Clinic, and therefore the bridge and entrance he had never seen, were at the opposite end of the Inner World from the warehouse sections. He pushed past Arthur, Emma and even Michel, to stride hurriedly to the water's edge.

One close look at it was enough. The current of this water was nothing like the current of that into which he had fallen—not more than a lazy two or three miles an hour in speed, though the water itself, when he went down on one knee and dipped his fingers into it, was as icy as the stream into which he remembered falling.

The current was flowing from his left to his right. He looked to his left, at the small boats and canoes moored near the end of the ledge.

"There's something wrong here," he said, his voice booming strangely under the rock ceiling which here was at least fifteen to twenty feet in height, arching out over the underground river, "boats brought upstream normally tie up at the downstream end of their moorage—"

A snapping sound and a shout from Michel brought Bart to his feet and spinning around. Behind him, the door to the tunnel was closing; and now revealed where they had been hidden by an outcropping of rock and the opened door itself, were Chandt and four Steeds—all dormitory Leaders, Paolo among them—each with a blindfold now hanging loosely around his neck, each holding one of the strangely lumpy-looking rifles Bart had first seen in the hands of a sentry at one of the doors to the Tectonal room.

Chandt had just used the lash of a long whip to wind around Michel's two wrists and jerk them together. The pain and the shock had caused Michel to drop both knife and gun; and both weapons were now skittering down the slight slope of the smooth rock to plunge over the edge into the water and disappear.

But Michel had not been so stunned by the shock that he had not recovered in time to grasp the lash above where it wound around his wrist, and a jerk of his arms had pulled the whip-handle out of Chandt's grasp. The Commander of the Steeds watched almost philosophically as the whip-handle, clearly heavy and weighted to serve as a weapon on its own, went skidding down the rocky incline to disappear also into the water.

Michel pulled the lash-end from his wrist and watched the weight of the drowning handle yank the lash across the ledge and out of sight in its turn into the dark stream.

"So," said Michel savagely, "our Emperor doesn't keep his imperial word after all."

Chandt ignored the words. He was busy reaching into the wallet that hung from the belt around the waist of his tunic. He produced a rolled up sheet of heavy-looking paper, of the same gray color on which the Emperor had written the pronouncements he had handed to Michel, earlier this morning. Bart looked directly at Paolo, who stood at the far end of the line from Chandt. Paolo avoided his eyes.

"You too?" said Bart. Paolo did not answer, but continued to look away.

Chandt had his paper out now. He held it up before him and read aloud from it in Latin as fluent as any Hybrid's, or any Lord's or Lady Lord's.

> *"To our Commander of Steeds:*
> *Three spies and members of a conspiracy under the renegade former Lord, Vincent Saberut, who some years back fabricated a false report of his own death while on the surface of the world, have introduced themselves to the Inner World secretly as slaves.*
> *These spies are Bartholomew Saberut, son of the renegade former Lord named in the above paragraph, and two other humans, Arthur and Emma Robeson; and these, having stolen various important documents from the X Collection of the Library, documents having to do in detail with the construction of the Tectonal, are presently trying to escape with these back up to the surface.*
> *With them, and to be considered no more than an innocent dupe of these spies unless proved otherwise, is our well-loved nephew Michel Saberut. You are directed to apprehend and return all four of these individuals to be dealt with according to our justice. Such is the importance of the documents they have stolen that, while every effort should be made to return the four alive and in good health for judgment, you are authorized if necessary, to put them to death; if that is the only way they can be kept from going free onto the surface with what they carry.*

> (Signed)
> *Zoltaan, Emperor*

Chandt reached into his wallet, pulled out a thick wad of papers, smiled at them and returned them to the wallet with the letter.

"The fugitives," he said in a calm conversational tone of voice, "clearly seem to be attempting to escape. Steeds, aim—"

The weapons, which had been held generally pointing in the direction of Bart and the others, came up to the shoulders of the men holding them, their muzzles aimed at the party by the water's edge. All, that is, but one.

"Wait!" shouted Paolo.

He had stepped away from the line of his fellows and his own weapon was up, but covering the other dormitory Leaders and Chandt. "They're not trying to escape! What're you talking about, Chandt? That letter sent us here to bring them back, not to shoot them down like turkeys in a pen! Drop your slicers, every one of you, or I'll cut you all in two!"

The other three Steeds stared at him for one long moment, then let go of their weapons as if they were red hot.

"Now, kick them into the water!" said Paolo; and the three obeyed.

Chandt had turned to look at Paolo. Chandt's face seemed vaguely puzzled and concerned.

"Paolo," he said, "you're getting upset over nothing. Of course we're not really going to shoot them. That's just the form of arrest I have to go through . . ."

As he spoke, he was walking toward Paolo. Paolo's weapon wavered for a second, and in that second, Chandt had spun about on his left toe and lashed out with his right foot in a kick that he was now just close enough to reach Paolo with. His toe drove into Paolo's body, up under the ribs on Paolo's right side; and the force of it lifted the dormitory Leader up on his toes. The weapon in his hand whined suddenly like a lost kitten and a bright green fan of light leaped momentarily from its muzzle, missing Chandt but literally cutting down the three other dormitory Leaders as if the light was something solid with a razor edge. But then the weapon dropped from Paolo's hands, and he himself dropped to the rock and lay still.

Chandt spun back and made a dive for the weapon Paolo had let go, but it was already skittering across the smooth floor of bare rock and as they all watched, it too slipped over the edge and disappeared into the dark waters.

Chandt straightened up and turned to face Bart and the others.

Michel began walking toward Chandt.

"Well now, Leader of Steeds and slave of an Emperor," said Michel, "the odds are a little more even. Perhaps you'd care to try to arrest just me, with your bare hands?"

"Michel! No!" cried Bart. "Look out! He's not just what you think he is—"

But Michel paid no attention to him. He was close to Chandt now, his arms half held out before him as if inviting Chandt to make the first move. Chandt was backing away, circling out from the rock that had been at his side, until his back was now to the group at the water's edge and Michel was between him and the wall.

Realizing suddenly that Michel would never listen to him, Bart began to sprint forward. But at the sound of a step behind him, Chandt wasted no more time in backing up. Instead, with a suddenness that took even the oncoming Bart by surprise, he met Michel, on the other man's next stride toward him, in midair with both heels lashing out in a lightning double kick at Michel's chest.

Michel had just checked his balance after the step forward and the powerful impact of Chandt's heels lifted him, for all his weight, and smashed him back against the rock behind him.

His head slammed with a stomach-twisting crack against the raw-cut rock and he slid down it to huddle without movement on the floor.

At the same time, in what was almost a rebound from the impact, Chandt had rolled over in midair and dropped back down onto his feet, facing the oncoming Bart in a half crouch, one leg a little forward of the other and his hands up at waist level and open, waiting.

Bart stopped, checking himself so suddenly his leg muscles creaked, but happily still a good two strides from Chandt.

For a long moment they simply stood, facing each other. Then Chandt took a step forward—and Bart took one back.

Now it was Chandt who advanced and Bart who backed away, circling on the ledge that had become far too narrow an open space for Bart's liking. What Bart had suspected had been true. Chandt was a master at what Bart and Michel's father had been expert in—what he had called the "tricks" of hand-to-hand conflict.

"You were sent to kill us, weren't you?" said Bart as they moved about each other, two partners in a set dance.

"I obey my Emperor," said Chandt.

"I'm right though, aren't I?" said Bart. "Everyone would know that Michel had left on a mission to the upper world. You were to kill us and get rid of our bodies. In time it would be forgotten that we ever went, or were—except perhaps the other Hybrids who'd known him would remember Michel from time to time."

"You could almost have been a Mongol," said Chandt. He smiled—and Bart found himself shocked when he saw it. "Who was it taught you?"

"My father," said Bart, "by himself in the upper world when I was growing up. The man you knew as Vincent Saberut."

"I remember," said Chandt. "I liked him. He came to me of his own accord for teaching. Few Lords do that. The Lords and Ladies must learn, but they're seldom eager to know, as he was."

They were still circling, Bart still backing away, Chandt advancing. The pattern and the situation were plainly as clear to Chandt as they were to Bart. At arm's reach, Chandt was by far the superior, and deadly. If he could get at Bart with his arms or feet while withholding his body, he would have the fight won. But if Bart could get a grip on Chandt's body from some position where the other's lethal skill could not be used, then Bart's superior strength could make him the winner. Whoever lost would die— because it would not be safe for either to leave the other alive; and if Bart died, Emma and her brother would die within seconds after Chandt reached them.

"He was a good pupil, your father," said Chandt. "One of the best I ever had. But he was only a pupil—"

Suddenly, he was coming at Bart through the air, as he had come at Michel.

Bart, balanced and ready, spun away from the lethal heels, which flashed by his chest—and felt his neck barely caught a split second later by the fingers of one hand on an outstretched arm.

For the moment, strength paid. Bart's neck and body muscles were powerful enough that he was able to complete his spin, tearing loose from a grip that would have held most men and been the beginning of the end with Chandt as victor. Having spun, Bart leaped backward again, while Chandt once more landed on his feet, turned, and stood facing him.

"Ah!" said Chandt. It was the sort of audible, near sigh of satisfaction a wine connoisseur might have made on first tasting a superb vintage. He once more began stalking Bart and they circled each other at some ten feet of distance, in silence.

Behind Chandt, Michel stirred, raised his head, put his hand to the back of it and stared at the moving forms of Bart and Chandt.

"Help me, Michel," said Bart, without taking his eyes off Chandt. "But be careful. Very careful."

A lesser individual might have looked behind him on hearing Bart's words. Chandt's gaze did not shift a millimeter from its focus on Bart. But he smiled.

"Don't have to tell me that," muttered Michel, almost drunkenly, pulling himself to his feet. "I knew what he taught, but I thought I was strong enough—never mind."

Chandt and Bart were continuing to circle, so that Chandt was coming around to where he could see not only Bart, but Michel also.

"Don't get in line with me, Michel," Bart said. "Keep moving. Try to keep behind him."

Chandt smiled again. Michel obeyed. He began to move around behind Chandt, who to all appearances completely ignored his presence. As he did so, the somewhat drunken look in his eyes, which had matched the thickness of his voice when he first came to, began to clear. He was squinting his eyes, though, and Bart suspected that he had a headache—it was amazing that he could move at all, after the blow he had taken.

Behind Chandt's back and out of sight of the Steed Leader, Michel lifted his right hand and made a pushing movement forward toward the corresponding side of Chandt's body, meanwhile lifting his eyebrows questioningly.

Bart did not dare make any obvious acknowledgment with Chandt's gaze sharp upon him; but after a few seconds, he lifted his own right hand a few inches, the hand opposite the other side of Chandt's body. He made the move as if unconsciously, all the time keeping his gaze locked with that of the Leader of the Steeds.

He still focused on Chandt; but Michel was within his field of vision and he waited for the other to make either another signal or the actual move he had already signaled he was ready to make.

They had grown very close in just this short time of knowing each other; and, even without specific evidence, Bart believed he sensed things in Michel that other people probably no more than suspected. First among these was the fact that, while to a casual glance he and Michel were very much opposites—he, stolid, taciturn and a loner, while Michel was vibrant, quick-tongued and social to an extreme—Bart had come to feel that beneath Michel's exterior was the same sense of difference and loneliness that he himself had always felt.

Now in this moment when everything depended on their working together against Chandt, it seemed to Bart he could feel something like a flow of energy back and forth between Michel and himself—not exactly as if they could know what was in each other's minds, but as if each could feel what the other was feeling, so that it was almost as if they shared one body that was in two places.

He waited, therefore, for the feeling that Michel was about to attack Chandt from the back, confident that he would know it was coming a split-second before it came, even though Michel had in no way signaled him. And he felt that Michel felt and understood this, too. This circling could not go on much longer with any safety. Chandt was the master, they were not. The longer the stalemate was prolonged, the greater the chance that Chandt would spot some moment of opportunity that would give him an advantage in attacking either or both of them at once.

Then, Bart felt the impulse from Michel, and the other threw himself at the side of Chandt's back that was on Michel's right. In the same moment, warned by the flow of feeling between them, Bart leaped at the other side of Chandt from the front.

Chandt's reflexes were unbelievable. The second they were in midair, his arms were both up before him and he was spinning about in a movement that would have had them flying by harmlessly, one on each side of him. But the double attack had been just a fraction of a second too unexpected and quick for him to complete the defensive maneuver. Michel missed him completely, but Chandt's spin brought him into direct collision with Bart, who grabbed him with both arms about the body and locked his hands together behind the other man's back, setting his chin into the hollow between Chandt's shoulder and neck.

Bart had been prepared to accept punishment from the free arms of Chandt, once he had his hold; and he had been determined to hold on, regardless. Nonetheless, the first blow of a fist from Chandt between his shoulder blades felt as if the other had hit him there with a heavy hammer. In spite of his determination, the breath was almost driven from his body, and for a second he felt his grip weaken—but then he tightened it once more.

A second blow bounced off the back of his head, but this time it was no harder than the blow of a fist from any ordinary man, and a third blow slid off his shoulder so lightly it was almost a tap.

He knew then that Michel had wisely managed to capture the

arms and legs of Chandt with his own. Michel and he had achieved what had been their only hope, gaining positions in which the advantage of their own massive but relatively unskilled strengths could be brought to bear on Chandt, in a situation where the Master of the Steeds could not use his much greater skill against them.

Bart set his chin deeper in the hollow between Chandt's neck and shoulder and strove to get the power of his shoulder muscles into the grip of his arms. His fists were locked together against the middle of Chandt's back. That back with its taut muscles was like carved wood, but Bart knew if he could get the full leverage of his arms against it, it would have to give.

. . . And slowly, it did give. He felt the lesser muscles of the other man, rod-hard from long training as they were, beginning to bend and give before the unrelenting pressure he was putting on them, as Chandt's body was slowly being bent backward.

Bart reached back in his memory for something else his father had taught him. Slowly, he closed his concentration down, shutting out the rest of the world about him, more and more, until nothing remained but the effort between him and Chandt. His arms tightened. Chandt gave, bending backward until he arched at an unnatural angle.

Bart's face was buried in Chandt's shoulder. Chandt's mouth was only an inch or so from Bart's left ear. There was a moment in which they stood together, hardly moving; and a faint breath, barely strong enough to be called a whisper, sounded in Bart's ear.

"Done . . . well . . ."

Then something gave inside Chandt and he hung limply backward in Bart's arms. Bart lowered him gently to the rock and stood for a second looking down at him. Chandt had fallen on his side, as if asleep. His eyes were closed, his face was like his face in sleep.

Suddenly, remembering, Bart turned to Paolo, three long steps bringing him to the other man. He knelt beside the dormitory Leader. Paolo lay on his side, but he still breathed, if raspingly and shallowly. The whole lower right side of his chest was caved in and the broken end of a white rib bone had pushed itself an inch through the skin revealed by his torn tunic.

His eyes were open, but they focused on nothing—not even Bart, who put his face down close to the other's. A quantity of blood had run from his mouth and was still draining slowly in a trickle down the slope of the ledge.

"Paolo," said Bart. Paolo paid no attention. Bart put his lips as close to the other's ear as Chandt's had been to his.

"Paolo, man," said Bart softly. "Thank you. We owe you our lives. Paolo, thank you."

For a moment Paolo's eyes cleared—or perhaps it was only Bart's imagination. But it seemed to Bart that for a moment those eyes focused on him. Paolo made a sound in his throat, as if he was trying to speak, but it only came forth as a hoarse and bubbling noise.

His eyes closed; and he stopped breathing.

Bart got to his feet, feeling very stiff and old, suddenly, as his muscles reacted to the strains he had put them to. He was sore all over. He turned to see Michel and the others grouped once more by the water's edge and the moored boats, watching him.

Emma scooped up Chandt's wallet.

"This will come in useful," she said.

"We'd better go," said Bart. His voice sounded strange in his own ears, and his skin seemed to be tingling with heightened sensitivity to the air about him. "What about gear—was there any here for us?"

"No," answered Michel. His voice was also altered and strange. It was as if both he and Bart had in the last few minutes become different men.

"We'll find some," Bart said, "somewhere downstream. We'll find the outer world and supplies, maybe one or the other first—but both, sooner or later."

He pointed.

"Take that biggest canoe. It'll hold us and everything we end up carrying with us. Michel, do you know how to use a paddle?"

"Yes," said Michel.

"Then you get aboard first. Take the bow. Emma and Arthur, you take the middle. I'll paddle at the rear and take care of the steering."

"What do we sit on?" asked Arthur, hesitating at the edge of the canoe, which Michel had already pulled in parallel to the ledge. Wincing and stepping down into the very center of the frail-looking vessel, Arthur got in. Emma followed with much less ceremony and much better balance.

After they were all in, Bart cast off the mooring line and picked up a paddle. In the prow of the craft, Michel also had a paddle. He was obviously unskilled with it, but they added the impetus of their paddling to the slow movement of the stream, which proved to curve to the right, so that almost immediately the ledge, with its grotesque pattern of still bodies, was left behind.

After the lighting of the ledge it had seemed at first that they were moving into utter darkness. But after a moment, to Bart's surprise, there was a snapping noise from off to the right, and a light mounted on the side of the tunnel came on. A brilliant swath of light from some device perched there lit up the tunnel before them.

The rock ceiling remained high. The air had a somewhat less damp smell now than it had had back in the tunnel. If it were not for the lights on the walls, Bart thought, it would have been possible to believe that they were not moving at all, but paddling a canoe that floated in place in an unvarying watery cavern. As they left the light on the wall behind, however, a new one snapped on before them, and that continued.

Eventually, the lights on the wall began to seem dimmer, and they became aware of illumination up ahead that was overpowering them. A little later, and it became clear that this new light was daylight; and in a moment after that the curving bed of the underground river turned them so that a speck of light at the left of the tunnel ahead of them grew rapidly into a rough half-moon of brilliance that was day.

A couple of minutes later the canoe glided out from under a moss and pine-studded rock face into the quiet expanse of a dark blue body of water perhaps half a mile across, with thick Canadian forest about its shores. To their left, the shore's rocky face descended to a shoreline only four feet above the water line, and a few dozen yards beyond, it bulged out to hide further view of that part of the lake, almost touching a small island that seemed so close to the shore that at first glance it looked as if an active person could have jumped from one to the other. Actually, the two were about thirty feet apart, and the dark water filled the space between them.

chapter
twenty-five

"NOTHING IN SIGHT," said Michel up front, resting his paddle across the bow of the canoe. "But there's got to be something, otherwise they wouldn't have sent people this way. So we go around the shoreline until we come to something. The only question is—which way? Want to flip a coin to decide?"

"No. Wait a minute," said Bart. He had put his paddle in the water and with a single strong stroke, started the canoe turning in place upon the water, so that in the canoe they all faced back toward the shore that had been behind them. Bart's eyes, more woods wise than those of the others, scanned the shore. He began to paddle toward the point where the shore was only a matter of a few feet above the level of the lake.

"Let me take a look around ashore, first," he said.

The canoe reached the shore, and Bart grabbed the limb of an overhanging spruce and pulled himself up onto the land. He had brought the mooring rope with him and he tied the boat to the spruce.

"I'll be back in a couple of minutes," he said.

He walked into the woods. It was strange to feel the springy yielding of earth, tree-needle carpeted earth, beneath him after all these months of hard rock or soft carpet; and to smell the scents of the Canadian northwoods forest. Plainly it was summer, here among the mountains; and for the first time he found himself wondering about the amount of time he had spent in the Inner World. In the mine he had kept track in his head of the time that had passed, as well as he could; but since awakening in the Inner World he had been too busy—had too much occupying his mind—to worry any longer about the time passing.

For the first time in a period too long to easily estimate now, he not only felt freedom—he smelled and tasted it. For a moment the thought even crossed his mind that all he had to do was keep going and he could be free of everyone, including those he had left in the canoe behind him.

But the thought was no sooner born than the memory of Emma blew it away like the white seeds of a dandelion in a young day's first breeze. He began to work at what he had come up here to find out, evidence of some sort of passage on foot through these woods.

He found sign, the faint fragment of a long-unused trail now almost overgrown, the ashes and burnt wood-ends of an ancient fire. He continued past the fire, and the trail led him to the shore again—on the other side of the bulge of land that nearly touched the small island and had hidden the further shoreline from those in the canoe. He found an open space between the trees that grew thickly right to the water's edge, and looked out across the lake and down along the shore.

He turned his head and called back over his shoulder.

"Can you hear me, back at the canoe?" he yelled.

A medley of voices answered him from the distance. Only one of them was clear. It was Emma's, and she said, "Yes. We hear you, Bart!"

"This is the way! Paddle around between the island and the shore!" he called back.

He waited and they came, sliding smoothly on the still water as Michel pulled the canoe forward from his position in the bow.

As soon as he saw the canoe poke its nose around the curve of the shore, he turned his eyes back on what they, too, would now be seeing. About a hundred yards farther up the shore another river fed into the lake. But this was no quiet stream like the one by which they had arrived here; it was a surface river from high up, furious and foam-toothed, three to five feet deep with enormous boulders sticking their heads up out of the water that bobsledded down the slope of the mountainside.

Here, where he stood, the water was behind the back-eddy from that torrent, and its surface was as smooth as it had been where they had emerged. Here, where there were no currents to toss craft around, a small wooden dock, attached to the shore and supported by two heavy log piles at its far end, gave mooring space to half a dozen canoes, some of them badly in need of repair before they might be put to any working use.

From the dock a trail, worn down to the bare rock and earth by boot and moccasin, led up the slope to a little hollow, where a log building too large to be a simple cabin hunched itself down in the shelter of mountainside and pine trees. Only the ever-present sprinkling of brown needles from the nearby trees kept the path from complete earth-nakedness.

He walked down to the dock and out on it to catch the bow rope Michel tossed him, and pulled the canoe in, tying it up. Together they all went up the path to the log building, opened its door, which was on the side facing the wild river, and let themselves in.

They stepped into an interior enclosed by the same logs that made the standing sides of the cabin. The floor was made of rounds of tree wood, chinked with clay. There was remarkably little space free for standing or sitting. What space there was stood opposite the door, against the far wall of the building, and contained a short counter behind which rose shelves loaded with a multitude of sacked and boxed foods. A round iron stove with stovepipe sticking straight up through the roof sat off to one end of the counter and was encircled by a few rough chairs—made of axe-split lumber from the look of them—around it. Some furs had been thrown over the chairs to cushion them.

Behind the counter was a tall, bald-headed man in perhaps his forties; and facing him from the other side were two men in the homemade leather and fur clothing of trappers. These all turned at the sound of the opening of the door.

"Just a minute," said the bald-headed man behind the counter, in French. He winked broadly at the two trappers, making no attempt to hide the wink from the newcomers. "I'll be back with you in only a moment."

He came around the counter and approached Bart and the others.

"Well, neighbors!" he called out in English, in a hearty voice. "Didn't expect to see you until next week. Come on in back, and make yourself comfortable!"

With his back to the two trappers, he frowned heavily at them, then turned and led them down an aisle between the piles of barrels, boxes, bales and other goods and through a wall made up of the same sort of materials into a room of about the same size as the clearing around the counter. This room, however, held another stove, a bunk against the one small area of wall that was left exposed. Some chests covered with furs made for more comfortable chairs.

"Take your ease, folks!" he boomed out again in English, in what seemed to be a voice pitched deliberately to be heard by the trappers in what passed for the other room. "I'll be with you in a bit—not more than half an hour, say."

He turned to leave.

"Say, wait just a minute!" said Arthur. "Don't you know—"

"Shut up!" said Michel. He spoke softly, but some months of

being a slave who did what any Hybrid told him to, had trained
Arthur. He shut up.

They took chairs and waited. There was laughter and some talk,
still in French, from the other room. Most of what was said was
indistinguishable. Bart and the others waited in silence.

At last there was the sound of feet moving across the floor, of the
door opening and closing; and a moment later, the bald-headed
man had rejoined them, dangling from one hand a liquor bottle
with a long green neck.

"Forgive me," he said. "But I have to keep up my appearance as
a trading post."

He looked at Michel.

"I didn't get a call saying anyone was coming," he said in
English. "Somebody must have been asleep at the switch. But—"
He looked at Michel. "—you're Michel Saberut, aren't you?"

"That's right," said Michel, "and this is Cousin Bart Saberut,
Vincent Saberut's son—"

"Pleased to meet you, Cousin," said the bald-headed man.
"I'm Lehrer Green. Vincent passed through here more than thirty
years ago. I was an apprentice in my second year on the job here,
then. I never knew he had a son—beyond Michel, here."

"Bart was born after Vincent left," said Michel smoothly.

"Ah," said Lehrer, accepting as unnecessary to be said Michel's
implication that Bart's father had left behind him an impregnated
concubine. The trader held up the bottle.

"I don't know if you're interested," he said. "This is part of the
special supplies we keep on hand for just such situations as you just
ran into out there. Good brandy for the French, whiskey for the
Scots and English—even a bottle or two of vodka for the occasional
Russian. I hint I stole several bottles from the luggage of some
company supervisors who were up here inspecting; and then sell it
to them at a bargain price. They can't wait to get out of here for fear
they might have to share it with me. If either you or Bart would like
a drink, Michel—"

He glanced at Emma and Arthur.

"I assume these two are slaves?"

"Oh, yes," said Michel carelessly. He produced the original
order given him by the Emperor. "But I don't want them outfitted
as servants—at least at first. And I'd appreciate your not talking
too much about our coming through here, even to our own people.
Our mission's a little on the special and quiet side."

"You don't have to ask me!" said Lehrer. "Do you think anyone would hold this post as long as I have without having discretion? No one going through here is told about anyone else—with the exception of my mentioning your father, which I did only because you did, and your relationship to him. Plus the fact, I assume by this time he's dead.''

''He is dead,'' said Bart, a little shortly.

''At any rate, if either one of you want something to drink, I've got some fairly good wines, too, for my own use—''

''No, thanks,'' said Michel. ''Our business doesn't leave us time to sit around.''

''Certainly, certainly,'' said Lehrer, putting the bottle aside on the top of what looked like a flour barrel. ''Now what do you need?''

''I'll let Cousin Bart tell you that,'' said Michel. ''The first leg of our trip is going to be through the woods, bypassing civilization. We'll need some cash—about ten thousand dollars in Canadian and the same in American currency, but perhaps fifty thousand in large denomination English pounds; and about the same amount of value in gems—small and easy to carry.''

''I'll get busy right away,'' said Lehrer, and went off.

There was a look of shock on Arthur's face. Bart guessed that it had been the first time the other had realized what kind of wealth his masters commanded.

''Quick!'' Michel was saying in a low voice. ''Help me find it!''

''What?'' asked Bart and Arthur together. Emma ignored them. She had opened the smaller suitcase she had been carrying and begun rooting around in it. Now, pulling out something that looked like a map, she gave a small exclamation of satisfaction and shut it back up in the suitcase again.

''Lehrer's call box from the Inner World—ah, here it is,'' said Michel, uncovering a screen like the ones with which Bart was now familiar. ''I could kick myself for not having thought of this while we were sitting around. I'm no engineer, but I ought to be able to put one of these out of action temporarily . . . there!''

He had opened the box and he came up with a small metal part, which he slipped into a trouser pocket.

''That'll hold him from getting any word in about us, if they find what's happened to Chandt and his Steeds. But this will make him suspicious if he tries to use the box soon; we want some kind of interruption in communication that won't attract attention later. Bart, can you look around outside this cabin—probably on the side leading back to the underground river we came down on. There'll be a buried wire running from the cabin here to the Inner World, whether it goes back to the river and up the sides or bottom of it, or along the surface until it comes to a hole drilled down into some part of the Inner World. Find that and break it—make it seem like it broke by accident, or because some animal chewed on it or something—can you do that? Then I can put this piece back in with no danger.''

''Once I find it, yes,'' said Bart. ''I'll go look now.''

He passed out through the way their host had gone, and waved to him as he passed. The other was busily moving boxes to get at something stacked behind them.

''I suppose you've got an outhouse out there somewhere in back?''

Lehrer straightened momentarily to point.

''Yes. Sorry,'' he called. ''But we couldn't risk anything less primitive in a place like this. I did manage to put in a heating system if you know where the switch is to turn it on—but in the summertime like this, you won't need it. Just go straight out back—you'll find it behind that first screen of trees.''

Bart went out and turned right. This side of the building, he was happy to see, had no windows in it. He went slowly along the outside of the building and around a farther corner, examining the dirt at the foundation of the house. If there was a wire running out of there from the inside, Lehrer would want to get at it in case of breaks or other problems—not only in the summer, as now, but in the nine other months when the ground was frozen. That meant it would probably exit the house just at or just under ground level, but that there would be some mark on the building to help Lehrer locate its exit point. Farther out in the woods, the wire could be buried down below the likely digging range of animals; but here, the wire should be both accessible and marked.

After a moment, his eye picked up a piece of bark off the lowest visible log of the building. That a piece of bark might have been broken or rubbed off a building that had been here this long was not surprising, but this piece was almost a perfect square some three inches on a side. On closer examination it turned out to have been put back over the exposed bare wood with some sticky substance to hold it there while yet making it easy to remove.

Bart did not remove it himself, but dug with his fingernails into the loose soil, pine needles and other detritus just below it. After a few seconds he found it, a wire coated in some flexible material of a dull reddish gray that matched with the color of the ground around it.

A lifetime of habit sent Bart's hand to his belt for the knife he had not worn for nearly two years. Frustrated, he looked around on the ground, found a couple of shards of granite with sharp edges, and started macerating the wire between them until it parted. When it finally broke, the two frayed ends looked not unlike the ends of a break chewed by some small burrowing animal; and to further the illusion, when Bart put them back in the earth, he raked in on top of them such loose earth and pine needles as a squirrel or other such creature might claw up while rooting for food.

He straightened and went on to the trees in the direction of the outhouse; but once beyond them he turned to the edge of the fast-moving river. He squatted to wash his hands in the cold water, cleaning under his fingernails with the sharp edge of a broken dry twig to get as much of the earth out as possible.

When he stepped back inside the building, everyone there was gathered at the counter in the main room, near a stack of woods clothing, blankets, and sacks. Michel and Lehrer had their heads together over a large piece of paper spread out on the wood surface of the counter. At the sound of the door opening, Michel looked up.

"Bart!" he called. "Come over here and look at this map!"

The map had names printed plainly on it, with the false trading post near its center. The name "Shunthead" was plainly to be seen not far off. Running from the trading post in the opposite direction from the mine, however, was a chain of lakes. The first of these was the lake the trading post was on, which was nowhere near as small as it had seemed. They were simply on one narrow arm of it, and the main body curled southward toward a chain of farther lakes. On one shore of the last of these was a square marked "Fort Shadwell."

From Fort Shadwell, a road was indicated stretching out to the southwest, off the map; an arrow paralleling it underlined the words "to the coast."

"What about it, Bart?" asked Michel as Bart also bent over the map. "Does this tell us what we want?"

The question had a double meaning, for they had discussed the direction of their going the night before at Pier's; and Bart had told Michel that they would by no means be going southward and coastward, but up into the woods, to sit out a winter in a cabin they would build. By doing that they could let their trail get cold for any hunters sent by the Emperor. In the spring they would move on again, bypassing any nearby settlements until they were far to the east and could slip, unnoticed, into some fairly large town to take up roles as different people.

"Looks like it ought to work fine for our purposes," said Bart.

"That's that, then," said Michel.

He folded the map up and pushed it into a pocket of the bulging backpack at his feet. "By the way, that one's yours, Bart. I explained to Lehrer here about my weak back."

Bart now noticed that there were three backpacks as well as a small stack of firearms and other gear; and of the three, one was the large one into which Michel had stuffed the map and two were smaller—obviously for only two of the three other people—who had to be Arthur and Emma if Michel was hinting that for some reason he was not going to carry a pack.

This was puzzling, but it could wait to be explained once they were well away from the post. They would not need the backpacks, anyway, until they left the lake to head into the woods.

"I'll help you get the other gear down to a canoe," said Lehrer. "You'll want something bigger than the one you came out in. That can wait here until some of the bunch from inside come out on one kind of business or another."

They moved their gear and supplies down to the dock.

"I'll pack the canoe," said Lehrer, who was obviously used to dealing with people whose experience with such things had been minimal or none. "You may think you know how after the training course they put you through—"

Bart and Michel exchanged significant glances.

"—but you still may learn something by seeing me do it," went on Lehrer, continuing to work. "Just remember that a badly loaded canoe can overturn on just a breath of wind—and *that* you can get at any time. Also, remember the advice you had to stick close to the shoreline, no matter how much of a long way around it looks, because a real wind or a sudden rain that hides sight of any shore, can come up in a moment . . ."

He continued packing.

"Well," he said at last, standing up. "There you are."

He watched as they took their places in the craft, nodding in approval as they stepped into the middle line of it to enter, then raised his eyebrows as Michel took the bow position and Bart the stern.

"You're not going to have the slave paddle?" he asked, staring at

Arthur. "He looks strong enough for a good day's work—"

"Not to start off with," said Michel. "I've been inside all my life and I want to see what this feels like." With his paddle he swung the bow of the loaded canoe away from the dock, Bart helping a little less so that they turned to face away from the shore. They turned their bow toward the same gap between island and land they had passed through earlier, for their supposed route down the lakes to the south and Fort Shadwell.

"Good luck!" Lehrer shouted after them. "Remember that business of staying close to the shore!"

They saw him turn back up the dock toward his trading post as they passed from sight around the bulge of land that came out toward the island.

"Pull in to shore," said Emma unexpectedly, cutting short Michel, who was also starting to say something. Bart looked at her in the center of the boat, where she knelt facing him. There was a stern look on her face and she had open in front of her the small suitcase she had carried all this way.

As Bart automatically turned the prow of the canoe toward a low point in the bank of land alongside, she held out to him a piece of paper from the open suitcase.

"I think I can follow this all right," she said, "but you're the woodsman among us, Bart. Why don't you look at it?"

As the prow touched the earth and rock of the lake shore, Michel, looking bemused, stepped out with the mooring rope in his hand and looped it around the lower trunk of a nearby spruce.

"Go ahead, Arthur!" said Emma, urging her brother forward and leaving the canoe herself behind him, so that Bart unthinkingly followed her and came ashore himself, still studying the paper she had handed him.

It was a map; and, as she had said, not too difficult a one to follow. The exit of the underground river, the shoreline with its bulge out toward the tip of the island, and a rectangle with the words *trading post* printed neatly beside it in English, were all easily recognizable at the bottom of the map. They stood out clearly in the lines of black ink in which the map had been drawn. There, also, at the approximate equivalent of the point where they now stood, a dotted line led up the slope away from the lake, roughly parallel to the shore, for a short distance to an "x" marked *lightning-struck tree stump*. At that point it turned left at an angle marked *40 degrees* and proceeded for a rather longer distance to end at a curved line that looked the rough outline of a camel's hump.

Beside the hump was the legend *large boss of rock. Looks solid but is actually hollow. Follow directions on back of map.*

Bart turned the map over and found its back half filled with a series of sentences, set down in a neat list and numbered consecutively.

"What's this?" he asked, frowning.

"I know," answered Michel in a cold voice, "and so should you. That bag must have the equipment Pier mentioned confiscating from some of our earlier, more eager, cousins. Isn't that right, Emma?"

"Yes," she said.

"You mean—" Bart broke off, suddenly aware of Arthur's curious, sullen face, and realizing why neither Emma nor Michel were putting into plain words what Emma had carried from the Inner World. "But Pier was definite about not—"

"Marta is a little more practical than he is," said Emma.

"But . . ." Bart's mind scrambled still in some confusion. "Eventually—I mean, if we follow what's here on this paper, Pier's got to guess what Emma carried away with her and who's responsible for her having it. What if he simply asks Marta?"

Emma smiled.

"He won't ask," she said. "He'll guess, but he won't ask. He'll know that if he asks, she'll tell him; and what she'll tell him is something he knows he mustn't hear. His honor is precious to him; but nowhere near as precious as Marta."

"I suppose you're right," said Bart, staring at her. It was not the first time he had been made aware of the flint-hard practicality Emma could show under certain conditions. She and Marta were evidently much alike.

"It's her grandchildren she's thinking of, you know," Emma reminded him, more gently. "Our children, but her grandchildren."

Bart nodded slowly.

"Well, you're right about the map," he said. "There'll be no trouble following it." He stepped over to the mooring rope and tied it more securely around the tree trunk to which Michel had attached it. Then he paused for a moment and looked out across the empty lake. Untying the rope again, he waved a hand to Michel.

"Give me a hand," he said. He picked up two of the packs from the interior of the canoe, having to step down the steep bank and into the water to do it; and held them up to Michel. The latter nodded and took them, handing them in turn back to Emma, who with Arthur's slow aid deposited them back in the trees. Within a few minutes they had emptied the canoe; and then Bart and Michel lifted that from the water, and it, too, was hidden.

"Let's move, then," said Bart. "It's past noon, already."

"What is it?" asked Arthur as they all, including him, began to move away from the lake. "What's on that paper?" But no one, including his sister, answered him; so he followed in silence.

Bart took the lead and the map. The true distances covered by the lines of ink on the paper were not indicated there; and he was a little surprised to find his way to the lightning-blasted tree stump mentioned, in less than fifty yards. Looking back along the way they had come, he chose two of the taller trees they had passed and took a bearing that was approximately forty degrees to the left of the line of travel they had been following up until then. He also looked back at the way they had come, to familiarize himself with its appearance for the return trip.

If the tree stump was that close to the lake edge, then their destination could not be much farther—he suddenly made the connection in his mind. Almost certainly Lehrer Green not only knew what was at the place to which they were headed, but probably had some routine duties there, from time to time. Naturally, then, it would be close to his trading post . . . or rather, his trading post would have been set up close to it.

In any case, it meant that what the map pointed them to could not be much farther from the stump than it had been to the edge of the lake behind them; and, sure enough, they had covered only a little more than the equivalent of that distance when they came out into an open area where a number of trees had been cut down, and a large outcropping of granite rose from the slope around it.

The outcropping was about the size of a three-story building. Following the directions on the back of the map, Bart led them around it to its far side, to a smaller boulder of some whitish-gray rock that was unlike the brown granite of the outcropping itself and did not look as if it had originally occupied the place in which they found it.

Bart passed the map to Emma and got down on his hands and knees searching around the base of this rock. When he found a whitish patch on it, almost at ground level and almost between the small boulder and the outcropping—for the two stood close enough to touch at one point—he pressed the whitish patch inward.

It sank down into the surface of the boulder only a fraction of an inch, but the whole part of the boulder visible above ground leaned over on its side like an egg sliced across near one end and hinged at a single point. Revealed below it was not the buried part of the boulder but a lighted opening equipped with steps descending below ground level.

"Ah!" said Michel.

Bart led the four of them onto the steps and down. Emma came last and the minute her head had descended below ground level, the boulder righted itself over them; and they were sealed within the tube of the staircase.

Bart counted the steps as he descended. There were a hundred and fifty-one of them. They brought him at last to an ordinary door-sized entrance beyond which was a well-lit room, its center dominated by a round, polished metal shaft some yards in thickness. It not only looked like the shaft of the Tectonal which Bart had seen in the Inner World, it was turning like the shaft he had seen. Its top vanished into a heavy metal cap braced with girders that ran from it to the surrounding wall, which was also circular, also of metal.

Bart drew a deep breath.

"Right," he said.

He led the way up to the shaft and knelt at its base, glancing at the last lines of instruction on the back of the map. There was a thin silver collar, nearly a foot wide, that surrounded and almost touched the moving shaft. It extended out over the floor. Bart used the point of the sheath knife given him by Lehrer, as part of his woods outfit, to pry up the edge of the collar. For a long moment it resisted; and as he grimly increased the pressure he was putting on the point of the knife in trying to force it between collar and floor, he began to wonder if he was asking too much of the blade—the directions on the back of the map had called for a screwdriver to pry up the collar.

Then, with an almost musical sound, the entire twenty feet or so of ring sprang free from the floor and hung loosely around the turning shaft, being dragged along with it as it rotated. Bart got up and walked around the shaft until he met what he was expecting—a point where the ends of the ring came together.

Taking hold of both ends of the parted ring, he pried them apart. They came reluctantly at first, then more easily; then stiffened to the point where it was obvious he would never be able to spread the ring enough to take it off the shaft. Michel came to aid him, but it was obvious that even with Michel's help—and Arthur's as well, r what it was worth—the ring could not be taken from the shaft.

They ended by propping the ring at two opposing points with a uple of their backpacks, so that it tilted up on one side enough to low nearly four feet of space between it and the floor, at the point here Emma and Michel knelt with the small suitcase open and a ctangular package in what looked like waxed paper on the floor eside it.

From one end of the package came what seemed to be no more an a hair-thin thread, leading to a roll of such thread wound on a indle. At one end of the spindle, the thread ran to another, entical spindle, and this to a third that Emma was now carefully ting out of the suitcase, while Bart held the piece of luggage open r her.

They went on extracting more of the connected spindles. When ey finally finished emptying the bag there was a long row of indles laid carefully out on the floor, each one connected to the e beyond it by a loose length of the threadlike material that ound it. In addition, there was a small, boxlike affair with a short, rrated, but thick piece of metal projecting from one end of —rather like a key with a block for a handle.

"Is that all of it?" demanded Bart, staring unbelievingly at the agile-looking thread and the package, which was less than four ches thick and not even three feet in length.

"It's plenty for its purpose," answered Michel.

He took up one of the connecting lengths of thread between the cond and third fingers of his right hand. "This is brittle, but it's t remarkable longitudinal strength. Enough so that less than the enty pounds of it we've got here can hold the weight of the plosive—" He tapped the rectangular package. "—and either u or I can hold them both and lower the package a good two and a lf miles into the tube, there."

He pointed to the girders strengthening the cap that were easily reach overhead.

"Then, when we've got it down as far as we want it, I set the ner with the setpiece, here, for anything up to fifty minutes. At e end of that time it'll trigger off the charge in the explosive—" e pointed briefly again at the rectangular package. "It goes off, d blows the shaft apart at that point."

Arthur made an odd sound, somewhere between a gasp and a oke.

"And then what?" said Bart skeptically. "They pull out the

broken pieces down there and put a new shaft in. It may take them few weeks, even a month or so to make a new shaft and set it i place—''

"You don't understand," Michel interrupted him. "This sha has tremendous length and weight; and it's delicately balanced. Th forces turning it are tremendous and they're coming nowaday mainly from the magma currents below, rather than any drivin apparatus in the Inner World. After the explosion the broken piece will try to keep turning. The shaft'll break into dozens of piece and probably pierce the tube that contains the shaft in as man pieces, or more."

"So," said Bart. "Perhaps six months to fish it all out and fi it."

"More like a year or two," said Michel. "The whole Tecton: will have torn itself apart. And by the time they get it replaced an working again, the concentration of currents in the magma wi have been lost from the gathering of them that's been going on fc over eighty years. It'll take as long again—perhaps as much as hundred years—to rebuild such a concentration of forces again an get back to the point the Tectonal's at now."

"A hundred years, Bart," said Emma, looking up from the ope suitcase, beside which she was still kneeling. "A hundred years fc the world to save itself."

"You can't do that!" shouted Arthur, lunging for the loop c thread leading from the explosive package to the first spindle "Don't you realize what you're doing? They might let us gc otherwise—but they'll hunt us all down like wild animals if we d something like this!"

Michel's arm shot out, knocking the lighter man back and almos off his feet.

"You interfere with this, and they won't have to hunt yo down," growled Michel, reminding Bart eerily of Paolo. "I' wring your neck like a chicken's, myself!"

He turned to Bart.

"Watch him, Bart," he said. "I know how to do this and yo don't—so it's going to have to be up to you to keep him away fror us while I let the explosive down and set the charge."

Bart avoided looking at Emma. On her part, Emma said nothing

"Don't worry," Bart said. "I'll see he doesn't interfere."

He stood up and turned to face Arthur. But Arthur made n effort to move from where Michel's shove had sent him. He onl stared at Bart with a malevolent hatred.

"You're killing us all," Arthur said, "and it's you who pretend to love my sister!"

Bart did not answer. He kept his eyes steadily on Arthur, hearing behind him the rustle of paper and occasional muttered bits of conversation between Emma and Michel. The minutes slipped slowly by.

"All ready," announced Michel's voice at last. "I've set it to blow in thirty minutes. That should give us time to get down to the lake and the canoe, and still let us be near when the explosive goes off. We don't want to leave until we know that the job's been done. That agree with your thinking, Bart? If you've some objection, I can still change the timing on that box."

"No," said Bart. "Thirty minutes'll be fine. For one thing, I can take us back directly instead of making the dogleg we made on the way up by going to that tree-trunk first. Let's go."

They went, leaving the open suitcase, and the propped-up ring still around the turning shaft. They climbed the stairs and stepped out into the midafternoon sunlight. Bart carefully swung the fake boulder back into place. Unbidden, the thought came to him that the motion of setting it up was the same motion with which a gravestone might have been raised into place. But he said nothing of this to the others.

They had the canoe back in the water and were reloading it when they felt the reaction of the Tectonal's breakup.

It was not the sound of the explosion itself that reached them, for that relatively small shock would have been contained by the miles of vertical shaft-tube and the closed room above its top end. What they were made conscious of was the actual breakage of the great shaft itself.

The first signal came without warning, like a sharp, momentary tap on the soles of their feet—as if they were mice scurrying about the rafters on the upper side of a giant's ceiling, and the giant himself, annoyed by the sounds of their movements, had reached up to bang with his massive fist on the ceiling's underside.

This was followed by a vibration too small to produce any visible tremor in the surface about them, or even in their legs. A vibration that they sensed in their eardrums more than felt, but which was undeniably there as it rose in amplitude for perhaps a minute and a half, and then finally fell away to silence again.

"That'll be the shaft breaking and binding against the tube, all along its length," said Michel with satisfaction.

They climbed into the canoe and pushed off.

"Look!" said Emma.

They looked back to see something like a wisp of whitish-gray cloud, or part of a plume of smoke, ascending over the treetops farther up the slope. It did not grow, or continue, however, but drifted away on the slight breeze above the treetops, thinning out as it went until it was no more than a streak of haze, quickly disappearing.

"Let's go," said Bart again.

The others, who had stopped to watch the cloud, turned back to settling themselves in the boat again; Bart, in the stern of the canoe, swirled his paddle in the water, turning them so that they moved parallel to the land, headed past the opening of the underground river down which they had come. He intended to push on into the main expanse of the lake before heading out at a sharp angle toward the other shore, northward and away from the direct route to Fort Shadwell.

"No," said Michel, plying his paddle in the prow to turn the canoe back into the current from the entrance to the underground river.

Bart dug his own paddle in strongly; and the canoe, caught between two conflicting impulses, lost headway and began to drift outward into the lake on the slow current from underground.

"What's all this?" demanded Bart harshly. Michel looked back over his shoulder at the others.

"I'm sorry," he repeated, "but I'm going to have to go back. I'm not going with you. Forgive me for taking you back into danger a second time; but I didn't trust you to get by alone with Cousin Lehrer at the trading post. He'd met me; he knew me. That saved a lot of questions."

They stared at him in silence.

"It had to be this way," said Michel. There was a different note in his voice. "I'll try not to put the rest of you to any risk, if I can. If there're people—people come to check on Chandt and his Steeds—already at the ledge by the time we get close, we'll hear their voices well before we come around the curve into sight under their lights. If that's the case, I'll slip overboard and swim the rest of the way back. The current's not that strong; and once I get there, I can hide in the water between the boats until they've taken the bodies off; and there's a chance for me to slip out and go back the way we came."

"Hold it," said Bart, backing his paddle against the current to hold the craft where she was. "I'm sorry, Michel, but you've got to give me a better reason than that, why we should risk taking you back.''

"I've said I'm sorry." Michel's face was unhappy. "It's just that I can't go with you. I didn't realize it earlier, but I never could have. I've got to go back. As I say, I hate putting the rest of you at risk to do it. But it's too far for me to swim in water that cold; and if I'd taken a canoe from the dock, no matter how good a reason I gave him then, Lehrer'd have guessed the truth later on when he heard I was back below. Two days after that, the whole Inner World would have known—not just the Emperor and the Guettrigs—that you were outside on your own, knowing all about us down there.''

"That's not the answer I need," said Bart, still holding the canoe in place. "I want to know why you think you have to go back. Did you plan this from the start?''

"My God, no!'' said Michel emphatically. "You wouldn't think that of me? Pier found himself a family in you and Emma; and so did I. You have to understand. Our father left for the surface before I was old enough to really get to know him, and my mother died in less than six months after that. So it seemed to me I was alone in the world; and I built a sort of shell, which was me, the way everybody knew me, and lived alone in it, until that moment when you proved to me I wasn't alone.''

"What is all this?" demanded Arthur.

"Be quiet, Arthur," said his sister.

He gaped at her. His face twisted in anger and his mouth opened. Then he closed it again and sat silent. Michel, ignoring him and Emma, was staring hard past them at Bart.

"You can't imagine what it meant to me to find out I had a brother—even a half-brother," he said. "Your being there made my father real to me. It made me someone with a family, just like everyone else in the world. That's why what Pier said to us last night suddenly reached me and made sense to me. Just as he said, I had my own self-made Book inside me. But I'd been refusing to look at any part of it that pretended I was like other people. When I did I saw that it was Pier I agreed with—not our father, for all I'd worshiped the idea of him all these years. The Inner World has to straighten itself out, or be straightened out by people on its inside.''

He paused. Bart felt the need to say something, but could not think of the words he wanted.

"It's all right for you," Michel said. "You were born up here. You belong here. But I belong down there; and my duty's down there, just as Pier's is. I've got to go back. It was Pier's talk that made me see it. I'd heard it before, but now it's real. And the only possible thing for any of us is to follow his own Book; and most of us do. Tell me, Bart, why did Paolo do what he did?"

Bart floundered.

"Paolo?" he said. He could not dodge the question after what his half-brother had just said to him, but it was hard to put what he felt into words. What was worse, it triggered off a strong feeling of guilt in him for not having recognized what was in Paolo, earlier.

He would never forget what Paolo had done; and he could not be sure—that was the hell of it—that in Paolo's place he would have done as much for Paolo. Then he suddenly realized that it was not necessarily a reciprocal matter. It was a case of the inner Book Pier had talked about, all over again; and he was ashamed that Michel should have recognized it before he did, himself. The feeling of guilt lifted from him and the words he needed came.

"Michel," he said slowly, "I think—I'll never be sure, but I think—Paolo did what he did because he was the sort of person who ought to have lived a few hundred years ago, when the world would have fitted him better. Laws and regulations—they didn't mean a thing to Paolo. There'd always been laws and regulations, there always would be. Someone would make them, arbitrary rules that he had to obey in order to stay alive. But that's all they were—arbitrary rules. They didn't have any meaning of themselves for him."

He stopped to look into Michel's eyes.

"Am I making sense to you?"

"Very good sense," answered Michel. "Go on."

"All right, the rules meant nothing, except that under certain conditions he had to obey them," said Bart. "What did mean something to him was his own code, his own Book—and that was very simple. Anything went; but if someone was a friend to you, you were a friend to him. That's all there was to it—"

"It was enough to make Lorena fall in love with him," said Emma softly.

"And it was enough to make him go up against Chandt, the one man he was really afraid of—and that cost him his life," said Bart harshly.

"But he held to his Book," said Michel from the bow of the canoe as they floated on the gently swirling water, kept in place by the movements of Bart's paddle. "And if he had a Book and the Emperor has one and other people—like Pier—each have their own—you can't expect me not to have one, can you, Brother?"

Bart looked at him; and in fact Michel's face seemed changed, enough so that he seemed to be looking at a man he had never seen before.

"I'm sorry, Bart," said Michel. "Our father believed what he did, and you probably believe he was right. Pier doesn't. Pier believes that people like the Emperor have to be fought inside the Inner World, and I'm afraid, after all, it's Pier I agree with. I didn't realize that until I saw Paolo die for the way he saw the world. But I do now. That's why I have to go back."

Bart felt he should argue with this, but somehow he could think of nothing to say that fitted at this moment.

"I just didn't realize how deeply I agreed with Pier, with what he said at his home, just before we said goodbye to him and Marta," went on Michel. "It wasn't until I saw what Paolo was willing to do that I realized I didn't have any choice with my own way of looking at the worlds, both outer and Inner. Bart, Pier needs me back there. All the Liberals need me back there."

"The Emperor'll kill you the minute he finds out you're back," said Bart.

"You're wrong," answered Michel. "The one place I'm completely safe from him is openly living back in the Inner World. He admitted this himself, remember? He can't even take the chance of trumping up some kind of false charges against me so he can act, because even true charges wouldn't be believed by the majority—Hybrids and Lordly class alike. No, there, in the lion's mouth, I'm safe; and there I can do the most damage to what he wants."

There was a moment of silence in which everyone waited for Bart to react. He ended it, finally, with a sigh; then dug his paddle in deeply and sent the canoe's nose forward toward the opening of the underground river. They moved into shadow, into darkness; and as they came into the curve, a lamp switched on on the wall of the cave, lighting their way around the curve.

"We'll hear anybody up ahead on the ledge long before they see this, what with the bright lights there," Michel told them.

After that, there was very little said. They reached the landing and there was no one there but the dead. Nothing had changed. No one had come yet. Michel get out onto the rock. He shook hands with Bart and Emma lifted her arms to him. He reached down, picked her up out of the canoe, and they hugged each other for a moment, wordlessly.

Then he lifted her back down into her place in the center of the canoe.

"Goodbye," said Michel.

"Goodbye," said Bart, as he backed the canoe once more into the current of the river that immediately began to carry them away again downstream.

"Goodbye," said the others, even including Arthur.

They went away; and the ledge with Michel standing on it looking after them grew smaller in the distance; then was cut off from sight entirely as the curving of the river put a rock wall between them and the ledge. Arthur, without being given orders, had moved up to the front of the canoe to take up the paddle. Somewhat to Bart's surprise, he was of some use with it. The automatic lights on the rock walls once more lit their way out into the sunlight.

Once out on the open lake Bart turned the canoe and, behind the screen of the island, headed away on a slant across open water in a move that would have worried Lehrer, who had thought of them all as amateurs at northwoods travel. The change of direction swung them generally more and more west until they had passed that point of the compass and were headed north.

"This isn't the way to Fort Shadwell," said Arthur as they began to approach the lake's farther shore.

"No," said Bart economically from the stern of the boat. He used his paddle to swing the canoe parallel to the shore, but Arthur dug in his own paddle and turned the bow back toward a nearby possible landing spot.

"I thought as much," Arthur said. He produced one of the revolvers they had gotten from Lehrer Green. He held it casually, but it was pointed generally past Emma, in Bart's direction. At some time he had gotten it from among the other gear in the boat. There was a note in his voice Bart had never heard before.

"Then here's where we part company. I want a rifle, my pack, and enough food and gear to get me on foot to Fort Shadwell. It only ought to take me a week or so longer to get there that way than it would've by boat. I'll also take a third of that money Michel got from what's-his-name—Lehrer—if you don't mind."

"Arthur," said Emma, "you're being foolish."

"That's exactly what I'm not being, sister dear," said Arthur. "What was foolish of me was to spend all these years taking care of you when I could have been making something of myself out on my own. Well, now you've got this chunk of bone and muscle to take care of you; and I give him to you freely. As Michel said back there, we've all got our Book; and I suddenly realized what mine is."

He gestured with the revolver at Bart.

"You paddle into shore," he said. "Just to make sure everything goes smoothly, I'm going to step out first and keep this gun on you while you split up our possessions."

"You damn fool!" said Bart. "It was Emma who took care of *you* all those years—mainly because you didn't have enough sense to take care of yourself. What are you going to do with the money? Try to make yourself a fortune as a flash gambler?"

"Just paddle," said Arthur.

"Do what he says, Bart," said Emma. "If Arthur's determined to go, we can't keep him."

"You're right about that," said Arthur, rising and stepping onto the muddy shelf of land upon which the canoe had pushed its prow. He held the revolver steady on Bart, as Bart used his paddle to swing the canoe side-on to the shore. "Now, get busy laying out my stuff."

Bart did so, regarding Emma with more than a touch of surprise. She seemed unusually calm about letting Arthur leave them after all these years of watching out for him and making a home for him.

"It's all right, Bart," she said suddenly, apparently reading his thoughts. "Arthur had to make up his mind to leave us someday."

Good Lord, thought Bart, she must have been seeing this change coming in Arthur for some time. Well, the man had been altered by his time as a slave in the Inner World, and maybe even, as he said, by what Michel had said. In no way had it made him any more likeable; but maybe it had given him a little more common sense and backbone. Bart finished dividing up the food and gear and making the pack ready for Arthur. He laid the rifle and ammunition, both for a long gun and for the revolver, on the ground beside the pack and straightened up.

"There you are," he said to Arthur, and—disregarding the revolver—turned his back on the man to get back into the canoe and take his place in its stern. It was only then he saw that Emma had moved up into the bow and taken up a paddle.

"Emma, you can't do that!" he said.

"Certainly I can. Just as well as Arthur," she replied and pushed off from the land. She looked back at her brother. "Goodbye, Arthur. God keep you safe."

"Don't worry about me," said Arthur, who was already putting on the shoulder straps of the pack. "Just try to stay alive yourself with the kind of company you keep."

Bart put his paddle in the water and helped turn the canoe back on its original course, parallel to this shore, which ran only about another two hundred yards before ending in a bend which opened on a wider stretch of lake. Arthur was left, unseen behind them.

They glided rapidly toward that open water, which widened out into a very wide stretch of lake indeed. The trees of its far shore were a solid line of green with the distance—Bart estimated that straight across would be a good four to five miles. But the day was clear and almost windless, and he was no amateur with a canoe in any case. And he had been reading the weather as far back as he could remember; and this time of year, under these conditions, it was not likely that there was wind or a rain squall lurking out of sight just over the horizon.

Now, back above ground in his own kind of country once more, Bart's instincts were reasserting themselves. Emma, he could feel, was indeed as good a paddler as her brother, although her keeping up this sort of effort for the rest of the day seemed unlikely. The sunlight sparkled along the long sheet of water before them, and the sky was blue, with just a few free-floating high clouds of pure white. He could smell the water, the pines, the spruce, and all the land around the water. They smelled good.

He could feel the stretch of his arm and shoulder and back as he pushed the paddle against the water. He could feel the muscles working clear down his legs and the hard bulge of calf muscle against thigh muscle as he knelt to paddle. The back of his head warned him that those same muscles, unused this long time to kneeling to such work, would be stiff and perhaps painful tomorrow—or even later on today; but that did not matter.

What mattered was that he was back in his own country at last. Arthur had miraculously removed himself as an obstacle between Emma and himself; and now finally there was no reason they could not settle down as they should have long ago. His solitary years were over; over so suddenly that he could not really feel what the new life was like.

That feeling, like the stiffness of his muscles, would come tomorrow and in the days after. Meanwhile he felt happily, if rather strangely, adrift, wondering about himself and Emma in the years to come, about the world, about everything. He looked into himself and was surprised to see how little he understood of what he saw. A sudden chill made itself felt inside him.

"Emma?" he said to her small sturdy back, bulky in the heavy jacket.

"Yes, Bart?" her voice floated back to him.

"What's my Book—my Book, inside?" he asked. "I can't seem to find any I've really got."

She laughed.

"You? Of all people?" she said. "Of course you have. Everybody does. Don't worry, you'll find it there. You just have to wait until you can put it into words for yourself."

She would be right, he told himself; and was comforted, in the warm silence that followed as they paddled toward the farther shore and to the north. She was always right.